SCANDALOUS

The Victoria Woodhull Saga
Volume II

FAME, INFAMY, and PARADISE LOST

Also by Neal Katz

OUTRAGEOUS

The Victoria Woodhull Saga, Volume I

Rise to Riches

OUTRAGEOUS is the 2016 winner of ten literary awards including three Gold Medals: IBPA Ben Franklin, Bill Fisher Award for Best First Book by a Publisher, the IPPY Award for Best Historical Fiction, and Gold Medal for Historical Fiction/Personage by Reader's Favorite. Other Awards: Finalist in the Historical Fiction category of the 2016 Next Generation Indie Book Awards, Second Place winner of the IndieReader Discovery Award for Best Fiction, Best New Fiction in the International Book Awards for 2016, Finalist in two categories Independent Author Network Book of the Year, Chantecleer Goethe Award Finalist, Shelf Unbound Notable 100, and one of IndieReader's Best Books of 2016.

SCANDALOUS

THE VICTORIA WOODHULL SAGA
VOLUME II

FAME, INFAMY, and PARADISE LOST

NEAL KATZ

TOP READS PUBLISHING, INC

Vista, CA

FIRST EDITION

ISBN-13: 978-0-9964860-9-5 (paperback)
ISBN-13: 978-0-9964860-8-8 (hardback)
ISBN-13: 978-0-9986838-0-5 (ebook)

Library of Congress Control Number: 2018931405

Scandalous: The Victoria Woodhull Saga, Volume II: Fame, Infamy, and Paradise Lost
is published by:
Top Reads Publishing, Inc.
1035 E. Vista Way, Suite 205
Vista, CA 92084 USA
www.topreadspublishing.com

For information please direct emails to:
publisher@topreadspublishing.com

For more information about The Victoria Woodhull Saga, visit:
www.thevictoriawoodhullsaga.com

Cover design, book layout and typography by Teri Rider
Set in Minion Pro

Printed in the United States of America

26 25 24 23 22 21 20 19 18   1 2 3 4 5 6 7 8 9

To all women, #MeToo

Change is in the air we breathe.
Be strong, be bold, lead us forth!

No man is an island,

Entire of itself.

Each is a piece of the continent,

A part of the main.

If a clod be washed away by the sea,

Europe is the less.

As well as if a promontory were.

As well as if a manor of thine own

Or of thine friend's were.

Each man's death diminishes me,

For I am involved in mankind.

Therefore, send not to know

For whom the bell tolls,

It tolls for thee.

For Whom the Bell Tolls by John Donne, 1624

"And the Truth Shall Make You Free"

Speech by Victoria Claflin Woodhull
November 20, 1871
Steinway Hall, New York City

I sung of Chaos and Eternal Night,

Taught by the heav'nly Muse to venture down

The dark descent, and up to reascend…

Long is the way and hard, that out of Hell leads up to light.

Arise, awake or be forever fallen.

Paradise Lost by John Milton, 1667

Contents

Part I

FAME

Part II

INFAMY

Part III

RUN FOR PRESIDENT

Part IV
PARADISE LOST

PREFACE

The world has changed dramatically since *Volume One, OUTRAGEOUS: Rise to Riches* was published in 2015. The #MeToo movement has toppled powerful people and illuminated the deeply ingrained mistreatment of women. Bringing truth to light was my primary purpose for writing the series, and now with the perpetual news cycle of more and more women—and men—coming forward, I believe the topic is revealing further depths of deep-seated gender prejudice and abuses of power.

One thing you will discover while reading *Volume Two, SCANDALOUS: Fame, Infamy, and Paradise Lost*, is the first published #MeToo event. Much like the modern exposés in *The New Yorker* and *The New York Times*, on November 2, 1872 Victoria and Tennessee published two exposés in their *Woodhull & Claflin's Weekly* newspaper. Both articles are quoted verbatim in the text of this book to maintain the clarity and ferocity of their voices.

The first article covered the misconduct of the "most famous man in America," the Reverend Henry Ward Beecher. The well-researched article delivered the facts and background for the outspoken moralist being nothing more than an abusive and prolific adulterer and charlatan.

The second article covered the brutal treatment of women at an annual high society, New York City gala event called "The French Ball." The night of sanctioned public debauchery and abuse of young women in 1869 led to the kidnap and repeated rape of two fourteen year old girls, one of whom died from the abuse. Horrid? Yes. New? Sadly no.

Because I believe the internal thoughts of people are critical for character development, I write in a style called *magical realism*. Visions, trances, dream state, and seeing of future events are all treated as though they are literally happening. I chose Victoria and Tennie (or perhaps the reason Vickie chose and continues to advise me) because we share many common experiences. In lucid dream state, I have interviewed almost all of the major characters, and they have provided some of the incredible truths presented in the book.

I too have lived with the burden of sexual child abuse from the opposite sex parent. A mother's abusive treatment of her male child remains a taboo subject even today, rarely discussed.

The narrative sounds real because I personally have suffered the indignities of arbitrary legal prosecution, financial devastation after huge successes, and even imprisonment. Like my heroines, I made terrible mistakes, and I have survived and thrived again. Mine eyes have also seen the glory of Love in my own near-death experience, and love continues to guide my life today.

Some background on my thought process may help you enjoy your adventure even more. The book you hold is volume two of three planned for *The Victoria Woodhull Saga*. *Outrageous: Rise to Riches* is followed by *Scandalous: Fame, Infamy, and Paradise Lost*, and either one could be read independently, but better in sequence. The third volume is tentatively named, *Audacious: Paradise Regained*.

I used to think Historical Fiction qualified as an oxymoron. Which is it, history or fiction? I've come to learn that "history" from its first record is a shadowed reflection of what actually occurred. The account is influenced by many variables, including worldview, political agenda, philosophical and religious beliefs, economics, gender, race, origin, education and what the historian ate for dinner the night before! In other words, no two people will witness a given event and depict that event in the same manner, or even within a close proximity. Have some fun and play the childhood game of broken telephone again. You'll know what I mean.

As I write, I carefully select what I focus on and how I present it so that you may learn about, enjoy, and experience the past. This leads me to write complex multi-dimensional characters that do not easily fit into any preconceived molds. The motivations of people matter to me, so I present them, especially the underlying psychological profiles, as the protagonists do stupid things that infuriate us. I tend to not focus on what kind of eggs were prepared for breakfast, rather I try to communicate the feeling of an emotional trigger, perhaps piercing a yoke and watching it spread across the plate, after an ill-fated pregnancy.

To accurately represent the times and especially the personality of Victoria, this volume contains many direct quotations of her speeches and newspaper articles as originally printed. To help you identify these passages, they are offset as block quotes. Despite numerous suggestions to the contrary, I have left the original texts intact, without posting "[sic]" every time there is a grammatical error or awkward word to our modern ear. Likewise, Victoria is unwilling to use a lower case "c" when describing her hero, mentor, and husband, the Colonel. The word "woman" meant both a single woman, and also all women and womanhood.

You will discover that Victoria embraces and promotes revolutionary ideas and theories. The motivations and manipulations behind financial and economic events fascinate me. I either research to discover or devise a logical coherent explanation for market events. I endeavor to render sometimes complex mechanics into reasonable understanding.

For example, here are some inflationary factors: A five-cent loaf of bread in Victorian America would cost five dollars today, so a one hundred multiple. However, while a million-dollar fortune would logically be equivalent to a one hundred-million-dollar net worth today, economists claim that the estate of the wealthiest man in America, Commodore Cornelius Vanderbilt of $105 million in 1877 would be equal to the power of $210 billion today—a two thousand to one ratio. The point being, net worth inflationary factors are a huge multiple of ordinary cost of goods inflation.

Which brings us back to where we began—another oxymoron. Life is not simple, but oh my, glorious when we learn that living Love makes us radiant, and enables us to manifest almost anything. I confess I felt daunted by the success of Volume One, winning or placing in twelve of fourteen award competitions entered into by my publisher, Teri Rider of Top Reads Publishing, Inc. (Please read the Acknowledgements at the end of the book. It really does take a village to get a book out.)

Daily, I sat to write with acute awareness of the razor-sharp sword of Damocles above me, held in place by one horsehair to prevent it from slicing me in half. I wanted to create a Volume Two that was not just as good as, but even better than Volume One. You be the judge! *Please* let me know what *you* think. Oh, one more request—please be so kind as to write a review on Amazon, Goodreads, and any of your favorite booksellers' websites.

Upward and Onward.
I hope the year 2018 will be remembered in history as The Year of the Woman.

Neal Katz
Village San Andres Huayapam,
City Oaxaca, Mexico

Part 1

FAME

Chapter 1

NIGHTMARE

15 East 38th St., New York City
Night of the Woodhull & Claflin Brokerage
Grand Opening, February 14, 1870

T*he pain was excruciating.*

Someone pinned me down on my stomach as two scalpels cut into my back.

I screamed.

The knives cut deeper, from the top of each shoulder and down to the base of my spine. I imagined the bloody "V" they must have carved into me.

I was about to pass out, but I felt them making holes by hammering spikes through my skin and bones. I felt a searing pain and I could smell my own flesh burning. I tried to struggle to get to my feet, but they held me down too tight.

I pleaded with them to make the pain stop.

The pain increased. It grew unbearable.

I screamed.

Finally, it stopped. I tried to stand up but lost my balance. My upper body burdened me. The heaviness made all my movements awkward. I stumbled. My legs could barely support the new weight.

I stood alone at a cliff over a deep chasm. I could not see a bottom to the canyon. I did see an endless abyss. Then out of nowhere an angel with white wings swooped into the sky. I turned to face her. At first I thought the angel beautiful and magnificent in her lofty flight, but then

3

she started plummeting at me like an evil spirit. She pressed a baby to her bosom, and she flew so close I had to duck to avoid being hit. She cursed me as she passed, hurling spells at me.

Her words hit me like claps of thunder, and I stumbled backwards. With each pass she maneuvered me closer and closer to the edge. Inch by inch the Angel moved me closer to falling into the dark abyss. This possessed spirit intended to force me off the promontory.

She plunged towards me, and I saw her eyes had no color or life in them. They looked like cold black coals. I cried out in fear. Looking into her eyes, I lost my balance and fell off the cliff. I tumbled head over feet in a free fall, plummeting to my death.

I knew I was going to die.

Suddenly, a pain worse than childbirth in my back and under my shoulders made me forget about falling. Something tore at my flesh. Something ripped me apart. I suffered agonizing, tormenting pain.

Suddenly huge black wings unfurled from my body. I flapped my massive black wings and soared above the canyon rim and up into the heavens. I became an avenging black angel flying directly at the evil angel with white wings. I cast epithets at her and the baby boy clutched in her arms.

My words became lightning bolts.

One crackled so close she dropped her precious cargo. The baby boy fell toward the earth. She arced down and caught the baby, then flew at me. She turned into a monstrous serpent and hissed at me and coiled to attack. She spoke odd words that sliced into me like daggers. The winged serpent hissed in tongues like something possessed. I bled from cuts on my flesh.

I pleaded with her to stop. I promised I would not seek revenge if she would just stop. The pain amplified. My fears grew worse. She did not even hesitate. She kept up her assault of razor-sharp words.

I fought back, casting my words as cannon balls, which exploded on her scales. We waged war, on and on, both of us tattered and torn. We became exhausted but kept fighting. I felt it would never end. I beseeched the serpent to please cease hostilities, but to no avail. I quickly wearied. All of my being wanted to rest.

Then everything went black, cold, and damp.

The stone floor and walls of my dungeon were covered in a dank slime. Everything felt slick and sickly. I could not get warm.

Someone I knew stayed near me in the prison for a short time and then disappeared. I was alone for a long time. No one came to visit me, except the shadow of my jailer. For the longest time, a rat scurried back and forth across the slimy cold, my only companion. I appreciated the company, and would talk to my visitor. Not even the rats wanted to stay very long in the damp, frigid darkness.

I called out. No one could hear me. My words had lost all their powers.

I tried to see in the dark. I suffered from hunger, exhaustion, and filth. I listened for any sign of life or someone other than the rodents to speak to. I began crying out, wailing, and shouting as loud as I could. I pleaded for someone to come and take me away. I begged to see daylight. When no one appeared, no one answered, and no one came, I cried myself to sleep.

Nothing… only cold, damp, darkness.

Then fear. What if nobody ever came?

I screamed for Demosthenes, my spirit guide, to come visit me, to keep me company. I pleaded for just a glimmer of his shining green light.

Nothing.

I pleaded for my sister, Tennessee, but she did not appear or speak to me. I tried to contact my longest and dearest friend and lover, Rosie, but I could not conjure her image nor hear her voice.

I was abandoned.

I was completely alone.

I heard shouting and someone shaking me. I felt a harsh slap on my face.

"Wake up!" My sister Tennessee shouted at me, but she seemed far away.

My husband's voice urged, "Victoria, please open your eyes!" I felt his strong hands on my shoulders, shaking me violently.

I blinked my eyes open. Colonel James Harvey Blood came into focus, and right beside him Tennie. They were looking at me. The look on their faces made me realize something was terribly wrong.

"What happened?" My voice croaked. I looked at both of them.

My husband sounded upset. "You were crying out in your sleep, screaming in pain, and then you started whimpering." Dismayed, he continued, "I couldn't wake you." I motioned to the side table, and my husband gave me a glass of water. I gulped it down very quickly. "You were suffering, moaning in your sleep. I had to go wake Tennie to see if she could help me bring you back."

"I didn't wake up?" I asked, still confused.

"No!" Tennie exclaimed. "You were writhing and thrashing in your sleep. Then you started screaming about wings, big black wings." Her eyes filled with horror. "I tried to enter your dream to lead you out of it, but I couldn't." Her desperation frightened me. "I had to slap you several times before you finally woke up." She lowered her head and added softly, "I'm sorry, Vickie."

"I don't understand. This has never happened to me before." I could not recall ever being so lost in a dream. I reached out with one hand for my husband sitting in front of me to hold it, and with the other I reached for my sister sitting on my side. Each of them welcomed my hand.

I immediately cringed and dropped their hands. James' hand was stone cold, and Tennie's felt like a burning log. I could almost smell my flesh burning. Tennie saw my reaction. She grabbed my shoulders and made me face her.

"Tell me your dream, Victoria," Tennie commanded in a voice a full octave lower than normal. "All of it. Leave nothing out."

I began to tell them the dream, as best I could remember it:

"Demosthenes, my Majestic Guardian, protector and spirit guide since childhood, appeared to me.

"He spoke to me. 'Victoria, your work is about to begin!'

"'What work?' I asked. 'How do I start?'

"'You will know,' he said, and smiled the familiar smile a loving parent would bestow as a blessing on a child. He turned to leave and started to fade away.

"'Wait!' I called after him. 'Please, I beg of you, tell me more.'

"He turned back and became corporeal again. 'To change things,' he began, continuing to smile lovingly at me, 'you will use words.' He became radiant, illuminated in a shimmering emerald light tinged with highlights of bright gold. 'Spoken and written!' He nodded his head and once again turned to leave. Hesitating, he turned his shoulder and forewarned me: 'Your road will be filled with great joys… as well as great hardships.' He walked away, the gold tinged, green vapors following him, and evaporated into the ethers.

"Then I found myself with you, Tennie, arriving in our nation's capital so I could address our leaders. First, we had to repeatedly run and survive a gauntlet of smelly men in the lobby of a big hotel overflowing with people who pushed and shoved in every direction. The faces of the people in the lobby jutted right in front of us, aggressively arguing a certain point of view. We had to struggle and push them away, just to get through.

"When my time to talk to the leaders arrived, I was timid and unsure. My speech faltered and I thought I would completely fail, but, looking up, I saw emerald vapors and knew Demosthenes stood nearby. I started talking, and the cadence of my speech gathered speed and became the cadence of galloping horses. Upon my summation, almost everyone stood, shouting and applauding my speech.

"The same scene repeated itself at a grand hall where I stood up and spoke to a large group of mostly women. Once again, at the commencement, I waivered, and then Isabella Beecher put her arm around me, and I also felt Demosthenes close by. Once again my weakness and timidity departed, and I delivered a powerful oration.

"I saw myself on many stages in huge theaters and halls, talking to throngs of people. The enormous assemblies terrified me. I imagined myself standing before them trying to speak but unable to utter a single word, completely mute. I would look for one familiar face. I would find either you, Tennie, or you, my Colonel, and I would instantly calm down and start talking. Once I began, I fell into the flowing rhythms of words and images, moving the crowds to passion."

I paused to drink some more water.

Tennie wanted me to continue telling the dream. "Can you remember what you said, Vickie? What were the speeches about?" My husband nodded, affirming the question. I continued.

"Even though the locations and types of people changed, the speech remained the same. I advocated universal suffrage. I declared woman must attain full citizenship with the right to vote and equal legal rights. I argued every woman should receive equal pay as a man for the same work. These were the pillars of my temple. My passion created a tempest. I fomented social and domestic revolution.

"At the conclusion of each appearance, wherever it took place, the audiences would stand up and cheer. I basked in their adoration.

"I saw myself, with both of you, laughing at our predicament. Our clothes were covered with big splotches of black printer's ink. By the door across from a mechanical printing press, there were neatly bundled and tied stacks of newspapers. I saw clearly the names in the heading of the first page, *Woodhull and Claflin's Weekly*, below which a banner read "UPWARD & ONWARD."

"As our popularity grew, a national political party nominated me as their candidate to run for President of the United States. Elizabeth Cady Stanton acted as my campaign manager. I selected Frederick Douglass to become my running mate."

My husband interrupted me. "But darling, none of this would make you cry out in pain. Try to remember something to do with big black wings."

I trembled, and shook my head. "*No!*"

I heard my voice in the distance. I looked up into both their eyes. I saw them both through a filmy cloud, imploring me to finish giving the full account. I didn't want to. Despair gripped my soul, and I wanted to evaporate into the air.

"You must continue, Victoria," my sister ordered.

"Just as everything was going perfectly, someone or a group of people attacked me. They held me down while someone performed a violent surgery on my back. They carved a deep bloody V into me. Then out of nowhere an angel... *oh no!*"

I stopped as I recognized the face of the malevolent angel. I felt my stomach turn. I started drifting away, leaving the room and trying to disappear so the white angel would not see me.

"Victoria!" Tennie's sharp voice brought me back. "Stay focused. Stay with us, *here*, in your room. Go on!"

"Go on, sweetheart." My husband cradled my face and caressed my cheek, nodding his head for me to continue to finish describing the dream. Their presence, his gentle concern, and their support gave me courage.

"A white winged angel with the face of Harriet Beecher Stowe swooped down. She flew at me like some evil spirit. Clutched in her arms was a baby boy. She pressed the baby Henry Ward Beecher to her bosom. She flew close and cast spells upon me."

I convulsed and cried as I completed telling the nightmare and the terrifying ending. "I lived a long time in a dank, dark dungeon. I had been forsaken."

My husband held me from behind with his strong arms and rocked me back and forth. Tennie hugged me. Despite their solace, I kept whimpering the same phrase, over and over again.

"I was completely alone."

Chapter 2

SWEET SUCCESS

40 Broad St., New York City
Late Winter, 1870

Our new brokerage firm, Woodhull, Claflin & Company, thrived. We were young, rich, and increasingly famous. I was thirty-two and Tennie C. twenty-five. We made a point of remaining newsworthy and were reported on almost daily by one newspaper or another. This made us enormously popular, usually controversial, and increasingly successful.

Controversy made good and free advertisement!

It mattered not to us if our success resulted from our being the only women-owned-and-managed brokerage firm, or from our affiliation with the Commodore Cornelius Vanderbilt, the richest man in America.

My sister loved the man three times her age, and prided herself on being his paramour. Regardless of what others accused, the two of them adored each other as if Cupid himself had loosed the arrows that struck their hearts. We were often guests at his home, for dinner or afternoon tea. The Commodore had recently married his distant relative, Frank Armstrong Crawford, a Southern-belle relative about my age. Defying all convention, Tennie often stayed the night to sleep next to her beloved. There could be no intercourse, as the Commodore had contracted the French disease, or syphilis, from his youthful whoring. Tennie had discovered other ways to satisfy and mystify the older gentleman.

My husband paid dearly to earn the respect and honor that was his due as Colonel James Harvey Blood, war hero. The Colonel—I cannot imagine belittling his bravery and accomplishments by writing his title with a lower case *c*—had survived six bullet wounds leading his troops of the 6th Missouri. He now served as our director of operations and took care of all the paperwork and most of the trading. My Colonel combined a passionate intellect with a worldly acumen and uncommon business sense. His presence at the brokerage firm allowed Tennie and me the time and freedom to promote our business. An active and vocal spiritualist, my husband's passions seemed unlimited. We privately enjoyed a joyfully robust intimacy.

Sometimes, a line of women overflowed from our reception area into the street. They waited patiently to hand us their money in one form or another to open an account for us to manage. We wrote down all the names and then marked the sum and form of deposit, either cash, gold, silver, or bonds. We asked the clients to choose their own level of risk tolerance. Many of the women would only trust another woman with their life savings, which they had surreptitiously sequestered from their husbands. Many had probably heard of our association with the Commodore.

The financier Henry Clews, president of the Fourth National Bank and principal of the brokerage firm, Livermore, Clews and Company, the second largest seller of war bonds, opened accounts with us. Tennie parlayed a check hand-signed by Vanderbilt in the amount of seven thousand dollars, payable to our firm, to entice Mr. Clews and the Fourth National Bank into becoming clients. Henry publicly proclaimed he knew for a fact Commodore Cornelius Vanderbilt personally backed the firm. Mr. Clews assumed every purchase or sale we made executed an order, or at the minimum, coordinated in concert with the almighty "Titan of Wall Street." In part, this was true.

With everyone eager to follow our actions, we were creating market trends just by taking our early positions. When the sheep followed, we would take our profits. It was a self-fulfilling prophecy, and our portfolios, both personal and clientele, earned exceptional profits.

Even nervous and thin Jay Gould, sallow mastermind behind the Gold Scandal in September that brought the national economy to the brink of collapse, opened an account at our brokerage. I handled his transactions personally, although the Colonel executed the trades. He requested the account be held in a "street name." Thus, his name did not appear on any ledgers. We would execute orders for Gould, and we often piggybacked his purchases, no doubt as he had planned. He in turn had a standing order to piggyback on our purchases of other stocks. He also assumed we would be acting on instructions from the mighty Vanderbilt.

Our trades made money for Gould and also all our brokerage accounts. On Mr. Gould's large-volume trading account, we earned brokerage fees of about one thousand dollars every market day!

As I had imagined when I first learned about the brokerage business, Woodhull, Claflin & Company made fees on each buy and each sell for our clients, whether the client made money or lost.

Tennie and I would sit for meetings in two unique chairs the Commodore had commissioned for us. They were shiny black lacquer on walnut wood. The arms and legs were carved and tooled with bear-claw ends in front and scrolls against the backrest mantle. Plush stuffing and two distinct designs in satin and silk created a dramatic effect. I chose the British design with gold lions on a deep red brocade and gold ribbons. Tennie delighted in the gift from her lover, a royal blue satin background with cords of yellow gold sewn on the sides with matching golden embroidered velvet *fleur de lys*—the stylized iris of France. We both felt like royalty.

Business flourished.

We were having fun!

"Lizzybeth, I'm glad I have caught you alone." I traveled on a cold, snow-filled day up to the offices of *The Revolution* to solicit the help of my dear friend and loving mentor, the woman I considered my true mother, Elizabeth Cady Stanton. "I want you to help me set up my own regular soirees."

"Of course I'll help you, Victoria." Lizzybeth rose from behind her desk and gave me a kiss on each cheek. We sat in two of the chairs in front of her desk. "It is the least I can do to repay your generosity in saving our paper. The $10,000 you gave me back in May stretched the bounds of generosity. I fear I will not be able to repay the debt."

"What debt? *Gave* is the right word, Lizzybeth. You…"

"It's not that, Vickie," Lizzybeth interrupted. I looked at my friend and saw an uncharacteristic gloom shrouding her aura. She wore distraction as if she had donned a hair shirt as punishment. I reached over and took both her hands in mine.

"What's wrong, my dear?" I inquired gently.

She guided me to the divan and we both sat down. I rarely saw Elizabeth Cady Stanton as anything other than totally resolved and determined. Now the woman beside me appeared shaken. This worried me.

"Our little enterprise, *The Revolution,* is not doing well." Lizzybeth paused to release the deep sigh of a foregone conclusion. "Once Mary Livermore and Lucy Stone rallied the Bostonians to publish the *Woman's Journal and Suffrage News* with the active support of businessmen, and the popularity of contributing editors like Henry, Catherine, and Harriet Beecher, our subscriptions have plummeted to less than half."

I shuddered at the mention of Harriet Beecher Stowe. "They are a cunning and mean-spirited bunch," I commiserated. "I am happy to contribute more. I told you, the day I gave you the money. I'm not expecting it back. We will treat any new monies on the same terms." She still bowed her head. "Come on!" I reached and lifted up her chin. "Please let go of whatever burden is weighing you down on my account."

She smiled wanly, weighed my offer for a moment, and surprised me. "No!" She jumped to her feet. "You have already been too kind. I will never permit myself to take another dollar from you." She pushed both hands in front of her as if she were pushing away my own hands filled with cash.

"All right, Lizzy." I looked at her. "What else distresses you?"

"Teddy Tilton has arranged for the continuation of *The Revolution* with Laura Curtis Bullard buying the paper. Susan and I will continue to contribute articles, but we will not be the exclusive editors." She looked up, her eyes filled with tears. "Susan and I feel we have lost our child." Defeated, she returned to the divan.

"Something else is wrong." I began to lose my patience and rapidly tired of mental guessing. "Come out with it, Elizabeth!" I ordered. "Whatever troubles your soul today, tell me now."

"The conventions loom on the horizon," she cried out. "They are a mere couple of months away. They have sold out Steinway Hall, and our meeting at Apollo Hall will leave half or more of the seats empty in a much smaller theater. We will look pathetic!" Her anger replaced desperation. "I want a reconciliation, and I have told them thus, but there is still a great divide. They are impossible!"

My friend spoke about the simultaneous annual conventions, scheduled for mid-May in New York City. Her splinter group, the National Woman Suffrage Association, organized and formed in outrage and protest against the American Equal Rights Association convention last year. The N.W.S.A. sought full equal rights for women, including recognition as persons under the law in addition to suffrage, through a sixteenth amendment to the U.S. Constitution. The N.W.S.A. allowed only women to be full members, and no men were allowed in the top leadership. I told them I thought this a mistake. Lizzybeth served as president of the association.

On the other side, the highly successful and well-financed American Woman Suffrage Association formed by the elite Boston

Brahmins led by Lucy Stone, her husband Henry Browne Blackwell, Julia Ward Howe, and Mary Livermore encouraged significant male backers and appointed them to key positions. The A.W.S.A. elected the popular Reverend Henry Ward Beecher, a man who disgusted me with his hypocrisy, president of the association. They sought woman suffrage without any mandate for legal rights for women.

"They are so elitist and arrogant!" Lizzybeth declared.

The Boston group intentionally scheduled its meetings on the same days as the N.W.S.A. convention to demoralize and undermine our smaller group. The two factions would be simultaneously competing for endorsements, newspaper coverage, and funding..

I thought back to the dream I had nine months earlier. In it, I had a clear vision of the impact of this great divide between women. I had watched this chasm swallow up the entire woman suffrage movement for four decades. I saw the women who could not work together wage war, grow old, and decay, their bones withering away before women were able to legally cast ballots across the nation.

I shook my head to clear the vision.

"Lizzybeth, there is time to plan and prepare. We are months away from the meetings." I sought to assure her. "I know dear Mr. Tilton is diligently working on finding a resolution and unifying the factions." Indeed, the tall, handsome, and broad-chested Theodore Tilton dedicated himself to unifying women in order to present politicians and the public a compelling solidarity on universal suffrage.

"I'm sorry, Lizzybeth."

"For what?" She paused. "Oh, it will all be fine." Lizzybeth stood and went to sit at her desk. The resilient and optimistic Elizabeth Cady Stanton returned. I thought I could hear her brilliant mind working through a new challenge. "Yes, Vickie, dear, I think it will be a marvelous idea for you to host a series of soirees."

"Oh, I know it is the heart of winter," I explained, "and not the most opportune time to get people together. But I thought if I held them early in the evening and served sumptuous, hot dinners downtown at our offices on Broad Street…"

"Not to worry at all!" She took out a piece of parchment paper embossed with her initials and started making lists. "Let's plan the first few together!"

Virginia, a red-haired, Irish waif whom we came to call Ginny, became our receptionist. Ginny broke through the police line to offer Tennie and me a hope candle on the Grand Opening day of Woodhull, Claflin & Co., a Registered Brokerage. A huge Irish policeman punched her full force in the stomach, and she collapsed on the ice-covered street. The brute picked her up with one hand and swung his second to pummel her in the face. I ran to intercede and, just before the punch landed on my head, the police captain wielded a tree-limb club with a burnished burl end, and smashed the arm of the assaulter.

As our receptionist, Miss Ludwith turned out to be extremely competent and, like a sponge, absorbed knowledge of the business. Ginny became an irreplaceable asset for all of us. Tennie took her shopping and purchased several outfits for her to wear at the firm. Attractive, appreciative, and smart Virginia had an increasingly long list of responsibilities. She became a constant and welcome reminder that, if we could only give women a chance, they would rise up and take their rightful positions, likely to outperform men.

Ginny ushered in Anna Dickinson, and I welcomed my dear friend. "So good to see you again, Anna." The diminutive Queen of the Lyceum traveled throughout the country delivering her impassioned speeches to large audiences. She also served as a founding board member for the N.W.S.A.

"Once Elizabeth told me about your inaugural soiree, I had the Lyceum managers change my schedule so I could attend." She paused and beamed a radiant smile at me. "Congratulations, dear!" Nodding her head at the offices, she added, "On everything!"

"Thank you, Anna. You are so kind."

"I have also insured our old friend, The Beast will attend." We both laughed at the reference to the United States Representative from Massachusetts, General Benjamin Butler.

"I look forward to seeing The Beast once again."

Anna's features had been the subject of many cartoons and caricatures. Her short-cut, black, curly hair, gray eyes, prominent nose, and full mouth gave her a signature look.

We left the front offices and went behind the heavy wooden screens to a plush parlor my sister and I usually designated for the private and exclusive use of women.

Anna sat on the deep-green velvet divan, and I sat down in a red leather tufted wingback chair. Though smaller than I in stature, and four years younger, Anna had a booming voice she mixed on the stage with her passion for social causes. The combined impact had been mesmerizing audiences throughout the country for a decade. Exuberant, she turned to me, her eyes like crystals.

"So good to see you again, Anna."

"Vickie dear," her words came in a rush. "Do you remember when I told you one day I would introduce you to my promoters and secure a place for you as a traveling lecturer on the Lyceum circuit?"

"Of course I do, Anna. We met at *The Revolution*. You were exhorting General Butler to bring pressure to bear on Governor Geary in Pennsylvania to reverse the death sentence and free the poor, young immigrant girl, Hester Vaughn." I smiled at her and nodded my head in respect.

"Yes. We won that small battle," Anna declared.

"I am glad the governor finally acquiesced." I smiled.

"Thank you, Victoria, for arranging first class passage for Hester to go back to England. Due to your generous annual gift, she is studying to become a teacher."

"My pleasure to join forces with you, Anna. You are so persuasive every time you speak!" I did not seek to ingratiate myself with Anna, I simply stated a well-known fact.

"Which brings me to why I'm here today." Anna's enthusiasm filled the room and her smile warmed my heart. "I have mentioned you to several agencies, like the American Literary Bureau in New York, Redpath's, Fall's, and the Boston Lyceum Bureau." She spoke nodding her head up and down.

"Thank you," I paused, somewhat confused, "I guess." I looked up at her and queried, "I have to ask: What on earth for?"

"They book most all of the Lyceum engagements across the country." Anna was excited and encouraging, but I realized I missed the point of all this.

"Anna, dear, I don't…"

"You're ready!" She announced.

"Ready for what?"

Anna laughed gleefully. "Ever since you rendered Frederick Douglass speechless, I have been waiting for the perfect time to place you on the Lyceum stages. The time is now!"

"But Anna," I stood up and started to pace the room. "I am too busy here promoting the new brokerage firm," I protested. "And we need constant publicity to expand."

"Victoria, listen to me." She patted the divan, motioning me to come sit beside her. I did so and she clasped my hands. "You are always telling me you want to have a widespread impact, become a leader. You say you were told as a child you were born for greatness."

"Yes." I confirmed. "My Majestic Guardian came to me early in my life. Demosthenes foretold I would become powerful. But, I am, Anna. It has all started happening right here in New York City."

"You are rapidly becoming a well-known person in the New York area. Victoria, once you start touring the Lyceum, you will become a prominent *national* figure." She beamed her radiant smile. "Just like me!"

I knew the history of the Lyceum lecture circuit. Josiah Holbrook formed it in 1826 in Millbury, Massachusetts, choosing the name of Aristotle's gathering place to promise stirring intellectual discourse. Authors such as Ralph Waldo Emerson, Henry Thoreau, Nathaniel Hawthorne, and Harriet Beecher Stowe had first reached audiences and built demand for their books by reading sections of their work to crowded auditoriums. Impassioned orators such as William Lloyd Garrison, Frederick Douglass, Susan B. Anthony, Lizzybeth, and the Reverend Henry Ward Beecher became nationally known due to their appearances on the Lyceum stages.

The reigning monarch and most highly compensated speaker on the Lyceum circuit patiently held my hands.

She said, "Since Whitelaw Reid is the managing editor of Greeley's *Tribune*, we can build your success through the papers. He certainly built mine."

Anna told me her history. "Whitelaw has been enamored with me since William Lloyd Garrison published my abolition essay in *The Liberator* when I was fourteen. In 1860, when I was eighteen, Whitelaw declared me the 'Angel of the Union.' In 1863, he proclaimed me the 'Joan of Arc' for the Union forces, and my reputation grew rapidly."

Anna paused and squeezed my hands. "I am about to announce my extended sabbatical and conduct a grand farewell tour. I am ready for a private life. I want children and the joy of living at home with the man I love."

"But Anna, which one?" I blurted. We both laughed.

"Neither of the two you are thinking about." Anna looked radiant as she beamed a happy, coy smile. "We'll get to that later."

Anna redirected the discussion. "I intend to appoint you as my heir apparent, teach you, and eventually anoint you as my successor. Mr. Reid will help," once again Anna raised her eyebrows over her smile, "With the right motivations, of course."

Anna and I had an early dinner at Kurtz's cavernous restaurant at 60 Broadway, just one block from the office. She talked about her initial plans for my new career. Although I was eager to share my good news with my family, I needed time to think through the ramifications. Listening to Anna, I became aware that despite her reassurances, I did not feel ready. Crowds terrified me.

At the end of the meal, I told Anna, "I will consider it."

"Great! We will start next week with appointments in New York." When I saw her smile and confidence, I had to present my position more emphatically.

"Sweet Anna, thank you. Alas, you are more confident in my abilities than I. You have no idea how terrified I am of public speaking and crowds in general."

"You only have to…"

"Please do nothing more until I ask you to do so." I cut her off. I saw her disappointment, but she acknowledged my request with a nod of her head.

That evening I shared Anna's proposal with the Colonel and Tennie. Both of them thought the opportunity of my becoming a Lyceum speaker provided a perfect next step. I consulted with my constellation of adopted family, close friends, and mentors. Yes! Everyone unanimously agreed. They all encouraged me to soon be traveling and speaking on the Lyceum circuit to huge crowds at the largest venues in the country. Lizzybeth strongly supported the project and told me she would join me as often as she could.

I fretted over the decision about the Lyceum and Anna's generous offer. Even though everyone expressed support, something was not right. Nightly, like Jacob, I wrestled with angels in my sleep. I panicked about engaging the huge, white-winged angel with Harriett Beecher Stowe's face. In my imaginings I kept seeing myself with no words, standing totally dumb in front of crowds.

Finally, one night I went to sleep, asking Demosthenes to give me some sign or signal as to what I should do. That night my Majestic Guardian appeared in a dream.

"Come walk with me, Victoria." I peered out the window, and a beautiful bright path appeared. As soon as our hands joined, his shimmering green and golden light illuminated us both. We walked along well-kept paths through a beautiful garden. I felt serene and infused with wonderment.

"Behold!" He paused and pointed out a young sapling of an apple tree.

"And now..." Demosthenes motioned toward the tree, no longer a sapling. It offered its first fruit of a few shining red apples. We strolled some more, only to end up back at the same place.

"Some things take time." Demosthenes smiled at me. He made all conflicts and worries melt away. This time the tree outsized the old apple tree behind my childhood home in Homer, Ohio, and stood laden with big, shiny red apples.

Rachel, my departed childhood neighbor, teacher, and friend, sat on a bench nearby. She beckoned me to sit with her. I was filled with joy and raced up and embraced her. We sat and marveled at the big apple tree. I felt so happy to see her again. We sat close together, happy in reunion and admiring the abundance of bright red apples.

"Deep roots bear shiny fruits." Rachel sang....

Upon waking I remembered the entire vision. I would indeed become a speaker, but not yet. Like the apple tree, I needed more time before becoming a powerful and prolific bearer of fruits.

My decision not to immediately embark on a speaking career disappointed everyone except Tennessee. She looked into my eyes and simply nodded her head.

"When the time is right," she confirmed.

"Victoria, I am happy to introduce you to my escort this evening," Anna smiled coquettishly, "Mr. Whitelaw Reid."

"What a pleasure," I said as Whitelaw bowed formally and kissed my hand.

"Horace Greeley brought Mr. Reid to New York to command the daily operations at the *Tribune*." Of course I already knew this, but gazed approvingly as Anna praised her escort.

The tall and elegant man had an easy air of confidence about him. His dark hair gave way to deeply set, penetrating eyes. As his most distinguishing feature, other than his natural affability, he sported a large moustache that rivaled my husband's.

Two weeks earlier, Mr. Reid published an article, "Women in Wall Street," which was kind to me and Tennie. I was grateful Anna had enticed Mr. Reid to attend our inaugural soiree. The event would be featured in the morning papers. "This is wonderful, Anna. I am most appreciative."

Whitelaw let go of my hand, turned, and hesitated. After a long moment, the tall gentleman smiled, bowed, and kissed Tennie's hand. I saw a spark dance between their eyes, as if a nymph playfully enthralled a most willing satyr. Tennie laughed demurely and allowed the gentleman to escort her into the gathering. Her gray-blue eyes were sparkling.

"Well, you and Tennie C. will have to help me occupy Reid or Benjamin." Anna smiled at me coyly. "They both want all my attention." We exchanged knowing smiles. "Looks like Tennessee already commandeered the situation!"

"She usually does," I replied, and we both laughed.

Anna went into the parlor to visit with Isabella Beecher Hooker and Lizzybeth. Isabella had expanded her activities and advocacy for the N.W.S.A., and she and I talked regularly. Susan B. Anthony, with her usual stern countenance, sat by Lizzy's side like an eagle jealously guarding its prey, so no one else could partake.

The contrast between the two of them always amused me. Elizabeth dressed beautifully and exuded an inviting disposition. Tonight she wore a flowing dark green ball gown, a set of pink pearls adorned her neck, and pink ribbons were tied in her curled, blond hair.

Anthony always looked like a strict schoolteacher ready to commence an elementary class. She groomed her hair unappealingly, pressed back and gathered tight. Her black, utilitarian frock made her look unapproachable. Everything about her conveyed a disapproving demeanor. I don't think I ever saw the woman simply laugh. I could tell the two actively mourned their loss of their shared venture, *The Revolution*.

The tall and handsome bond financier and banker, Henry Clews, spoke with a distinguished British accent and a perceptive financial mind. Henry engaged in a conversation about the stability of the economy with Matthew Hale Smith, another Wall Street personality, and with General William S. Hillyer, who had served President Grant as his wartime chief of staff.

My dear friend and personal financial advisor, John Pierpont Morgan, who had on several occasions given me in-depth tutorials on complex financial matters, joined the others. As always, J. P. held a tall glass full of whiskey.

Morgan addressed a group of financial men. "I am concerned about the scarcity and high prices on the C.M.A. shares. The construction costs are a multiple of what it should have cost, by all reckoning. An unusually large portion of shares seem to be held in street names, making it impossible to know who owns the stocks. Quite unusual."

J. P. was voicing his contrarian position regarding a darling of Wall Street, Crédit Moblier of America. During the construction of the transcontinental railroad, the Union Pacific Railroad contracted C.M.A. to construct the eastern leg. U.P.R.R., through C.M.A., competed against the Central Pacific Railroad to reach the joining point. Substantial federal land and mining rights incentivized both groups to reach the joining point first. When the "Golden Spike" joined the two tracks at Promontory Point in Utah on May 10, 1869, all the grants went to the Central Pacific, backed by Leland Stanford, Collis Huntington, Mark Hopkins, and Charles Crocker.

"I'm staying away from the bonds, Henry. They smell like rotten fish." J. P. concluded.

"I didn't know you were a railroad engineer, John," Clews responded. "This is what makes the markets so interesting." He paused to exchange a knowing smile with Mr. Smith and General Hillyer. "Sad your father's bank will not profit on the bonds. We did some great business together during the War."

"I know it does not take $180,000,000!" I saw J. P. turning red, so before he could present the logic behind his conclusion, I hooked his arm and guided him away.

I calmed him down. "They are not all as smart as you, J. P. They will find out in time."

"You are right, of course," He said, and started looking for new whiskey to fill his glass. "I will hold my counsel to those who seek it." He bowed to me. "Thank you, Victoria."

"We should all thank you, kind sir. Your tutoring of the Colonel and George enables our firm to grow."

"Then we shall share our gratitude and I will remain your humble servant." He set off to find more drink.

Knowing General Butler would come, I purchased some of his guilty pleasures, a box of doughnuts injected with a jam crafted from Bourbon whiskey. He could eat the doughnuts in public and enjoy himself without betraying the fact he consumed his precious, barrel-aged Bourbon.

General Butler arrived and found himself trapped in an animated discussion with Lizzybeth and Susan. They were relentless. He kept looking over at Anna, standing by Mr. Reid, along with Tennie.

I overheard Lizzy commenting, "Rumors are swifter than truth and near impossible to disavow."

"Rumors are more deadly than bullets." When General Butler responded in his high-pitched, squeaky voice, the room silenced like a battlefield before the first shot. "At least in war, you have the ability to fight back, outmaneuver your enemy." He addressed the entire room. "Rumors inflict deadening wounds without killing you. They take on a life of their own, continuing to inflict pain and damage, until in some distant future they are either eventually forgotten or you die."

Anna left the side of Whitelaw Reid and joined the conversation. Nervous laughter broke out. Anna's beatific smile lit up the room as she forged ahead. "But dear Beast, leader of men and pillar of fortitude, surely we can choose to ignore what other people may say."

"I will defer to my nightingale." The General smiled and kissed Anna's hand. "But I know of no other instrument so savage, persecuting, or relentless as rumor."

As we all finished the dinner catered by Delmonico's, Tennessee invited the men to cigars, which caused the slightly inebriated gentlemen to laugh in good humor. General Beast seated himself next to Anna, with Whitelaw on the other side. Tennie obviously enthralled both Whitelaw Reid and Henry Clews. Truth be told, Tennie enthralled any man who still had a pulse. She sat most alluring in her revealing, royal blue ball gown and stunning white pearls. Her eyes shimmered like a crystal glass chandelier. My sister rose in her place, acknowledged me, and spoke.

"We have stormed the gates, Victoria and I. Never before has woman been allowed to become a stock and gold trader. Now crinolines, pantaloons, and petticoats," she paused, allowing the men to form vivid pictures of her words, and smiled to all, "and even trousers-wearing women stand willing to compete in the world of finance, previously a fortress declared for men only."

"Here! Here!" The high, squeaky voice of The Beast sounded.

"Here! Here!" Everyone responded.

"We will play equally with men. We ask no special favor or consideration." Tennie concluded with an open challenge. "Let our account balances determine who excels and who falters."

The next day, *The New York Tribune* published a story on the front page under the headline, "See Who Wins!" The byline credited the managing editor, Whitelaw Reid. The article recounted in generous detail our first soiree. After the article, everyone wanted to be invited to one of our gatherings.

Our fame grew.

Chapter 3

PRONOUNCEMENTS

New York Herald
April 2, 1870

As February passed the mid-mark, I had to do something special, something dramatic now that I decided not to accept Anna's offer. I wanted to pursue my path of becoming eminent. I remembered how Rosie, my longtime friend, lover, and former co-actress in San Francisco, taught me to recognize the power of the press.

I set out to have tea with Rosie at her current place of business, Annie Wood's house of nocturnal entertainment, one of the "Seven Sisters," the most prestigious and expensive brothels. Annie managed her elite bordello with an iron fist. "Rosamund," Rosie's professional *nom de bode*, held the reputation as the highest priced courtesan in all of New York City.

I waited in the parlor room where I normally met with her. Occasionally the loud, bawdy, voluptuous, and insatiable Josie Mansfield, our dear friend, co-actress, and lover from the San Francisco days, would join us. Every time I sat in this room, great things followed. I assumed the men who frequented the establishment felt the same.

"Vickie!" Rosie swept into the room. Her beauty took the air from the room. I gasped.

"How can you look younger every time I see you?" I voiced my amazement.

"Because, dear, I'm a ..."

"*Witch!*" We proclaimed in unison.

I had learned over the last twelve years to listen very carefully to anything Rosie had to tell me. Rosie taught me how to distill and prepare tinctures and oils from flowers, spices and herbs. The one she called "Thieves" protected us from disease when we toured the war-torn South. She called herself Pagan and said people would call her a witch if they knew about her rituals and practices. I thought the rituals beautiful and rich with meaning. Rosie saw the future as clearly as Tennie.

"My, you are looking full of woe," Rosie laughed gently. "What have you been up to, my little dove with an eagle's heart?" She drew me to her, and kissed me full on the lips the way she had taught me. Our lips formed over our opened mouths and our tongues danced playfully. We would exchange licks and bites of the other's lips. I savored the kiss. We had spent hours kissing this way, back in San Francisco, nibbling playfully, deeply connected, lips not parting for hours. After a few moments, I broke off the intimacy. Rosie cocked her head at me. "Well, you certainly have something on your mind."

"I do love you, Rosie," I apologized.

Rosie tossed her head back and a resonant, heavenly laughter emitted from deep inside her. "I've known that from before we even met." She continued to laugh. It always surprised me such a rich sound emerged from so slight a frame. She motioned me to sit down next to her. "So, tell me, Vickie, what thoughts are running through those gears clicking away in your head?"

"Anna Dickinson visited me and wants to help me launch a new career as a speaker on the Lyceum circuit." I paused. Rosie waited for me to continue. "I decided not to accept her kind offer," I announced sadly. "And I have been thinking..."

"You made the right decision, Victoria, you are not ready, not yet."

"Rosie, may I ask you..."

"Do not despair. You will be soon enough."

"What I..."

"I already know what you want." Rosie giggled.

"But, I haven't even…"

"Stop! Don't talk when I am interrupting you!" Rosie cut me off again, laughing at her own joke. "April second, dear girl." Rosie proclaimed. "And make it bold!"

"What?" I shook my head. "How could you possibly know why or what …?" I stopped and looked at her. "I wanted to visit and talk with you." I thought a moment. "Did Tennessee…?" I caught myself mid-question and realized that of course Rosie would know my purpose. She always did! Many times in the past Rosie would know my mind well before I knew it myself.

Rosie watched the puzzled look on my face turn to full understanding. Her jubilant laughter filled the room like cascading waterfalls. I loved Rosie's rippling, dulcimer-toned laughter. She reached for my head and guided it to rest on her heart, as she had done countless times before. I always felt completely safe when she held me close. She ran her fingers across my hair, gently pressing my head closer to her. She held me like a guardian angel. She kissed the top of my head. I felt completely loved and protected.

"You will become a great orator, Victoria. I knew over a decade ago, remember? I told you so."

"Yes, I remember." I recalled the moment Rosie combed out my hair late one morning after we had entertained the men, and held one another tenderly while we slept. I smiled, remembering our lovemaking and how Rosie taught me new things. She was amazed when I showed her just how well I had learned. I had confided my frustration about not fulfilling my destiny as promised me by my Majestic Guardian. Back then, Rosie comforted me, telling me to be patient, and assuring me I would become powerful. She had prophesized, "Victoria, you will play to masses."

"But not yet!" Rosie returned me to the present. She peered into my eyes. "My little dove, you need to build your name and recognition while giving your new roots here in New York time to dig in deeper. Then you will start to harvest the fruits of your endeavors." She hesitated a moment, then, making a quick decision, concluded, "This will give you the strength to survive strong gales."

I felt as if Rosie had witnessed my dream about the apple tree. I should have known up front that Rosie would voice my innermost thoughts. I turned and implored her with my eyes.

"How, Rosie? Tell me, what should I do?"

"Please, Victoria, just go ahead and do it!" She glared at me. "Don't be coy about it, and never look back." She hesitated for a moment, and added, "There will be a price to pay, but that never stops 'The Woodhull'!" Her peals of laughter enlivened the room.

"Rosie, is it possible we are talking about the same thing?"

"I do believe so. You want to declare yourself in the papers as a candidate for President, to be the first woman to ever do so. This way, more people will know your name, and listen to you."

"How?" I shook my head from side to side. Rosie just laughed and placed my head back on her bosom.

"Publish your intention on the second of April," Rosie intoned, ignoring my question. "It will herald your arrival as a force to be reckoned with." I could feel her smiling without seeing it. I heard her heart quicken. "A most propitious day!"

"A most propitious day!" I whooped and leapt to my feet, pulling Rosie up to give her a big hug. Every time Rosie had identified a most propitious day in the past, truly wonderful things had started happening. I now expected marvelous things would result from this new most propitious day.

"Thank you, Rosie!" I reached to pull Rosie close to kiss her goodbye. She pulled back.

"Understand Vickie, your path will not be simple. There will be successes, but also great hardships and moments you will feel completely alone."

Rosie, her voice void of joy, suddenly looked so sullen it scared me. For just a moment she appeared to be an ancient crone, with gray hairs and her face contorted by age. Confused, I looked away.

"Completely alone…" I whispered as I recognized the words from my nightmare. Rosie must have heard the dread in my voice. I thought I would cry.

"Listen to me, Victoria." She turned my face to hers and I saw only the youthful Rosie I knew so well. "You are resilient and you will overcome every adversity." She smiled. "Your fate, my dear."

"Rosie, sometimes I fear the struggle. I worry I will be abandoned and left completely alone." My eyes filled with hot tears.

She beamed at me with so much love I had to smile in return. "Use your words, Vickie, in every way you can. You will live a long and wonderful life. You will live to see many of the changes you seek." She winked at me and consecrated her words with the traditional benediction, "So mote it be."

Taking my leave, I remembered what Demosthenes said to me in my nightmare the night of the Grand Opening. My road would be filled with wonderful joys, but I would endure great hardships. I felt a chill down my spine.

I assembled the best team I could think of to help me announce my candidacy for President. The incredibly wise and learned Stephen Pearl Andrews thought it "bold and the perfect time!" The strapping, handsome wordsmith and firebrand intellectual Theodore Tilton joined Pearly and my dear husband to help me forge and fashion a proclamation for the papers to print.

I would induce a trance or prompt myself in my dream state to talk out loud. My dear husband would write down my words verbatim. Once the themes and primary content were down on paper, my *Le Trois Mousquetaires* dedicated to the protection of their queen would sit and discuss my dictations. We would modify them for the greatest impact and the finest presentation. Sometimes the ideological debates were quite lively.

At my request, and the exchange of a promise for exclusive reporting of some future stories and a fee, Whitelaw convinced James Gordon Bennett to publish in the *New York Herald* on April 2, 1870, my "First Pronunciamento":

> *As I happen to be the most prominent representative of the only unrepresented class in the Republic, and perhaps the most practical exponent of the principles of equality, I request the favor of being permitted to address the public through the medium of the Herald.*
>
> *While others of my sex devoted themselves to a crusade against the laws that shackle the women of the country, I asserted my individual independence; while others prayed for the good time coming, I worked for it; while others argued the equality of women with man, I proved it by successfully engaging in business; while others sought to show that there was no valid reason why women should be treated, socially and politically, as being inferior to man, I boldly entered the arena of business and exercised the rights I already possessed.*
>
> *I therefore claim the right to speak for the un-enfranchised women of the country, and believing as I do that the prejudices which still exist in the popular mind against women in public life will not soon disappear, I now announce myself as candidate for the Presidency.*
>
> *This is an epoch of sudden changes and startling surprises. The blacks were cattle in 1860; a Negro now sits in Jeff Davis' seat in the United States Senate. Political preachers paw in*

the air; there is no live issue up for discussion. The platform that is to succeed in the coming election must enunciate the general principles of enlightened justice and economy.

I anticipate criticism; but however unfavorable the comment this letter may evoke, I trust that my sincerity will not be called in question. I have deliberately and of my own accord placed myself before the people as a candidate for the Presidency of the United States, and having the means, courage, energy, and strength necessary for the race, intend to contest it to the close."

By: Victoria Woodhull

The declaration had its desired effect. My popularity, and perhaps notoriety, grew. I learned again controversy generated press, and the free advertising benefitted business. The volume of new accounts at the brokerage soared.

Not all the newspapers were kind. A pernicious cartoonist, strikingly in the style of Tom Nast but not signed, published a vicious depiction of me. *Pandora's Voice Box* had me standing on a stage as *Pierrot* in a simple, billowing, white clown outfit, with a single tear flowing from one eye, wearing a false crown, and a sash that read "Would be President." A gargoyle-like monkey named Free Love and two satanic dogs named Spiritualism, and Equality performed tricks at my command. In the background a treasure chest with an engraved "P" lay open and bare. A white dove named Hope escaped by flying away.

Several written editorials were equally malicious. I tried not to pay any attention to the many vicious articles about me. I failed miserably. Mostly they claimed I could not have written the words I published, as I had no formal education. It hurt to have my name dragged through the mud by journalists who held no regard for facts. Had they already forgotten President Lincoln taught himself? They obviously did not know the Commodore Vanderbilt, their royalty, left school after the third grade, same as I.

I formulated a plan. I sent a message to Whitelaw asking him to visit.

Whitelaw Reid, always generous with his time and published support, came to our offices. I believe part of the stimulus for his desire stemmed from the fact Tennie would join us. It would be queer of any man not to be interested.

"Thank you, Whitelaw, for coming over." We sat down in the back parlor.

"Always a pleasure, Victoria." He turned, rose from his seat, and smiled broadly as Tennie entered the room and sat directly across from him. "Good to see you again, Miss Claflin." He bowed to her. "How may I be of service to you two ladies?"

"Please, Whitelaw, call me Tennie." She leaned into the space between them. "We want to undertake an enterprise if you think it wise, and if you are willing to advise us."

"I believe I and the *Tribune* are duty bound to assist you in any way possible. The two of you certainly help sell a lot of papers!"

"Good!" I declared. I stood up and started pacing the room.

Tennie spoke from her seat. "We are hurt and tired of the mockery much of the press make of us. They are cruel!"

Whitelaw listened intently, while continuing to look at my sister. "You know it is just business, Miss… Tennie." He seemed almost apologetic. He glanced briefly in my direction. "Does it really matter to you what they say, Victoria, as long as they are writing about you?" His voice revealed he genuinely cared.

"I used to think not." I let my exasperation show. "The meanness frustrates me. Using us as a distraction from the important, real issues pains and disheartens."

Whitelaw, to his credit, sighed deeply. "I confess, I know that to be true!" He talked with me but could not remove his eyes from Tennie.

"Vickie and I have talked about it, Whitelaw. We want your candid advice, and thereafter, direction on how to publish our own weekly paper." Even I found my little sister enchanting. As she leaned in talking to him, he almost leaned out of his chair. "We want to report, entertain, and present the serious issues of the day of interest to both men and women." She smiled at him. "We want to promote open debate."

Whitelaw leaned back into his chair. Suddenly, he got up and started pacing the parlor with long strides. I sat down and we watched as an internal unspoken argument seemed to rage inside his head.

"Well! It has never been done before." He spoke with his back to us. When he turned around, I am sure he saw the looks of disdain on both our faces. He smiled. "Yes, I know, precedent has never stopped Victoria Woodhull nor Tennessee Celeste Claflin." Then he chuckled. "Do you two see a bullfighter's red cape no other woman sees and imperatively charge at the target?"

Tennie chided alluringly, "Why, Mr. Reid, are you calling us bovine?" She widened her eyes and pretended to be shocked. We all laughed, breaking the tension in the room.

"No! Most certainly not! Although you two do seem to have a monopoly on boldly marching where only men have gone before." Tennie rose and marched directly toward him. He took her hand, and she allowed him to return her to her seat. We all laughed further.

"As to the question at hand, please share your thoughts, most illustrious and accomplished sir." I spoke the entreaty in a Southern belle accent. Whitelaw chuckled.

"Well, if anyone could do it, it would be you two." He nodded at me, and gazed adoringly at Tennie. "You have the resources to afford building up the subscriptions. I dare say, you can generate sufficient interest to sell enough papers in the interim." He nodded his head several times and concluded, "I don't see why not!"

"Thank you, Whitelaw." I appreciated his benediction.

"Will you help us?" Tennie pushed forward. "Will you advise us, introduce us to the right people, and provide consultations to allow us to do this well?" My little sister had become a consummate woman of business.

"Tennie, surely you understand there exists an inherent conflict of interest, given my position at the *Tribune* and working for Mr. Greeley." Whitelaw stopped and sat down. Still, he had demonstrated he wanted to help.

"We have anticipated that, Whitelaw!" I said, and Tennie nodded her agreement. She looked at me, imploring me to continue. "What if we agree, right here and right now, we will always provide you personally an advance copy, as soon as it goes to the typesetter, at least a day prior to publication. You would have exclusive information for the *Tribune*."

"You two really are far more clever than nearly all men. You are amazing!" He looked briefly at me and for a long while at Tennie. He weighed his decision, and then his face showed a cunning grin. "It would make the decision easier if Miss Claflin would agree to deliver each advance copy and dine with me."

Before I could respond, Tennie stood and kneeled in front of Whitelaw and placed both her hands on his thigh tops. He flinched and smiled. She looked up into his eyes and affected her own Southern belle drawl.

"Why Mr. Whitelaw Reid, the pleasure would be all mine."

My sister and I were going to publish our own weekly newspaper! Whitelaw advised us and, true to his word, found us an older, yet still good Koenig & Bauer steam-powered printing press and dependable men to maintain and operate the equipment, cut the pulp paper, set the type, and then print, fold, and bundle our weekly.

Woodhull & Claflin's Weekly would be the first major newspaper founded, owned, and managed exclusively by women. Whitelaw even sent a few out-of-work reporters he knew to be excellent to work for us. At Whitelaw's suggestion, we set the price at ten cents a copy or four dollars for a year's subscription... a twenty percent discount on the single-copy price.

Everyone involved, even Rosie, agreed a most auspicious day for the first edition would be May 14, 1870. We would issue our first paper the same day both woman suffrage conventions commenced in town. Thus, Tennie and I would once again be doing in business what others were only talking about. They spoke words while we took action.

I would use my words... *in print.*

Chapter 4

IRREPARABLE DAMAGE

New York City
Spring, 1870

My husband arranged for his brother George to join the brokerage firm to manage all the advertising, paperwork, and organization. The two men worked closely with J. P.

The Colonel called a meeting of the key people in the firm after closing one early April day. George joined us as we assembled in our rear offices. I wondered if James already knew my news and had convened the meeting for my announcement about the newspaper.

Ginny, our proficient and dedicated assistant, hovered by the door, not sure whether to come in or continue closing up. "Virginia, George and I will put things away this evening," the Colonel spoke. "Why don't you go ahead on home?" Ginny never questioned our intentions, nor we hers. She took her leave.

Tennie and the men lit Cuban cigars, a gift from Vanderbilt, and the pungent smell of thick, gray smoke filled the room. Tennie wore a cropped business jacket over a starched white linen shirt, and pants, which outraged many. The pants brought her attention and emphasized her prodigious bosoms. My sister attracted the notice of men regardless of what she chose to wear.

"He is completely out of control, Victoria," my husband pronounced, starting the meeting.

I realized the first agenda item would be the behavior of a man I hated, feared, and yet chose time after time to try to salvage, Reuben Buckman "Buck" Claflin, my father.

"Do we have to discuss this, James?" I tried to avert the discussion. I had good news to share and I did not want to spoil it by talking about my terrible father. "I would prefer..."

"Yes. We do!" The Colonel raised his voice and hand to cut me off. "It is bad enough he buys the most expensive clothes he can find at the best shops in town and charges it to the firm."

George nodded his agreement and added, "When you and Tennie are out, he hangs around the office and sometimes talks with the clients."

"I already know. Is all this really necessary?" I wanted to discuss my news and plans for the weekly. I tired of the constant complaining and bickering about Buck. No one had to tell me to what degree Pa was evil. I knew better than anyone. I looked at James, saw the intensity of his ire, and knew better than to ignore him.

"I told you, yes," repeated the Colonel.

My exciting news would have to wait. I settled in to listen to the charges pile up against Pa.

"Vickie," Tennie spoke up, betraying her complicity with the others to confront me about our family, "this really is important. We have to do something. Please listen."

"Fine! He buys some clothes and charges our account. I understand!" I thought I could quickly appease the three of them.

"No. You don't know!" The Colonel shouted. His confrontation made me tremble. "George, tell her what happened."

"Victoria, I take full responsibility. This is all my fault." George spoke to me sincerely contrite. He lowered his head.

"Nonsense!" The Colonel raised his voice at his brother. "Give her the facts, man!"

"Three days ago, your father milled about and talked with some of the clients while James attended to meetings." George looked up at me with so much guilt I had to respond.

"George," I said, "I do not hold you accountable for whatever Buck did. I know he is a scoundrel of the lowest order. Just tell me the sordid details."

"I had to run an errand down to the exchange to lodge a purchase order, and Buck convinced me to leave the doors open. He said he would mind the shop." George bowed his head to his chest.

I lost my temper. "And stop feeling so damn guilty!" I yelled before I could hold it back.

The floodgates opened and George divulged the story as if expelling poison. "Yesterday, a finely dressed, and quite young woman came in and told me she wanted to change her preferences on her trading ledger. She was willing to assume more risk than she first indicated."

"Get to the point, George." I demanded.

"I asked what her name was. She surprised me when she said Astor was her family name, as I knew I would have paid special attention to that family name on a new account card. Her first name is Emily and she is the great-granddaughter of the patriarch, John Jacob Astor."

"Really?" I was genuinely surprised. "We will be trading on behalf of Astor money?" I remembered studying long hours about the Commodore in the magnificent library on Lafayette Street. The Astor library was part of the legacy of the Commodore's predecessor as the wealthiest man in America.

I realized George was waiting on me. "Go on, George!"

"I looked through our client ledgers and found no Astor clients."

He hesitated until he looked up and saw my nostrils flare. "Please, just give us all the information."

"I remembered the day she said she came in. Ginny lunched at Kurtzman's, and I had to get to the exchange before closing. Your father offered to sit at the front desk in Ginny's stead until her return."

"What did you do with Emily Astor, George?" I interrogated.

"I covered for the firm, informing her that one of you," he pointed to Tennie and me, "typically picked up and reviewed all new account ledgers to add your own comments. This fact pleased the young lady immensely and she asked me to thank you for the personal consideration. She stated she would love to meet one of you. Upon my request, she handed me her deposit receipt. It was quite a large initial deposit." He stopped and looked ashamed to continue.

"Go ahead, George, tell her how much." The Colonel commanded his brother.

"The receipt identified our acceptance of five thousand dollars in bearer bonds drawn on The Bank of New York."

"That is a large deposit!" Tennie declared.

I stood up to speak, but my husband raised his hand to arrest my motion. It irritated me to be so openly directed and forcibly controlled. I sat back down. Obviously, the Colonel seethed with a deeper rage than I had calculated.

"Finish, George," the Colonel ordered.

"I checked our deposits, there were none for this sum on that day or after. I checked everywhere for her ledger card, as she said she signed one, but there is no client ledger card in the young lady Astor's name."

"Damn it, George!" My husband shouted. "Tell her who signed the bloody receipt."

"Oh, s-s-sor- sorry, J-J-J- James" George started stammering as he often did under great pressure. "The receipt was signed 'Reuben b- -b-ba- Buckman c c-Ca- Claflin, Manager.'"

I recoiled. *Pa outright stole from the firm.* I had borne witness to every manner of heinous act by Buck, but he was reaching new depths. Five thousand dollars was an enormous sum of money, almost fifteen years' wages for a laborer. I closed my eyes and took a deep breath, trying not to feel like the helpless little girl Pa hurt when I was only nine.

My mind left the room. I viewed my nine-year-old self stumble out of the shack we lived in and stumble my way to the river behind our home. I remembered the pain and convulsed. Buck raped me. I hurt so bad I wanted to die. I saw myself sit in the riverbed, gather my shift, wash the blood out, and then wash the blood and that sticky white fluid from Pa off my legs.

I saw a shimmering green light emerge from where the water whispered to me. I watched as my Majestic Guardian rose up from the swirling waters and spoke to me.

"You are but a little girl, Victoria. I will protect you. You will rise up from this river, rise up from these poor surroundings and rise up to live in a great house of great wealth in a city far away by the sea, with docks crowded with ships. You will become their leader…. All this shall come to pass."

"Victoria!" I heard Tennie's voice reaching to me from a distance. Slowly the memory dissolved and I returned to the room. I turned to my sister and saw she had a worried look on her face. She knew I had fallen into a vision or memory. I looked up and saw that my Colonel knew it as well. As he looked at me with compassion, his anger softened.

I took three deep breaths with my eyes closed to join the present. I blinked my eyes open and turned to George. "What did you do?"

"I had no choice." George spoke plaintively. "I withdrew the amount from your principal account and deposited it into a client trust account in the name of Emily Astor."

Before I could address George, the Colonel spoke. "Thank you, George, you did well. You may leave us."

George stood to depart.

My husband said, "Brother, before you take your leave, could you tell Victoria and Tennie what the firm spent on expenses in the month of March."

George looked down. He hesitated. He avoided all our eyes and talked directly to the floor. "t-t-tw-w-twenty th-th-th-thousand d-d-d-dollars." He exhaled and quickly withdrew.

Few people spent that much money in a lifetime, let alone in a single month. "Surely it is because of our opening day and setting up our home." I suggested.

"No, Vickie, it is not." James would not compromise an inch today. "First, the Commodore made a gift to Tennie by covering all the costs of our opening day gala."

"How is it possible we spent so much?" I wondered. No matter how rich we were, we could not survive our current level of spending. "Where did it all go?"

"Our family!" Tennie spat out the words. "It gets worse." Tennie gasped for breath several times as she spoke rapidly. "Mama Roxanne steals my jewelry and pawns it at shops down in the Five Corners. I could almost bear it, if these were not the precious, irreplaceable gifts to me from my beloved Cornelius. I have to hire Josie's friend, Mr. Harper to threaten legal enforcement of stolen goods to force the pawnbrokers to sell them back, always with a handsome profit to the shop."

"I didn't know, Tennie." I apologized.

"There is a lot you don't know," she released a built-up pressure. Her voice got higher and louder as she became despondent, "Our sisters steal both our clothes and then chop them up to make them fit." She looked me in the eyes, "Our entire family is out of control." She finished, shouting at me.

"Indeed!" James turned on me. I have rarely seen him so adamant. "What are you going to do about it, Victoria?"

I turned away, hurt by the brunt force of my husband's manner. Being so directly confronted by the facts, I thought about it. Our home housed and provided for ten others besides James, Tennie, and myself, and my two children. My son Byron had grown into a big boy at age fifteen, but he had not matured emotionally or mentally. He required constant monitoring and care. Zulu Maud, my thriving, shining light of a daughter, would celebrate her tenth birthday in April. She regularly demonstrated her incredible intelligence, and I employed tutors to provide her the classic education denied me.

We also supported and housed my parents, my two older sisters, one of their husbands, and four of their grown kids. And then Dr.

Canning Woodhull, my first husband and father to the kids, moved in and helped take care of Byron. All together, the Colonel, Tennie, and I paid for the upkeep of fifteen souls.

I so wanted to share the great news that Tennie and I were starting our own paper and publishing the first edition to coincide with the opening of the suffrage conventions. I had been elated, but now all excitement had evaporated. I looked over at Tennie. She looked focused on the immediate problems of our family and not our future.

After some time sitting quietly, I realized the Colonel and Tennie were waiting to hear from me. I found my voice. My words satisfied no one, but I sought to end the meeting.

"I will contact young Emily Astor and ask her to lunch."

"*And?*" My husband demanded.

"I simply cannot abandon my family. I made an oath in my youth to protect Tennie. They are loathsome, but I will not put them out on the street." I turned away from my husband. "It is a terrible burden," I paused, "… a terrible burden." I despised my inability to break from my family. I wanted to but simply could not.

"A burden you place on us all. One day, Victoria, you will lift this burden and kick your entire family of takers, other than Tennie and the kids, out of our lives." James shouted. "How can you hold the utter fantasy that one day they will love and embrace you instead of treating you worse than an animal?" He hesitated. I hoped he realized his words were cutting me deeply. "I, for one, await your awakening day, to rid our lives of this pestilence!" My husband walked away disgusted.

His words slashed through me. I felt a rupture. Something fundamental broke in that moment between my husband and me.

We lost something precious, forever.

"Mr. Tilton, you look dreadful. Has something bad happened?" I asked.

"Not necessarily!" he pronounced. At his request, I met with Theodore at the office of *The Revolution* with Elizabeth Cady Stanton and Susan B. Anthony.

Theodore, a man for whom I held ever-increasing high regard, knew that the woman suffrage movement, to have any chance of securing political support, must be united, the factions reformed in solidarity. Any division would fortify an already nearly insurmountable opposition.

Many people were arriving in New York City to meet and set the agendas for the two simultaneous suffrage conventions in little more than a week. Mr. Tilton had hardly slept for several days, working well into the late evenings trying to broker a reconciliation to be announced at a consolidated convention.

Teddy rose from his chair and paced between the desks of Susan and Lizzybeth. He seemed unaware of our presence. He paused and then looked pleadingly at Elizabeth.

"Just say whatever it is you came to say, Theodore." Lizzybeth meant to be courteous, but her tone betrayed her impatience.

"The split can be reconciled," Teddy proclaimed.

"Truly?" I failed to hide my shock and disbelief. As much as I wanted to support and encourage dear Theodore, I had little hope for any positive resolution.

My mind left the room. I remembered last year, seeing the evil I had not seen since my childhood. The so-called Boston Brahmins' eyes turned into either burning red flames or cold black coals. I remembered my vision about the factions fighting for decades. I knew there would be no unification. I saw it.

"They offer reconciliation!" Theodore's rich, baritone voice brought me back to the room. He continued. "Elizabeth, you will be named a senior officer of a new United Woman Suffrage Association. In return you will disband the N.W.S.A. upon commencement of your convention on May 14 and pledge your support for the U.W.S.A. The

United convention will be conducted at Steinway Hall commencing May 15!"

"This is wonderful news!" Lizzybeth exclaimed. She looked at Teddy and saw what I also saw. He looked troubled. "Then why the long face, Theodore, and why are you pacing so incessantly?"

"There are details to be worked out." Teddy stopped pacing.

"This is better news than I had expected from those elite, self-righteous, cackling, old biddies." Elizabeth clearly rejoiced that the woman suffrage movement might yet be undivided. She thought for a moment and then asked, "Will the platform of the new U.W.S.A. seek a new constitutional amendment for universal suffrage and full legal rights for women?"

"In time, yes." Theodore answered carefully. "They want to campaign for the vote first, and thereafter pursue equal legal standing of women, once women can vote." He looked despondently toward Susan B. Anthony.

"I've had a vision." I declared to the three of them. "If there is not an immediate unification of the movement, the split will prevent women getting the vote for half a century to come." I hesitated, but then went on, facing Elizabeth and looking into her eyes. "In fact, you will all grow old and wither away before women can legally vote throughout the country."

"Absurd. You have no way of knowing that!" Susan sneered.

"It could very well come to pass!" Theodore supported me.

We all turned to Lizzybeth to see her reaction. I could see the strains of emotions cross her face, as clouds block the sun to cast shadows on the prairie. She too knew the lack of a unified effort would spell political disaster.

"It is so hard to compromise on the principles I know in my heart are right." She gazed across the office space, speaking directly to her partner, Susan. "Perhaps we have to compromise to amalgamate and move our agenda forward, one step at a time."

Susan sat still as stone. She paled before our eyes.

"I truly think it best," Theodore offered.

"I concur!" I affirmed.

Susan asked warily, "Once we disband and pledge our support, then Elizabeth and I will be allowed to serve as officers of the U.W.S.A.?"

"I fear not." Theodore collapsed into a chair. He spoke as if confessing a sin.

"I don't understand." Confused, Lizzybeth looked at Teddy. She shook her head from side to side, trying to dislodge the fog obfuscating her thinking.

Susan B. Anthony stood up, placed two fists on her desktop, and leaned as if ready to spring at Theodore. Color flushed back into her face. She seethed, "They will take you back Lizzy, but they repute me."

Elizabeth sat back deep into her chair. "Theodore, is this true?"

"Sadly, yes. I tried, Mrs. Stanton, truly I did." Teddy's eyes welled up and overflowed with his frustration. "I told them this would hurt you; make it more difficult for you to agree."

Elizabeth Cady Stanton gathered herself and stood up. She walked over to Susan and took her hands still balled into fists. She kissed first the right and then the left. Lizzybeth then placed a hand on Susan's shoulder and kissed her on the cheek. Susan fought against tears.

Lizzybeth spoke in a flat monotone that sounded like a death toll. "Theodore, tell them their terms are unacceptable." Her resonant voice continued the funereal dirge tolling woeful tidings. I heard the universal suffrage movement being laid to rest. "They know I will not betray my followers or my friends. They can have their convention and we will have ours." She lowered her head to rest on Susan's shoulder. She squeezed Susan's hand.

"I feared as much." Despondent and fatigued, Mr. Tilton stood up. "I will take my leave."

Lizzybeth walked back to her desk and took out her embossed personal stationery. "Theodore, you tried, and I thank you for your efforts, but it is not meant to be. I do have one last request of you in this matter." She wrote a short note. She folded the vellum in half and placed it in an envelope. She lit a match and reached for a wax candle. Her seal closed the envelope imprinted with an ornate crest formed by the letters E. C. S.

"However I can be of service, Mrs. Stanton." Teddy volunteered.

"Please deliver this sealed note to Mary Livermore."

"Mrs. Stanton, I will do as you ask." He struggled for a minute, but made up his mind. "May I know, what does the note say?"

"Yes." Lizzybeth looked across at Susan and then stood up with an air of dignity and respect. "My response to their proposal reads, in all capital letters:

OVER MY DEAD BODY!

Theodore's carriage stopped at my residence. The man looked like a little schoolboy. His eyes looked into mine, seeking comfort.

Teddy had become a close confidant and political advisor, helping me write, edit, and refine my candidacy announcement. Often, we worked late into the night. I comforted him when he confessed to me his cuckhold by his wife Libby and Teddy's former employer and mentor, the Reverend Henry Ward Beecher. We became quite intimate and shared our thoughts openly.

I learned the erudite and poetic Theodore Tilton for several years wrote Reverend Beecher's Sunday sermons and distributed them to be published in the papers. Finally, I understood the irreconcilable dichotomy between the loftiness of Henry Ward's words and his all too worldly licentious behavior. As I sensed on the day I first met Henry Ward, he sat on a throne of moral righteousness as a usurper.

"Prior to delivering Mrs. Stanton's note, I must at least try to persuade Mary Livermore and the A.W.S.A. to include Susan."

"It won't work, Teddy." I could not encourage his further effort, nor shield him from the inevitable. "It is not to be." I reached for his face and turned his cheek to face me. "Please come in and join us for dinner. You should allow yourself to relax."

"I must try!" The man said solemnly. "I fear all is lost!"

Tennessee came home early one evening, rushed into my arms, and broke out in tears, heaving deep sobs. My sister almost never cried, so I knew something must be very, very wrong. I held her for a long time to let her shed her tears. After a long while, she started to calm down. I cradled her head against my heart.

Suddenly, she shoved me aside and cast an angry glare at me.

"I've lost him!"

"Tennie, what happened?" I asked. She looked away from me, biting her lip to stop the flow of new tears. I could see her teetering between despondence and fury.

"What happened?" Tennie mocked me in a tone so full of bitterness and vitriol I turned away from her. "Don't you move!" I froze and turned toward her.

"Sister, I can't help without knowing the facts." I took one step in her direction and she raised her hand to prevent my approach.

"*Help*?" She grimaced a hideous smile. "*Know the facts!*" She mimicked me. Her voice had an edge to it sharper and more dangerous than the honed blade of a butcher knife.

I felt fear, not for myself, but for Tennie. Tennessee's emotional development had been forged in the fire of abuse and pounded out on the anvil of trauma. I looked at her. I dropped my arms, lowered my shoulders, and opened my palms to her. I looked into her eyes and thought I saw a frightened little girl.

I knew the feeling.

I could not help it. Without moving or sobbing, a single tear flowed from my left eye down my cheek. Another streamed from my right. I blinked my eyes and stared at Tennie with more tears flowing down my face. I dared not move. As softly and as gently as I could, I implored my sister, "Please tell me what happened." I gazed at her with nothing but total acceptance, love and compassion. Tennie turned to me, giving in to her need for affection.

"Oh Vickie, please stop crying. It will get me going again. I'm not sure I'll ever stop."

I sniffled my nose and did my best to hold back the tears running down the sides of my face. I opened my arms to allow her to step into my embrace, if she wanted.

Tennie stepped into my arms and I held her protectively. I did not ask any questions. I gave her time. As she calmed down, keeping her head against my chest, she screeched.

"I've lost Cornelius!"

We sobbed together. I rocked her back and forth. While holding her, I felt convulsions rack her body. I shuddered; somehow her prophecy was coming true.

I gasped as though an ice dagger had plunged into my heart. I also felt the short hairs on the back of my neck standing straight up. I guided Tennie to the divan. She told me the entire tragic tale, beginning in a monotone.

"My beloved summoned me. His note said he suffered, quite ill. I went to 10 Washington Place, and Edward, the butler, showed me into the downstairs library." She looked up to me. "You know Edward, he is usually very friendly with me, and we often exchange a few words. Tonight, he behaved strictly formal and did not converse with me. Not even one word.

"I heard shouting upstairs. I heard a frail voice and I heard a female, Southern drawl. Finally, I heard a strong male voice. The

Commodore, his wife Frank, and William were having a terrible argument. I heard my own name shouted several times.

"I stood up, proceeded to the doors, and opened them to go upstairs and support Corney. Edward stood immediately outside the door, as if standing guard. He dolefully shook his head at me and then he motioned me to go back into the library. I glared at him. He looked apologetic, but determined."

Reliving the moment, my sister stood up and became quite animated. She continued, "I shouted out, 'Corney, I am here to heal you! I'll make you better!'

"Edward shocked me when he placed his hand at the small of my back and gently pushed me back toward the library. *He touched me!* I wheeled around and yelled toward the stairs. 'Cornelius, they are keeping me from seeing you. I can help you!'"

I could not control my reaction. "Tennie, Edward touched you?" I knew Edward would never touch either of us, unless given specific orders.

Tennie continued to pace. "I heard a weak cry. Cornelius pleaded for them to allow me to administer to him. They shouted their replies, and I did not hear another sound from my lion. The shouting stopped.

"I heard Frank and William as they trampled down the staircase and the doors to the library burst open. The two of them, looking like galloping horses, suddenly stopped. Before I could say anything, Frank assailed me.

"She spoke in her Southern drawl, softly but with venom. 'I have waited long enough. I am his wife, not you! You are not to come back inside my house!' Her nostrils flared as she glared at me.

"I responded, 'Corney summoned me. He wrote he needed my treatment. Even Dr. Linsly has told you how effective my treatments are in restoring Cornelius.'

"William snorted like a wild beast. 'We will not discuss the manner of your *treatments* in the presence of a true and respectable lady.'

"Frank leveled an accusation at me. Despite her drawl, she sounded like any other girl in a brothel brawl. 'He caught the grippe from exhaustion and exposure the night of your grand opening.' She raised her hand in anger as if to strike me. 'I knew it would prove too much for him. But he insisted on being there till late at night, even though he went *to you* already fatigued.' Frank concluded by shouting at me, 'This is your fault!'

"'Let me see him!' I pleaded with them. 'If the Commodore tells me he no longer wants to see me, I will make no further attempt to see him.'

"Frank spoke in her slow drawl as if to spit in my direction. 'I will have you removed from this premise as the trash you are!'

"I stood up and declared. 'I am going upstairs to see my friend, my benefactor, my mentor, and *yes*, my lover!' As I opened the door, William forcibly grabbed my arm with his left hand and spun me out the library doors and into the foyer.

"I cried out, 'Unhand me, you brute! You're hurting me!'

"'Throw her out!' Frank screamed.

"William hurt my arm." Tennie stopped her pacing for an instant and rubbed the top of her right arm. She looked up at me, imploring with her eyes.

"In the foyer, Edward stepped forward to assist me, but William hissed at him to step back. William pulled and shoved me toward the front door. In the foyer I screamed out, '*Corney!* They won't let me see you! I love you!' No answer.

"William opened the front door with his right hand and whirled me around to force me onto the landing and face him and Frank. I cried out, 'I need to see my Corney!' I shouted, 'He summoned me!' I begged them, 'Please let me heal him.'

"Frank turned to me, her eyes widened. I saw it, Vickie. I saw the look in their eyes you have told me about. Frank's eyes had burning red flames in them. William's were cold black coals.

"They slammed the door in my face."

I rose and grabbed my sister. I held her close to me. We both wept openly. She tore herself away and looked at me with the utmost despair. Her voice sounded as if it came from beyond this world.

"I have never felt so alone," she moaned.

I shivered with the familiarity of this feeling. I sought to comfort her. "You will see him away from the house. You will! It will be all right." I tried to reach out to her.

Tennie looked directly at me. Her eyes blinked and she appeared shocked. She spoke quietly, "I have lost the only man I will ever truly love." She moved away from me. I felt helpless.

I dreaded what would come next. Eyes filling with new tears, my sister reminded me of what I already knew. When we came to New York and I planned on meeting Cornelius, Tennie had a vision; she would fall in love, be abandoned, and never love again.

Tennie spoke coldly, "I told you so."

Chapter 5

HAYSTACK HENRY AND THE BEECHER FAMILY

New York City
Spring, 1870

"Thank you for seeing me on such short notice, Victoria."

Isabella Beecher Hooker had traveled from her home in Nook Farm outside of Hartford, Connecticut. I invited her to attend our next soiree. She responded, asking to see me beforehand. She came to our brokerage business office on Broad Street, and we sat in the back room.

"Of course, dear Isabella. It is the least I can do, given all the hard work you do for the cause." I looked at her flush face and asked her directly. "Dear, are you excited over some news, or has someone upset you?"

"You always see things so clearly." She bent her head toward me in acknowledgement. "And you are always unafraid to speak your mind." She looked across at me, "I envy you!"

She hesitated.

I waited patiently as she seemed to organize her thoughts. "Take your time," I said.

Isabella had become a central figure in the N.W.S.A., promoting it actively. Her broad flat nose, protruding chin, wide forehead, and deep-set eyes looked like they had taken an impression of her older stepbrother, Henry Ward, and molded Bella's features into it.

Isabella, at age forty-eight, recently joined the movement. Over a year ago, she started touring throughout the Midwest, giving lectures on universal suffrage. She championed the N.W.S.A. cause, and her Beecher name opened doors closed to both Lizzybeth and Susan.

Recently, Isabella had worked long hours travelling up to the Northeast, hostile territory, to promote and solicit support. She focused primarily on raising funds to fill the treasury and pay the costs for the upcoming convention.

Following the precepts of her eldest stepsister, Catherine, Isabella had focused her life on supporting her husband and raising three children. Catherine Beecher's popular book *Treatise on Domestic Economy*, published in 1842, had been for three decades the predominant handbook for the conduct of a married woman. The book admonished women to stir things up only in the kitchen, serve your husband dutifully, procreate bountifully, and provide a warm hearth, home, and bed. The book proscribed to mind-numbing details every aspect of domestic life, from how to bake bread to how to wash, dry, and fold clothes. All this written by a childless spinster, still a virgin at age sixty-nine!

"Sometimes the members of the Beecher family are simply horrible!" Isabella immediately raised a hand to cover her mouth as if she had cursed the Lord.

"I know the feeling. Families can be terrible burdens." I tried to comfort her. "Believe me, I know."

"You simply could not imagine the magnitude of limitations placed upon me as a member of my family." She let all the air out of her lungs, which collapsed her chest, making her look older and frail. She looked so defeated it alarmed me.

I nodded my head, trying to encourage her. "Go on." Apparently, this opened some last linchpin to release the floodgates of her emotions.

"Each one of my brothers and sisters is holier and more exalted than the next! They get it from my father." She laughed a derisive laugh. "At least publicly." She stopped.

"I don't understand."

"Of course not. How could you? That is the very point!" Her words and demeanor compounded my confusion.

"Perhaps from the beginning, dear," I suggested. I had no idea what path she tread.

"Thirteen offspring all in all remained to answer Lyman's call." Isabella sang in a sing-song voice the names of her sisters and brothers. "Roxana begat Catherine E., William, Edward, Mary…" She smiled at me like a little girl repeating her lessons word for word.

Enthused with her accomplishment, she continued calling out the names of her siblings as if reciting a school rhyme, "Harriet who died at three, George, Harriet Elizabeth, Henry Ward, and Charles. Roxana died when Henry Ward was three and Charles, two. Harriet, (my Mom), begat Frederick C.— he died at two—Bella (me), Thomas Kinnicut, and James Chaplin. Fifteen young Beechers did Lyman seed, thirteen grew up to be tall." She looked up at me. It felt like she sought my approval.

"You had twice as many brothers and sisters as me." I declared. "Were any of them tender and close to you?"

"No! My life has been full of rigid expectations. Harriet is eleven years older and acted more like my aunt than my sister. Now she is firmly against me! She finds out where I am going and poisons the people I am to see with rumors and innuendos." She stopped short, embarrassed.

"Innuendos? About whom?" I queried.

"About Lizzybeth and Susan. About Theodore Tilton, and about…" She paused.

"Finish!"

"You!" It pained her to utter the word. "And Tennessee. My entire family is vehemently against us."

I waived my hand, dismissing the entire bunch of them.

"They are a powerful group," Bella warned.

"The rest of your family act as if they alone stood on Mt. Sinai to receive the Almighty's Ten Commandments and formed a private circle to dance with Moses!"

"Harriet is the worst. She is a political force to be reckoned with." Bella looked into the distance. "All because of a book she never even wrote." Isabella for the second time covered her mouth as if she gave voice to forbidden words.

"What on earth are you talking about, Bella?"

"I've said too much, Vickie, forgive me. I really should never, ever talk about it."

I felt exasperated. Isabella's thoughts were so disconnected. I sensed she had come with some other purpose. I grew impatient. "Is our conversation at its end?"

"No. Please." Her eyes filled with tears. "Victoria, please be patient with me for a few more moments." She gathered herself and proceeded down a forbidden path. "*Uncle Tom's Cabin* is not an original work!"

"What? Are you sure, Isabella?" This news did not completely surprise me. I already knew Henry Ward Beecher rose to fame on words he did not write, and sat on his throne of morality as a false king. I found it entirely plausible Harriet Beecher Stowe obtained the literary pinnacle, political rectitude, and moral righteousness through pretense.

"Yes." Isabella sighed wearily. "I witnessed the process there in her home." Again, Bella looked aside, viewing the past. "I saw Harriet transcribe the diary of a runaway slave who escaped to Canada." She hesitated and then exclaimed, "It is outright plagiarism! She copied for hours at a time the book entitled "*The Life of Josiah Henson, Formerly a Slave, Now an Inhabitant of Canada, as Narrated by Himself.*"

She stopped only to peer into some other memory. "Harriett also copied whole passages from the Grimke sisters' book with Theodore Dwight Weld, *American Slavery As It Is: Testimony of a Thousand Witnesses.*" Isabella concluded, "By the time she finished, the two volumes were worn to the point of pages separating from the binding."

"Bella, why are you telling me all this?"

"I have to tell someone, Victoria. Besides, I need your help."

"You can ask without telling me your family secrets."

Isabella looked at me dolefully. "They are too much for me to bear. There is no one else I can talk to. Most people will simply cut me off and defend my family, even to me. The entire family methodically thwarts my efforts."

I sighed. "After the war, you'd think families would not allow themselves to become split over disagreements."

"It gets worse, Vickie!" She raised her voice in exasperation. "They are so elitist, haughty, and judgmental."

I chose not to tell her about what I saw in her sister Harriet's eyes. "Surely out of thirteen siblings you must have some allies and supporters."

"Rollie-Pollie has been kind. It started after I married John and started having children, living my life according to exact dictates of the *Treatise*." She mentioned Catherine's book with contempt.

"Bella, dear, I am trying to follow you, but who or what is Rollie-Pollie?"

"Haystack Henry!" She declared, looking at me.

"I am not stupid, my dear. However, I have no idea what you are rambling on about."

"Sorry," she recanted the look. "About the time I was born, Henry Ward was a plumpish boy. He did not excel in his lessons, and he constantly earned Father Lyman's wrath."

She chuckled to herself, no doubt with the memory of stories she had been told. "Henry Ward would entertain our neighborhood kids by appearing in the barn on top of bales of hay, elevated to look like Father's pulpit in church. Haystack wore an old pair of farmer's blue goggles to imitate Father's bi-focal spectacles. Henry performed the caricature by mimicking to near perfection the original intonations, cadences, and oratory art of the sermons delivered by Father. Haystack would raise his voice then lower it to a whisper. Part of the joke rested upon the fact the words were often just jumbles of sounds, completely unintelligible!" Isabella paused. Clearly, she enjoyed telling the stories she had heard about her decade-older brother.

"After spreading his short corpulent arms wide and combing back his hair as a gesture of the zeal he felt, just like Father, Haystack would bow his head solemnly and conclude by diving and rolling head over heels down the hay to land at the feet of his audience. He stood up to the cheers and shouts of his fellows."

"I am happy for you. Glad you have fond memories and a present closeness with Henry." I hesitated, but this time I chose not to curb my tongue. "For my part I find your brother a contemptible man."

"You don't know the half of it, Victoria. As I grew up from a small girl, I heard about Haystack's romantic affairs." She stopped and her face reddened.

"I already know more than you think. Theodore has told me about his wife and your brother." Isabella snorted at this. I continued, "I also know about the Bowen wife and daughter. I first met your brother in person when, full of sorrow over the departure of the wife of Moses Beach, he failed to deliver his sermon. Chloe Beach's new baby resembles Henry to an astonishing degree."

Isabella was shocked I knew so much. "Does everyone know?"

"No, I believe not!" Truthfully, most of it I guessed at. Isabella just confirmed my suspicions.

"It's despicable, Vickie." She now spoke conspiratorially. "He has bedded scores of his parishioners. Many of his conquests are the wives, sisters, or daughters of his most ardent backers and deacons of the church." She cried out. "You can look amongst the congregation and see his facial features repeatedly imprinted on many young boys and girls."

I sat stunned. I had guessed at Henry Beecher's moral corruption, and cared not about any man's personal choices. The sheer volume of improprieties impressed and approached farce. The pomposity of his righteousness in the face of such unbridled promiscuity galled me most. I thought Henry Ward both odious and obnoxious. The high and mighty Beecher clan fascinated many but disgusted me. I turned away from my anger and returned to the point of Isabella's visit.

"Enough of your family, let's leave them behind. You said you need something from me."

"Yes. Thank you." Faltering, she explained. "With my family negating my every effort, well in advance of my arrivals to distant regions, I have failed miserably at my purpose. They frustrate and stymie my every step." Isabella looked so dismayed my heart went out to her.

"How can I help?"

"Victoria, I have failed the National terribly. We do not have enough money to hold the convention in a few days. I have avoided telling Elizabeth and Susan—they already have too much to worry about. I am desperate." Her hands shook and it looked to me like she cruelly bullied herself inside her own head.

"How much?" I asked.

"I don't understand. How much what? How much did I raise?" Distressed to distraction Bella couldn't think straight.

"It is a simple question, Bella. How much money do you need?"

"To properly hold the convention?"

"Yes. What sum will allow us to end this conversation, hold the convention and help the delegates who need lodging?"

Sheepishly she looked up at me and muttered, "One thousand dollars." She added, "I'm sorry Vickie, I have no right…"

"Shush!" I stood up and walked over to my desk, opened my bank draft book and proceeded to write a check for the amount of two thousand dollars. I dried the bank draft with a blotter, and waved it back and forth as I walked back to Isabella. I looked at her sternly, but then smiled.

"Let's agree that this," I handed her the cheque, "is the fruit of your efforts."

"Oh my! This is too much." Bella gasped.

"This must be our little secret. I don't want Lizzybeth, Susan, or anyone else to find out you came to me."

"I won't tell anyone. Ever!" Bella promised solemnly. "I know you are busy, so I'll take my leave. Thank you, Vickie." We hugged. "I am ever so excited to attend your soiree."

She left extremely grateful. I did not let myself be comforted by her vow of silence. The woman simply could not hold a secret!

I felt soiled. Yes, I, who had seen the very worst of human behavior. I felt unclean, hearing the hypocrisy of Lyman Beecher's progeny. Once home, I took a long hot bath and tried to wash the filth and stench of the Beecher family off my soul.

I opened the door to our bedroom wearing only my towel. I loosed the knot. "Tenderly, please."

My Colonel was incredibly gentle and patiently coaxed me to arousal. He accepted I did not want to talk. James held me close to him through the night. Surrendering to him and nestling in his arms, I felt safe.

Chapter 6

UPWARD & ONWARD:
WOODHULL & CLAFLIN'S WEEKLY

New York City
May, 1870

The only other time I had felt this angry happened after our arrival in New York City, when I realized the widely popular Henry Ward Beecher, a lecherous adulterer, lied and denied his own conduct.

Other people fueled my anger. The imbecilic, myopic self-centeredness exhibited by the leaders of the A.W.S.A. deepened the chasm splitting the suffrage movement at the exact moment that only reconciliation would forward the cause. While I had already seen the outcome in my vision last year, their sheer arrogance and imperiousness infuriated me.

The Reverend Henry Ward Beecher, his sister Harriet Beecher Stowe, the hearth-and-home moralist old maid, Catherine, and all the other Beechers, save dear Isabella, encouraged and executed a methodical obstruction to progress. This provoked me further. One single family may have had a more detrimental influence on our times than any other. My knowing they were morally corrupt, plagiarist, adulterer, and all the while two-faced about it, made it unbearable. I wished I could bring the entire house of Beecher down around them—excepting Isabella.

The Commodore Cornelius Vanderbilt and his family did not escape my rage. I knew his new Southern belle of a wife, Frank, and his son, William, were controlling him against his wishes, but really! He'd seen Tennie thrice since William and Frank rudely threw my sister out of 10 Washington Place and told her never to return. Tennie met her Corney at the best rooms in the best hotels. They rendezvoused at the Hoffman House, where we first opened our brokerage offices, the new, fancy Fifth Avenue Hotel, with its mechanical car draying people up the many floors of the tall building, and the Astor Hotel.

While Tennie told me they enjoyed the luxury of both the surroundings and each other's company, she always returned home suffering from melancholia. Could no one else see that the two truly loved each other? My little sister constantly revived the health of the Commodore. Did no one in his family care a jot for his being well?

No, sir, I think not! I thought of my address at the offices of *The Revolution* when I confronted Frederick Douglass.

I wanted to devise a clever way to shoot a cannonball across the bow of the Beecher clan and also place on notice those of the old blood aristocracy, as well as the *nouveau riche*, that no one could hide from the printed word.

I hoped my plans would be well received by our inner circle.

"This time you will have to listen to reason, Victoria!" My husband raised his voice to make sure I heard his imperative. The Colonel had assembled our closest friends and advisors at the printing office of the *Woodhull & Claflin's Weekly*.

The Colonel, Whitelaw Reid, Teddy Tilton, Stephen Pearl Andrews, Tennie, and I sat on desks and equipment for lack of chairs. As I scanned the room, I thought the others all looked like jurors who were ready to find someone guilty and condemn them to the gallows.

"Don't you all see how perfect my plan is?" I turned to the jury. "Theodore, are you familiar with Mary Wollstonecraft?"

"I know her only by her reputation. I am aware of her sympathetic work on the French Revolution, *Vindication of the Rights of Men,*" Theodore answered, "but confess I have not read it. Nor..."

"I've read both!" The thin, reedy voice of Stephen Pearl Andrews interrupted the mellifluous Teddy. "Mary preceded her times and she paid the price with ignominy." He pulled and stroked his long full, beard from the moustache down to just above his chest. "She lived and promoted free love openly, before any other woman in modern times. Those in power used her affairs with women and several men while married to obscure and diminish her groundbreaking work, *A Vindication of the Rights of Women.*"

Pearly's face flushed with excitement whenever he spoke from his immense body of knowledge. He continued, "Mary wrote the treatise in 1792 to refute the pompous traditionalist Charles Maurice de Talleyrand-Perigord's 1791 report to the French National Assembly, stating that woman needs no education except for the prosecution of domestic duties, and is fettered and confused by any additional exposure to thought." Pearly paused, wondering what to say next. I wanted to laugh in joy at his acumen, admiring the mechanical gears precision, the fine watch piece of his mind. But they were assembled to keep this woman's work further suppressed.

"Thank you, Pearly." I walked over to alleviate the dear man from more explication and kissed his balding head. "You always amaze me with the power, breadth, and instant recall of your knowledge."

"One is glad to be of service," Pearly bowed, "I am honored to be asked and to contribute my humble part." His high-pitched voice expressed his gratitude. I turned around to face the others present.

I declared, "The front page of our first edition can present a brief biography of Mary and an excerpt from *A Vindication* as an entrée to address, refute, and denounce Catherine Beecher's intolerable opposition to universal suffrage."

"Victoria, all of us here..." James began to speak, but I interrupted him.

"Catherine Beecher must be removed from the mountaintop of authority from which she has demeaned women since the 1840s through her accursed *Treatise.*" I took a deep breath. "In fact, it is time to dethrone all the Beechers. I despise their duplicities!" I shouted.

I looked up and saw what could only be described as stern, unsympathetic faces, as if everyone else knew we were attending a funeral and somehow, I was not informed.

"Whitelaw, please…." The Colonel took control. "She will accept it better coming from you than from me." My husband nodded in deference to the highly accomplished newspaperman who had agreed to advise us on this venture. Whitelaw turned to address me directly.

"Victoria, I admire your passion and further commend you on the cleverness of using Mary Wollstonecraft as a kind of Trojan horse to usher in the attacks on the conservative stand relegating woman to serve their husbands from the hearth inside the home." He stood up and towered over everyone else except Theodore Tilton. "However, I simply cannot support your plan."

"Why not?" I demanded.

"Because it would incur the wrath of the entire Beecher clan, and—mark my words—they are formidable. You would also alienate the financial backers of the Reverend Henry Ward here in New York. They make good money on him and will not suffer an attack without retaliating."

"Whitelaw, you told me once controversy is good advertisement!"

Whitelaw dropped to one knee so our eyes were on the same plane. "Vickie, please listen, these men are all-powerful. Horace Greeley has known this for decades, and *The Tribune* avoids certain names and conflicts no matter how compelling a story might be." He stood himself up. "If we at *The Tribune* have to be careful, do you really think your first edition dare throw all precautions to the wind?"

"Yes!" I pointed to my sister and paused to let my emphasis fill the room. "We have made a great fortune doing what others would call 'throwing caution to the wind,' haven't we, Tennie?"

Before Tennie could answer, Theodore spoke up. "Perhaps a long-term campaign to start out slowly and build momentum would win the day. This is not a time to be reckless." Theodore expressed his genuine concern.

"I want the first edition to be bold, not namby-pamby." My plea sounded too plaintive to my own ears. "We formed the *Weekly* to have a voice and speak with passion."

My husband's voice filled the room. "Victoria Woodhull! You are the most stubborn woman I have ever met. I wanted to do this gently and allow you to come to your own informed and rightful conclusion." The Colonel exhaled, shook his head, and shrugged his shoulders. "You leave me no alternative!"

Against my will I sought the eyes of my husband to find a softness I could not find in his voice. I only saw pain in his eyes, not even anger. I realized then I would have to give up my intention to lead with Mary Wollstonecraft. The woman would have her just recognition another time.

"Can't we compromise?" I tried to negotiate.

"No!" The Colonel's voice boomed. Instantaneously, my husband transformed into a judge polling a jury.

"Whitelaw, what say you?"

"Regretfully, I do apologize, Victoria and Miss Tennessee, but if you insist on a direct assault on the Beecher family in the first edition of the *Weekly*, I must withdraw my support and involvement."

"Thank you, Whitelaw." My husband responded.

"Before you move on, Colonel Blood," Whitelaw added, "I want to mention, Tennessee and I have come up with a viable and engaging alternative, yet it remains very aggressive and dramatic. It involves quoting from the French author, George Sand."

Everyone in the room knew the *nom de plume* for the provocative female author who denied her nobility and insisted she be called Amantine-Lucile-Aurore-Dupin, not the Marquise of Dodevant. She avowed free love and lived it too, having had several affairs, most notably with the actress Marie Dorval, the French playwright, Alfred de Musset, and of course, her tumultuous affair with the Polish composer and pianist, Frederic Chopin.

Seeing me shaking my head from side to side, the Colonel called his next juror. "Pearly, your advice, please."

"Woefully, dear Victoria, I think it best to temper your outrage and build your readership, at least as a first step. There is a precedent…"

"Enough for now, Pearly. Thank you." James interrupted. He continued to call the roll of assembled jurors. "Mr. Tilton, please."

Theodore rose and filled his strong breast with air. Then his shoulders sagged as he expelled all his breath and lowered his head to his chest. He confessed, "Sadly, I must concur. In time, we can build loyalties and a constituency, and perhaps then address the wrongdoings of the Beechers. Certainly no one here wants Beecher exposed to the public more than I. But we must build methodically, and only strike when fully prepared. I counsel restraint and moderation. Please listen to us, Victoria." He sat down, looking forlorn.

My husband spoke, addressing me alone. "Victoria, please see I do this to protect you, not to dictate to you or control you." He bent his torso toward me. "I love you, my dear." His eyes filled with moisture. "It pains me greater than I can express to gather your closest advisors to deny you… anything." Returning to his resolve, "We have all discussed this. If you insist on the front page of the first edition using the Wollstonecraft lead to attack the Beecher family, you shall be working completely alone."

The Colonel shocked me. He knew my greatest fear. It hurt to have it thrown in my face as a matter of argument. I looked up to

Tennessee. A bright smile spread across her face, her eyes sparkled, as she bobbed her head up and down.

"What?" I asked, bewildered, and raised my hands upward, extending the fingers and turning the palms up. I raised my shoulders, while shaking my head. "What?" I repeated.

"It will be *grand!*" Tennie exclaimed. "I like this Sand lady! This will make for a great premier edition." I recognized my usual exuberance and conviction displayed by Tennie. She circled the room, "Gentlemen, we've work to do!" She allowed each man to kiss her hand as I sat in my chair. "Why, she even wears pants!" She raised both hands to her face to mime exaggerated shock. Then she laughed gleefully. "Just like me!" The gentlemen joined in the laughter.

A quote from Amantine Dupin or George Sand convinced me I had made the right choice in agreeing with my counselors:

The world will know me someday. But if that day does not arrive, it does not greatly matter. I shall have opened the way for other women.

However, in my case I knew I would be known, as promised.

From the moment the meeting ended, everyone pulled together to make a great first edition. The paper listed J. H. Blood as the managing editor. George, my brother-in-law, contacted the advertisers who had placed ads when he managed a New Jersey newspaper. Most were happy to work with the Blood brothers again, and many to be somehow involved with Tennie and me. This gave *The Weekly* a great head start.

The nameplate would read: "WOODHULL & CLAFLIN'S" arching over the word "WEEKLY." I still insisted the banner under our name read: "UPWARD & ONWARD," as if Tennessee and I carried a flag!

The front page featured literature and intellect. The left column commenced with a poem titled "*Speak No Ill!*" The balance of three columns consisted of an excerpt from a novel by George Sand, *In Spite of All*, translated exclusively for the *Weekly*. We decided to also feature culture on the front page of our premier publication.

The second page powered headlong into politics. We presented a laudatory article on Elizabeth Cady Stanton in a column titled, "*Live People.*" The first paragraph of our story read:

> The Woman Rights Movement, involving as it does the larger half of the human race is of profound significance. It agitates both hemispheres. It is pre-eminently a radical movement, for it seeks to remodel the framework of society, so far as the relations of the sexes are concerned, and professes to place women on a footing never yet conceded to them in the history of mankind. Exceptional instances have occurred in our time, wherein, from extraordinary merit, or under peculiar circumstances, that precedence or equality has been granted to individuals as of special privilege, which is now demanded on behalf of the whole female sex, and as an indefensible right. There is a rapidly growing public opinion in favor of more extended female employment in all public and private capacities; of more liberal educational advantages; and of an equalization of wages between the sexes.

The article provided a brief history of the woman rights movement, followed by a highly complementary depiction of the physique, intellect, fashion, manner, and passion personified in Elizabeth Cady Stanton.

I made sure fifteen hundred copies were distributed at the commencement of the meeting of the A.W.S.A. at Steinway Hall so they could read about the excellence of the woman their leadership maligned.

To address our place as female brokers and women of finance, the third page featured a response by E. G. Spaulding to an article, which excoriated him for his role in establishing the greenback currency as legal tender. The response ended with a group of testimonials from leading politicians and cabinet members. I harkened to Whitelaw's advice. It is always good to quote powerful men. They enjoy seeing in print their words followed by their names.

The next two pages summed up the week's activity with a story of a train wreck in England, a sports page featuring baseball scores and schedules, along with boating news. Next, after the sporting news, we printed a deliciously barbed French gossip page, direct from Paris. The luscious descriptions of French society concluded saying the high society in Paris eagerly awaited the arrival of *Woodhull & Claflin's Weekly*! It was all they could talk about.

Pages six through ten spoke only of politics, woman suffrage, education, equal wages, and labor unions. The lead article called for a sixteenth amendment granting woman suffrage and full legal standing.

One article dared to mention the limited perspective of Catherine Beecher on the educational requirements of women and her declared opposition to woman suffrage. The article's primary focus, however, identified and praised the new woman universities establishing themselves to afford women equal educational opportunities. The column to the right publicized the British Women Suffrage Bill introduced by John Stuart Mill, based on his essay, *The Subjection of Women*, as presented to the conservative House of Commons.

Page twelve reported on the stock exchange, and appropriately for a women-owned newspaper juxtaposed an article on fashion in New York. Mostly about Tennie, the story reported on how our brokerage firm defied conventionality in every manner. We listed the top seventeen railroad stocks, always headed by the Commodore Vanderbilt's New York Central and Harlem, the largest corporation in America.

After three pages of diverse advertising, thanks to George and my husband, the *Weekly* ended with the entire back page dedicated to entertainment and the theatrical events in and around New York City. We published reviews of running plays, and playbill listings of the coming week. After all, I once had a brief career as an actress in San Francisco!

Sixteen pages in all provided something of interest for just about everyone. Many people helped and contributed.

From May 10 to May 13, the Colonel, Tennie, and I labored at the printing office alongside the pressmen. The black printers ink splattered our clothes. In the wee hours of the morning of May 14, the three of us laughed, swabbing fresh ink on each other in exhilaration and sheer exhaustion. Just as in my dream, the wall, which held the door to the street, could hardly be seen behind the clean, twenty-five copy stacks, freshly bound in string, of the first edition of *Woodhull & Claflin's Weekly*. We printed four thousand.

I used my words. We had a platform to reach out and disseminate our thoughts. Once again, we sisters, Woodhull and Claflin, bypassed barriers and entered into arenas where no woman had yet dared to tread.

The simultaneous and opposing conventions of the National Woman Suffrage Association, chaired by Elizabeth Cady Stanton, and the American Woman Suffrage Association, led by the Reverend Henry Ward Beecher, gave the press an opportunity to jovially discredit the concept of universal suffrage, saying women could not even get along among themselves, let alone join forces to form an advocacy in solidarity.

I thought of Mr. Whitman's powerful poem *O Captain! My Captain!* Like our assassinated President, the woman suffrage movement lay upon the deck, "Fallen cold and dead."

Chapter 7

MOMENTUM

Spring to Fall, 1870

Anote arrived the day before we were to issue the third edition of the *Weekly*. General Butler asked me to meet him after dinner, "To discuss the issues at hand." The general apologized for the late hour and late notice, also for inviting me to his room. He wrote, "I can only excuse my request by explaining I must return to Washington, D.C. earliest in the morning."

I made my way to the Hoffman House, where the manager immediately recognized me from when Tennie and I had offices in two parlor rooms upstairs. The man happily informed me of General Butler's room number, in fact the suite of our old office. The manager nodded to me courteously and informed me, "He always asks to stay in your old suites." I nodded to him in return and thanked him.

I made a point of entering the bar and viewing the naked, bathing maiden exquisitely painted by William-Adolphe Bouguereau. I stopped and admired her scandalous beauty.

I knocked on the door to my old office. The high-pitched voice beckoning me to come in identified the occupant, General Benjamin Butler, the Congressional representative from Massachusetts. I opened the door and found the general in good spirits, no doubt having drunk plenty of bourbon. His face was a ruddy color, his nose a shiny red, and his eyes twinkled. He looked like someone had added a pair of short, fat legs under a bullfrog! Appearance aside, a brilliant, powerful and cunning man welcomed me.

"Good of you to come, my dear." He kissed my hand. "How have you been, Victoria?" His squeaky voice hid the fact the man before me had been a victorious war general and now moved events in the Capitol as a forceful and innovative politician.

"Quite busy, kind sir. Thank you for taking the time to see me."

"Yes, yes. Welcome. Well done on the first edition of your new weekly. I am already an avid reader."

"The very reason I registered you as a subscriber and you'll have the *Weekly* delivered to your offices in Washington." I smiled at him.

He motioned me to the velvet divan and he sat in a chair opposite. "I'm glad I found the time, Victoria. You sent word you wanted to see me? What can I do for you?"

"You are kind and generous, dear Beast." He smiled at my use of his nickname for having imposed strident wartime laws in the occupied territory of New Orleans. "I am dismayed and seek your counsel."

"Well, Victoria, you are here; I am your willing accomplice. Just tell me what you want."

I had to concentrate to ignore the contradictions between the prowess of the man before me, the sound of his voice, and the body it emitted from. I decided to just come out with it—all of it.

"This whole Richardson affair makes me furious. We *must* proceed with force to a sixteenth amendment granting woman suffrage and full legal standing!" Then I added, "I'm sorry for shouting."

"I always admire your passion, Victoria." U.S. Representative Butler said with a twinkle in his eyes. Then he deflated, letting out a long deep sigh. He reached for one of his cigars and started rolling it unlit around his mouth. He drummed the fingers of his left hand on the nearby table.

I referred to the recent acquittal of Daniel McFarland, accused of the murder of Albert Richardson. The accused admitted he sought out the deceased, who actively and openly conducted a love affair with McFarland's wife, Abby. McFarland shot and fatally wounded Richardson in front of several witnesses.

I vented my anger. "The verdict of not guilty by virtue of insanity constitutes the all-male jury declaring to the world a wife is chattel, to be treated as property."

"Victoria, I know the circumstances. I have read all the accounts."

I stood and paced as I spoke. "And the insult of not allowing Abby to testify, to tell the jury what her husband told her of his premeditated intentions to commit murder."

"I agree with you. While technically justice may have been served, the ruling sacrificed equity. Victoria, what do want me to do about it?"

I kneeled in front of General Butler and placed my right hand on his knee. I looked up into his eyes. "You are a good man, General." My eyes became moist, "How dare they? The jury condones the murder and then the judge grants custody of her boy to the man who had repeatedly beaten both wife and child?"

"Acknowledged, Vickie, not letting her testify based on her gender sets a bad precedent. However, legally much of what she would say would be thrown out as hearsay." He placed his hand on my head to comfort me.

"Can you imagine what it felt like for Abby to watch her lover die and then have her son ripped from her arms by the judge?"

"I am most sympathetic." He lifted my chin, paused, and smiled. "I also clearly recall your lecture to Mr. Frederick Douglass the day we first met. Remembering your brilliant arguments, I will say, No! I cannot imagine the pain and indignity the woman must have felt." I smiled too and let my head rest on his thigh, remembering the day we met at the offices of *The Revolution*.

"Thank you, General." I stood up as another wave of emotion seized hold of me. "Then, the impudence of that old maid, Catherine Beecher, God Almighty I hate that family, to publish her article in both the *World* and the *Tribune*."

General Butler adjusted his position in the chair and took a long sip of his bourbon.

I imitated an old crone prattling, as I quoted Catherine Beecher: "Woman may separate from her husband for abuse or drunkenness and not violate law, but neither party can marry again without practically saying, I do not recognize Jesus Christ as the true teacher of morals and religion."

As I finished, I looked up to see if I had gone too far. "Did Christ die so Catherine Beecher could unilaterally interpret his teachings?"

The Beast listened intently, excited and fully engaged. "Go on Vickie, I can see you have more to air."

I continued, "And the pure gall when all knew Richardson would not survive, the sanctimonious Reverend Henry Ward Beecher had the impudence to marry the dying man to Abby Sage McFarland, an already married woman!"

"Catherine Beecher's article does present a full rebuke and condemnation of her little brother, Henry Ward." The general chortled at the very public family infighting.

"You are above all else, dear Beast, a righteous man guided by the light of justice." I returned to my seat on the divan.

"Victoria, I am first and foremost a man. Still, I try to see all matters from the point of view of both men and women." He paused to pour himself another full glass. "Still, it is surprising the Reverend Beecher would conduct a full marriage ceremony between a married woman and a man about to die." He sipped the whiskey. "Not so hard to understand, given Henry Ward's…" He stopped mid-sentence. The Beast hesitated to continue.

Exasperated I asked, "Do all you men assume no woman knows what is going on?" I laughed. "The only reason the Reverend performed the marriage of a married woman to a dying man was that he wanted to wed Libby Tilton, with the benediction of the Almighty. Henry doesn't care that he is married, and she's still married to Theodore."

"You are a remarkable woman, Victoria." My knowledge of events surprised the Beast.

"Then help this woman forward the cause and put an end to the ownership of all women through matrimony. Help me get approval of a sixteenth amendment."

"You ask for a lot, Victoria, perhaps too much of a politician who has to foresee the limits of the arts of compromise."

"Am I not talking to The Beast, the General who declared all women as prostitutes and their properties forfeit, if they impeded the Union cause? Did you not, as Commander of the New Orleans territory, issue the first emancipation proclamation in the form of the military order declaring all escaped slaves were proper military contraband and thus freed?" I looked into his eyes and challenged him. "Am I not speaking to that very same leader of men?"

"Yes, yes, yes. But age and politics have mollified me." He took another swig of his bourbon. "I still love to antagonize the old guard and create controversy, but I have learned to be measured in my strategies and only attack when there exists a tactical advantage."

"Then really stir things up!" I stood up and recommenced my pacing. "Invite me to address Congress. I will show you the speech prior to delivery. Let a woman advocate to the lawmakers the necessity of a sixteenth amendment granting woman suffrage and legal standing."

"Victoria, no woman has ever been invited into chambers except to visit Representatives who choose to meet."

I halted in front of him. "Do I look to you like a woman afraid to be the first? To do anything?"

The General seemed at a loss for words. He hummed and hawed and looked at me with intense eyes. "You would be surprised how Washington works. Everything, and I mean everything, is bought and paid for in one manner or another. I hope I do not offend or disappoint you."

I laughed. "Not in the least, silly man. I prefer to know what others may call harsh realities, so I don't have to waste my time and effort trying to figure it all out."

"You are a rare woman indeed, Victoria. I have always been a keen admirer of your accomplishments, and your beauty." He stopped and seemed to be waiting.

I thought for a few moments and came to a decision. "It has been a long day. The whole McFarland story, and especially Catherine Beecher's article consigning woman to conjugal slavery, makes me feel covered in filth." I sighed and put the back of my right hand to my forehead. "Would the Representative of the State of Massachusetts kindly allow this humble woman to use his wash basin and pitcher to bathe?"

A wide grin spread across General Butler's face.

"And would the gentleman be so kind as to hand me a towel and help dry me off when I am… refreshed?"

"It would be my profound pleasure to honor your request." He held out a hand, indicating. "I am sure you are familiar with the alcove, right there."

"Anything else, my dear Beast, before I commence… to undress for my bath?"

"Only, thinking about it, and weighing all the different and diverse elements of the equation, I see no reason not to stir things up a bit in Congress." He spoke eagerly. "You must understand it may not change anything for now, but it will provide me more leverage later on." He smiled and announced, "I *will* have the Judiciary Committee issue a formal invitation for you to make an address. That I can do!"

I leapt into his arms, hugged the man, and planted kisses on his sweaty forehead and jowls. He turned red.

I untangled from him and stood with my hands on my hips. "General, how do you contend with nearly all others being far less than you… in wit, intellect, charm, and vision? How do you do it?"

"Flattery will get you everywhere!" General Butler said, laughter erupting from his bulbous body. "I believe I could correctly ask you the same question, Victoria." He slightly bowed his head to me. "Much like you, when they cannot match me they complain all the more."

"So true! Thank you, my dear, dear General Butler." I kissed his cheek again.

"It will take time, Victoria, but upon my return to Washington I promise to set things in motion."

I walked past the man and started to disrobe so I could use the fresh water and washbasin to clean my naked body before going home. I left the drape open. The General sat back in his chair and watched.

In fact, the General assiduously toweled me off, making sure absolutely no remaining droplets clung to any portion of my skin.

At the conclusion, he muttered, "Thank you, Victoria."

"Just make sure I receive the invitation, dear Beast." He nodded.

Men are so ridiculous.

The Beast's promise to secure an invitation to address the Judiciary Committee of Congress fortified my resolve. I forged ahead, defining a full platform. In the subsequent issues of the *Weekly*, we adopted a strategy of reprinting a powerful article from one of the popular daily newspapers. The first article originally appeared in *The World* on the International Workers Union and the influence of the German authors Karl Marx and Friedrich Engels. *The World* reciprocated the compliment, publishing quotes from the *Weekly*. We widened this reciprocal and mutually rewarding practice, increasing both our subscription bases.

I used the third edition on May 28, 1870, as a herald for a new recurring political column delivering my message to create a new constitutional amendment:

SIXTEENTH AMENDMENT.

WOMAN AS A SOCIAL ELEMENT.

… It is useless to attempt to blind our eyes to the present social condition; facts too numerous and hideous, stand to prominently before us. We cannot escape them if we would, and should not if we could. Nor will it mend matters to gloss them over and label them sound, when they are only putrid. Unveil New York at midnight—or, as for time, at midday—the scenes disclosed would show our social system to be ripe for revolution.…

… Public prostitution is but nothing compared to that practiced under the cloak of marriage. … Let every woman who abhors prostitution in her sisters equally abhor licentiousness in her brothers.

… The scales of justice woman has been weighed in have been fearfully against her, and in favor of men. She demands that they be balanced; and we demand in the name of all that is still pure and holy, that woman shall no longer shield man. From such an equality as must arise from such practice, and from the additional equality that can only flow from pecuniary independence on the part of woman, can the most perfect beauty and purity of marriage be evolved. Round it will gather a halo of light and divinity from which all baseness, impurity and license will shrink in shame, and woman become a social element of power and importance.

I would wait for General Butler's invitation, but I would not sit idle.

By the time I reached Washington, D.C. and spoke to the Judiciary Committee of the House of Representatives, the amendment would have momentum.

Upon arriving home late one winter evening after the election in the second week of November, 1870, I found a letter from General Butler, embossed with the seal of the House of Representatives.

He did it!

The House of Representatives of the United States of America formally invited Mrs. Victoria C. Woodhull to appear before the Judiciary Committee on January 11, 1871. He confirmed I would be the first woman ever so invited. I was so excited I almost failed to read the rest of the text.

In the balance of the letter, the Beast admonished me to abandon my plans to present a proposal of a sixteenth amendment, which I had been publishing articles about in our *Weekly* all through the summer and fall. General Butler warned me a sixteenth amendment granting woman the vote would be "dead in committee." There existed almost no inclination throughout Congress to pass another amendment on suffrage at this time.

I felt like my feet were knocked out from under me, and I had been punched in my stomach while falling. What evil was this? I had planned to convince the politicians to pass a sixteenth amendment to achieve universal suffrage. I had envisioned the speech. Now I had the invitation I sought, but no argument to present. I paced the room and then broke down crying. I went upstairs and flung myself onto the bed and sobbed a good long while.

I felt fear! What could I possibly say to all those distinguished representatives in the Capitol? I did not want to make a fool of myself, and thereby all women. I felt the burden too much for me. I panicked.

I stayed in my own private hell. I avoided talking to anyone until I could come up with some kind of plan. Lucky for me, the days were short and during the Yule season business slowed down.

Three days later, preparing for bed, my husband spoke to me. "Victoria, something is wrong." He looked into my eyes. "You have not been yourself for the last couple of days." He motioned me to sit on the bed facing him. I started to cry. "What's wrong, Vickie?" He lifted me into his arms.

"I don't know what to do!" I wailed. "Sorry, James." He tenderly reached for my cheek and caressed my face with his fingertips.

"I can't help you, Vickie, unless you tell me: What is going on?" He waited for an answer.

After a few moments, my dear husband continued, "Whatever has come up, we will find a way to deal with it."

I sheepishly reached for the letter hiding under my pillow and handed it to James. After reading the first paragraph about the invitation, he looked up and exclaimed, "Why, this is fantastic news!"

"Read on." My voice sounded like a heavy flat iron press.

James quickly read the balance of the letter and looked at me. "I see." He smiled as if he saw some inside joke I did not understand.

"What's so funny?" I jumped off the bed and stood across from him.

"I know Victoria Woodhull, and she is intrepid." I could feel his beam of confidence penetrate me. "The Victoria I know will see a way to make this into a triumph. I am certain of it."

"And if I don't?" I held on to my fear, but I knew the Colonel had spoken the truth. I was dauntless and would find a path. I let out a deep breath and reached for my husband's hands. "I know you are right." He kissed my hand.

James embraced me. I motioned to the bed, but he stood up. "I want you to sleep deeply, Victoria. That is when you have your best revelations." He pulled back the blankets and helped me lie down, covering me with the goose down blanket. "I am going down to the study to read a while." He kissed my forehead. "Tell me your dreams when you awake, my dear love."

I sighed and fell asleep.

The room filled with a luminous green and golden light. Demosthenes appeared and motioned me to join him. I got up to put on a robe, and suddenly we were in an ancient library, perhaps the one in Alexandria. Slate and wood shelves held a few bound books, but mostly scrolls.

"Why am I here?" I queried.

Demosthenes smiled his loving smile. Walking down a corridor between the shelves, he stopped, turned, and sorted through several scrolls. He found the one he wanted and upon touching it, the scroll gleamed with shimmering green and golden light.

"Will I be able to read it?"

"No." Demosthenes laughed to the point his whole body shook. "But you will be able to write it!"

I looked at him. He seemed quite pleased with himself.

"How am I…"

He spoke softly and kindly. "You will use your words, Victoria, just as I have told you."

Demosthenes then took my hand and showed me how to open the scroll. At the top, there were letters like the ones I had seen when he first etched his name in marble in front of me, and they transformed into our recognizable alphabet.

Once I held that memory, the foreign letters started dancing and then transformed themselves into green letters tinged with the purest gold and formed a single word centered at the top of the scroll:

"MEMORIAL"

In the distance, I heard Demosthenes' laughter fade away. Then I heard my voice talking out loud. I must have been talking in my sleep, the way I do when I am in a trance.

As I surfaced from the depths of my slumber, I became aware of a scratching sound. I thought there might be rats in the bedroom. Alarmed, I opened my eyes to find the Colonel feverishly writing notes on a sheaf of papers supported by a book, with his ivory-handled, steel-nib, iridium-tipped pen. He dipped the tip into the small inkwell at the round table and continued his rapid composition.

"Just a minute, Victoria, I think I have it all down."

"What do you mean, James, have all of… what down?" I yawned.

"Why, your Memorial!" Disoriented, I remembered the green and gold dancing letters, then watching them settle down at the top and center of the scroll Demosthenes showed me, and how they formed the word, "Memorial."

"I'm confused, dear husband. Are you talking about my dream?" I looked at him while still trying to become fully alert. "But, I haven't told you about it yet."

"Oh, yes, you have." He answered while continuing his rapid writing. He emitted a loving laugh. He reminded me of Demosthenes' laughter in my dream and I found myself momentarily back in the library in Alexandria. I shook my head several times.

The Colonel finally put down his pen and cast a radiant smile. He stood up, placing the current sheet behind several others, and came to embrace me in bed.

"What is going on? Please tell me!"

He sat upon the edge of the bed, faced me, and explained.

"I have been your dutiful amanuensis through the dawn, diligently transcribing your dictation." He seemed very pleased with himself.

I raised my right fore and middle fingers to my temple, the sign I did not understand a word.

"Oh, sorry, dear one. No need for Webster's Dictionary right now. *Amanuensis:* a scribe or recorder of speech to writing."

"What did I say?"

"Everything!" I looked for a bump on his head from a fall. "Just as I said, Victoria, the answer would come to you."

"Please, James, say one thing I can understand."

"You have your Memorial to present to the House Committee in Washington!"

Over the next week, all my counselors, the most intelligent men and women I knew, worked on the Memorial, refining it to a finely honed presentation. On November 19, *Woodhull & Claflin's Weekly* proclaimed:

SIXTEENTH AMENDMENT

DEAD IN COMMITTEE

From then on, we began publishing the arguments for woman suffrage with full legal standing according to my dream.

I was ready!

Tennie and I traveled through rain and thunderstorms to Washington, D.C. on the shortest day of the year, December 21, the day of Yule, the winter equinox. Our train, the "Pennsy" (The Pennsylvania Railroad) finally crossed the Potomac River on the Long Bridge toward the capital and stopped at the brand-new station, still being built at 16th and "B" Streets. Walking on planks placed as a path through the ubiquitous mud, we presented our luggage tickets to the drayage porter under the sign WILLARD HOTEL and rode in a carriage to the famous establishment on 14th Street and Pennsylvania Avenue.

Once inside the lobby, I finally understood why President Grant had proclaimed, "We should line up all those damned lobbyists and shoot them."

The stench, heat, and thick clouds of cigar smoke were stifling. We were barely making headway and constantly being jostled about, when a pair of young military men saw Tennie. As is so often the case, they came to her aid. The handsome officers parted the crowd like young Moses at the crossing of the Red Sea.

I remembered the passage in Exodus when after Moses and all the men sang their praises to all powerful God, Miriam, the prophetess, sister of Moses and Aaron, grabbed a tambourine to lead all the women to sing and dance their own celebration of the miracle of vanquishing Pharaoh's army. I liked Exodus 15 because women exalted God equally, albeit separately from the men.

We finally arrived at the front desk. When we presented our names to the registrar, he looked at us in amazement. He quickly went and got the manager, who walked up to us declaring, "Welcome to the Willard." He bowed formally and added, "Mr. Willard himself has placed you in the Presidential Suite. The same suite houses visiting heads of state and our own Commodore Cornelius Vanderbilt."

I looked at Tennie, and she shrugged her shoulders. My heart quickened as I knew the reference to her "old goat" pained her. She did not react at all other than to smile, but I saw a dark cloud flicker across her blue-grey eyes.

"Of course, he did." My sister confirmed with confidence, as we were both accustomed to deferential behavior. "Now, could you kindly show my sister and me to our rooms. The lobby is louder than the trading floor of the stock exchange during a frenzied, stampede sell off!"

"Of course." He then paused, remembering something. "Did you get the name of our drayage porter at the station?"

"Yes," I answered, and gave the man the card exchanged by the porter for our luggage tickets a short time ago.

"Excellent. This way, please." The manager himself escorted us to the stairway.

The only disadvantage of staying in the top floor of a hotel is all those stairs. I want to see a man climb all those flights with a full padded crinoline, multiple layers of petticoats, and the yards and yards of fabric we are forced to wear. I think the poor man would faint!

However, the climb was worth it.

On one side of a walnut double door, a shiny brass plaque stated, "Presidential Suite." Inside awaited a luxurious abode with a large sitting room and beautifully ornate gold-leafed furniture—just like at home. The manager wished us a pleasant stay and turned to go.

"Does the suite have a bathing tub?" Tennie inquired.

"Yes, it does."

"We would like to get out of these clothes and take a bath." Tennie smiled fetchingly at the manager. The poor man actually blushed. "Could you have some men bring up some fresh waters? Warm would be nice."

"I will do it immediately, Mademoiselle!"

On a center table a huge bouquet of fresh flowers, rare for the dead of winter, held a card. I opened it, expecting to see the signature of the Beast, my dear General Butler. To my surprise, a short note invited Tennie and me to dinner day after tomorrow. The note ended by stating, *Antonia wants to meet such admirable women of conviction. Joseph Willard, Proprietor.*

"Who is this Antonia Willard, and why does she want to meet us so much?" My sister asked.

I told Tennie what I knew about Mr. Willard and Antonia. I had studied the entire history of the Willard Hotel prior to staying at the establishment.

I turned to Tennie. "Antonia may be one of the few women who had once been more ostracized than we. Union Captain Joe Willard served on the staff of General Irvin McDowell, who established his tactical headquarters in a home owned by Edward R. Ford in the city of Fairfax, Virginia, a Confederate town. Captain Willard informed the owner his home would be appropriated."

I paused and went to the table with a pitcher of drinking water, filled a cut crystal glass and drank.

"Go on Vickie, but please make it short, as I am tired from our travels."

"Willard interacted daily with Ford's flirtatious 23-year-old daughter, Antonia, a stunning beauty mature beyond her years. The amicable Union captain succumbed to the guiles of the classic Southern belle."

"Don't they all." Tennie snorted. "Just like at Annie's!" We both laughed.

"At 41 years old, Captain Willard fell in love with young Antonia and spent whatever time he could with her, despite the fact he was a married man. He also brought her back to Washington, D.C. She lived in a suite of rooms a few floors below."

"Really, Victoria, be done or let's stop. Could you pour me a glass?"

"Always the impatient one!" I said. Tennie sat down in a blue satin wing chair. "The military exposed Antonia as a spy for the Confederacy in 1863. Upon her arrest, she stayed in the old Capitol Prison, where "Wild Rose" Greenhow, the Washington socialite and Southern spy ring leader, also served time."

"Oh my!" Tennie expressed. "Now this is getting interesting. What happened?"

"Joe Willard used every chit and favor garnered over decades to arrange for Antonia's release, and he finally succeeded after seven months. In 1864, Willard divorced his wife and married his true love. It is said Antonia has never been the same since her horrid imprisonment."

"Well, dinner should be interesting." Tennie paused and her face looked like she had seen an ominous vision.

"What is it, Sister?"

Before she could answer, a knock on the door interrupted our conversation and several men brought in warm water. Tennie went off to bathe, and I joined her shortly. We never did talk about what she saw. I did not pursue it. I hoped Tennie had not viewed the abandonment I repeatedly saw in my nightmares.

I could not discard nor suppress feeling the fear of my dream the night of our gala opening about being abandoned in prison. I was increasingly apprehensive as the dinner approached.

Joseph Willard was a charming, true gentleman—he reminded me of my Colonel. Mr. Willard arranged a sumptuous meal and told stories about several visits of the Commodore Cornelius Vanderbilt. We all laughed at the Commodore's favorite story about oysters and Benjamin Franklin's horse. Antonia discreetly touched her husband's arm when he began another Vanderbilt story. He nodded and changed course immediately as if she had tugged his reins.

Throughout the meal, Antonia, who must have been a stunning beauty a few years prior, now looked sallow and frail, appearing decades older than our common age. She was reserved and retiring. Honestly, it was hard to image her young, vibrant, and in the midst of intrigue.

"I am a subscriber to your weekly. It is one of my great joys." The softness of her Southern lilt was interrupted by a fit of coughing. While she hid it well, I saw a blotch of blood spread across the linen, right under the embroidered "W" on her napkin. She was so frail.

Back in our rooms, Tennie grabbed my arm. "You know that she will not live but a few months."

"Yes, I know. That poor young woman." I turned to Tennie full of fear. "What did they do to her in prison?"

"They broke her spirit." Tennie announced.

General Butler invited Tennie and me to stay at his home in Washington, D.C., for Christmas Eve. I always marveled at how we

Christians thought that we invented a holiday to celebrate the birth of Jesus Christ, when the early Christians had taken all the traditions and rituals of the Pagan holiday of Yule.

Rosie told me when the Romans brought Christianity to England, the churches purposefully coincided new religious holidays at the same times as the long-standing Pagan ones. Confused peasants simply attended church to honor their traditional Pagan holidays, as all the visual trappings were the same. Easter at the vernal equinox derived its name from the Saxon goddess of spring, Eastra, or the images of the German goddess Ostara.

The last ten days of 1870 and the first ten days of 1871 were filled with Tennie and me, often joined by Isabella Hooker and Susan B. Anthony meeting every elected official who would see us. Many took the meeting to simply meet the notorious sisters and to have the occasion to gaze upon Tennie. We realized we were entertainment, an item of interest, as if we were part of Mr. P. T. Barnum's show. Very few took what we had to say seriously. Few made any attempt to appear to listen. They preferred to gaze at Tennie with unguarded lust.

On the eve of the Memorial, Isabella Hooker informed me that the National Woman Suffrage Association convention scheduled to open in the morning at the same time I would present to the Committee, would be postponed until three in the afternoon. Several members of the N.W.S.A. wanted to attend and lend their support in the morning. I knew they were trying to be supportive, but I felt more pressure having them at the meeting. We all hoped that the eight congressmen on the committee would finally listen... and then take action.

My anger grew. These men in power sat in their exalted positions and simply protected the status quo, no matter how unfair to women. My time to present the Memorial had arrived.

Chapter 8

MEMORIAL: HOUSE JUDICIARY COMMITTEE

The Capitol
January 11, 1871

January 11, 1871, was a good day.

A light snow fell to settle upon the Capitol building, forming a beautiful white blanket. To compensate for the chill of the snow, the mud everywhere hardened, so it was actually easier and safer for everyone to get to where they were going. The skies were so dramatic, turning dark grey, then the sun bursting through with golden brilliance only to be obscured again by more heavy, dark, moisture-laden clouds.

I was confident and knew the text. Once James had written down my dream talk, everyone we knew and trusted helped fashion the exact words. Pearly, the Colonel, Theodore, and Whitelaw would explore points and counterpoints, ultimately arriving at a consensus. Lizzybeth, Susan, and Anna Dickinson reviewed and suggested equally important, female points of view. My Memorial presented balanced intellect, legal argument, oratory, and, most important of all to me, passion.

Tennie and I bought matching dark silk dresses, elegantly tailored with folds and creases to look like unfurling flowers. We both wore deep royal blue neckties. Our haircuts imitated the cropped style of men. We both donned identical alpine hats, each with a long, white ostrich feather.

I decided to wear an elegant brown duster. Tennie draped herself in the most exquisite, flowing, dark emerald green taffeta shawl. Tennie's light peach and cream complexion against the emerald green and royal blue rendered an angelic countenance. Our attire hinted at masculinity, yet we remained deliciously feminine.

We had breakfast delivered to our rooms, a privilege of the Presidential Suite. General Butler arrived joyfully disappointed that we were already in full costume. Tennie and the Beast ate heartily, but I worried over my presentation and kept reviewing my notes. I drank some strong tea. I simply could not eat.

"Just be yourself, Victoria!" General Butler continued eating. "The gentlemen will be transfixed!" He cut a large chunk of sausage and dipped it in some cream, took a bite, then continued in his high squeaky voice, so in contrast to his intelligence and presence. "Best eat something, girl. Always good to have something in your stomach before a battle."

"He's right, Sister. You will need your strength today." Tennie placed a peeled boiled egg on my plate.

The Beast laughed when I pushed the egg around my plate and watched it roll. "You are definitely going to stir the pot. This will be fun." He continued eating and talking with gusto. "All those old blowhards are going to have their comeuppance."

"But will they *listen*?" I inquired.

"My dear," the General began, "best not to think you will vanquish the entire Philistine army with a single pebble from a slingshot." The General paused to fork his remaining sausage onto a large clump of bread torn off the end of the loaf and consumed the entirety with a few large bites.

"You will be fine, Victoria. You always are." My sister smiled at me. "Besides, Demosthenes will be with you."

"Yes." I appreciated the reference to my spirit guide, but I could not feel his presence.

General Butler rose from the table. "We'd best get going." He wiped his face on the linen napkin embroidered with a "W." Gurdie, my Viennese sewing teacher back in Chicago, would have approved of the exemplary stitching.

"Yes." I realized I spoke in monosyllables. Not good!

"Victoria, Victoria," General Butler laughed. Then quietly and kindly, like a doting father, he cupped my head in his hands and placed a gentle kiss on top of my forehead. "As I said paramount, just be yourself." He withdrew his hands and chuckled to himself over some thought. "You are Victoria Woodhull. All you have to do is to *Woodhull it!*"

"*Woodhull it!*" Tennie chimed in gleefully.

I did not share their mirth.

The Honorable Representative to the United States Congress General Benjamin Butler escorted me into the chamber. He guided my left arm, and I held Tennie tight with my right. Several members of the House Judiciary Committee were milling around talking amongst themselves.

The smallness of the room surprised me. Reportedly, the large marble hall where we were scheduled to meet had filled with the smoke of a malfunctioning furnace; or so we were told, albeit we could neither see nor smell any signs of smoke. A long rectangular mahogany table polished to a high gloss dominated the limited chamber. Eight chairs faced the entire room. Tennie sat next to me on my right across from the row of chairs.

To my surprise and delight I found Isabella Beecher Hooker, Susan B. Anthony, Ernestine Rose, and Paulina Wright Davis, and others from the N.W.S.A. seated in the second row of the small gallery. Reporters stood or leaned against the set of bookcases behind the Committee members and flanked them along the side walls.

In front of each chair, a four-page copy with a cover sheet read:

THE MEMORIAL
OF VICTORIA C. WOODHULL

General Butler shook hands with another committee member, Representative William Loughridge of Iowa. Five other representatives huddled around a thin man with a hawk-like, chiseled face, Representative John Bingham of Ohio, the author of the fourteenth amendment and primary contributor to the fifteenth amendment—a powerful man.

Bingham had gained national notoriety for prosecuting the conspirators in the Lincoln assassination trial. As a result, Mary Surratt, who owned the boarding house where John Wilkes Booth and the other conspirators stayed or met, became the first woman sentenced to death and to be hanged by the federal government. I had met and talked with Bingham before. The man simply hated all women, no doubt including his own mother.

The chairman called the meeting to order, rapping his gavel. He thanked me for accepting the invitation to appear before the House of Representatives Judiciary Committee. He confirmed the full text of the "Memorial" had been presented to the distinguished members of the Committee. He concluded his remarks by asking me to present my arguments.

I stood.

I placed my fists upon the tabletop, paused, and began. I recited from memory the opening of my Memorial:

> To the Honorable Judiciary Committee of the House of Representatives of the United States:
>
> The undersigned, Victoria C. Woodhull, having most respectfully memorialized Congress for the passage of such laws as in its wisdom shall seem

necessary and proper to carry into effect the rights vested by the Constitution of the United States in the citizens to vote, without regard to sex...

I stopped and looked up. I saw the face of John Bingham sneering at me with disdain. I felt he judged me for reciting something they had already read. He gazed at me as if he pitied me, but with a contempt—nay, a hatred—for me, a woman daring to speak to this exalted assembly of men.

I felt the wind as it slowly swayed the limp body of Mary Surratt, as she swung to and fro... dead by hanging, to and fro... slowly twisting... to and fro. I could feel the breeze on my face, as I looked into her lifeless eyes. The horror and indignity were gone now, as she swayed... to and fro. She looked so calm, her struggle over. Only her body was left moving like a pendulum, swinging dead Mary Surratt to and fro... to and fro.

I felt a sharp grip on my hand. Tennessee squeezed my fist. Bingham snickered loudly and looked away from me. My stomach ached and I wished I had eaten something.

I didn't speak.

The room filled with tension. General Butler leaned over his table, physically imploring me to continue. Isabella looked worried and kept nodding her head toward me, mouthing the words, "Go on! Go on!" Susan B. Anthony sat ramrod straight, and her nostrils flared just below her hawk-like black eyes. Tennessee dug her nails into my hand, almost breaking the skin.

Then the room filled with a luminous green and brilliant golden glow. I felt the hand of Demosthenes at the small of my back. I looked to my left and heard him whisper. "*Use your words, Victoria.*" I took a deep breath and looked directly at Representative John A. Bingham.

"I believe, sir, you are the author of the Fourteenth Amendment and acknowledged architect of the Fifteenth Amendment." He looked startled that I had singled him out and addressed him directly. He arrogantly nodded his head, confirming his accomplishments.

"Good. Thank you." I started speaking clearly, quietly, but with passion. With each point I made, I increased my volume slightly, the way I had learned from Mr. Frederick Douglass.

> Neither the State of New York nor any other State, nor any Territory, has passed any law to abridge the right of any citizen of the United States to vote, as established by the Fifteenth Article of Amendment, neither on account of sex or otherwise;
>
> Nevertheless, the right to vote is denied to women citizens of the United States by the operation of election laws in the several states and territories, which laws were enacted prior to the adoption of the said Article XV. No distinction between citizens is made in the Constitution of the United States on account of sex, but Article XIV of Amendments to it provides 'no State shall make or enforce any law which shall abridge the privileges and immunities of citizens of the United States, nor deny to any person within its jurisdiction the equal protection of the laws.'

Having quoted his words to him, I paused and glared at Bingham. He returned my gaze, looking insulted, shocked, and appalled. *Good!* I thought to myself. I continued.

> Congress has the power to make laws which shall be necessary and proper for carrying into execution all powers vested by the Constitution in the government of the United States; and to make or alter all regulations in relation to holding election for Senators and Representatives, and especially to enforce, by appropriate legislation, the provisions of the said

Article XIV;

The continuance of the enforcement of said local election laws, denying and abridging the right of citizens to vote on account of gender, is a grievance to your Memorialist and to various other persons, citizens of the United States, being women,—

Therefore, Your Memorialist would most respectfully petition you honorable men to make such laws as in the wisdom of Congress shall be necessary and proper for carrying into execution the right vested by the Constitution in the citizens of the United States to vote, without regard to sex.

I stopped.

The room remained still, silent.

Then it erupted into pandemonium. There were shouts of "Here! Here!" and "Well said!!" as well as "Absurd!" and "Preposterous!" There was a standing ovation as well as boos.

The chairman repeatedly rapped his gavel. "Order! Order!" Finally, John Bingham stood up and shouted, "I will clear the room, unless there is order right now."

Once the chairman restored order and everyone had settled back into their seats, Representative Bingham questioned me. "Are you finished?"

"No!" I shook my head. I looked directly at Bingham. "You, sir," I pointed an accusing finger at him, "have said to me," I imitated his haughty Midwest accent, "'You are no citizen! You are a woman!'" Many in the crowd openly jeered the man. He again ineffectually pounded his little mallet.

Glaring at Bingham, I proclaimed. "I am a woman. You sir, will never know and can't possibly understand the hardship and suffering this entails. It is bad enough you personally dismiss half of the human race. Must your laws reflect your hatred?"

There were cheers from the gallery.

I stood up, defiant. "I am a citizen of the United States of America." The crowd shouted, applauded and gave me strength.

One by one I captured the eyes of each committee member. "As a citizen, I have a Constitutional right to suffrage!" More shouts of approval provided a staccato accompaniment to my cadence.

I leaned over the table and pointed at Bingham. My voice rose on a huge wave of emotion. "If you deny our right to vote, *you, sirs,* are in contempt of and defile the very Constitution you swore to uphold."

Before sitting down, I warned them all, "Do so at your own peril!"

The small chamber erupted. John Bingham tried to restore order, but could not. He rose, nodded to the other members, and quickly fled the chamber.

Tennie kissed me. I looked across the table to General Butler, who smiled and nodded his head up and down. He bent his head toward me, winked, and silently formed the words, *Well done.*

I was glowing!

Isabella and Susan followed us all the way back to The Willard. As Tennie and I sat down to order lunch, the two women asked if they could join us. I did not feel like company, but before I could reply, Tennie said, "Why, of course, we'd love for you both to join us."

I thought the parsimonious Miss Anthony might simply want a free lunch. Then, I thought of the way I had looked for a friendly face in the committee chamber and found both women before us providing the much-needed support. "Yes, do join us."

Isabella started to speak. "Victoria, in all my…"

"Please let us order our meals before we have any discussion." I felt ravenous. My stomach churned, completely empty. I looked over at Tennie and remembered the bountiful breakfast she ate. I motioned to a waiter to take our order, then changed my mind and instructed him, "Waiter, please commence our meal immediately by bringing tea for all of us, and some warm bread and butter... honey, too. As quickly as possible!"

After we all placed our orders, Isabella turned to me. "Victoria, you were simply amazing the way you spoke to the committee, especially Representative Bingham."

"Yes, indeed." Susan Anthony added, not quite void of emotion.

Tennie asked the question I myself had thought, "What can we do for you ladies? We have already donated generously to the National Woman Suffrage Association—in fact we have underwritten the entire convention."

To my relief the bread arrived, and I lathered on the fresh butter and watched it melt into the coarse, dark slice. It tasted like manna in the wilderness.

"We acknowledge and are most grateful for all your generosity." Isabella looked over at me. "Susan and I have talked it over and we would like to invite both of you to sit upon the dais at the N.W.S.A. convention later this afternoon."

The conversation paused as we were served our meals. Tantalizing aromas of sage and rosemary wafted from my steaming plate of mutton stew.

"Seems odd you did not invite us before now, given our extensive support." Tennie always jumped to the bottom line.

"Not fair!" Susan could be as direct as Tennie. "We were scheduled to commence the same time as your presentation to the committee, but we all wanted to be there to support you. Once we knew your timing, we did not want to draw attention away from you." Though she was normally austere, Susan appeared genuinely upset.

"It's true," Isabella declared, and then continued, "We want to ask you for one more favor, Victoria." She paused and looked over at Susan.

"Really, sweet Isabella, just speak your mind." I found Isabella's timidity exhausting. I returned my focus to the plate in front of me.

Susan spoke instead. "Victoria, we came here to enlist you to make the opening address this afternoon. We want you to be the first speaker."

I put down my knife and fork. I remembered how lost I felt before the Committee and seeing Mary Surratt sway from her gallows. I trembled.

"We really do want you, Victoria. The convention will rally around your words," Isabella added.

"I want you to take my place and deliver the commencement address." Susan declared, "You can use your text from the Memorial." I rarely saw Susan B. Anthony wax reflective, but she did. "In this age of rapid thought and action, telegraphs and railways," she shrugged her shoulders and tapped her chest, "this old stagecoach won't do."

Susan's words shocked me. I had never heard her talk so candidly or admit any limitations. I turned to Susan and asked her frankly, "Does LizzyBeth want me to appear?"

"Very much so," Susan answered without hesitation.

"Do it, sister." Tennie encouraged. "Isabella, Susan, and I will get the entire Washington press to attend the convention to hear you."

"Yes, we will," Isabella chimed in. "Many were not coming, but once they hear you will be speaking, after your performance before the Committee, they will drop everything to attend."

I looked up at Tennie, knowing only she could see the dread and fear in my eyes. She looked back at me confident and reassuring. She nodded her head ever so slightly and winked at me.

"Very well," I said. "Please do make sure all the press are there." I looked at my steaming plate of stew, which I had tasted and eagerly enjoyed just a moment ago. Conscripted, I could not eat another bite. My stomach flipped with the anticipation of another speech. I looked wistfully at my food. I stabbed a piece of the lamb, swirled it in the rich gravy, and abandoned the fork on the plate.

"What fun!" Tennie blurted. She whispered something to Isabella, who I believe started to blush. "I know the perfect outfit to wear."

True to her word, as I struggled to write a few thoughts on some paper, Tennie dressed to make as much of a statement with her costume as I did with my speech.

She eagerly stripped off her clothing, tossing pieces every which way, and proceeded to quickly dry wash. She applied more rose and jasmine oils, gifts to us from Rosie.

She overdid the oils and it made me think of the ladies when they would quickly prepare for the next encounter. A quick splash of cheap parfum to strategic parts of the body was commonly known as "a whore's bath." I thought my association harsh. Tennie returned to the room with her new outfit; I joined her exuberance.

"So, tell me, what is this?" I queried.

"Today I will debut the latest in woman fashion." She giggled ebulliently. I smiled, I thrilled to see my sister excited. I knew how she suffered, not being able to see her Corney. My sister stood unclad. She felt completely comfortable without as much as a strip of cloth to cover her nakedness.

The outfit she displayed declared a revolution! She held up each garment as she narrated, "Pants of dark blue satin, buckled at the knee over these light blue, sheer stockings."

"Oh my!" I could not contain myself.

"Shush, Vickie, I am not done." She quickly turned from stern schoolmistress to enchantress. "This dark blue blouse with the deep "V" to my waist will end where the pants end." She motioned downward to her knees and then back up her chest. "This white linen shirt will be underneath the blouse with this white collar and cravat." An image of the Commodore came to my mind.

"My calves and ankles will be visible through my stockings above these blue sequined slippers."

"And your corset, my dear?" I inquired.

"They are so restricting and uncomfortable." She jostled her body and placed her hands to lift each breast and dropped her hands. Only her hands dropped. "I simply do not need one!"

We both broke out laughing. I thought this outfit would have been risqué even for Tallahassee back at Annie Wood's establishment. I decided to dress the same as I had for the committee, simple, elegant, and, I hoped, imposing.

"It will be interesting to see which makes the greater impression: my words or your wardrobe." Our laughter filled the room.

Later that afternoon, we sisters attended the National Woman Suffrage Association convention in Lincoln Hall. True to their word, the three fates, Susan, Bella, and Tennie, had summoned every reporter in Washington, D.C. In addition to my address, there would be a world premiere of the newest clothing. Miss Tennessee Celeste Claflin would introduce a striking departure in woman fashion.

I sat in the middle of the dais, with Tennie to my right and Isabella Hooker to my left. Also, seated in the row facing the audience, were Lucretia Mott, Elizabeth Cady Stanton, Paulina Wright Davis, Susan B. Anthony, and Josephine Griffing.

Lizzybeth hugged me before sitting down and spoke into my ear. "You did well today, very well." She hugged me again, before letting go. I felt the warmth of a loving mother.

Isabella called the meeting to order and named each one of us on the dais. She saved my name for last. "Last, but certainly not least, we are honored to have Victoria C. Woodhull on the dais." A few of the women cheered. "Earlier today over at the Capitol, Mrs. Woodhull asserted woman's right to suffrage under the Fourteenth Amendment," Thunderous applause filled the hall.

Susan introduced me as the commencement speaker and told of the stirring victory at the Committee this same day. I rose to speak.

Once again, I tensed as panic seized me. I looked helplessly to the large crowd, and then turned my eyes to Isabella, seeking refuge.

Calls came out from the crowd.

"Speak!"

"We want to hear you."

"Tell us."

Uneasiness filled the large hall.

I thought of my Demosthenes, but could not feel his presence. I started to speak meekly, softly.

"I appeared before the House of Congress Judiciary Committee today, a few hours ago."

"Louder!"

"We can't hear you."

Isabella slid a glass of water over to me and I drank it eagerly. Tennie encouraged me from her seat. I turned to face the crowd.

I found my words. "Woman deserves the right to vote as much as any man!" There were shouts of approval. "We are citizens of the United States!" My voice boomed out before me. Luckily, the crowd interrupted my speech with another standing ovation.

I explained the logic of the Fourteenth and Fifteenth Amendments, granting the right to vote to woman, as we are all citizens. Several times standing ovations halted my speech. I continued:

> Let women issue a declaration of independence sexually, and absolutely refuse to cohabit with men until we are acknowledged as equals in everything, and the victory would be won in a single week.

Laughter collided with applause.

> If the very next Congress refuses woman all the legitimate results of citizenship, we shall proceed to call another convention expressly to frame a new Constitution and to erect a new woman government.

The cheering lasted a long time. I considered stopping, but I wanted to incite and impassion.

> We mean treason! We mean secession on a thousand times grander scale than that of the South. We are plotting revolution. We will overthrow this bogus Republic.
>
> And we shall plant a government of righteousness in its stead... *of woman, for woman, and by woman.*

The tumult lasted several minutes as I took my seat.

Paulina Wright Davis shouted for order. When none was to be found, she adjourned the meeting until the morrow.

The morning papers gave the convention the moniker, "The Woodhull Convention," and others reported of "The Great Secession Speech." One reporter said I looked so resolved and confident I appeared "One of the forces of nature behind the storm, a small splinter of the indestructible."

Tennie's outfit left everyone dumbstruck. I know many disapproved, but no one who attended would voice such opinion. The press freely castigated my sister as often as they rapturously described her appearance. There were as many stories about Tennie's liberating costume as about the speech. I rejoiced for her.

All acknowledged that the sisters Woodhull and Claflin had stormed Washington, D.C. and conquered.

Chapter 9

ORATORY

The East Coast
Winter–Spring, 1871

U pon our return to New York City, the brokerage office was overflowing with new depositors and requests for speaking engagements. I sought the counsel of my friend Anna to help me manage the requests.

"Vickie, will you let me make you the queen of the Lyceum circuit?" Anna was excited that she might implement her old plan to have me tour with her, culminating in declaring me the new headliner of the Lyceum. "We can alternate being the last speaker each evening."

"Dear Anna," I tried to proceed gently, "I could never surrender the control of my engagements to the bureaus. The men who manage you take too much of your fees."

"But Victoria, they also secure the highest fees paid at every appearance I make."

"I'm sorry Anna, your offer is genuine and kind, but I will not subjugate myself to any man negotiating on my behalf, nor dictating to me when and where to go."

"Victoria, you know you have my undying support. I will contribute to your success, however I may."

In fact, Anna, Lizzybeth, and Isabella used their extensive contacts and relationships built over their lifetimes to provide me with planning, hospitality, and comfort wherever I traveled to speak.

The incredibly wise and learned Stephen Pearl Andrews thought it "about time!" The strapping, handsome wordsmith and firebrand intellectual, Theodore Tilton, joined Pearly and my dear husband to help me forge and fashion the speeches and then the press releases to print in our *Weekly* and the local papers in advance of my appearances.

As for the speeches themselves, they were… captured. I would induce a trance or prompt myself in dream state to talk out loud. My dear husband would write down my words verbatim. Once the themes and primary content were down on paper, my *Le Trois Mousquetaires*, dedicated to the protection of their queen, would sit and discuss my dictations and modify them.

Tennie contributed too. She seized every opportunity to leave New York City and journeyed to pre-arrange my travels, securing the best locations available at the lowest prices possible. Cornelius had begun listening more closely to the plaintive requests softly spoken in the mellifluous Southern accent of his wife Frank Armstrong Crawford. The giant of industry's new wife with her conspirator, the patriarch's son, William, increasingly exerted control over the household. Tennie and her lover could no longer have their liaisons at the city's best hotels.

I believed Frank and William were more concerned with the amount of control they could exert over the eventual estate than with Corney's health. No wonder his illnesses worsened.

I feared my increasing notoriety—the majority of stories reporting my statements were pejorative—would hurt our business. This worried me.

"James, does it hurt our business when the papers continually castigate me?" I asked my husband one evening when I was back home.

He held me close to him, pressing my head to his chest. "In fact, the opposite, my dear." He kissed my forehead. "Consistently, when you are widely maligned, we experience a windfall of new accounts at the firm and a surge in subscriptions at the *Weekly*." If

I had any remaining doubts, James helped me forget them through our exquisite lovemaking.

I continued to incite the press and provoke public debate with challenging declarations in my speeches and in interviews. I wrote in the *Weekly* of becoming disillusioned:

> Rude contact with facts chased my visions and dreams quickly away, and in their stead I beheld the horrors, the corruption, the evils and hypocrisy of society, and as I stood among them, a young wife and mother, a great wail of agony went out from my soul.

Circulation grew.

> Woman's ability to earn money is better protection against the tyranny and brutality of men than her ability to vote. I demand equal pay for equal work.

Accounts increased.

> Hundreds, thousands, aye, millions of human beings, men, women, and children wander the streets of our cities and highways of our country, hungry, and cold, vainly seeking in this land of plenty, where physical want should be unknown.

Speaking requests inundated our offices with higher and higher offers.

I was the last speaker on slates of highly distinguished speakers on any given evening. I would follow the likes of William Lloyd Garrison, Wendell Phillips, Sojourner Truth, Henry Ward Beecher, Walt Whitman, sometimes Anna Dickenson, and even Mr. Frederick Douglass. I always spoke to sellout crowds, from Maine to South Carolina.

Wherever I spoke, I could always find the face of Tennie or my Colonel in the crowd. This would settle me down, and after a few words I would find the cadence and the rhythms would become their own imperative.

We had the advantage of traveling first class for free on any railroad or boat under the influence of the richest man in America. At the mention of the Vanderbilt name, we were immediately treated as royalty. In rare instances when challenged, we produced a hand-signed note on the Commodore's embossed stationery, requesting anyone who read the note to treat Tennessee Celeste Claflin and Victoria Woodhull as his personal guests.

I diligently quoted from the most current *W & C's Weekly* in each speech. Every night I hired pretty young girls to sell five hundred copies before the performance. Circulation grew as subscribers, city by city, signed up at four dollars for a year to receive the *Weekly* through the post.

Henry Ward Beecher was the only one to voice an objection about the sale of the *Weekly* and subscriptions in the lobbies. He continued to display what I considered a licentious attitude toward me and every other woman who crossed his path. I told the young girls to shun him. I knew he did not remember our meeting in his offices after his failed sermon, because, after all, to him I was only a woman. The man continued to vex me, and I him.

The speaking engagements excited not only the audiences but myself as well. Anna told me it would be so. She was right. My blood pumped fast as I modulated my voice from soft whispers to rising crescendos.

> The spirits are coming back to tear your damned system of sexual slavery into tatters and consign its blackened remnants to the depth of everlasting hell.

While I became the headliner, the cast of additional speakers changed by geography. I received encouraging compliments from many of the great orators of our time. Walt Whitman, the poet who had praised us at the grand opening of our brokerage firm, was always so kind and encouraging that I felt loved as if by a father. In turn, I let him know how much I adulated him and his writings. I was surprised he remembered my favorite poem was Crossing Brooklyn Ferry. Mr. Whitman told me, "I don't hear that very often." I cherished the gentle man.

Frederick Douglass was particularly beneficent.

"I want to congratulate you, Victoria," his deep voice rumbled, "on your meteoric rise in popularity and influence." The famous man spoke to me after we shared the stage through several ovations in upper New York near Albany.

As the curtains closed, he continued, "Now that the Fifteenth Amendment is ratified, I pledge my loyal and unwavering support to the cause of woman suffrage and perfected legal standing. That's what I promised Elizabeth Cady Stanton at our meeting at the offices of *The Revolution*." He paused and I could see him contemplate how much more to say.

"I beseech you, most learned and accomplished of men, I will willingly receive any advice or direction you generously afford me."

"*Ha, ha, ha!*" The pedagogue laughed robustly. "I pride myself on not being caught in the same snare twice. Your entreaties are worded sweetly, young lady, but we both know your tongue is cuttingly sharp!"

"I will take that as a compliment, thank you, sir. Still, I ask you to share your thoughts."

He turned serious. He shook his head side to side. "Be careful, Victoria!" His eyes filled with a sorrow that only a life filled with too much pain can summon. "Much like me, you bear a burning passion for change. This will attract many, including those vehemently, rigidly, and perhaps violently opposed to you." His powerful shoulders tensed, seemingly oppressed by some huge weight I could not see. "Change will not come without a price for either my kind or womankind." He shirked his shoulders as if releasing a large bale of cotton. "The truth is that you and your sister have already invaded realms originally exclusive to men—white men!"

"Thank you, Mr. Douglass, coming from you…"

"We are past that formality, Mrs. Woodhull." I better understood LizzyBeth's dedicated loyalty and attraction to the man standing before me. "Simply call me Frederick. It is easy. Even the frogs can say it." He reached out to me and took both my hands the way a father would reach out to a departing daughter. "You are building momentum, my dear young lady, and while that has its own appeal, and you certainly bring fervor to your cause, but beware: There is an unseen danger the more recognized you become. This danger builds in direct proportion to your increasing fame. Many will exalt you, but others will swear to destroy you."

"I have received threats…"

"These are not idle. You need to pay attention." He pressed my hands and then looked off into the distance. "Sadly, while the First Amendment guarantees each individual the right to speak freely his and, yes, her mind, it cannot guaranty freedom from the consequences. Were it otherwise, and all would be welcomed into a fraternity of respectable intellectual debate, my heart would be much gladdened." The way he spoke was intoxicating.

Frederick took a deep breath and then continued. "But our world is formed with deep chasms and divides, not lofty ideals." He looked intensely at me and continued.

"Choose your battles wisely, Victoria. Know your enemies at least as well as you know your friends, and tally your detractors with as much accuracy as you tally your account ledgers." With a long sigh and a lowered voice, he concluded, "Always know your full reckonings, so you are never caught by surprise. I assure you, without the distraction of specifics, to do otherwise can be devastating."

I could not help but hear the echo of the Commodore Cornelius Vanderbilt when he delivered the exact same admonition to me about constantly knowing my entire portfolio positions of cash, stocks and bonds. A chill ran down my spine.

"Thank you, Mr... Frederick."

"I add my congratulations on your success, young lady. Be alert and try to envision and foresee the consequences of each choice you make. At the risk of redundancy, I reiterate, not doing so can invite catastrophe."

The reactions to my speeches and growing popularity seemed to unravel the tight, dry guardians of moral certitude. Members of the A.W.S.A. were about to descend upon our little Isle of Manhattan like invading hordes from the North. Once again, the family Beecher played a central role in malevolent attacks upon us.

I met Elizabeth Stanton on a bright April day for lunch at the historic Tontine Coffee House at the northwest corner of Wall and Water Streets. Before the war of 1812, the four-story Federal style brick building had served as an active market for everything from stocks and bonds to vendor wares. We both ordered soup and sandwiches. We sat immersed in a gathering of young voices for change mingled with merchants and financial people in a potpourri as diverse as the ingredients in the establishment's soups.

"Frederick sends his warmest regards. I talked with him up in Albany," I said.

"I know, he wrote to me. He is rightfully concerned for you." Lizzybeth went on, "Catherine Beecher, her sister, Harriet Beecher Stowe, along with the repellent Reverend Henry Ward Beecher have personally written and signed letters delivered to every member of the N.W.S.A." She handed me a copy of one of the letters. "They charge each of our members to be very careful, admonishing them to make certain and be very clear about the woman speaking on our behalf. You, Victoria."

"I am not surprised."

"Vickie, before you get upset, I want you to hear what I wrote to Lucretia." Lucretia Mott was the eldest and most venerated leader of the N.W.S.A. Lizzybeth unfolded a sheet of her stationery and read to me from a copy of her letter.

"I have thought much of the attacks on our dear Woodhull, and all the gossip and innuendo have brought me to this conclusion. It is a great impertinence to pry into any of her affairs. How should we feel to have everyone overhauling our antecedents? Woodhull stands before us today one of the ablest writers and speakers of the century."

"Thank you, Lizzybeth."

"And this, Vickie." She opened another piece of paper. "Susan practically tore the paper underlining almost every word." Lizzybeth read out loud, "Not until we catechize and refuse men, will I consent to question women. And it is only that Mrs. Woodhull is a woman, a member of an enslaved class, that we ever dream of such a thing. What would have been thought of our founding fathers stopping to trace and investigate every volunteer revolutionist joining the Continental Army?"

"Lizzybeth, I would not be able to stand without the moral support and active advocacy all of you continuously generate. I am very grateful."

My mentor laughed. "Stop being so formal with me at your side." She motioned to our bowls and plates. "We will need sustenance for the battles to come."

"Indeed. Let's eat." I said lightheartedly. I realized hidden from view, my stomach was churning.

Being caught in the middle, the anguished Isabella Beecher Hooker brokered a meeting. I met with her oldest half-sister,

Catherine Beecher, the regressive old spinster who had written the code of conduct for married women with children.

Catherine brought a chill to the door of our house. I could feel it before she clanged the large brass claw. I opened the door to the woman who conducted a letter campaign to discredit me.

"I will not enter a home of impropriety," she declared.

I thought of accepting her decision and shutting the door in her face. Instead, I suggested we take in the brisk winter air. "If you want to wait a minute or two, I will summon our phaeton for a carriage ride through Central Park."

As Catherine sat on the velvet seat inside my brougham, she commenced without the slightest regard to courtesies.

"Young woman, perhaps because of your youth, a misbegotten fervor, or likely the lack of a proper education, you have embarked on a disastrous path..."

"So, we are to be friends, then." I interrupted her.

"Impertinence is not a shield. It only reveals a base weakness." She averted her eyes to continue. "You create an unholy, toxic concoction; a devil's brew, mixing the teachings of free love, the baneful influence of spiritualism, your fascination for the demi-monde, and the moral poverty of thousands of women who, but for desperate temptations, would be pure. Your mixture is inflammatory and explosive, yet you pour it onto the foundations and footings of the family and state. I have no doubt you seek to burn us all to cinders."

"I had no idea you thought me so powerful, Catherine."

"*You* are not. But as an instrument of the devil, your impact is magnified ten thousand times." She went on with a vehemence forged far beyond the reaches of reason. "I suppose that I can understand, given your lack of breeding. One with proper upbringing would simply not behave in this manner." She stared straight ahead, not even acknowledging my presence in my own carriage. "You are possessed by some powerful malignant spirits, or you have been touched by Satan himself."

She seemed to finally exhaust her desire to demonize me. I realized that the evil she saw in me, in fact, lived in her own holier than thou spirit. I looked at her and almost shrieked—I saw her head covered with a swarm of little flying devils with rats' tails, buzzing around her.

"You are misguided, Catherine." I tried to clear the image of the buzzing devil rats from my mind, unsuccessfully. "Many great people that you admire already accept and live my theories of social freedom, though they are not ready to condone it publicly, nor become an advocate, as I am. You decry free love, while your own exalted little brother, Henry Ward, the most popular preacher in America, openly practices it."

"Stop! Do not speak another word!" She screamed.

"I do not condemn him. I applaud him. If only he had the courage to join me in preaching what he practices."

"*Evil!*" Catherine shrieked. She drew herself in to the farthest corner of the seat. She hissed, "I know my brother is unhappy, but he is a true husband. I will vouch for my brother's faithfulness to his marriage vows as though he were myself."

"Then you would bear false witness." I spoke calmly, but firmly. "You have no positive knowledge to go on. And you have no such direct experience yourself."

"*Evil.*" She formed a cross with both index fingers. "*Wicked.*" She lifted both her hands to cover her ears. She rocked herself back and forth. The flying devils with rats' tails scurried around her hands. "Mrs. Beecher is a horrible woman, but Henry Ward, unfaithful? No! Never! I will hear no more of it."

"But you will, as there is more to hear. He is in concubinage with several of his parishioners' wives—it is common knowledge." I had to press the point one step further. "If you were a proper person to judge, which I grant you are not, you would see that the facts are both true and fatal to your theories."

Catherine raged, "Victoria Woodhull, I will strike you for this. I will strike you dead." White spittle covered her chin.

I tried to answer her. "Cath…"

"*Stop!*" Catherine exploded.

She alighted from the carriage awkwardly. Her voluminous skirt over her heavy crinoline threw her off balance. Once on the ground she scampered away. I saw a trail of flying, rodent demons follow her like a personal storm cloud.

"Victoria." the high squeaky voice belonged to Stephen Pearl Andrews. I was descending the staircase on my way to gather my things and go to the offices of the brokerage. I started to put on my lighter spring matelasse jacket as the sun promised warmth that mid-April morning. He said, "What do you know already about the Paris Communards?"

"I have heard of them, of course." I raised my arms to bend him toward me and kissed his prominent, balding head. "Honestly, I have not had time to pay attention to them. They have seized control of the city of Paris and profess social change. Right?"

Pearly nodded, his eyes twinkled, his tell signal that his mind was fully engaged. "And so much more. Perhaps I can fill you in on the details…"

"Yes indeed, Pearly." Before he could reply, I went on, "But not right now. In fact, not today. I have to attend to this Beecher problem."

It took a few days for us to find the time, but when Pearly explained that a militant, working-class insurrection had seized control of Paris, I made the time and listened closely.

Pearly updated me from time to time with news. Together we decided that I would request to speak at the upcoming convention of the Labor Reform League at Cooper Union on May 8. I believed the causes of labor rights and universal suffrage could gain strength individually by becoming associated.

The patriarch, Peter Cooper, introduced me personally as he had my dear friend, Anna Dickenson, before Tennie and I arrived in Manhattan. I had not conversed with him since one of the earliest soirees, where we first met little over a year ago. I was thrilled to shake his hand once again.

"Thank you, Mr. Cooper, for always saying nice things about Tennie and me." I held his hand tightly.

"My privilege and honor, young lady." He bowed slightly, such an elegant elderly gentleman. "I am most fortunate to bear witness to your mercurial rise." He kissed the top of my right hand. "Well, the people are waiting, let us commence."

As he walked to the stage, the theater manager approached him and excitedly motioned to the doors.

"There are throngs of people outside without tickets, Mr. Cooper. We are completely sold out."

Mr. Cooper turned toward me and winked. "Of course, there are. They want to hear the famous Victoria Woodhull!"

"Should I bolt the doors and turn them away?"

"No! Not at all." He said emphatically. "Invite everyone in," he ordered, "And do not close the auditorium doors." Mr. Cooper motioned his right arm across the hall, "Have them sit or stand wherever they can. No one will mind." Mr. Cooper was a great populist. On stage his glowing remarks introduced me to the Labor Reform League. The entire hall was packed with humanity.

I commenced my speech identifying the wrongs that beset us, and included several references to the continuing rule by the Communards in Paris. I concluded my opening remarks, thus:

> There is no escaping the fact that the principle by which the male citizens of these United States assume to rule the female citizens is that of self-government, but, in truth, it is that of despotism; and so, the fact that poets have sung songs of freedom, and anthems of liberty have resounded for an empty shadow.

For over ninety minutes I presented the viewpoint that:

> We who demand social freedom simply ask that the
> government shall be administered in accordance with
> the spirit of the proposition that all men and women are
> born free and equal and entitled to certain inalienable
> rights. It means that every person is of equal right as
> an individual, and that he or she is entitled to pursue
> happiness in whatever direction he or she may choose.

I closed my speech by citing the last portion of Lord Alfred
Tennyson's poem, "The List Tournament," from the collection, *The
Idylls of the King*, about King Arthur and the knights of the round table.

> *The love that I cannot command is not mine;*
> *let me not disturb myself about it,*
> *nor attempt to filch it from its rightful owner.*
> *A heart that I supposed mine has drifted and gone.*
> *Shall I go in pursuit?*
> *Shall I forcibly capture the truant and transfix it*
> *with the barb of my selfish affection,*
> *and pin it to the wall of my chambers?*
> *Rather let me leave my doors and windows open,*
> *intent only on living so nobly that the best*
> *cannot fail to be drawn to me by an irresistible attraction.*
> *The New Era.*

> We are denounced as wishing to reduce the sexual
> relation to simple promiscuity, while our faith and our
> contention are that perfect freedom would annihilate all
> temptation to promiscuity. We denounce promiscuity
> and licentiousness with all our might, and shall protest
> against them to our latest breath.

I stopped. There was a long silence. Then applause filled the hall. The resounding ovation continued for the better part of an hour. At one point the clapping of hands became repeatedly unified into one loud thunderclap of deafening solidarity.

Even the *New York Times,* always contentious with anything Tennie or I did or said, proclaimed my address a complete success.

Before we could celebrate, we were informed that Pearly's wife, Esther Andrews, had died. He locked himself into an upstairs room at our home and would not come out until Tennessee affirmed to him that Esther had successfully crossed over to the Summerlands and her spirit was at peace.

Lizzybeth joined the household to review my speech and organize the commencement of the N.W.S.A. convention, two days away. Her strength and dedication were a comfort to all of us.

Intent on stymying any growth or support for the N.W.S.A., the A.W.S.A. opened its conclave on May 11 at Steinway Hall. We, the N.W.S.A., commenced simultaneously at the smaller Apollo Hall. I delivered the keynote address. Unlike last year, this time the popularity was reversed. The Apollo was filled beyond capacity, standing room only. Steinway Hall had obvious vacancies. This time they were impaled on their own spears of elitism, judgement, and segregation.

The N.W.S.A. convention represented several diverse factions. spiritualists, working women, labor reformers, businessmen, and politicians intermingled. Knowingly or not, all of them sat among ladies of the oldest profession.

Elizabeth Cady Stanton introduced me. Lizzybeth had fought to give me a seat of honor, next to Lucretia Mott, the venerated grand dame of the movement. "As we prepare to celebrate the twenty-third anniversary of the Seneca Falls Convention throughout the coming week, it gives me deep and heartfelt pleasure to introduce the woman I believe has become the standard bearer and protagonist of our doctrine. Please welcome the true heir to the Seneca Falls proclamation, Victoria Woodhull."

As I rose from my seat, I was embraced by two signatories to the Seneca Falls *Declaration of Sentiments*. Loud applause and shouts accompanied my walk to the lectern. I was prepared. I would confront marriage and woman as property, then state my case for universal suffrage clearly, and finish with a call to action!

I have had ample occasion to learn the true worth of present political parties and I unhesitatingly pronounce it is as my firm conviction if they rule this country twenty years to come as badly as they have for twenty years past, that our liberties will be lost or the parties will be washed out by such rivers of blood as the late war never produced.

Why do I war on marriage? Sanctioned and defended by marriage, night after night there are thousands of rapes committed, under cover of this accursed license. I know whereof I speak—millions of poor, heartbroken, suffering wives are compelled to minister to the lechery of insatiable husbands when every instinct of body and sentiment of soul revolt in loathing and disgust....

I have asked for equality, nothing more.... Sexual freedom means the abolition of prostitution both in and out of marriage, means the emancipation of woman from sexual slavery and her coming into ownership and control of her own body, means an end to her pecuniary dependence on man, means the abrogation of forced

pregnancy, of antenatal murder of undesired children
and the birth of love children only.

The crowd interrupted me with applause after each phrase,
sometimes cheering as I raised and lowered my voice to make my point.

Rise! And declare yourself free.
Women are entirely unaware of their power. Like an
elephant led by a string, they are subordinated by their
own acquiescence to those who are most interested in
holding them in slavery.

I restarted the argument that I fully believed:

Let women issue a declaration of independence
sexually, and absolutely refuse to cohabit with men until
women are acknowledged as equals in everything, and
the victory would be won in a single week."

Laughter and some gasps filled the hall. I concluded with the
incitement to revolution first spoken to the N.W.S.A. in Washington, D.C.

We mean treason. *We* mean secession on a thousand
times greater scale than was that of the South. *We* are
plotting revolution! *We* will overthrow this bogus
Republic and plant a government of righteousness in
its stead.

Cheering erupted and filled the hall. Women waved white hankies
in support of the movement. The same unified clapping of hands that
filled Cooper Union now filled the Apollo.

As I returned to my seat, Lucretia Mott stepped forward and with
tears in her eyes embraced me and placed my head on her chest. She

kissed the top of my head. She released me and took my left hand in her right hand and lifted it to the rafters. We both waved to the crowd.

The hall exploded in the frenzied excitement.

Solidarity at Apollo Hall!

We were one!

Part II

INFAMY

Chapter 10

HUBRIS

New York City
May, 1871

I woke up the next morning unusually late. The sun rose high outside the windows. I had allowed a sense of accomplishment entice me to succumb to slumber's tender embrace. I felt joy remembering the thunderous applause last night.

"Colonel." I heard no response. I realized he must have gone to the brokerage firm. On Fridays, we needed our weekly ledgers reconciled. I found a copy of the *New York Daily Tribune* downstairs on the end table near our sofa. I knew my speech would be printed. James had opened the paper to page four and drew an arrow to an editorial under the name of the founder and senior editor, Horace Greeley. Mr. Greeley and I shared no mutual regard.

> For ourselves, we toss our hats in the air for Woodhull. She has the courage of her opinions! She means business. She intends to head a new rebellion, form a new constitution, and begin a revolution beside which the late war will seem but a bagatelle, if within exactly one year from this day and hour of grace her demands be not granted out of hand. This is a spirit to respect, perhaps to fear, certainly not to be laughed at. Would that the rest of those who burden themselves with the enfranchisement of one-half our whole population,

now lying in chains and slavery, but had her sagacity
and courage.

These certainly were not the words of Horace Greeley, who held
no such respect for women. I smiled as I recognized the cadence
and eloquence of the managing editor, Whitelaw Reid, a man who
supported Tennie and me. He was our knight and champion.

My husband interrupted my revelry by coming home distraught.
"Victoria, I fear I have made an egregious mistake. It may imperil
us all." The Colonel doffed his hat, and tossed it on a side chair. He
clasped both my hands as he kneeled before me in the drawing room
downstairs. His eyes filled with tears.

I still glowed from the success of my speech last night. I would
have been much happier to explore exquisite love-making instead
of hearing about some error at the brokerage. The Colonel looked
alarmingly grim. His melodramatic tone and behavior startled me. I
resented it.

"Surely, it cannot be that bad, James." I batted my eyes flirtatiously
and asked, "Perhaps there is a way for us to commemorate our success
last night. It was marvelous."

"Not now." James winced and stood up, moving away from me.

"Husband, we have suffered losses before, certainly there is no
cause to bring you to the brink of tears… nor the precipice of anguish."

"Please stop." James pleaded. He started pacing around the room.
"This has nothing to do with the firm." He grimaced and then his look
turned to doubt. "At least I hope not."

"James! Whatever it is, please do two things for me; slow down, so
I can understand your statements, and," I took a deep breath to calm
my impatience, "tell me what is afoot."

Just then the front door opened and Tennie walked in. She dressed
in her typical business attire, gentleman-styled trousers, a short
waistcoat over a starched and pressed, linen pleated shirt. Typical for

Tennie, she moved freely beneath the shirt buttons confirming for anyone mildly curious, my sister did not favor the corset. Somehow the top two buttons were open.

Bustling into the room, she said, "It is so warm outside. We are going to have a hot summer." She stopped and looked at the two of us for the first time. She turned to the Colonel, "So you've told her!" My eyes must have narrowed and I bit my lower lip. Tennie's eyebrows rose up her forehead as her eyes widened in surprise. "Oh, I guess not."

"Enough!" I expressed my anger. "Out with it. What do you two need to say?"

"*Not fair*, sister. We did not want to distract you before your keynote last night. You were fantastic, by the way."

I turned to my husband.

"I am guilty of letting my hubris get the better of me," James confessed.

Without knowing it. I instinctively raised my right index and middle fingers to tap my right temple.

"Sorry, Victoria," James explained. "Remember the fatal flaw we talked about when I read the Greek tragedies to you?"

"Oh, you mean blind pride and arrogance?"

He flinched. "Yes."

Impatient as always, Tennie narrated. "We are all at fault!" Tennie pointed at me, at the Colonel, at herself, and at the stairs, to apparently include all the inhabitants of the house. "All of us." She sat down.

"Vickie, just before your address at Cooper Union I sat in the Essex Market Police Court." James declared.

"What?" I didn't know anything about this.

"Tennie and I decided to protect you, so you could focus on the 'Labor' speech and the keynote address." He stopped to pour himself a glass of water, drank a gulp, and recommenced his pacing. "Your sister, Polly, provoked by her husband Benjamin, whom we house and feed," he shot me a withering look, "convinced your mother to file a complaint against *me,* charging me with threatening her life or putting her in an asylum. She claimed that I have, and I quote, 'stolen the sentiments of daughters Victoria and Tennessee, alienating their affections.'"

"But Ma can't read! Those can't be her words."

"We all know that, but not the court. You have weaved so many fairy tales about your family, the public will believe anything." The Colonel's guilt did not prevent him from showing me his built-up anger over my family.

"Enough, both of you." Tennie's narrow ability to contain her impatience reached its limit. "The fact is that come Monday we all have to appear in court for a hearing on these charges."

"But why?" I shook my head, completely confused. "Surely the judge must know these are false accusations."

"He does." James covered his eyes with his right hand, squeezed his forehead, and started rubbing it vigorously, as if to remove some mark. He took in a deep breath and let it out, "I made an egregious error."

Tennie stared ahead and sat still as a porcelain doll on a shelf. She scared me.

I commanded, "Say it!"

"Yes, the judge saw the scam." James looked paler than I remembered ever seeing him. "The judge turned toward me and declared in open court, 'The worst thing specifically charged against you is living with your wife and not agreeing with your mother-in-law. The complaint is dismissed, unless you insist on a trial.'"

I lost my patience. "Then what is all this wailing and drama? He dismissed the case."

"*No!*" James bellowed. "I…" He hesitated and bowed his head to his chest.

Once I realized that he had come to a full stop, I demanded, "You *what?*"

"I insisted the complaint *not* be dismissed." He cringed. "I wanted to protect my good name and yours, and yours." He gestured first to me and second to Tennie. "We are to appear in court Monday at 1:00 in the afternoon."

"That's not all." Tennie stood up and fetched a piece of paper from her trouser pocket. "I receive this from Corney." She stepped forward to hand me a letter.

"Just read it out loud." I waved her back to her seat.

"My dear little sparrow, a pirate has just left this letter with me... An old woman came in who said she was your mother. I believe from what she said her mind is addled. She said that she had been told to get $300 out of me in exchange for the enclosed letter. I told her to read the letter to me. She could not. I believed she did not know what she had been put up to.

"I told her, no. My intimacy with you is honest, square and pure. I know you as an intelligent woman—more than most—who honestly earned her own living. I write this to you to raise the alarm and put you on your guard. The parties behind your mother mean you harm."

I sat still, stunned, immobile. I hated my sister Polly and her husband. My James was right; I should have never let them cross the threshold of our house.

Prior to going to court, we all agreed Colonel James Harvey Blood, my dear husband, would do all the talking. When called to testify, Tennie or I would remain unemotional and detached, answering only the question directly asked.

"This is not theater, nor is the witness chair a podium to make speeches." The Colonel went on to impress upon Tennie and me how court behavior had strict rules one must adhere to. "Speak only if you are questioned. *Never* speak out of turn. Don't volunteer anything."

James even prevailed upon Tennie to dress in complete compliance with conservative norms. She resisted, but finally complied. She even agreed to wear a corset, in court.

All counsel aside, the well-intended plan was, in fact, wholly impractical.

The courtroom filled with reporters and gawkers. I recognized many of the newsmen. It seemed every newspaper in the city sent a representative to cover the proceedings. The coverage would be enormous.

Before Judge Ledwith could read the charges, Tennie stood up and shouted. "There is a crime here. These allegationists, including my mother and my sister and her conniving husband, Benjamin Sparr, have held us hostage for too long." Wiping tears from her eyes, she continued, "When we first started here two years ago, we thought a row in the papers with these relations would hurt us." She gasped for air, "We agreed to pay them a ransom to leave our premises at Great Jones Street, and gave them $1,500 to move west and embark on their own fortunes."

The reporters rumbled and wrote feverishly, trying to capture all of Tennie's words.

"Counsel, please contain your client." The judge ordered.

Tennie ignored our lawyer and went on. "When they refused to move out after taking the money, we summoned the police to evict them from our dwelling. But they remained living in our house." Some reporters guffawed.

My mother Roxanne stood to interrupt her out-of-order daughter, and reviled my husband by pointing at him. "He said he would not go to bed at night unless he washed his hands in my blood!"

Tennie sat down when Judge Ledwith started rapping his gavel. Mama drew a cross on her chest and then clutched to her heart the Bible she had brought.

Roxanne could not be stopped. "I say here and call heaven as my witness that there," she pointed to where we sat, "is the worst gang of communists and free lovers in that house who ever lived—Stephen Pearl Andrews and Dr. Woodhull and lots more such trash…"

Ma's own attorney, Mr. Townsend, interrupted, "Keep quiet, old woman!" and tried to stand in front of her. She pushed him aside, to much laughter from the gallery. She continued haranguing until the judge ordered her to sit down and be quiet or be removed. Ma glared at her lawyer and then turned and glared at the judge.

The press could not control additional laughter. A circus atmosphere filled the courtroom. The reporters looked like sharks circling the waters, knowing there would be a feeding frenzy.

Ma's attorney handed a slip of paper to the court bailiff who announced, "Polly Sparr for the plaintiffs, please come to the stand to be sworn in."

Polly swore to tell the truth.

"Mrs. Sparr, do you know the man called James Harvey Blood?"

"Colonel Blood is aptly named."

"Objection, your honor, counsel asked if she knew him, not her opinion of him."

"Sustained."

Polly shouted out. "That man, right there," she pointed at James, "he became a ruthless murderer in the War and would sooner kill a man than walk away from him."

"*Absurd!*" My husband leaned over the table and shouted.

"Counselors," the judge roared, "either control your clients or you as well as they will be charged with contempt."

The judge's words meant nothing to Polly. "He threatens to kill my husband, and he threatens to murder Mama in her sleep, or abandon her at the asylum on Blackwell's Island."

"*Preposterous! I…*" The Colonel stopped when his counsel, Mr. Reymert, forcibly grabbed his shoulder.

Townsend rushed to Polly and unceremoniously grabbed his client by the arm and told her, "Shut up!"

John Reymert, Esquire, stood and nodded to Mr. Townsend, plaintiff's counsel, who nodded back, consenting to allow Mr. Reymert to cross examine.

He asked Polly, "Mrs. Sparr, did anyone ever hear Colonel Blood issue such threats, as you claim?"

"I heard his thoughts!" Polly stood up and shouted.

The courtroom burst into laughter.

"What's so damned all funny?" said Polly. The question increased the comedy. "My husband, Dr. Sparr, could hear him thinkin', and Ma knew his thoughts."

After a couple of minutes, the judge, who had to stop laughing himself, restored order and laughter subsided. Mr. Reymert patiently asked one last time, "Mrs. Sparr, can you name anyone who actually heard Colonel Blood verbally issue a threat out loud?"

"You think I am stupid! I can know the thinking of a man without it being said out loud or anyone else having to hear it."

The Judge laughed audibly.

Mr. Townsend handed another slip of paper to the bailiff.

"Victoria Claflin Woodhull, please approach to be sworn in."

"Objection. Mrs. Woodhull is married to the Defendant." Reymert asserted.

"Your honor, the fact appears to be in question. May I proceed?"

"Overruled," the judge announced. "Mrs. Woodhull, please approach and be sworn in."

I testified I had married Dr. Canning Woodhull at age fifteen to escape my childhood home. I stated my good Colonel Blood and I had been together for a decade. We had married, then divorced, and then remarried. I explained how Tennessee and I supported as many as twenty family members at our home on Thirty-Eighth Street.

"Why do you think your mother and older sister would bring this complaint if it were not factual?" Townsend asked me.

"Objection."

Before the judge could say anything, I answered. "It is not factual, it is absurd, obscene, and cruel, and you know it." Chatter filled the courtroom. "The logic or reason you seek, though it be void of all reason, is my family wants to separate Tennessee from me. They want her to travel and support the lot of them by telling fortunes and doing healings. *Greed* is the reason behind these proceedings."

I looked up. Reymert's head rested in his hands. James glared at me. I volunteered information, exactly the opposite of the instructions. Townsend smiled broadly. He inquired, "Mrs. Woodhull does Dr. Woodhull, your first husband, live under your roof?"

"Yes."

"Have you seen Dr. Woodhull?"

"Yes. I see him every day. We are living in the same house."

"Do you, James Harvey Blood, and Dr. Woodhull sleep in the same bed?" Townsend demanded.

Reymert jumped to his feet and shouted, *"Don't answer!"* He turned to the judge, "Objection, inflammatory and indecent."

Clamor beset the courtroom and again, it took the judge time to restore silence. During the outbreak, the Colonel looked at me with the most forlorn face I had ever seen. I could not help myself; I looked away. I saw the judge shaking his head slowly, solemnly, from side to side. He looked at my husband, took a deep breath, and grimaced, as if to say, "This did not have to be."

"Sustained."

Townsend spoke, looking directly toward Colonel Blood, "So Dr. Woodhull does not *sleep with Mrs. Woodhull*? Do I have it right?" Before anyone could answer or object, Townsend declared, "The plaintiffs rest."

Reymert gave the bailiff a slip; he called Colonel James Harvey Blood to the stand. The Colonel sat silent and glared at Townsend with a ferocity learned by men in battle. Reymert positioned himself between them to draw James' focus off Townsend.

"You are a decorated war hero who received multiple wounds, correct?"

"Yes, sir."

"Why, colonel, does the prior husband of your wife live under your roof?"

"My wife's boy fell when he was young. He needs daily medical care and treatment. The best person to do this is his father, Dr. Woodhull."

"Who pays all the bills for upkeep and maintenance of how many people living in the house?"

James replied, "All in all there are eighteen souls. The Woodhull & Claflin brokerage firm supports the entire lot of them."

Townsend waived any cross-examination.

Reyment had Tennie called to the witness stand. As she passed the Colonel on his way to his seat, he whispered to her, "Keep it short!"

Tennessee Celeste Claflin turned to smile at the reporters. "C-E-L-E-S-T-E is my middle name, in case any of you don't know me!" Apparently, Tennie would not be bound by her promises of restraint. She must have left them at home, along with her corset!

The newsmen cheered in great merriment. Abandoning formality, she smiled to the judge, glowered at Townsend, tenderly kissed the Bible, and pressed it to her untethered bosom. She swore to tell the truth to the court.

Before any question could be asked, Tennie spoke out. "I have long endured the presence of Mr. and Mrs. Sparr and nonetheless supported them."

"Objection, your honor, counsel for the defense has not asked a question."

"Sustained."

Reymert asked, "Have you ever witnessed Colonel James Harvey Blood become violent or threaten anyone?"

"Colonel Blood is a gentle and noble man. I never saw or heard any use of violence by this distinguished war hero, against Ma or anyone else. In fact, his response to her bitterness was kindness, perhaps too much so. Honestly, I don't know how he did it. That man," she stood and pointed at Benjamin Sparr, "has been blackmailing people through my mother."

Judge Ledwith stopped the monologue. "You are out of order, Miss Claflin. Your allegation is altogether irrelevant, if it is objected to, I will rule it out."

Townsend called out. "I object, but can anyone stop her from talking?"

Tennie held up a packet of letters tied with a red ribbon. "This stack comprises blackmail letters forwarded to me. I cannot imagine how many more were sent. These appear to be signed by my ma. Only, she can't read or write."

The courtroom burst out laughing. Judge Ledwith yelled at Reymert to control his witness, and rapped his gavel repeatedly. "Order. Order. *Order, God damn it!*"

Tennie continued like an unbroken filly, "The penmanship is masculine and of that deceptive man." She stood up and raised her index and middle fingers toward Benjamin Sparr to curse him. "You will suffer unendurable pains for this!" She sat back down to continue her monologue.

"Miss Claflin, cease talking!" The judge ordered.

"But, your honor, I am the *victim* in this case. I escaped the degradation of a life where I suffered greatly. My father is a mean and wretched man who forced me to do all manner of things." She stopped to breathe and I sought her eyes.

Finally, she looked solely at me. I slightly shook my head side to side and mouthed the word, "No."

Tennie shifted direction. "I do have genuine healing powers, more than any of you can accept. Commodore Vanderbilt knows my power." The courtroom gallery went crazy.

The judge rose from his chair. "Tennessee Celeste Claflin, *shut up!*" He rapped his gavel. He ordered the bailiff, "Remove her from the witness chair."

Tennie shrieked in pain, grabbing her chest as if a lance pierced her heart. "Judge," she proclaimed while gasping and breaking into tears, "I love my mother. I want her to love me."

Tennie leapt from the witness chair and ran to where Ma was sitting next to Polly. She grabbed the head of the old lady and started smothering her with loud smacking kisses. A tug o' war ensued with Polly and Tennie jostling Ma back and forth. Ma cried out, "You're both hurting me!"

"Order!" The judge bellowed. "Colonel Blood, stop this at once!" My husband rose and went over to the scene of battle and firmly placed his hands on the frenzied Tennie.

"Come away, Tennessee," he commanded, and dragged her away from Ma. "Enough spectacle for one day."

After a momentary flash of anger, Tennie acquiesced and returned to sit by me. She put her head on my shoulder and whimpered quietly. I held her hands.

The judge called for order, while glaring at the Colonel, blaming him for all this unnecessary waste of the court's time. James bent his head in shame. The judge summoned the two lawyers to the bench and whispered to them, and they nodded their heads in agreement.

As the lawyers drew away, the judge took charge of the case. He recited what was admissible and what was not.

I thought to myself, *How did this all happen? All the stories Tennie and I promoted about our happy childhoods and excellent lineage, shattered, obliterated in a single afternoon.* I placed my hands in front of me to try and hold on, to stay present. *What now? I felt helpless. My mind started to leave the courtroom. I started floating away.*

My husband crushed my hands in his, bringing me back to the proceedings. The judge concluded his statements. "This trial is adjourned. I am ruling, as I should have at the initial hearing, Plaintiff's suit has no foundation. This case is closed."

The judge retired quickly, but took the time to cast one last accusatorial scowl at my husband.

James looked pale as a ghost. I walked as fast and far away from him as I could.

Amidst chaos, upon arriving home I received an invitation I could not refuse.

> *Come to me my darling.*
>
> R

Beneath the single initial she drew a beautiful rose in full bloom. The tips of each petal were delicately highlighted in rouge. Rosie, my best friend and confidante, had summoned me. I admitted to myself I could use some of her tender love and care.

When I entered the sitting room at Annie Wood's bordello, decorated in antebellum style, a manservant dressed in light blue velvet livery escorted me into the chamber rooms and knocked at Rosie's door for me. Then he retired.

"Come in." The most melodious voice I'd ever heard beckoned me. I opened the door and found Rosie in a sheer nightgown with thin single threads of gold and silver running the full length. She was sitting in front of her mirror, combing out her long, auburn curls, and she looked like a goddess.

"I hate my family!" I sobbed.

"I know." She stood and welcomed me into her arms, placing my head against her heart. I accepted her comfort and sobbed all the more. She gently kissed the top of my head and rocked me back and forth. We stayed this way for several minutes, as I continued my bawling.

We heard a quick double knock on the door, then a pause, and then a single knock. After a short moment, Molly Ford, one of the top seven madams in New York City, whisked into the room.

"Good, you are here," Molly said. Rosie released me so Molly and I could kiss each other's cheeks. "I am here for a brief moment with Rosie. Very dramatic, Victoria! Your family has certainly given the press plenty of fodder."

"How could you know already? We left the courthouse shy of an hour ago."

Molly patted my hands. "In New York City, gossip is quicker than gunshot, and much more deadly. I hope you are ready for the storm." She turned to Rosie. "You are so lovely. It will be a shame having to miss you. When you come back, please come see me first." She swept out of the room as quickly as she had come in.

"Miss you?" I repeated. "Is there something you want to tell me, old friend?" I winced at the harshness of my tone to the one person I knew beyond all doubt truly loved me. Suddenly, I realized I had stained her exquisite gown with both my tears and tinges of my light rouge. Red splotches smeared over her heart.

"I am so sorry, Rosie. You of all people do not deserve that tone. I have destroyed your gown." The wetness made the sheer material seem to disappear, revealing even more of Rosie's exquisite body, with which I had an intimate familiarity.

"Don't fret, Vickie, a little salt is always good." She smiled beneficently, like when she first taught me pagan rituals and used salt crystals to create a purifying circle. I smiled at the thought.

We chanted in unison, "Tears always cleanse the soul."

"But I do have something serious to discuss." Rosie took my hands and led me to sit with her on her dark red and beige silk divan adorned by gold fleur-de-lys on both colors. "Within the fortnight, I will travel to Europe and make my home in either Paris or London." Rosie practically squealed with delight. Her hazel eyes sparkled with flecks of gold. She really was a magical creature.

"Come with me, Vickie. We can travel together. Bring your darling sister and husband if you like. Just…" She paused and became very serious. Her tone dropped a full octave. "Just let us away!"

"Something is wrong. You've had a vision. Tell me what you have seen."

"I have told you all along there could be difficult times ahead, and they seem to be advancing rapidly." She squeezed my hands, "It will be so refreshing to start over." Rosie stood and circled the room. "You have money now, and I have so many contacts in Europe. Will you join me? Please?"

I looked up at her. She exuded enthusiasm. For a moment, I thought it would be a great release to leave behind everyone but the kids, Tennie, and my Colonel. I looked into Rosie's eyes. "But how and where would we live? How would we make money? I have so much to do."

"Trust me." Rosie looked at me intently.

"I can't just abandon my candidacy for President." I stood up. "Everything I have worked for is here in America. You of all people know I am not afraid of a fight."

Rosie came over and knelt in front of me. She placed her head against my midsection. I held her close with my hands. After a few moments, I kissed her head, and reached under her armpits to lift her up.

She smiled at me. "I know your courage, young one. But as I am much, much, much older, please harken to what I am about to say."

Rosie never aged, she simply remained vital and young. I reflected again, "I cannot abandon all my hopes and aspirations."

"Vickie, my darling. Whether you join me now or years hence, we will be together again. Europe awaits you… and Tennie! You will find peace there; but peace may be boring to you now, yet perhaps a comfort in time." She lifted my chin and kissed me softly, delicately. "Whatever other lessons you may have to learn through hardship, remember to make decisions with your inner knowing and reason, along with your fiery passion."

We kissed deeply. I felt Rosie wanted to remind me of the many different forms of passion. She knew I had made up my mind. She accepted it, and she wanted to connect so deeply it would last until we could be together again. It was delicious.

"If you ever need shelter, Victoria, or a home to stay in, Molly has the keys to a number of properties I have invested in. Just ask her."

I began second-guessing my decision. I felt fear. "Will it really be that bad, Rosie?"

"Need not be, my lover." She hugged me in a long embrace. As I turned to go, Rosie chastened me, "Just remember your Proverbs: *Pride goeth before destruction, and an haughty spirit before a fall.*"

We kissed a last time.

Even before the door closed, I already missed Rosie.

Chapter 11

WORDS OF ATTRITION

Summer, 1871

E very paper in the country as far as San Francisco, California, carried the story of the trial. Not one supported any of us. No one sympathized. The new game in the press—discover and publish something more sensational about Victoria Woodhull and her preposterous family. I hated it!

News assaulted the N.W.S.A. convention every day during the week-long anniversary celebration of the Seneca Falls Conference. The day after my keynote address, the press called the convention the "Woodhull Convention." Now all the attacks on me and my family compromised the meeting. To stop the ship from taking on more water, the N.W.S.A. elected Theodore Tilton as an officer to counteract Henry Ward Beecher's involvement in the A.W.S.A.

While they had little stomach for it, I demanded Pearly, Theodore, Tennie, or James read the daily articles to me out loud. I failed to complete the accounts reading on my own, as my tears prevented it. Often, when being read to, I would slap the papers out of their hands in disgust.

The Colonel read the exposé on Buck and me written in the The *St. Louis Times*:

> The father, Reuben Buckman 'Buck' Claflin was a
> con man. He stole monies out of envelopes placed in his
> fiduciary care at the Homer, Ohio Post Office. Though

he was never prosecuted, local people confirm that he collected monies from the townsfolk to rebuild a gristmill and instead invested the money in a fire policy for several times the price of a new gristmill. After a mysterious fire on the evening after he purchased barrels of kerosene, he and the family were run out of town.

Victoria herself has a scandalous history. She operated a house in Chicago in a grand and peculiar style. She moved to our sedate city of St. Louis and she appeared as the proprietress of a clairvoyant institution. Many local citizens claim to have thought that she was of dubious character.

While he initially refused and advised me to not read any of the accounts, Pearly read to me the article published by *The Cleveland Ledger*:

The unfortunate fact remains that Mrs. Woodhull has inserted herself as a prominent figure in the Woman Suffrage Movement. Now that her shameful life has been exposed, it will follow that the enemies of female suffrage will point to her as a fair representative of the movement. In Cincinnati, many years prior, she was the same brazen, snaky adventuress that she now is.

The Colonel read me an article Horace Greeley wrote that lambasted the N.W.S.A. for adopting a resolution immediately after my keynote address. The headline read:

FREE LOVE IS FREE LUST!

Upon completion of the keynote address by Mrs. Woodhull, the N.W.S.A., enthused beyond reason, adopted this reckless resolution:

> All laws shall be repealed which are made use of by government to interfere with the rights of adult individuals to pursue happiness as they may choose.
>
> Enthralled with a reckless younger woman, the elder leadership must now distance themselves from the Woodhull, as she is one who has two husbands after a sort, and lives in the same house with them both, sharing the couch of one, but bearing the name of the other, perhaps to indicate her impartiality.

"*These insults*, I simply cannot abide them!" I ran sobbing into the arms of my husband. I felt I had been crying non-stop the last four days. "I want to fight back, James. You know what a vile creature Greeley is to his poor wife, Mary."

"Please calm yourself, my dear." My husband tried to divert me. "We are in this mess because of my wanting to fight the slanderous charges of your family against my person in public. *Hubris!* And I put you and all we have worked for in harm's way."

"Enough!" I wrested myself away from his embrace. "I don't want to hear any more of your confessions." He looked at me with woe in his eyes. "I want to retaliate. I want to fight back!"

"We've talked about this, Victoria. It will only make things worse." He tried to reason with me. "All this will all go away quicker if we simply leave it."

"I *cannot!*" I shrieked. I looked up to see James not just surprised, but alarmed. I calmed down enough to continue without shouting. "I do not have your constitution for bearing things without taking action." I winced hearing the words and realizing them a cruel parody of his choice to proceed to court. "I know I should not, but I have to... respond."

The Colonel gathered himself to his full height. "Then kick your *damned family out*. Show the world you don't tolerate false accusations."

"How long have you been holding that in, dear husband?" I spat the words.

"Years! And clearly too long!" James shouted at me.

"I can't just throw them out onto the street."

"*Why not?*" He shouted. "They wouldn't hesitate throwing you and the kids out." He pleaded with me, "Rent them a home, if you must, but get them *out of our lives!*"

I retaliated, "It is not your choice to make!"

He looked at me, stunned by my words. Much more softly, he said, "I know you don't mean that. None of this would have happened if you had done what I asked time and time again. Get rid of the lot of them, they hate you."

"So, *you* blame *me* for the court fiasco? How clever." I said with disdain.

Red flushed up his neck and covered his face. His rage filled the room. "I..." he stopped talking and shook his head. James bumped into me as he walked past me to exit the room.

He almost knocked me over.

I needed to react to the public attacks. I also had to focus elsewhere than on my family and home. I remembered everything Pearly had told me about the Greeley household. I befriended Mary Cheney Greeley to comfort her in her solitude, imprisoned by her husband outside the city and used for his lust and as a breeding mare. I wrote a short statement in our *Weekly*. I printed what many knew to be the truth, yet no one else dared say out loud, let alone place in print:

> Mr. Greeley's home has always been a sort of domestic hell. I do not mean that Mr. Greeley has proven an unfaithful husband. To the contrary, he has been held up for all to witness as a model husband in that

particular, and for that reason the fault and opprobrium of domestic discord has been wrongfully heaped upon Mrs. Greeley.

Whoever has troubled himself to inquire how much of the discord was attributable to Mr. Greeley discovered that the husband has had more to do with the souring the temper, unstringing the nerves, and completely disorganizing the machinery of a delicate woman's organization.

The Beecher family in particular seemed to delight in the Woodhull witch hunt. Catherine and Harriet wrote gleeful letters admonishing Stanton and Anthony for bad judgment.

Two days later, Henry C. Bowen, one of the first backers of Reverend Henry Ward Beecher, who had profited handsomely from the Reverend's popularity, published his assault. Theodore Tilton read to me Bowen's attack in his *Brooklyn Daily Union*, where Teddy himself served as managing editor. Teddy did not know about the article until he saw it in the paper.

No subject discussed during anniversary week excited so much attention as the question of suffrage for women. This excitement was not a little fanned by the sudden revelation of facts in the private life of Mrs. Woodhull. The esteemed and unfortunately misdirected ladies, Mrs. Stanton, Miss Anthony, and Mrs. Hooker had been foolish to have given a prominent place to the Woodhull *Weekly*. That despicable newsprint, with its coarse treatment of all the sacred things of human life, is enough to condemn anyone whose name is associated with it.

"How dare he, Teddy?" For the moment, Teddy was mute. He was shocked his employer did not even advise him of the article. I tried to console him. "I'll show the whole Beecher clan I mean business!"

Towering over me, he counseled. "Victoria, I know you feel injured, and this is far from the field of fair play," He paused and lowered his torso to look me straight in the eye. "Remember before the first edition you wanted to take on the Beechers?"

"Of course, I do. I listened to you all then, and look what it has wrought."

"All of what you have accomplished is due to the fact you did listen and *not* start a war with this all-powerful family and their backers."

"My conclusions differ, Theodore." I pivoted away from him. "Perhaps we would not be in this predicament if I had brought the battle to them much earlier."

"Victoria!" He grabbed my wrists and forced me to face him. I had never before seen him be physically aggressive. "Even Henry Bowen, one of the most powerful men in all of New York State, had to compromise and make peace with Reverend Beecher."

"Don't be stupid, Teddy," I challenged. "I already know the Reverend cuckolded Henry Bowen prior to his wife's death. Then the Reverend proceeded to bed Bowen's daughter."

Teddy winced. My words drove home the dagger of his own wife, Libby's pregnancy last year as a result of her affair with the Reverend. I was being cruel. I lowered my head. For a moment, he remained silent.

He collected himself. "The best way to move beyond all this is to let it be." He lifted my hands and kissed them.

"I still have to fire a warning shot at this murder of holier-than-thou Beecher crows."

"*Vickie!*" He shook my shoulders. "*Please* listen to one who is at least as aggrieved as you." He let go of me. "I *strongly* advise you to resist the temptation, Victoria." He hung his head in sadness. "In the end, it will do you more harm than them."

Despite Mr. Tilton's admonitions, and against the advice of everyone I knew except Tennie, I loaded the cannons and fired my warning shot in the next *W & C's Weekly.*

> Without pretending to a perfect knowledge of, or caring a fig about, the history of the personnel of either branch of the woman movement, we are led to suspect that this over-pious, over sensitive, Boston wing have much more to conceal than their more progressive sisters of Apollo Hall. To answer Mrs. Livermore and her cohorts, it is rather a delicate thing for those 'who live in glass houses to throw stones.' We all very well know that most people's lives are encased in these transparent brittle tenements.

I wasn't done. I released the following statement to the *Times* and the *World* to publish:

> Because I am a woman and because I conscientiously hold opinions somewhat different from the self-elected orthodoxy, which men find their profits in supporting, this very group assails me, vilifies me, and endeavors to cover my life with ridicule and dishonor.
>
> I do not intend to be made the scapegoat of sacrifice to be offered up as a victim to society by those who cover over the foulness of their lives and the feculence of their thoughts with a hypocritical mantle of fair professions, and by diverting public attention from their own iniquity in pointing their fingers at me.
>
> I am open. I say what I mean and do not hide my thought or conduct. I believe in Spiritualism. I advocate Free Love in its highest purest sense, as the only cure

for the immorality by which men corrupt and disfigure God's most holy institution of sexual relations.

My self-appointed judges preach against Free Love publicly, yet practice it secretly. For example, I know of a specific man in a neighboring city, a public teacher of eminence, who lives in concubinage with the wife of another public teacher of almost equal eminence. All three openly concur in denouncing offenses against morality.

Hypocrisy is the tribute paid by vice to virtue. So be it. Pardon me, if I decline to stand up as the frightful example others anoint me. I shall, however, make it my business to analyze some of these lives and will take my chance in the matter of libel suits, for I only speak or write what is true.

Chapter 12

STRANGE BEDFELLOWS

New York City
Early Summer, 1871

"I am under fire, Theodore."

"It pains me to see you suffer so." My champion opened his arms wide and offered his embrace. I needed it. "I am sorely outgunned! They have so many resources."

Not only did I suffer attacks from every quarter, but my husband did nothing to temper his anger with me. We still had not resolved the family issue. Also, he had advised against printing my defense and notifications. I would not be passive and accept being cast into the role of victim without a fight.

I continued venting to Theodore. "They have a multitude of loud cannons bombarding daily in rapid succession." I embraced the big man tighter, and he responded by holding me close. "We are so small. Once a week we load our single-ball musket and try to answer the thunder all around us."

With his left hand in the middle of my back pressing me into him, and with his right securing my head against his chest, I heard the rumbling of his voice from deep inside.

"Victoria, you are right!" He pressed his lips against my hair. "They are too many, and your single paper issued weekly cannot reach enough people to counteract the wretched characterizations they promote."

Placing his strong hands on my shoulders, he gently kissed my forehead. Then he moved me back enough so that I could see the intensity in his eyes. As he did so, I looked for answers.

"Victoria, remember when we talked about writing a biography about you?"

"Yes."

"Newsprint can have a devastating impact, but it is, in many cases, ephemeral as the next day's news fast becomes the focus. Perceptions can be mitigated if corrected, the record set straight in a more enduring form, like a book."

I stepped back from him. "Teddy, I do not have the time to write my life's story. My time is consumed with running the firm, preparing for speaking engagements, preparing for the election, and battling your prior benefactor, the ignoble Henry Ward!" I heard myself shouting. Then the words came between sobs and tears, "I'm so sorry, Teddy."

He held me close. "All of us who care about you and want to stand by your side have cautioned repeatedly against publicly antagonizing the Beecher family."

I pushed away his arms and turned my back like a petulant child not willing to hear something.

Anguished, he said, "Victoria! No one is wronged more than I."

The cruel cuckold of Theodore by his wife with Henry Ward infuriated me. Without turning around, I tried to assuage his pain. "I know. You are the injured one."

"I don't think you fully understand, Victoria!" He raised his voice. I turned around to face him, and offer solace. "The battle is not against the Beecher family alone," Teddy continued in a much softer tone. "They are influential enough, but their insurmountable alliances are formed by all the businessmen and politicians who derive their powers and line their pockets by associating with Henry Ward."

"Publish a biography?" I did not want to hear any more about the

Beechers' powers. I found the whole lot of them disgusting. "Do you really think it will help?"

"I do. This way we take control of the story, beyond the *Weekly*." He warmed to the idea and advocated for it. "So much so, I offer to pen it myself."

"I am surprised, Theodore. You have your own reputation to care for."

He paused and looked into my eyes. "T'would mean we will be compelled to spend many hours together, both during the days, and late into the nights, for me to learn everything about you."

"Everything, Theodore?" I asked, raising my eyebrows and batting my eyes. I believe the man actually blushed.

"For the sake of the book, of course," he quickly replied, albeit in a tone much higher than his norm.

I closed the distance and allowed him to hold me close. "Yes, then, for the sake of the book."

We worked often and close. When it started getting hot, we would go to the rooftop to work. Theodore and I would argue over my memories or the visions in my life. He found them too fantastical and wanted to "tame" the narrative. I would not agree and several times we approached a breach. We would retreat into physical intimacy and the argument would retreat as our surging blood entreated.

While I garnered some comfort from the time spent on the biography with Mr. Tilton, the press kept hounding me like a pack of dogs. I would not listen to anyone telling me to let it blow over, not to inflame the fires, not to respond.

Respond I did… as vehemently as I could. In the next *Weekly* I contributed this statement:

> Civilization is festering to the bursting point in
> our great cities and notably in Brooklyn… At this very
> moment, herculean efforts are being made to suppress

the most terrific scandal, which has ever astounded and convulsed any community... We have the inventory of discarded husbands and wives and lovers, with dates, circumstances and establishments. Confidences which are no longer confidences abound.

I would not stand quiet to be ridiculed nor swept away by anyone's contempt!

One hot June night as the temperature seemed to rise all day and failed to cool off when the sun went down, Teddy and I worked in the open air up on the roof. We sat in the double chaise I had designed. The chairs faced opposite ways and joined in the centers. Almost a bed, duck feathers filled the thick pads under sail canvas cloth. The backs collapsed, and each arm had a swivel piece, which, when lifted from the outside and fit into place, formed double accommodating writing tops.

To keep cool I wore only a soft-belted fichu, a small shawl made of silk and ribbons, which gave any zephyr access to coolly caress my near-naked body. Theodore had lit a few candles and wrote sitting nude, with the sheet covering certain parts.

Teddy recorded my narrative of saving my firstborn from certain death by sheer willpower. The air became still, having reached an equilibrium between hot and cool.

Suddenly, without a knock or any announcement, Tennessee flung the door open and walked up to us.

"Why must you torment me, Vickie? Will it never end? Does one of us have to die for it to stop?" Tennie's eyes burned with fury.

I stood up, leaving the sheet for Theodore. He quickly searched beneath the sheet for his cotton, drop-shoulder dress shirt with billowing sleeves and his short underdrawers. He stood up without finding his trousers.

I reprimanded my sister. "Tennessee, a knock or some announcement would be polite."

Tennessee just glared at me. I saw her as a wild horse. She could either charge or bolt away. I proceeded cautiously. "Sister, what has happened? Please tell me." I reached for her.

"Don't!" She yelled. "And don't 'Sister' me." She hissed more than spoke. "You only 'Sister' me when you know I am furious with you," she seethed, "and I am!"

"Okay, Tennie, but I don't know the cause of your fury." I paused to see if she would speak. I flinched when I looked at her and saw sparks of fire leaping toward me from her eyes. I closed my eyes and opened them, assuring myself my sister, Tennie, stood in front of me. "What has happened?"

"You steal them all from me." She bit her lower lip to try to hold back the tears. She glowered at me. Somehow, she realized I had no idea what caused her state. "You have the Colonel, and now Teddy, and everything you want." Her chest heaved, "Every time I start to love someone, really open up to him, *you destroy it.*"

"Not true!" I yelled back at her. "All I've ever done is protect you, make promises to keep you safe." I screamed, "*What have I done?*"

She would not relent. "I am so sick and tired of hearing about your promise to Pa so he would not touch me." She bristled. "Good God, Victoria, everyone else did!" "Then you use your promise to cover whatever misbegotten reason you have for allowing our family to live with us." She gathered her breath. "*Why?*"

Any escalation on my part would only inflame Tennie. Trying to control myself and speak as gently as possible, I begged her, "Please Tennie, tell me what happened."

She spoke in a torrent, as if a big boulder damming up a river suddenly exploded and the pent up waters rushed forth. "As always, since we started over a year ago, I went this evening to deliver our *Weekly* to Whitelaw." She looked to the sky and from side to side like a lost child. "He always takes me somewhere special for dinner, and then we retire to his home. I truly enjoy his company."

She took a deep breath and then resigned herself to continue. "The butler would not let me go upstairs. I had to wait for Whitelaw to come down," she gasped, "just like at Corney's.... I hate butlers!" She started wringing her hands while talking. "Whitelaw dressed casually, not for dinner out. When I asked if we were dining in, he looked at me with regret... or disgust?" She shook her head. "He said, with *your* latest attack against Mr. Greeley and Henry Ward, he could not see me anymore."

"Tennie," I stepped toward her.

"Then he bent down on one knee, took my hand, and kissed it, saying, 'I am so sorry, Tennie. So sorry.'"

"I..."

"Don't you dare speak!" She pointed at Theodore. "Does any man in the Beecher constellation keep his pants on?" She spat on the floor. "Go ahead with whatever game you are playing, sister," she chastised, "with your book and your lover."

Tennessee turned to go. After two steps, she half-turned and spoke over her shoulder. "We are bound, sister, but you have no care or regard for what happens to me. From now on, I make my own choices. I will not let you hurt me anymore." My sister stormed off.

"I should go," Theodore said as he started to get up. I came back to the chaise and lay on top of him to prevent it.

"Just hold me."

Tennessee, Stephen Pearl Andrews, Colonel Blood, Teddy Tilton, and George Blood gathered to discuss what to do next. We met in the back room of the brokerage firm, more comfortable than the Spartan office of the *Weekly*. This time we all felt the void from the absence of Whitelaw Reid and his guiding presence.

"I am fed up," I began. "We have to switch the focus and shine the full light of condemnation on Henry Ward Beecher, his clan, and all his co-conspirators. I want it off and away from me." There was silence.

"I have some good news that might help." The creaky, high-pitched voice of Pearly assailed our ears.

"I want to hear your news, Pearly; but first," I took a deep breath, "I want to publicly attack them, the way they are attacking us." I looked into unenthusiastic sets of eyes. "I want to expose Henry's hypocrisies and show him for the charlatan and usurper he is. I want to tell the world how the businessmen cloaked in propriety make coin from the church and everyone pays them indulgences. I want to expose the major newspaper owners and editors as nothing more than the bloodsucking, frightened sycophants they are."

The gunshots came from every direction. I realized I was surrounded.

"We will l-l-l-lose m-m-m-most of our ad-d-d-dvert-t-ti-tisers," George stuttered in his exasperation.

"There are other ways to fight back." The screechy voice of Pearl hurt my ears.

Theodore stood up to his full height, towering above me. "I implore you to disengage, and not further enrage. This is painfully personal to me, but I fear the damages to you will be far greater."

"You can't attack them," my husband spoke. "It will destroy everything we have worked for."

Tennessee challenged me, speaking coldly. "Are you capable of hearing the pleadings of the people who love you, who want to protect you and serve you, sister?"

Ignoring Tennie, I turned on my husband. "I've told you before," my voice sounded like hard, frozen ice, "Never tell me what I cannot do!"

Shocked as if I'd slapped him, Colonel Blood responded. "I am sorry, Victoria... a thousand times sorry I insisted on proceeding with the trial. That is how all of this started. I simply wanted to clear my name. I was wrong! It was arrogant and the result, disastrous."

I did not go to him to offer any comfort.

"I acted out of enmity, not logic," James said. "Victoria, *look* at the devastating consequences. I beg you, please allow me to protect you from making the same mistake yourself."

I wanted to go to him. Lay my head against his chest. Feel his arms embrace me. But I could not move.

Tennie spoke. "Sister, do you remember your nightmare a year and a half ago, the night of the Grand Opening?"

Her question jarred me. I had the sensation of leaving my surroundings and entering a trance. I started to disappear and I felt afraid. I sought a chair and stumbled. I think Tennie caught me.

"Stay here with me, Victoria!" Tennie spoke in a sharp tone.

I looked at her. I realized I had not thought about the nightmare in a long time. I thought her cruel to remind me of the pain and terror of being completely alone. I looked at Tennie and spoke with no emotion. "I remember."

"Your vision is but one option." Tennie held my hands. "You can choose another with the wisdom gained by what you saw in the nightmare." Her eyes were flinty, but they stayed a shade of gray-blue. I feared they would turn coal black.

Tennie reached for my face. She spoke gently, "Don't you understand yet, Victoria?" I heard the gentlemen in the room shuffle their feet, no doubt looking down or away, uncomfortable having to witness Tennie's obvious superiority as a spiritualist. "Our visions are not final rulings we are condemned to act out. Sometimes we have a choice; and having learned from our visions, we can choose a different path. We can manifest a different present, a different future."

"No." I felt the isolation and being alone. "I don't know."

Tennie grabbed my arms and shook me. "Really, sister? Are you truly so weak?" Tennie must have heard how hurtful her words were. She stopped.

I looked at her. She had cut me deeply in front of the others. My focus returned to the present. "I know your sight is far superior to mine." I took a few short breaths and found an anchor I could cling to. "I will not let them mock and belittle me—I mean us—without exposing them to the same measure."

"I have other matters to attend to." My sister abruptly turned away to leave.

"What?" I could not believe she would walk out before we collectively reached a decision. I shouted, "You can't just leave!"

Tennessee whirled around to face me. "Can't?" She challenged me. She nodded toward my husband. "Your favorite word, sister?" Her contempt and fury assailed me. She feigned a smile. "If I thought I or anyone else had the slightest chance to influence your decision, I would stay."

"Your name is in the banner, same as mine!"

"*For now!*" She sneered as she strode toward the door. "In the meantime, it serves *my* purpose."

Her departure stripped away all my resolve. I became passive, quiet, and inattentive. I tried, but I could not fathom why my youngest sister and closest friend would discard our love and abandon me. I felt like the earth itself had ruptured and created a huge canyon, leaving me standing precariously on the precipice. I could not speak.

The men conversed. The Colonel came to stand behind me and put his hand on my shoulder. I felt it, faintly. I drifted in and out of the conversation. After a time, I have no idea how long, I suddenly returned to the room fully alert.

Pearly conversed with Theodore about revitalizing a dormant national political party. He must have seen my focus return. With twinkling eyes and his high shrill voice, he delivered one of his dissertations on the philosopher Karl Marx, who inspired the Communards in Paris to revolt and seize power.

"Victoria," Pearly made sure he had my full attention, "I have spoken with this great man. I have received his blessing to publish his book *The Communist Manifesto* here in America. I have already begun work on a translation for the *Weekly.*"

"Our paper?"

"Yes. And the International Workingmen's Association World Council has granted me two new fully authorized Sections." He paused to smile at me. "Victoria, you will be the leader of Section Twelve, right here in New York City." His eyes gleamed with his vision. "We will build you a constituency to include all working men and women, and include every disenfranchised group that wants a voice. They will all join your American Equal Rights Party."

"Why, Pearly, to what end?" My thoughts seemed covered in fog.

"It's perfect," Theodore professed. "This way we can build support for your Presidential nomination. We can cobble together a political party." Teddy scratched his neck, envisioning it. "Much the way America creates a single cloak from all of our diverse lineages. We will forge a political melting pot of all the less fortunate. It will become a populist movement."

I could not tell which motivated Teddy more, avoiding an open conflict with his former mentor and saving himself and his wife embarrassment, or genuine excitement about this new party.

George nodded his approval.

As if hearing my thoughts, Colonel Blood concluded the meeting. "This certainly is a better alternative than attacking the powers that be." He paused, and then cautioned, "I am not sure how well the uneducated public will embrace these revolutionary ideas." He took a deep breath and spoke solemnly, "Just remember, almost all of the Paris Communards were slaughtered."

That summer, Theodore arranged for me to meet The Reverend Beecher. The purpose, a reconciliation and cessation of hostilities. We'd promise to protect him with silence in exchange for his supporting me by introducing me at several speeches in the coming months. I felt the taste of bile in my mouth agreeing to this, but it would be better than the distraction, cost, and energy of constant fighting.

The meeting took place at the home of Frank and Emma Moulton, a lovely wooden home with three floors and a basement. We sat in the formal room, where there were two dark brown velvet couches adorned with golden tassels at the bottom, and four dark brown linen-covered wingchairs forming a broad circle.

Emma Moulton graciously welcomed me into her colonial-style home, taking my hand into both of hers. Frank remained formal and quite reserved with his hands behind his back. A known connoisseur, he offered both Teddy and me fine French burgundy wine.

The Reverend Henry Ward Beecher, who had arrived prior to us, did not get up. The powerful man seemed terrified to meet me. He appeared to me more corpulent than when we first met in the office at his home that awful April day when the Colonel and I visited Brooklyn Heights.

Despite the heat, Beecher wore his clothes of authority, and he sweated profusely. His black frockcoat half covered the full vest over the high collared shirt and a black velvet bowtie.

The Reverend tried to direct the conversation. "Do you know I have my own spirit table I regularly practice on inside Plymouth Church? Why, I have even experimented with Mesmerism. I have to say, I am impressed by your oratory and passion." He attempted to foster a kinship between us.

I replied. "We are not here to discuss my passion, we are here due to your own passions, to offer you a way out."

"I am not so different from you, young lady. I actually admire you. I, too, know the marriage act often harkens the death toll of affections.

I am sad to so condemn each couple I marry." He smiled jovially, as if he did not just contradict his entire public message.

"Then why not proclaim your conviction and preach your true beliefs?" I challenged.

He turned pernicious, "Would you have me drive out all my flock? Should I preach to empty pews?" He waved his hand at me, as if he were some regal personage dismissing a minion.

"Excuse me Henry Ward," I fumed. "You are at risk here, not I. I have traveled here to offer you an escape from the dire circumstances of your own making!" I raised my voice. "You will *not* simply wave me away as if I were inconsequential."

He turned toward Theodore and bleated, "Why do you torture me with her? You were like a son to me."

I saw the torment in Teddy's face. I understood how important the Reverend once was in Theodore's life. This must have made the cuckolding all the more painful.

Theodore overcame or buried his hurt to take control of the meeting. "We must establish a congenial rapport, even if I myself find it *repugnant*," Theodore said. The Reverend flinched at his words. "Henry, I want you to introduce Victoria at several of her speeches and announce your admiration of her character."

"I don't have the courage to do it! I could be ridiculed!" Henry cowered.

"*And…*" Teddy continued to pronounce restitution like a judge in court, "You will write to your sisters, especially Catherine and Harriet, telling them to silence their defamation of Victoria."

I have never heard Theodore so upset. I think the vault holding all his emotions toward the coward before him finally blew open. "Harriett's thinly veiled novella, *My Wife and I,* published in *The Christian Union,* of which you are the editor, depicts Victoria as Audacia Dangyereyes." Teddy sounded like a prosecuting attorney presenting his case in court. "The book constitutes calumny and malicious character assassination." Theodore shouted, "Catherine openly calls Vickie and Tennessee 'the two prostitutes,' claiming 'only Tennessee exceeds Victoria's indecencies.'" Theodore bellowed, "It all must come to a halt."

More distraught than ever, Henry Ward's eyes filled with terror. He wailed, "They won't listen to me. I am much younger; they never listen to me." He turned pale and whimpered like a child. He turned, splotches of deep red starting to cover his face. He reared and attacked like a wounded bear. "I won't do it!" Henry Ward prostrated himself on the floor before Teddy. "Please, I beg you."

"Get up, Henry, I am not your confessor." Teddy recaptured his monumental patience, bent down and spoke softly but coldly into the ear of the prostrate cleric, "You will persuade them and bend them to your purpose, like you do so many others." Frank Moulton and Teddy helped Henry to stand up and then plop down into a chair.

"I do advise this," Frank Moulton counseled the preacher. "It may be the only way to avoid public ridicule." Emma caught the eye of Henry Ward and nodded her head in agreement. "Potentially, you could lose the Church," Frank concluded.

Henry sat up and turned on Theodore. "So, what if you tell the world about *your wife?* You can't hold that over me *forever.*"

The man before us was a chameleon of great ability. I stood up and addressed him. "You are a stupid and ignorant fool, Mr. Beecher!" I purposefully stripped him of any title of a man of faith. "You really think we women do not talk amongst ourselves?" I distanced myself a few steps, "Your affairs are numerous, sordid, and expressly prohibited by your precious Bible."

"Oh, no!" Emma Moulton exclaimed.

I wanted to expunge once and for all my hatred of his blatant hypocrisy. I pointed my index and middle fingers at Henry Ward. "*You are not* a holy man. You have forsaken Leviticus 18:17! It is forbidden to lay with both mother and daughter. Does the name Bowen mean anything to you? How about Beach? Morse? What is the count now? How many of your bastard children attend your Sunday sermons? Tens? Scores? Shall I call out the names of your lust's progeny?"

"Stop. Silence! *Stop her!*" Henry screeched while huffing and puffing his way to standing. He turned first to Theodore and then to the Moultons, blabbering in tears. "Please, make her stop!"

"I'll give you this, Reverend," I felt my pulse pounding inside my temples, "You are a prolific free lover and completely non-discriminating. You are truly a man of insatiable wanton and animalistic desires."

The preacher sobbed, pawing the air for assistance. Theodore towered over him. "Frank and Emma will provide you the dates you will appear with Victoria on stage and introduce her." Theodore expressed his total contempt for the man, "You disgust me. I once looked up to you like a father." Theodore stepped away from his former mentor and took my arm to guide me to the door. Teddy turned around and shouted, "Do I have your binding word, sir?"

Beecher cried out, "Yes! Heaven help me, *yes!*"

The press started hearing in early July of a new political group called The Victoria League. The League consisted of men and women who endorsed me for candidate and nominee of the Equal Rights Party for the 1872 presidential election. Different papers gave different names to the party. One called it the People's Party, another the Cosmo-Political Party. Whatever the name, the party constituted a movement and accepted both men and women equally. We let it be rumored the Commodore Cornelius Vanderbilt formed the League and served as its president.

The Golden Age, Teddy's paper, published an account of an unnamed reporter, allegedly to protect him from controversy, sent to interview the Commodore. This "special reporter" returned to the paper to state:

> When I asked the commodore if he were a Victorine, he quipped that "The only Presidency that matters to me is being re-elected as President of the New York Central." Commodore Vanderbilt further asserted that more people depended on him than on the federal government. He concluded by stating, "I'll take my corporate Presidency and leave the U.S. Presidency to the likes of the capable and highly intelligent Victoria C. Woodhull.

Most other newspapers claimed the interview a flight of fancy or blatant fraud, given the Commodore rarely offered any comments. Without the name of the "special reporter," the story was at best suspect. Through it all, Theodore confirmed and defended the story as true.

I decided to finance the resurgence of the Equal Rights Party. I wrote and published a formal reply to Victoria League on July 20. I accepted the endorsement and posited the impact of a woman for the first time, nominated for President of the United States.

> The right woman… would arouse such a tempest of popularity as the country has never seen and as a consequence should ride triumphantly on the tide of a joyous popular tumult to the supreme political position.

Stephen Pearl Andrews tutored me on the major points and purpose of the International Workingmen's Association, *The Communist Manifesto*, and Karl Marx himself, a close friend of Pearly.

I immediately saw the struggle between woman and man as a class struggle between oppressed and oppressor, proletariat and bourgeois. For centuries, European culture subjugated and suppressed all of womankind, even unwittingly, in the case of a few good men. Communism heralded the great change ahead. Pearly handed me his own translation, written in his hand, of *The Communist Manifesto*:

> The bourgeoisie, wherever it has got the upper hand, has put an end to all feudal, patriarchal, idyllic relations. It has pitilessly torn asunder the motley feudal ties that bound man to his "natural superiors" and has left remaining no other nexus between man and man than naked self-interest, than callous "cash payment." It has drowned the most heavenly ecstasies of religious fervour, of chivalrous enthusiasm, of philistine sentimentalism, in the icy water of egotistical calculation. It has resolved personal worth into exchange value, and in place of the numberless indefeasible chartered freedoms, has set up that single, unconscionable freedom—free trade. In one word, for exploitation, veiled by religious and political illusions, it has substituted naked, shameless, direct, brutal exploitation.

I also learned how the plight of the workingman parallels the plight of woman. I recalled my talk with Frederick Douglass at the offices of *The Revolution*, when I made it clear the plight of woman had much in common with the problems of the Negro.

Oppression is oppression, be it class, race, or gender.

Pearly handed me other pieces of paper to read between our private lectures. Pearly went on to explain the ideology.

> A similar movement is going on before our own eyes. Modern bourgeois society, [Capitalism] with its

relations of production, of exchange and of property, a society that has conjured up such gigantic means of production and of exchange, is like the sorcerer who is no longer able to control the powers of the nether world whom he has called up by his spells.

The less the skill and exertion of strength implied in manual labour, in other words, the more modern industry becomes developed, the more is the labour of men superseded by that of women. Differences of age and sex have no longer any distinctive social validity for the working class. All are instruments of labour, more or less expensive to use, according to their age and sex.

I learned why Pearly and Teddy were thinking we should form an amalgamated party driven not by its diversity but instead by its commonalities. Pearly handed me two more pages of his *Manifesto* translations, with several key words or phrases underscored. At the top, he printed in bold letters:

POLITICAL PLATFORM:

Bourgeois marriage is, in reality, a system of wives in common and thus, at the most, what the Communists might possibly be reproached with is that they desire to introduce, in substitution for a hypocritically concealed, an openly legalised community of women. For the rest, it is self evident that the abolition of the present system of production must bring with it the abolition of the community of women springing from that system, i.e., of prostitution both public and private.

The bourgeois sees his wife a mere instrument of production. He hears that the instruments of production are to be exploited in common, and, naturally, can come to no other conclusion that the lot of being common to all will likewise fall to the women. Our bourgeois, not content with having wives and daughters of their proletarians at their disposal, not to speak of common prostitutes, take the greatest pleasure in seducing each other's wives.

The Communists have not invented the intervention of society in education; they do but seek to alter the character of that intervention, and to <u>rescue education from the influence of the ruling class</u>. <u>Free education for all children in public schools</u>. Abolition of children's factory labour in its present form.

Excited, enthralled and enamored, I danced Pearly around the sitting room. I announced, "I want to meet Karl Marx."

"Perhaps in time." Pearly half promised. "I am working to translate all his works." Pearly sat down and patted the couch, beckoning me to join him.

I could not sit down. I twirled around the room. "I want to be the standard bearer for this revolution." I finally sat down next to him. "I will want to publish every word in the *Weekly*."

"We have his permission to publish his writings." Pearly's annoying voice camouflaged his brilliance and unsurpassed education.

"You shall my dear, you shall."

Hearing this, I turned to him and covered his face with kisses.

I did.

Pearly received the right to open two new International Workingmen's Association sections nine months earlier. Friedrich Sorge formed and headed the first section of the I.W.A., basically enrolling the German General Working Men's Union, formed in 1867. It spoke and wrote in German, exclusively. Other I.W.A. sections served groups with a single purpose, be it a language orientation or a specific trade or cause.

I was appointed leader of Section Twelve of the I.W.A. and proclaimed honorary president. The section shared offices with the *Weekly* in lower Manhattan, and we published the only American language translations of Karl Marx. Our first article featured Marx's discussion of the Paris Communards, *The Civil War in France.* We had to keep printing additional copies.

Our constituency expanded rapidly.

Henry Ward Beecher reneged the first opportunity he had to introduce me from a shared stage. He did so twice more.

Thursday, August third, grew hot and humid. The heat hung over the city into the early evening, making everything seem a little more difficult. I prepared to deliver my speech at one of my favorite venues, Cooper Union. Mr. Cooper offered to once again introduce me, but I told him Reverend Beecher had been granted the privilege. Mr. Cooper expressed his surprise by arching his eyebrows.

"Bowl them over, Victoria… you always do." He walked away to take his seat.

My speech, "The Principles of Finance," entailed an intricate discussion of the monetary system and how it suppressed laborers and women. Both workers and women were treated like animals. I wanted to yoke together the labor movement with suffrage and woman rights. Pearly coached me on the difficult concepts until I could believe I conceived them.

The crowd grew impatient as the minutes passed the eight o'clock start time. The crowd started pounding their feet and clapping their hands in unison, creating a thunderous roar.

Finally, Theodore went out onto the stage to introduce me.

The weasel Beecher sent no word. The man embodied absolutely no honor. He knew I expected him. I heard Theodore concluding his brief introduction. I had to focus.

I put aside Beecher and launched into my lecture. I started laying the foundation stones to build up to my goal, the unification of everyone other than the wealthiest ruling class. I discussed how banks preyed on the working man with high interest rates and high forfeiture percentages. I proposed nationalizing the banks to legislate rules forcing bankers to be of service to the lower class. I suggested a new national currency would create assets for a wider group of people, not just the richest. I told of a future where instead of *haves* and *have nots*, most people who were willing to work would have a fair share of America.

Of all papers, *The New York Times* reported I had mesmerized the crowd. They applauded my knowledge and ability to convincingly argue economic theorems. They mentioned that Theodore Tilton had given a stirring introduction.

Reading the praise, I held one thought. I wished I could tell everyone about the cowardice and dishonesty of one Henry Ward Beecher.

Tennessee declared her own bid for public office on the second day after my speech. She sought the seat of James Brooks in the Eighth Congressional District of New York, consisting mostly of German immigrants. The district spread east from Brooklyn to Jamaica Bay. Representative Brooks vied for his fourth term. Brooks served as the U.S. Government's appointed director on the board of the Union Pacific Railroad. This made him quite wealthy, sharing nothing in common with the constituents of the Eighth.

A strange assortment of bedfellows rallied behind Tennie. Henry Clews, the reserved and austere English financier and president of the

Fourth National Bank, advised her. The bombastic Jim Fisk, no doubt prodded by his concubine, my lover and friend Josephine Mansfield, openly supported her candidacy. Whitelaw Reid, distanced from me and the *Weekly*, remained loyal to Tennessee. Tennie's new beau, the tall, virile, and handsome Johnny Green, the new city editor of Benjamin Day's popular penny press, the *New York Sun*, gushed about Tennie to the brink of credibility.

Tennie declared her intentions on the August 5, 1871, front page of *Woodhull & Claflin's Weekly*. Directly under our banner motto: "UPWARD & ONWARD," the following appeared:

LETTER FROM TENNESSEE CELESTE CLAFLIN

I believe sincerely that the best interests of the country demand an immediate settlement of this great suffrage question. And believe the women citizens of the Eighth Congressional District of the State of New York to be as highly patriotic and as fully inclined to perform the duties which the rights of citizenship require of them as are those of any other congressional district And that the male citizens thereof, from their gallantry and courtesy, will as heartily and earnestly join with women to permit this settlement as would those of any other Congressional district, Therefore I offer myself to them as a candidate for the office of Representative in the Congress of the United States for the next regular term...

And I believe that the true men and women citizens of this district will accord every right, liberty and means of happiness to me equally with others, and will thereby acknowledge the great fact that I, as a citizen, have as clear a right to represent my fellow citizens in Congress as any other citizen has, provided that in other matters outside of right, liberty, happiness and law I may suit their tastes or opinions, and be deemed to possess the proper personal characteristics, independent of sex.

Upon the broad platform of equal rights to all citizens do I stand and solicit the votes of all citizens, women as well as men, urging as a special reason therefore that, by my election the Congress of the United States, through my application for a seat therein, may be compelled to acknowledge the right of women citizens to vote. Thus by your action will the question be determined for every other Congressional district in the country and for all women citizens.

In matter of general political policy, I believe in an enlightened application of the principles of freedom, equality, and justice, as far as the limitations of the Constitution will permit, and in modifying the Constitution whenever it is necessary so to do, that perfect political and social equality may be secured to every individual.

Respectfully,

Tennie C. Claflin

Tennessee spent almost as much time with Pearly as I with Theodore Tilton. She prepared for a speech to be delivered to the German-American Progressive Society at the biggest beer hall in the 8th Congressional District.

She delivered the entire speech in German!

Tennessee looked as respectable as a high-society lady, and at the same time irresistible. She wore a black cotton and silk dress contoured to her body and ending two inches above her ankles, revealing black silk stockings for a few inches above her low-cut, laced boots. She proved she wore no corset whenever she moved.

She was captivating.

Apparently, the 8th District *herrs* and *fraus* thought so, too. Her speech went well. Late at night, hundreds of Germans had crossed the ferry from Brooklyn and were marching up our street singing and shouting in response:

> "*Unser kleine schöne maidchen...* Tennessee!
> *Alles für...* Tennessee!
> *Unser...* Tennessee!
> Tennessee! Tennessee! Tennessee!"
> ("Our small beautiful maiden... Tennessee! All for...
> Tennessee! Our... Tennessee!")

Over and over again they chanted and then cheered. They brought with them kegs of beer and refused to disperse, even after their new heroine appeared on the roof in her nightgown. Tennie thanked everyone in German and asked the crowd to please go home. The drunken revelry continued for hours.

In the early morning, Tennie opened the front door and said goodnight. She blew kisses to the crowd and re-entered our home. With the sun rising over their homes in Brooklyn, they finally dispersed.

I was proud of my sister.

Because Tennie did not invite me to attend, I also felt left out.

Since Tennie had not come to the office, I returned home early the day after the speech. I entered our home and beheld on our red brocade couch, my sister in a partially unbuttoned nightgown entertaining Whitelaw Reid, who had abandoned ship when I published my warning to Henry Ward Beecher. They were sitting very close to each other, and Mr. Reid violated etiquette by not rising to greet me. The obvious reason—he had already risen.

Suddenly, the words I repeatedly spoke in my mind coming home in the phaeton, the congratulations and praise for such a tremendous feat, disappeared. Instead I spoke rudely.

"I hope you are proud of yourself, Sister!"

"Indeed!" She laughed her guttural laugh. She patted Whitelaw's thigh. "Why shouldn't I be?" She turned to him and shrugged.

"Because it won't amount to anything. You are just grandstanding!" I did not like the words I spoke. Yet, I could not halt the flow. "What is the point?"

Tennie jumped up and marched over to me, jutting her jaw and sticking her nose just inches from mine.

"*You* are going to lecture *me* about grandstanding?" She looked at me to see something. "Are you jealous, Sister?" She hissed the word "jealous."

"*No!*" I shouted. "Not at all." I shoved her to the side and sat down away from her.

Calmly, almost regally, she returned to a very crimson Whitelaw. She looked at me as if I were pathetic, or so I thought. She said nothing.

I said falsely, "I am only concerned that when you fail, you will tarnish our reputation."

Our exchange subdued Whitelaw's passion, as if a bucket of ice-cold water had been thrown on his lap. He got up, kissed Tennie's hand, nodded to me, and left without a word.

Exhaling fully, Tennie turned toward me. "Would that I could…" she took another deep breath, "tarnish our reputation. That would be a miraculous feat."

"We have to protect what little we have left." I argued. Even I didn't like my tone.

"Oh, stop it. It does not become you to be either stupid or naive. It is not in my power to diminish us ten percent of what you have already done and will continue to do."

"Why are you so spiteful? Why do you hate me so?"

"Really, Victoria? You think your race for President will yield any finer result than my declaring for Congress? These are attempts solely to make statements in the fight for suffrage, nothing more. We knew at inception they would fail."

"I can feel your hatred!" I started to cry.

"Then you have a powerful imagination." She paused and spoke very calmly, void of any emotion. "What upsets you the most, Victoria, is that I have become dispassionate toward you. Often, I simply remove myself mentally when you are ranting, willing to listen to no one, and making horrific mistakes." Her voice trailed off, and I know she viewed something in the past. Her voice became a flat monotone, "I leave your presence. Just like I did when Pa sent men up to use me."

That hurt. My stomach convulsed and I doubled over. I looked toward her to try and give her a little compassion. I couldn't. I felt wronged. I could not speak.

Tennie spoke in a far-away trance voice, "Our destinies are intertwined for a long time to come, Victoria. I will always support you, and act on your behalf, even when you make it difficult, like you are doing now. I will be with you for a long time to come." Her softness and distance were excruciating.

"I need you, Sister." I wailed.

Her voice returned to normal. "Yes, you do, so get over your fits of jealous rage and constant questioning of my loyalty. If you can't see the ardent support of all of us, right in front of you, then open your eyes." She stood looking down at me. "People who adore you, support you, and would sacrifice themselves for you, are invisible to you. The reason is simple: You are not loyal to yourself... nor to them."

Another spasm of pain racked my body. I watched Tennie come over. She helped me sit up and then sat next to me and put my head on her chest. She stroked my hair and spoke.

"Remember what you told me Rosie taught you over and over?"

"What?"

"Above all else, do ye no harm."

Chapter 13

FREE LOVE

New York City
Fall, 1871

Tennessee kept her word. Everywhere I went to give lectures, she went in advance to make arrangements. When she had something else to do, Colonel Blood would take over. I always knew at any gathering either my sister or my husband would be there for me to gaze upon and not feel alone. A few times when I became ill or exhausted, Tennie would deliver her own speech in my stead and receive thunderous applause and great accolades.

One or the other accompanied me on my lecture circuit. I used the "Woman Right to Vote–Secession Speech" I had been delivering for months. Trains took us to Philadelphia, Detroit, Pittsburgh, Chicago, and more. In Cleveland, *The Banner of Light* reported what a crowd of five thousand witnessed.

> It was a sight never to be forgotten to see that vast assemblage under the magic spell of an eloquent speaker—not what schoolteachers call eloquence, but the eloquence which comes from earnest conviction. There the look of the eye, the expression of the face, and the quiver in the voice all go to show that superficial thoughts have been laid aside and that the domains of earnestness, sincerity and fidelity have been fully entered upon.

I could feel the momentum as though riding on a train leaving a station. The Woodhull accelerated, and nothing would stop us.

In September Theodore published Tract 3 in *The Golden Age*, thirty-six pages called *Victoria C. Woodhull, a Biographical Sketch*. He charged a dime for each copy. The epistle canonized my memories. For the first time, I controlled the telling of my life story.

As with all things Woodhull or Claflin, the response contained the full spectrum from praise and adoration to contempt and vilification. Spiritualists clamored to have me speak to them at their gatherings. *The Sporting News* ridiculed the apparitions and visions in my life. On October 7, *The Day's Doings* caricatured Theodore's revelations by publishing a slate of thirteen absurd and grotesque drawings. While Theodore took the brunt, ostracized for publishing such a fantastical account, our fame and infamy grew.

In accordance with my détente with the Reverend Henry Ward Beecher, the *Weekly* from time to time kindly mentioned him in a positive light or quoted him as an authority on this subject or that. As I gave many speeches, Henry Ward Beecher continually violated and ignored our agreement, not once introducing me on stage or acknowledging me in print. The Reverend earned a new well-deserved moniker, "Oath Breaker."

My house filled with Theodore's melancholy, as we talked in the sitting room with the windows open for any breeze. Theodore sat on the red crushed velvet sofa and I across from him on the satin divan.

Theodore lamented, "I warned you the phantasmagoria would stretch credibility beyond its tolerance."

"Controversy is good." I tried to lift his spirits. "Conflicts make better newsprint. More people will read it."

Shaking his head, he moaned, "Credibility is better! I have become a laughing stock of the educated and literary." He paused to push his golden locks back behind his brow and continued in anguish, "I wish I hadn't listened to you."

I stated my belief. "The biography is sincere and true in detail..." Theodore flashed a look of anger as if he were accusing me in a court of law. "At least on the whole."

"The press excoriates me, not you!"

It pained me to see him so distraught. I thought it best to change subjects before he sank even lower. I stood and approached him.

"What about Beecher?" I lifted his chin to look up at me. "How many times must he disappoint us, Teddy?"

He responded to the question immediately. "Everything is all about Victoria Woodhull, isn't it?" He shook his head in disgust. "I have talked with the Reverend and Frank Moulton yet again." Theodore shouted at me. "You must not take any action against the Reverend. I do not want controversy and additional ridicule, especially now!" He realized he shouted and lowered his voice to continue. "We have to stay the course and forge amicable relations."

"Why, when he has violated his word and does not perform his side of the bargain?"

Theodore stood up, clearly exasperated. "He has promised me and sworn before the Almighty he will appear and introduce you."

My ire rose. "And you believe him? No wonder you are a cuckold!" I immediately raised my right hand to cover my mouth. I regretted the words as soon as I uttered them. "I'm sorry, Teddy. I didn't mean it."

I moved toward him, but he backed away. I reached out my arm, and he denied my touch. I looked up to his eyes. He would not look at me.

"Please forgive me." I pleaded with him. "I should never have said that. It is not what I think."

Coldly, without looking at me, Mr. Tilton concluded our conversation. "He will introduce you before the Labor League at Steinway Hall on November 20. I hope you will be happy!"

As he walked away from me, I could not resist. "He'd better."

It pained me to see only his broad back. He took a few steps, then hesitated. With a deep sigh, he dropped both his arms as if he cast something from his hands, releasing himself from some great burden... me.

An advanced copy of my biography caused John Gage to invite me and Theodore to Vineland, New Jersey, for a convocation of spiritualists on September 8. Theodore declined his invitation. However, my husband traveled with me, enthusiastic to meet many of the people he and Emma Hardinge had classified on index cards before she moved to Boston. Last year, Emma married William Britten and finally published her huge register, *Modern American Spiritualism*. Both James and I were excited to reacquaint with Emma.

I helped the spiritualist group with funding and brought a bundle of free copies of my biography. Twice, the organizers of the convocation asked me to address the assembly. Emma introduced James to many of the people who were given the "A" coding, meaning they were authentic spiritualists. James accepted their request that he serve as secretary of the meeting.

In addition to my two addresses, I commented and engaged in discussions, helped with the planning of future events, and encouraged all the participants. Pleased with my contributions, the group read aloud my entire biography, formally making it a part of the minutes of the convention.

At the end of the sessions the group approved:

> Resolved that we deeply appreciate the aid we have
> received in this Convention from Victoria C. Woodhull;
> that we hereby declare our firm adherence to the

principles of the Equal Rights Party, and that we will labor for the success of its able candidate.

The only damper on the entire trip, Mrs. Hardinge Britten told me several times that my social freedom speech did not adequately consider all the attending consequences. On our last day, she spoke to me while dining with James and me at our quaint inn.

"Victoria, have you considered the complexities, devastating effects, and horrific destruction on the families and children of those who practice free love?"

"The point, Emma, is equal legal standing. I am not promoting lust. Woman must be equal in every way." I replied.

"In any triad, at least one and possibly two families will be completely abandoned and destroyed. What is fair, Vickie? Should innocent children or abandoned wives suffer?"

I did not want to part with animosity between us. "Emma, I have cherished you as an older sister. I do not want to let a difference in ideology sever our relationship." She nodded her head in agreement, and I stated, "I will continue to speak out with the full knowledge you disagree."

"Yes." She smiled at me, a smile which coupled challenge with familiarity. "And if or when I publish my thoughts on the subject, I, too, will know that you disagree." The Colonel frowned and stood up. He escorted Emma to her lodging.

Prior to the close of the convocation, James and I were invited to attend the national American Association of Spiritualists annual meeting only a week away, in Troy, New York. We decided to take a few days and enjoy the beauty of upstate New York.

James and I savored the few days we had without the pressures of our daily regimen and responsibilities. We walked along the river, ate leisurely meals, read to one another, strolled around the park, and rekindled the long-missed passion of when we had craved one another. We sated that appetite diligently. It had been a long time.

Ginny shipped enough copies of the biography to distribute one to each attendee. I first addressed the Association at the commencement, then as the last speaker, talking about the spirits in my life. In the latter speech, I focused on themes such as primary and higher education of the children of spiritualists, and the freedom from persecution. After all, we were a mere two hundred miles west of Salem and its infamous witch trials.

John Gage nominated me to serve as president of the Association. On the second ballot, they elected me. The Association also endorsed and joined the Equal Rights Party.

Colonel James Harvey Blood and I were in love again. Such joy!

Choo, choo—I could hear the steam whistle blow. The Woodhull was gaining momentum.

Chapter 14

SABOTAGE

New York City
November, 1871

On Tuesday, November 3, 1871, Tennie and I registered to vote. Friday, November 7, was city election day. Six women joined Tennie and me at our home on Thirty-Eighth Street. Big Boss Tweed had once again hand-selected his slate of candidates.

For two decades, William Magear Tweed had held a stranglehold on New York City and influenced local, state, and national elections as the head of the notorious Tammany Hall regime. Due in large part to his corruption and taking of bribes, Big Boss became the third-largest landowner in the city; Vanderbilt remained number one, and Jacob Astor's family, number two. Tweed also served on the boards of the Erie Railroad and Jay Gould's Tenth National Bank. While lining his pockets, he paved the way for the legal and perhaps not-so-legal actions of Jim Fisk and Jay Gould.

Rosie warned me to never cross or embarrass this powerful man.

Two months earlier, Samuel J. Tilden, former New York State Assemblyman and recently the chairman of the Democratic State Committee, convened the Committee of Seventy. These respected, just, and honest men gathered to figure out the factual state of affairs of New York City. Henry Clews served on the committee. Days prior to the election, the committee secured indictments on Big Boss Tweed, Mayor A. Oakley Hall, and a gang of city officials, most of whom stood for re-election.

Despite the cold weather, we eight women marched a full mile, arms intertwined, down Fifth Avenue to Twenty-Third Street. We turned east and arrived at a furniture store on 628 Sixth Street, the polling place for the Twenty-Third District of the Twenty-First Ward of New York City.

I walked to the front of the line and turned around. "Good gentlemen and kind sirs," I took the time to make eye contact with the first several men in line, "Would you be so polite as to allow a few women to advance to the front of the line?"

One fellow spoke up. "You are Victoria Woodhull!" I nodded.

And another man asked, "Is your sister here too?" All the men agreed to let us go first, no doubt interested to see how the scandalous Tennessee dressed. Joining our band of women was our lawyer, John D. Reymert, who back in May represented the Colonel in the alienation of affections trial brought by my family.

Tennie and I presented our ballots to the three poll inspectors. Addressing them and the men who crowded forward to witness the scene, I spoke. "We have duly registered and submit our ballots to be counted."

"We can't accept them. No woman votes today," countered the Democratic inspector.

"By whose authority?" Tennessee demanded.

The man replied with authority, "Under the direct orders of Big Boss Tweed and Tammany Hall."

I declared. "That is unconstitutional by both the federal and state constitutions." I took both books from my satchel and held them high the way a preacher would raise the Bible. "We have registered and we have the right to vote as assured by the Fourteenth and Fifteenth Amendments of the U.S. Constitution, and the Second New York State Constitution." I presented the copies opened to the appropriate pages to the poll worker.

"My state constitution doesn't have that section!" The man argued while turning red and getting angrier.

John Reymert, attorney at law, addressed the man. "Sir, you have an outdated state constitution, which was replaced by the current constitution you just received."

"How do I know it is not a fake?" The man yelled at our lawyer. "We've done just fine using this one in all the other elections. These women ain't going to vote. That's *final!*"

Reymert turned to the Republican poll inspector. "What about you sir; do you support this illegal activity?"

Despite a murderous look from the Tammany Hall stooge, the Republican replied, "I believe you hold the ruling copies. She can vote."

Reymert turned slightly to stare directly into the eyes of the Democratic inspector. "Know, sir, lack of knowledge of the law does not negate a violation of it. You personally are liable up to the sum of $500 per violation for obstruction of the legal and due voting privileges of citizens. You personally will have to pay a $4,000 fine."

As Reymert spoke, I spied a tall young Irishman looking at his right palm. He had written down a list of names. Rumor had it, the Boss Tweed machine paid Irishmen $1.00 for every vote they cast. I moved over to grab the man's hand, exposed his palm, and shouted at the lout preventing our voting. "What is this? A list of names! How many times will this young Irishman vote today?"

"Take it up with Big Boss Tweed!" The Democratic inspector shot a glance at the Irishman, and the lad ran from the building. The boor finished his declaration by spitting on the floor.

The Republican inspector stepped up to say something, and the Democrat gave him a threatening stare and commanded, "Not a single word," and then yelled, "*Next!*"

I shouted so everyone could hear me, "Each one of you present, bear witness to the fact duly registered United States citizens and residents of New York State are being denied their constitutional right to vote! This gentleman, Mr. Reymert, will circle around, so please help us women, and give him your name."

The Democrat threatened the group of us. "Get out of here, and take all these women with you, or I'll have a policeman arrest the bunch of you!"

I had the last word. "We will leave. I already have your name! You will not get away with this, Quinlan O'Rourke! You are a shining example of a brutish and lawless man."

"Be gone with you." The man pointed us to the door.

We ladies returned to Thirty-Eighth Street.

The Sunday edition of the *The New York Times* published a letter from me.

> I have been refused the right of voting by the Democratic inspectors of my district, the Republican dissenting and desiring to receive my vote. Under the election laws of the state, the inspectors are, or I am, guilty of felony since either they prevented a legal voter from voting, or I attempted to vote illegally! And either they or I SHALL be convicted of the crime.

In the November 11 *Weekly* I published my "President's Message" to the American Association of Spiritualists. Some of the spiritualists started assailing me as a carpetbagger who invaded their convention. They went so far as to say I had a hidden agenda and used spiritualism as a false pretense.

My article filled five columns and identified all the different constituencies we were merging together: suffragists, spiritualists, labor, communists, and free-love advocates. I expressed my deep appreciation for the trust and vision of the Association.

The great and influential status of spiritualists has arrived at a state of readiness to intervene actively in the political affairs of the country.

How appropriate that together we spiritualists will harbinger and establish a government guided by the Good, True and the Beautiful to replace the present system, which is ruled by corruption and influence peddling,...

I tell you frankly that I feel myself called upon by the higher powers to enact a great role in connection with this great change.

Teddy came to our home in the early afternoon of Sunday, November 19. "Theodore, promise me you'll deliver this note into the hands of the Usurper. Please stay until the Oath Breaker gives you an answer." I handed him my sealed letter.

"You have my solemn word, Victoria. I will not fail you." The tall blond bent down to kiss my hand. I embraced him. I was so relieved he forgave for my cruel remark a few weeks ago. He asked me, "May I inquire as to the content of the letter?"

I immediately recalled when he had asked Elizabeth Cady Stanton the same question half a year ago. Her notification to the leaders of the American Woman Suffrage Association was succinctly written in all-capital-letters: "OVER MY DEAD BODY!" I remembered it sounded to me like the death knell of any united woman suffrage movement. The letter I handed Teddy still offered an olive branch to the most deplorable man I knew—besides Pa.

I picked up my draft and read it to Teddy. "Dear Reverend Beecher: For reasons in which you are deeply interested as myself, and in the interest of truth, I desire to have an interview with you, without fail, at some hour tomorrow." I started to pace the anteroom. "Two of your sisters have gone out of their way to assail my character and purposes, both by the means of the public press and by numerous private letters written to various persons with whom they seek to injure me and thus to defeat the political ends at which I aim."

I put the second page on top and continued to pace while reading. "You doubtless know it is in my power to strike back, and in ways more disastrous than anything that can come to me; but I do not desire to do this. I simply desire justice from those from whom I have a right to expect it, and a reasonable course on your part will assist me to it. I speak guardedly, but I think you will understand me. I repeat, I must have an interview tomorrow, since I am to speak tomorrow evening at Steinway Hall, and what I shall or shall not say will depend largely on the result of the interview."

"I will deliver the letter, Victoria," my knight said, and sallied forth on his mission. We agreed to meet early in the morning and head down to the Brooklyn Ferry to travel to the Plymouth Church and Reverend Henry Ward Beecher.

As Theodore and I rode in the phaeton the next morning, my mood turned darker and gloomier than the thunder booms, lightning, and pelting rain slanting toward us. I needed rest, not to travel in the cold and damp. I had become fatigued from speaking to large audiences across the northeast, having spoken in Pennsylvania and Hartford last week. Tonight's speech would be the most significant of my career. I would directly confront my critics.

Yet, here I sat having to spend half my day on a performance night to somehow force a backbone into Henry Ward Beecher. Even though the rains made it difficult to view, I saw the placards and banners that James, perhaps inspired by our rekindled love, and his brother George had put up all over the city, promoting the speech this evening. Even the ferry dock had several well-placed announcements.

The voyage unsettled me due to the roiling seas. I remembered while studying Vanderbilt how important it was for him to be able to set sail, or rather, steam across tumultuous seas. Being tossed about and feeling like I was repeatedly dropped off a cliff, I believe the Commodore gave not one thought to the comfort of his passengers. There would be no reading of Whitman on a day such as this. The challenge today was to keep breakfast in my stomach instead of on the deck.

A carriage brought us to the Moulton's federal-period abode. The smell of fresh-baked bread greeted us before the threshold. Frank and Emma were equally soothing. Emma served tea and hot biscuits with butter. We sat near the fire in the old, large hearth, and we chatted for quite a while as the tea became cold and I consumed several biscuits.

Frank stood up and advised me. "I am sure the delay is due to the Reverend's need to dress against the cold and wet."

I challenged, "You don't think he is simply too much of a coward?"

Frank verbalized my thought. "He has too much to lose."

Theodore rang the bell outside, heralding the arrival of the Reverend. I was shocked at the countenance of Henry Ward. Instead of the vociferous lion and powerful advocate, he appeared unsure of himself, meek, and afraid.

The Reverend spoke to no one in particular and could not raise his eyes to address me. "Were I to come, I believe I should sink through of the stage floor." I had heard that bleating lamb voice of his before. No one else spoke, so he continued. "I am a moral coward on this subject, and I know it, and I am not fit to stand beside you. You go there to speak what you know to be the truth; I should stand there a living lie."

Theodore was harsh. "This is your last chance to honor your word, Henry."

Frank was angry. "Have you wasted all our time trying to build a bridge of reconciliation? You must appear!"

Henry looked to both of them and cried out. "Do you think this thing will come out to the world? Will everyone know my indiscretions?"

Both Frank and Theodore nodded their heads, gravely confirming Henry's worst fear. Teddy spoke, "Nothing is more certain on earth or in heaven, Henry, and this may be your last chance to save yourself from complete ruin and damnation."

Like a child, Henry Ward tried to stand up, only to rest back down on the sofa. Beecher reached out toward Teddy, pleading. "I can never endure such a terror. Oh! If it must come, let me know of it twenty-four hours in advance so I may take my own life. I cannot face this thing."

I stood up and walked over to the bent head of Henry Ward. I found his cowardly plea stirred in me only a feeling of outrage. "That time has passed, dear Reverend." I hissed at him. "Be there this evening to preside and introduce me, or bear the consequences."

He fell onto the sofa, bumping Emma. Crying like a small child, he reached for her and plopped his head on her chest so she would comfort him. She looked up dismayed.

"*Enough!*" I shouted. "Theodore, I have a speech to give." Teddy looked like he wanted to make one last argument. I grabbed his arm, placing my hand on his, and half pulled him toward the door. We grabbed out coats, scarves, and mittens and without putting any of them on, and stomped out of the house.

Teddy tried to talk to me on the way home. I raised my right hand with my fingers up, stopping him. When I saw his face so full of remorse, I gently put two fingers upon his lips and shook my head from side to side.

I sought no comfort. I just wanted to focus on my speech.

I waited nervously for the large crowd to settle down in Steinway Hall. *Les Trois Mousquetaires*, James, Pearly, and Teddy, had helped me fashion a powerful speech. I was ready and everything was in place, except for Henry Ward Beecher.

I loved Steinway Hall for its acoustics. My voice would boom across the hall, and even my whisper would be heard by everyone. The crowd filled the Hall and people were standing anywhere they could, even outside. Some of the placards promised a sensational address, proclaiming:

> THE PRINCIPALS OF SOCIAL FREEDOM:
> INVOLVING THE QUESTION OF
> FREE LOVE, MARRIAGE,
> DIVORCE AND PROSTITUTION

Everyone attending came to hear me argue for free love. In the lobby, there were stacks of half-sheet, printed statements, which Pearly had written.

> She wishes it to be clearly understood that freedom does not mean anarchy in the social relations any more than it does in religion and politics; also, that the advocacy of its principles requires neither abandoned action nor immodest speech.
>
> Horace Greeley, Governor Hawley of Connecticut, and the Boston Exclusives are specially invited to seats on the platform.
>
> All lesser defamers should secure seats toward the rear.

In practice sessions, it took me one hour and twenty minutes to read the speech. I knew, on the stage it often took me half again as long to finish. For all its complexity and historic references, "The Principals of Social Freedom" could be distilled into one simple concept: *Equality*—one standard for all.

As the minutes ticked by after eight o'clock, the boisterous crowd became unruly. Unison chants of "Start it now!" filled the air, then thunderous stamping of feet. The hall seemed to quake.

Tennessee returned from viewing the crowd. "They won't hold much longer."

Theodore implored me. "Frank promised me he would bring Reverend Beecher. Please wait till they arrive."

"Victoria, dear, please do not wait for the cur." James smiled at me. "You are ready, go forth and conquer!"

Tennessee came over to me and told me to take a few deep breaths. "Stop if you lose your place, and try your best to stick to what you practiced." She smiled at me. "I know you are nervous, as you always are, yet you always come through." She raised my chin with her left hand. "You *are the Woodhull!*" She laughed and kissed me. Tennie and James went to find their seats.

At eight and fifteen minutes, Frank Moulton and Emma burst in, dripping wet. They looked downtrodden. The Oath Breaker had not accompanied them. Frank began to speak. "We did every…"

I silenced him with my hand. I stood up gathered my notes and proceeded to walk to the lectern alone.

Just before I parted the curtains covering the wings of the stage, Theodore spun me around and declared. "I will stand for you." He walked out onto the stage and informed the crowd that he would preside this evening and went on to introduce me.

After brief introductory remarks explaining his unscheduled presence at Steinway Hall, Theodore spoke with heartfelt passion.

> Five minutes ago, I did not expect to appear here,
> but several gentlemen have declined to introduce our
> speaker, one after another for various reasons, chief
> among them being objections to this lady's character. I
> know her, and I believe in her, and I vouch for her. As to

her views, she will give them to you, and you may judge for yourselves.

It may be, she is a fanatic. It may be, I am a fool. But before high heaven I would rather be both fanatic and fool in one than be such a coward as would deny this woman the sacred right of free speech.

Allow me the privilege of saying with as much pride as ever prompted me, I introduce to you, Victoria C. Woodhull, who will address you upon the subject of social freedom.

Theodore walked back to the stage left wing, offered me his arm and escorted me to the lectern. He bowed, kissed my hand, and left the stage the way we came.

As I reached the lectern, the noise reached a crescendo. It was so loud I could not hear my own thoughts. The standing ovation and jeers lasted several minutes. I rested my notes on the lectern and tried to commence speaking, but the crowd was too loud.

Finally, I walked in front of the lectern and raised and lowered my hands, motioning the crowd to sit down. I placed my hands on my hips and shouted. "You all came to hear me talk, *right*?" There was thunderous applause as I returned to the lectern and started.

My brothers and sisters, I come before the public at this time, upon this particular subject, notwithstanding that malicious and designing persons have sought to malign and undervalue my private life and personal motives, in a manner that shall complicate the righteous sentiment of these all-important issues. You are aware that my private life has been pictured to the public by the press of the country with the intent to make people believe me to be a very bad woman.

Thunderous applause and only a few shouts of derision welcomed my opening, and I was buoyed by the affirmation of the crowd. I continued with a history of the fight for individual freedom from the sixteenth century to the present, from Europe to America. Then I approached the central theme.

> The basis of society is the relations of the sexes. There is no escaping the fact that the principle by which the male citizens of these United States assume to rule the *female* citizens is not self-government but despotism.
>
> Our government is based upon the proposition that all men and women are born free and equal and entitled to certain inalienable rights, among which are life, liberty, and the pursuit of happiness. What we who demand social freedom ask is simply that the government of this great nation shall be administered in accordance with the spirit of this proposition. *Nothing more, nothing less.*

I paused as the crowd went wild again. I purposely quoted the banner of *The Revolution*. I looked up to where my dear Elizabeth Cady Stanton and her eagle protector, Susan B. Anthony, sat with Tennie in the front box seats. I smiled at Elizabeth as she stood up, threw me a kiss, and applauded.

I felt myself surrounded by spirits with whom I had communed. Demosthenes was standing right beside me. I pressed my argument for freedom from the slavery of marriage.

> Law cannot compel two people to love. The matter concerns these two alone, and no other living soul has any human right to say aye or nay. It is none of their business. Where there is no love as a basis for marriage, there should be no marriage!

The crowd seemed spellbound. I pressed on.

> I would not be understood to say that there are no good conditions in the present state of marriage. By no means do I say this; on the contrary a very large proportion of present social relations are commendable. They are as good as the present status of society makes possible. But what I do assert, and that most positively, is that all which is good and commendable now would continue to exist if all marriage laws were repealed tomorrow.
>
> I do not care where it is that sexual commerce results from the dominant power of one sex over another, compelling him or her to submission against the instincts of love. And where hate or disgust is present, whether it be in the gilded palaces of Fifth Avenue or in the lowliest purlieus of Greene Street. There is prostitution both high and low, and all the laws that a thousand state assemblies may pass cannot make it otherwise.

Pandemonium broke out. Cheers and shouts of approval were assailed by hissing and boos. The battle escalated to a point of frenzy. The crowd became so unruly I could not continue. Theodore reappeared on the stage to demand order. Suddenly, I could not feel the presence of my spirits.

I shouted a challenge. "Let the gentleman or lady who seeks to interrupt me, to inhibit my delivery, come forward on this platform and define their principles precisely and fairly!"

In shock, I witnessed my little sister Utica, born between me and Tennie and the prettiest of us all, rise in the box directly above my right. She wore a beautiful outfit, a comely new Parisian style dress, with blue and apricot silk faille and white silk roses. I had the tailors measure Utica for the costume specifically to attend this occasion. She looked beautiful, although I could tell she had mixed copious amounts of alcohol and laudanum. She leaned over the front of her box and shouted down, "How would you like to come into this world without knowing who is your father?"

I froze. Did anyone else hear derision in her voice? An anger built up and brewing over decades of jealousy? Sensing a fight between two women, the crowd cheered her words.

For a moment, I tried to seize the relevance of her question. There was none. It had one purpose—to upset me.

"There are thousands of noble men and women in the world today," I said, "who do not know who their fathers are." I paused and beheld the ugliness of the crowd. My temper flared. "God alone knows how many illegitimate men or women are in this hall tonight!"

A policeman took it upon himself to remove my sister from the theater, she yelled out. "Unhand me, you brute. I am her sister." She shouted. "My name is Utica!"

The crowd became belligerent. The assembly started shouting "Shame, shame, shame," at the policeman. When he kowtowed to their moral judgment and left the box, they all chanted, "Utica, Utica, Utica."

Theodore came out again and assured the crowd that Utica would have ample opportunity to address the entire gathering at the end of my speech. Terrified, my sister disappeared to the back of her box. Finally, the crowd settled down, but the earlier rapture had disappeared. Feeling a sense of urgency, I started fresh.

> How can young people who enter upon marriage
> in utter ignorance of that which is to render the union
> happy or miserable be able to say that they will always
> love and live together? They may take these vows in

perfectly good faith and good intention, then repent them in sackcloth and ashes within twelve months.

Now, let me ask, would it not rather be the Christian way, in such cases to say to the disaffected party, 'Since you no longer love me, go your way and be happy, and make those to whom you go happy also. I will seek my own happiness as well.' I know of no higher, holier love than this.

I had regained control of my cadence, and the crowd. Someone shouted from the main floor, "Are you a free lover?" Cheers and applause supported the question. *How dare they interrupt me time after time?*

Frustrated, I threw my notes on the lectern and marched out to the front of the platform.

Yes! I am a Free Lover! I have an inalienable, constitutional and natural right to love whom I may, to love as long or short a period as I can; and to change that love every day if I please, and with that right neither you nor any law you can frame have any right to interfere.

Shouts came from every direction. I feared the audience might riot. I pressed on.

When I practiced clairvoyance thousands of men and women from all walks of life, both living and departed, told me their tales of horror, of wrongs inflicted and endured. This led me to question whether the hollowness and rottenness of society, supported by laws which gave rise to so much crime and misery should be continued.

What can be more terrible than for a delicate, sensitively organized woman to be compelled to endure the presence of a beast in the shape of a man who knows nothing beyond the blind passion with which he is filled, and to which is often added the delirium and cruelty of intoxication?

I know I speak the truth. Love is that which exists to do good not just get good.

Boos and profanity dominated the scattered polite applause. I looked at the watch on my lapel. I had been standing for two hours. I was tired, but I needed to finish—on my terms.

Were the relations of the sexes thus regulated, misery, crime and vice would be banished, and the pale wan face of female humanity replaced by one glowing with radiant delight and healthful bloom.

I prize the good opinion of my fellow beings, every one of you. I would gladly have you think well of me, and not ill.

Contemplate this, and then denounce me for advocating freedom if you can, and I will bear your curse with a better resignation.

I bowed and left the stage to a tumult of applause, foot-stomping, and insults. Utica had fled the building.

Tennie was waiting for me in the wings. She embraced me. "Not exactly the written speech, Sister."

I looked into her cool, gray-blue eyes. "Why would Utica do that?" Tennie just shrugged. I squeezed her tighter. "Take me home, Tennie."

The next day I departed on a seven-engagement tour over thirteen days. Everywhere they wanted to hear the "Principles of Social Freedom" address. Within days, Tennie had booked another three engagements, so I would speak eleven times in a fortnight.

I became the highest paid speaker in the country, although Mark Twain, the *nom de plume* for the humorist Samuel Langhorne Clemens, rivaled me. The monies from the engagements helped with our monthly expenses. The brokerage firm, after the fiasco of the court embarrassment, earned much less money than it had before.

While traveling, I had the time to read many of the newspaper accounts of the Steinway Hall address. *The World* stated many were disappointed with my "high moral ground." *The Tribune*, normally my nemesis, acknowledged, "The social problem never had a bolder advocate than Mrs. Victoria C. Woodhull proved herself last night at Steinway Hall."

They were not all kind. Most castigated me for using words not normally spoken in public meetings, such as "sexual intercourse," "pregnancy," "rape," and "abortion." I was accused of being possessed. Henry Bowen, a founder of Plymouth Church, wrote in *The Independent* that my Steinway Hall appearance constituted "... certainly one of the dirtiest meetings that has ever been held in New York."

One paper went so far as to trot out the centuries-old hysteria whenever a woman started to gain attention. After calling me a witch, without using the word, it censured me as "a vile woman, possessed by the carnal power to captivate and destroy men." What would come next? Would they burn me at the stake, or banish me from the kingdom?

The Herald reported, "The argument was the most astonishing doctrine ever listened to by an audience of Americans. For an audience of three thousand people to applaud, or even listen patiently to the sentiments expressed last night is a deplorable state of affairs."

Theodore suffered the most.

First, the press ridiculed him for penning and publishing my *Biographical Sketch*. After the Steinway Hall address, he told reporters, "The printed speech, which I had the privilege to preview, did no damage. Her spontaneous, interjected remarks compromised her. She said violent things."

Despite the statement, the public dismissed Theodore as so love-struck as to lose all critical capacity. Teddy's speaking engagements rapidly canceled, and his subscription base at *The Golden Age* evaporated.

After each lecture, the same local regional newspapers praised my efforts. "A woman of remarkable originality and power." Another called me "The most prominent woman of our time." Many others vilified me.

At the end of a difficult fortnight of traveling and seriatim oratories, I felt completely exhausted.

Part III

RUN FOR PRESIDENT

Chapter 15

A PATCHWORK QUILT

December, 1871

Tennessee Celeste Claflin published her first book, *Constitutional Equality of the Sexes,* the first week of December. We were all proud and happy for her.

Stephen Pearl Andrews mentored Tennie's writing. The work relied heavily on the prophetic work of Judith Sargent Murray, who published *On the Equality of the Sexes* in *The Massachusetts Magazine* eight decades ago, in 1790, preceding by two years Mary Wollstonecraft's publication of *A Vindication of the Rights of Women.*

Elizabeth Cady Stanton gave me a copy of Judith Sargent's writing. Lizzybeth explained to me that although Judith performed higher than her brother in preparatory school, only he could go on to receive a higher education at Harvard College in 1769. At age eighteen, her parents forced Judith to marry the commercial seaman Captain John Stevens, and attempt to have kids. Unwilling to compromise her talents like so many other smart women condemned to marriage, Judith began a prolific writing career. Tennie's book opened with the preamble poem and prologue sentiments from *On the Equality of the Sexes*:

> *… Yet cannot I their sentiments imbibe,*
> *Who this distinction to the sex ascribe,*
> *As if a woman's form must needs enrol,*
> *A weak, a servile, an inferiour soul;*

*And that the guise of man must still
proclaim,
Greatness of mind, and him, to be the
same...*

*But imbecility is still confin'd,
And by the lordly sex to us consign'd;
They rob us of the power t'improve,
And then declare we only trifles love;
Yet haste the era, when the world shall
know,
That such distinctions only dwell below;
The soul unfetter'd, to no sex confin'd,
Was for the abodes of cloudless day
design'd.*

*Mean time we emulate their manly fires,
Though erudition all their thoughts
inspires,
Yet nature with equality imparts
And noble passions, swell e'en female
hearts.*

But our judgment is deemed not so strong—we do not distinguish so well.—Yet it may be questioned, from what doth this superiority, in this determining faculty of the soul, proceed. May we not trace its source in the difference of education, and continued advantages? Will it be said that the judgment of a male of two years old, is more sage than that of a female's of the same age? I believe the reverse is generally observed to be true. But from that period what partiality!

One is exalted, and the other depressed, by the contrary modes of education, which are adopted! The one is taught to aspire, and the other is early confined and limited. As their years increase, the sister must be wholly domesticated, while the brother is led by the hand through all the flowery paths of science. Grant that their minds are by nature equal, yet who shall wonder at the *apparent* superiority, if indeed custom becomes *second nature*; nay if it taketh the place of nature, and that it doth the experience of each day will evince.

—Judith Sargent, *On the Equality of the Sexes*, 1790

Tennie's book incorporated the parts of her lectures based on the *New Development* arguments I presented to Congress close to a year ago. The book was well received, though a few of the regular cartoonist detractors showed Tennessee in provocative attire with Stephen Pearl Andrew's arms around her writing on a pad with his pen. A second depicted a Tennessee puppet sitting on Pearly's lap as he pulled the strings to make her write.

The typical cruelty.

After a week of rest, I journeyed to Washington, D.C. to do my best to disturb and interrupt the A.W.S.A. convention. I dined with Major Joseph Willard, who once again placed me in the Presidential Suite. Joseph and I discussed the tragic loss of his wife on February 14, just weeks after Tennie and I had dined with the couple in January, short of a year ago. Tennie and I both knew she would depart quickly. We had no idea it would be so soon.

I offered my condolences and volunteered to try and reach out to Antonia in the ether world. He politely declined. I did not push the issue. Joseph still actively mourned his lost wife. The waiter appeared, and I once again ordered the mutton stew.

We discussed Antonia. "The Old Capital Prison destroyed her." Joseph lamented. "Prison broke Antonia's spirit and gave her consumption. She never fully recovered."

"I'm so sorry, Joseph."

"At least we had several years together. John Bingham convinced the jury to hang poor Mary Surratt. She did nothing more than run a boarding house."

I felt the same breeze on my face I felt last year viewing Mary Surratt swing to and fro. I tried to focus on Mr. Willard's words.

"Alan Pinkerton, the head of the then-new Secret Service, suspended habeus corpus to imprison the socialite Rose O'Neal Greenhow on the grounds of suspected treason. She successfully managed an entire network of spies and prior to the First Battle of Bull Run messaged General Beauregard the battle plan of General Irwin McDowell. Rose seemed to survive the Old Capitol Prison the best, perhaps due to the company of her eight-year-old daughter in prison, or perhaps because she had so many powerful friends in D.C. who could request favors and provide bribe money.

"She died two years after her exile to the borders of the former Confederacy. After publishing her memoirs and visiting the monarchs of Europe, Rose drowned on a ship lost at sea. Many claim she tried to return to North Carolina with new funding for the South."

He drew me into his melancholy. I knew Joseph needed to return to actively living his life. "What can I do for you, Joseph?"

"Will you accompany me to her gravesite tomorrow?"

I could only guess how many people had declined this same offer. Most people in this parasitical town could not afford to be seen at a traitor's gravesite.

"I would be honored." I tried to focus on the savory mutton stew filled with carrots, peas, and potatoes. My stomach churned. I spread rich, yellow butter onto the fresh, crusty biscuits. Alas, as before, my appetite failed me.

"Victoria, I'm afraid my grief has ruined your meal. I'm so sorry."

"More likely the travel and the clouds of cigar smoke in your lobby."

"Yes, the lobbyists are a rough bunch."

The gallant, retired Major Willard, a faint glimmer of his former self, accompanied me all the way up the stairs. At the door, he said, "It is a grand suite."

"Yes, it is, Joseph." I gave him a familial hug, and he turned to walk down the stairs in his solitude.

"Good night, Victoria… and thank you."

The next day we took his private phaeton drawn by four beautiful, chestnut Morgans. He laid an ornate wreath on Antonia's grave and started to weep. I went to comfort him, but he motioned to the driver.

"Please go back to the hotel, Victoria," he said ruefully. "I want to spend some time alone with my wife."

My heart went out to him.

The leadership of the A.W.S.A. would not let me speak. Only Mary Livermore would meet me.

"Why not let me appear, Mary?"

"Not possible, Victoria, and I think you know it."

"It will certainly increase your attendance, and I may unite your movement in your hatred of my message," I argued.

"Mrs. Woodhull, the A.W.S.A. is above you and your kind," she continued in her haughty elitist New England manner. "You will never address us, because we will not sully our communal purity."

As I was locked out of the convention hall, I hired boys to hand out copies of the most recent edition of the *Weekly* to every attendee. Sympathizers told me the podium issued instructions to throw the papers out.

A majority of women, not fully drawn in by the tepid oratory of Lucy Stone, nor the poetic verse of Julia Ward Howe, read the *Weekly* out of sheer boredom. I rejoiced hearing that during addresses by Beechers, Catherine Beecher, Harriet B. Stowe, and the Usurper himself, women fanned themselves with the *Weekly*, thus displaying the banner and the names Woodhull and Claflin throughout the hall.

I found a way to make my presence felt. I left satisfied.

I returned home late afternoon on Monday, December 11. An offensively pungent odor accosted me upon my arrival home. Our house smelled like the lobby at the Willard. In our sitting room, about twenty men and a few women, including Tennie, were talking loudly. The stench emanating from the laborers further challenged the olfactory nerves, especially mixed with odors of stale beer and cheap cigars. I could barely breathe.

I walked unnoticed into the middle of the room and screamed. *"Hello! I am home!"* The crowd quieted little. "Will someone, anyone, please explain to me what all these people are doing here?"

My husband walked up to me and began talking rapidly. "Yesterday the police threatened to arrest 150 communist supporters who had gathered at Cooper Union for a funeral procession to honor the execution of young General Louis Nathaniel Rossel. The police only arrested a handful of the leaders. The leaders who escaped are here now." I hadn't seen the Colonel so excited about a subject for a long time.

He went on. "You know the Thiers Government executed Rossel, who led the Communard forces of the Paris Commune, a fortnight past at Versailles."

"Yes." I read about the arrests circulating in today's papers. "Why would the police do that? Don't they know that will incite 10,000 supporters to march the next time?"

"Exactly!" The Colonel gave me a big hug and kissed me before continuing. "The French Sections of the I.W.A. have called for a massive funeral march this Sunday along the exact same route!"

As chairman of Section Twelve of the International Workingman's Association, I spoke to the room. "The Twelfth will show solidarity and join in."

James kissed my hands. "Precisely what we are coordinating, right now." He turned around and returned to the ruckus.

I took off my hat and cloak and asked our cook to prepare some strong tea for me and bring me something on toast to eat. I went over to kiss Tennie's cheek and joined the French section leaders.

We all talked until late at night. By the time we were finished, we had planned a unified solidarity march starting at Cooper Union on Sunday at one o'clock. There would be I.W.A. members, side-by-side with suffragists and spiritualists. Irishmen would walk with Negroes, and every religion would be represented. We even planned for a full row near the front to consist of three men marching arm-in-arm: an Irishman, a Chinese, and a Negro.

Tennie and I hired the only militia who would lead the parade. The Skidmore Light Guard, a Negro unit, would provide twenty-seven uniformed soldiers brandishing muskets. Two military drummers would lead, followed by an officer and three rows of eight men. Not only would the guard prevent police interference, it would present a military air to the procession.

Sunday at noon we assembled at Cooper Union. Charcoal stoves roasting chestnuts emitted whiffs of warm, aromatic smoke. A fierce cold belied the bright sunshine. The wind pierced exposed skin as if an icicle shard tore through the body.

The determined showed up in numbers, tremendous numbers.

Almost everyone wore some form of red—a patch, a scarf, a ribbon, a flag, or their entire outfit. I wore a black dress with black double skirt and a Basque waist. Tennie wore an all-black dress with double skirt and a heart-shaped waist. Black velvet trimmed my black bonnet, also adorned by loops of red, a white feather, white illusion strings, and red lace. Tennie wore a black felt hat trimmed with loops and ends of red grosgrain ribbon and a black feather.

Tennie on the right, the French section leaders, Stephen Pearl Andrews, Theodore Tilton, Colonel Blood in full military uniform, and I on the left formed the first line behind the soldiers. Tennie held a large red flag on the far right, and I carried the flag of the Twelfth Section of the International Workingmen's Association on the left. Banners of the different trade and labor unions spotted the ranks.

At the rear, six black Friesian horses covered in black cloths high-stepped, draying a coffin draped in black with red flags and red ribbons streaming from each corner top. On both sides of the catafalque, huge red signs declared:

HONOR TO THE

MARTYRS OF

THE UNIVERSAL REPUBLIC

At precisely one o'clock, the drummers started beating out a funeral march. The streets were jammed with spectators whose breaths created little clouds in front of their faces. Most of them would join the procession once the rear reached them. All along the route, despite the cold, families could be seen looking through opened windows.

We marched down Third Avenue into the Bowery. As we passed Fourth Street, crowds grew antagonistic and the police tried to push them back to avoid a melee. As we approached Third Street to the east, I had a premonition. I stopped. The Colonel caught the banner as it began to fall.

I heard the soft voice of Rosie eagerly urging me. *Turn them right, Victoria. Now. There is a dangerous crowd ahead. There will be bloodshed. Turn right!*

My husband's voice guided me back to the present. "Victoria, are you all right? What just happened?"

"Turn them right!" I shouted. "Quickly, Colonel. Tell the unit to turn right and march west on Great Jones Street."

"Why?"

"*Do it!*" I shouted. "Quickly, please!"

James returned the banner to my hands and ran ahead of the soldiers. He ordered the Lieutenant, "*Parade right!*" The junior officer did not have to repeat the command from a Colonel. The drummers took a sharp turn to proceed west down Great Jones Street. Before the corner, I moved to the side and gazed back. The march filled the six streets all the way back to Cooper Union.

The parade turned up Fifth Avenue and turned left on Thirty-Fourth Street. We were confronted by several mounted police officers, their horses breathing heavily, filling the air with moisture. The police captain, the same man who ordered the crowd to disperse last week and subsequently arrested six of the leaders, rode out from the others to talk.

Tennie and I, along with Pearly and the Colonel, walked to the front. Before anyone else spoke, I challenged the captain.

"To my knowledge, Captain," I called out loud enough for all to hear, "our procession has been orderly and without incident. Why do you now block us from proceeding down Sixth Avenue and completing our march? Do you intend to arrest us?"

The powerful man sat in his saddle and began to laugh. The other mounted police officers joined in, but they seemed nervous or jittery. Before I could speak Tennie stepped forward.

"Is this all a joke to you, Captain Byrne? I fear that in our mourning and solemnity we have not perceived the frivolity you and your men enjoy."

"*Enough!*" The thick Irish captain of police bellowed. His horse took two strides forward, narrowing the gap between us. He presented an imposing figure.

"Militia, *Ready...*" Colonel Blood ordered. Several of the militia aimed their rifles at the police, who responded by drawing sabers and firearms.

The captain shouted an order to his policemen. "*Stand down!* Goddamn it. Lower your weapons."

He looked at my husband. "*Colonel* Blood, *retired,* isn't it?" He spied the gold rectangle containing the Union Colonel rank insignia. "Would you kindly ask your men to return their muskets to their shoulders, before this turns ugly and gets out of control? You don't want to fire on policemen, do you?"

"*At ease!*" My husband ordered the soldiers. They followed his orders. I grabbed Tennie and started to recommence the march.

The captain blocked our path and shouted again. "*Stop* or I will have your pretty arses arrested. Blimey, you two women are hellfire!"

"Captain, I will not..." I couldn't finish my sentence as the captain cut me off again.

"Christ, lass, hold back a moment. I've come to thank you."

"What?" Tennie and I spoke almost simultaneously.

Captain Byrne dismounted, gave his reins to another policeman, and walked right up to us. He towered over my sister and me. He questioned us. "Who decided to turn right at Great Jones Street?"

"I did." I replied.

"Why?"

"I had a premonition. I heard a voice tell me that danger lay ahead."

The captain took off his hat and scratched his head. "Mother Mary and Joseph, unbelievable. You prevented a bloodbath. We were losing control of the crowds who were ready to attack the marchers. They were assembled one block east on Lafayette, all the way down to Houston. We would not have been able to stop them. Many would have died."

Then Captain Byrne did something very strange. With bleary eyes either from the cold or sentiments, he bent down and kissed my hand. "I would have lost many good men, and members of the public as well." Captain Byrne stood up and looked straight at me. "I am grateful… for your… uh… premonition."

I responded, "Thank you, Captain. I am sorry I was impolite before."

The captain rumbled a hearty laugh and spoke loudly. "Lady Woodhull apologizes for being impolite!" Everyone laughed a little, perhaps to ease the tension. He turned to me and said, "After getting us out of trouble back there, you almost instigated a battle, just now! We are not your enemy, woman. When someone needs us policemen, they are not so critical. They just start yelling, '*Help! Police, help!*'"

Remounting his horse, he shouted with an air of authority, "Marchers, proceed in an orderly manner and disburse when you get to the Union." He turned his horse around and led the policemen to ride off. The captain bellowed good-heartedly, making several of his men snicker or laugh, "We'll protect your pretty rears!"

We marched down Sixth Avenue, turned east on Fourteenth Street, then arrived at the conjunction of the major roads of Park Avenue, Broadway, and Fourth Avenue on Fourteenth Street, known as the Union.

Tennie and I, along with Stephen Pearl Andrews and most of the people who had been talking and smoking in our home when I returned from Washington, D.C., six days ago, laid wreaths and garlands at the base of the statue of President Lincoln.

It was a solemn occasion, and the decision had been made there would be no speeches. I complied, but it wasn't easy. After an hour of watching marchers reach the Union, with many more yet to come, we hailed a carriage and went home.

Celebrating winter solstice four days after the memorial march, a small gathering of close friends joined us at our home to celebrate Yule. Our assembly included Tennie with Johnny Green, Theodore Tilton, Ginny from the office, who attended to Byron and Maude, Pearly, James, and me.

Rosie, my lover and pagan guide, taught me about Yuletide. I remembered Rosie's explanation of the origins of Christmas.

"You'll find, dear Victoria…" Rosie spoke as she lit candles, invoked spirits, and conducted rituals in what she called "the olden ways," "nearly all Christian holidays, like Christmas, are based upon pagan rites. *Yuletide,* also the Roman, *Saturnis,* and the Egyptian birthday of Horus, son of Goddess Isis, all celebrate birth and renewal. Horus is usually shown suckling at his mother's breast. That is the source for the Christian figure, the Virgin Mother Mary.

"The Christians gave new names, but kept the meanings of the ancient holidays. Thus, during the early centuries after Christ, villagers would flock into churches, which put on lavish feasts, lit the same candles, and offered plenty of drink on the old tradition days.

"Over time, the original holidays were forgotten by most, and the Christian celebrations dominated. All the Church ever cared about was seizing land, wealth, and power." She sighed. "As it has always been."

I missed Rosie.

We drew a circle to summon the elements, drew the Quarters, North, East, South, and West, corresponding to Earth, Air, Fire, and Water. Ginny helped Byron light a red candle, and we invoked Father Sun God. Maude lit a blue candle and she invoked Mother Moon Goddess. We closed the circle, placing ourselves inside with the invoked spirits. Then we blessed a small Yule log to send a beacon to summon the return of the Sun King to rule over the longer days ahead. Byron shouted, and Ginny kept him from putting his hands in the fire.

Then we did a ritual Rosie had taught me. First each person wrote down something he or she wanted to get rid of in the coming times. We could write as many things as we wanted. After folding the papers and not sharing their contents with anyone else, we would burn the words, and release what we did not want.

Then we wrote down things we wanted to come to fruition in the lengthening of days ahead and we folded those papers as well. Then without sharing what we wrote, one by one we blessed our wishes and, as all of us intoned "So mote it be," threw them into the flames to be released into the spirit world to summon the events. When all of us had finished, we chanted, "And so it is."

Then we opened the circle, releasing the elementals by Quarters, thanking the Sun God and the Moon Goddess for joining us. We wished them well and asked them to go to other circles. We chanted, "The circle is broken and Magick is afoot. Blessed be! The circle is broken and Magick is afoot. Blessed be!" We kept chanting while some got up and danced around the room to celebrate the end of the long night and the coming return of light.

We drank strong mead and ate warm cinnamon buns and honey cakes, which filled the air with a blessed smell. Wisps of black smoke curled into the air from one kerosene lamp. Most of the illumination came from the fireplace and reflections of the joy on our faces.

When we all settled down and lit new candles, the conversation turned to the impact of the solidarity march. The high-pitched voice of Pearly pierced the air.

"I am surprised. The most identifiable impact is rampant polarization, with different factions splitting off and abandoning the synergistic whole we created, much greater than the sum of its diverse parts."

Several of us laughed. It was impossible not to. Pearly understood our love and endless amazement at his erudition, and also at his uncanny ability to almost always make something quite simple sound extremely complex!

"I am surprised," I spoke, "that the papers have made it look like the entire procession convened for the sole sake of showcasing Tennie and me."

Johnny Green, Tennie's *beaux de jour*, entered the conversation. "Agreed. I think the newspapers entirely missed the point and purpose of the parade."

James responded, "I think they had a rare occasion of high acuity and perception. For once they actually got it right."

We were talking about the reports of Tennie and me drawing all the attention, to the point of negating any other message. Many groups did not feel comfortable juxtaposed with strangers they otherwise would never agree with. Simple laborers walking next to women suffrage supporters in front of spiritualists, followed by radical sexual liberation advocates.

"What do you mean, Colonel Blood?" Johnny asked.

"Sometimes, it is of greater service and dedication to play less than the leading role." My husband spoke looking directly at me, leaving no doubt he addressed my behavior. "While not as obvious, often supporting something quietly and from behind the showcase creates a greater impact."

I countered my husband. "And who would have avoided the massacre if I hadn't been in front and listened to Rosie speaking to me?"

"True, my dear. And you also nearly caused a shooting skirmish with the police."

"I did not issue the orders! You did."

My husband turned a beet color. Tennie quickly intervened, "Why shouldn't we lead the parade? We certainly paid for it. At a nice profit to many, I might add."

James tuned to her and gently said. "Because, dear Tennie, we planned to have you in back of the hearse."

"So, we'd walk in horseshit for hours?" Seeing Tennie's faux disgust and pretend fainting, everyone laughed, even the Colonel. Enjoying the moment, my sister leaned forward and, looking up to James, pleaded, "Oh, please, kind sir, let me walk in front of the horseshit!" More laughter filled the air. James walked over to Tennie and kissed her on her head. The tension between my husband and me receded.

Tennie stood, raised her chin, stood erect, twirled a full circle, and proclaimed, "I for one will never apologize for drawing attention!" She smiled a coquettish grin and concluded, "After all, beauty is in the eye of the beholder." Several of the men guffawed and offered polite applause.

"Indeed!" The Colonel declared, "Better to have you both walk in front of the excrement." He paused, and then added, "Perhaps it is possible to be right, and prevent a massacre, and still be able to learn from the experience."

Theodore stood up, shifting the mood toward more serious discussion. "We are at a critical point in several of the movements. It is dangerous to lose constituents who return to their core imperatives." He paused and looked around the room. "There must be a way to bring all the diverse groups together."

"I do admit," I spoke from my seat, "in any restaurant or beer hall, each of these groups would gravitate to themselves and shun the others."

Theodore spoke out. "Therein lies the problem. It is too easy to remain isolated with just your own kind. Then, there is no political power."

Pearly stroked his few long strands of white hair. "Each time there is a faction that separates itself from the whole, it intensifies the splits. Factionalism will prevent the solidarity requisite to achieve critical mass and momentum. That is why I take such umbrage with that ignorant German *arschloch*, Friedrich Sorge. He will destroy the entire movement."

Sorge had ridiculed me, Tennie, Section Twelve, even the unassailable Stephen Pearl Andrews, and all the participants at the march. He accused all of the marchers of shifting the focus and purpose from the doctrine of the I.W.A. to the personal political ambitions of one Victoria Woodhull. He published all this in a German newspaper. The story became the most widely translated and reprinted article ever from that newspaper. Sorge promised to write to Karl Marx and the Central Convention to demand the dismantling of Section Twelve and banishing me, personally, from the movement.

Theodore said, "We are losing about half of the N.W.S.A. who wish to distance themselves from the I.W.A., spiritualists, and sex radicals."

The discussion and the whole situation frustrated me. I stood up and walked over to a small desk and pulled out a piece of bond paper from the center drawer.

"I want to read something to you all." I announced. "I quote this copy of a letter Lizzybeth sent to the papers endorsing me to the N.W.S.A." I unfolded the paper.

> Victoria C. Woodhull stands before us today a grand, brave woman, radical alike in political, religious, and social principles. Her face and form indicate the complete triumph in her nature of the spiritual over the sensuous. The processes of her education are little to us, the grand result is everything."

I declared my fatigue and need to retire. Pearly said he had an important announcement to make. My curiosity piqued, I sat down.

"I am happy to announce," Pearly began, "I have finished my complete translation of the 1848 original publication of Karl Marx's and Friedrich Engel's political pamphlet, *The Manifesto of the Communist Party.*"

Everyone stood and applauded Pearly. He waved his hands to quiet us down. "I have something to add." Tears moistened his eyes as he looked at me and at Tennie. "Courageous and enlightened young ladies, my Yuletide gift to you both is full authorization from Karl Marx himself to publish my translation, the first in America, in *Woodhull & Claflin's Weekly*.

Both Tennie and I rushed to Pearly to give him long hugs and kisses all over his face. The crimson lip marks were slightly darker than his bright-red blush. The other men shook his hand and patted him on the back. The Colonel gave him a big hug, as did Theodore, who lifted the man off his feet.

We distributed sherry glasses and poured to toast the dear man and our mentor, Mr. Stephen Pearl Andrews.

"Wait. I too have a publication announcement!" We all turned to James, waiting to hear what he had to say. He hesitated.

"You opened the gate, Colonel Blood, so go on, charge through." Tennie said, and turned to smile at me.

My husband presented me a tightly wrapped package.

"I thought we weren't giving gifts," I challenged, to cover my embarrassment at not having thought to give any myself.

"Please go on now and open it, Mrs. Woodhull," Ginny said. I think she was more excited than I.

James came behind the sofa and placed his hands on my shoulders. "Something we all worked on while you were traveling."

"Just trying to keep everything equal." Tennie said with a mischievous grin.

"What in the world is going on here? Is this a conspiracy?"

No one answered. Everyone waited for me to open the package.

"Open it, Mama." Byron took my hands and tugged and tore at the wrapping, trying to help me. Zulu Maud clapped her hands in excited anticipation.

"All right, By, I'll get it," I kissed him on the forehead.

"Byron, come sit by me." Ginny patted the place next to her on the divan, and Byron joined her. She patted his leg. He always calmed down when Ginny was near.

I opened the package to find five bound volumes with the same gold leaf title on a deep red-burgundy soft leather binding. The title read:

The Origins, Functions,
And Principles of Government:
A Collection of Speeches and Articles
By
Victoria C. Woodhull

Everyone clapped and cheered. I had no idea they were going to do this. Tears welled in my eyes. "Thank you all, every one of you."

I motioned to the kids, and they ran over and hugged me. "Happy Yule," I said to each of them. "Ginny, will you help the little ones go to sleep?"

"Yes, ma'am."

Little Maud held each person's face and looked into their eyes and solemnly announced, "You will have a wonderful year." When she got to "Uncle Pearly," she added, "And you will talk so I can understand!" We all laughed and applauded. Ginny took the kids upstairs to put them to bed. She would probably have to rock Byron until he fell asleep.

"Now," Tennie inquired, "if you will do me the honor, we can exchange our first books. You can dedicate yours: *Forever Together*, as I have done for you! Oh, and sign it, please."

James announced, "We now have four distinguished authors in our home." He smiled and nodded to each one of us. "Happy Yule, everyone."

"Happy Yule!" We all clamored.

"Blessed Be." Tennie and I spoke as one.

I heard Rosie join us, *And so it is...*

On December 23, my first book was delivered to bookstores for sale. On Saturday, December 30, 1871, *Woodhull & Claflin's Weekly* published the first American translation of *The Communist Manifesto*. As it turned out, 1871 was a very good year.

I was eager for 1872.

Happy New Year!

Chapter 16

POLITIC

January, 1872

"*Vickie, help me!*" Helene Josephine Mansfield, my former co-actress, lover, and personal spy inside her lover, Jim Fisk's and Jay Gould's offices during the gold scandal, burst into our home, shouting and running into the sitting room. I had just arrived home in the late afternoon of Saturday, January 6, 1872.

"Josie, dear, what has happened?" Josie's eyes were red and her cosmetics ran down her face. Clearly, she had been crying a long time. I stood, handed her a handkerchief, and guided her to our brocade settee.

"*He's shot him!*" She screamed in anguish before we sat down. I held her and rocked her big body back and forth.

"Who has shot whom, Josie?"

"Ned has shot Jumbo!" She sobbed. "Twice, once in the left arm and once in his belly." She opened the handkerchief, and filled the delicate lace with snot. She let it fall to the floor and continued to cry.

I knew part of the story from the press. I had cautioned Josie to be careful and not overplay her hand, well, her entire body. She ignored my advice. After meeting Jim Fisk at Annie Wood's brothel over four years ago, Josie became his dedicated mistress. Recently, Josie became enamored with a business associate and partner of Big Jim.

Edward "Ned" Stiles Stokes, a tall and handsome man, sported a long, burly mustache, not unlike my husband's. Ned owned an oil refinery in Brooklyn at Hunter's Point with Big Jim as a silent partner.

For over a year, Josie carried on relations with both married men. I remembered her account of a confrontation with Big Jim.

She told me, "Big Jim was so angry, he shouted, 'How dare you, Josie?' I replied, 'How dare I? You lie with any strumpet or chorus girl you wish, often several at a time… though I can't imagine why.'"

Josie continued, "He shouted at me, 'That is man's condition and prerogative!' Then I told him, 'What's good for the goose is good for the gander!'"

"Jumbo yelled at me. 'You are making a public fool out of me, Josie… After all I have given you and done for you.'"

"'Ha!' I said. 'You would have paid more if I simply stayed with Annie Wood. I see no reason why, when I completely satisfy the both of you as I have for a full year, I must cease. The two of you together barely satisfy *me*.'"

"He bellowed at me, 'Damn it, Josie. I love you… You can't put two locomotives on the same track and try to couple them when they head in opposite directions.' His face turned a dark red and he screamed, '*Get the hell out!*'"

Josie and Ned tried to blackmail Big Jim for $200,000, threatening to tell his wife of the affair and publish a stack of letters Fisk had sent to Josie over the years.

"Jumbo didn't take the bait. He surprised us by telling his wife, Lucy, of the entire affair."

This surprised me too. Truth is, Lucy would have had to be a mole living underground not to know the facts. Besides, Big Jim kept Lucy happy. She and her lover, Fanny Harrod, lived well in an elegant Boston home, all expenses, lavish gifts and travel for both women paid by her generous and promiscuous husband.

I coaxed her, "Go on, my dear."

"Jumbo used his Tammany Hall connections with judges to have Stokes falsely arrested on charges of embezzlement. I feared they'd take him to the Tombs down in Five Points. Instead, the police took

Ned to the Ludlow Street Jail. Jumbo used the opportunity to raid Ned's refinery and take it over by force. Big Jim even ousted Ned's mother, Nancy, from her home and the property she alone owned."

"What happened today, Josie?"

"They released Ned at noon." Josie wailed. "It wasn't so bad at Ludlow. They gave him a cell off the street, where he brought furnishings, his books, and several bottles of his private collection of wines. I went to see him often to keep his spirits up, and other parts." She smiled coyly.

"Today, Josie!" I wanted to find out what I could do to help.

"I was there when the prison released him. I wanted to take him to my new room at Annie Wood's. He would not go with me. He said he had something he had to do." Loud sobbing interrupted her narrative.

I held her hands and then placed her head on my chest. I waited for her to regain her composure. She continued between sniffles, "Apparently, Ned went home, showered, and got dressed. He arrived at the Grand Opera House just as Jumbo was leaving and overheard him telling his driver to take him to the Grand Central Hotel at 673 Broadway.

"I was already at the hotel to plead with Jumbo to stop fighting with Ned. I also planned to beg Big Jim to give me some money, anything at all. I am destitute!" she wailed, and collapsed on the divan sobbing.

Josie's way of relating facts exhausted my patience. I wanted to shake her and demand she get on with it, but I held my tongue. My longtime friend looked distraught enough.

Josie resumed. "I sat in the restaurant on the second floor of the hotel, waiting for Jumbo, when I heard gunshots." Josie started gasping for breath. "I ran out and down the hall to the main staircase, and there Ned stood, smoke still coming out from his Colt House Revolver. Big Jim lay collapsed on the stairs, his blood staining the new Brussels wool carpet."

Josie seemed to drift off.

"Did he die?" I inquired, trying to get her back to the present.

"What? Oh, no." Josie remained far off.

"Well, that is a relief!" I exhaled. "At least Ned didn't kill him."

"When the doctor came and saw the gunshot in the left arm and the black blood gurgling up from deep inside his belly, he tried to find the bullet and stanch the bleeding." Josie spoke very quickly now. "He couldn't do either. The doctor looked up directly at me and shook his head, saying, 'I doubt he'll survive the night.' I screamed."

I held Josie tight and placed her head on my heart. I rocked her for a long time until she finally stopped crying. Only after she finally calmed down did I ask her a few questions.

"Did they arrest Ned?" She didn't reply out loud, but nodded her head.

"Josie, what can I do for you?"

"I have no money, Vicky. Ned made terrible investments. I don't want to go back to Annie's and have to work the trade again."

I thought, *How dare she take advice from anyone other than me.* I let the thought go. Alas, Josie lived just as imperiously and spontaneously as I, if not more so.

"Josie, don't worry about anything right now. I'll message the Hoffman House to prepare a suite for you, and provide you every service you desire. I'll send a note to Annie too, asking her to send several outfits to you, and that you won't be needing to impose on her hospitality."

Josie looked up to me like a lost little girl, her voice a vapor. "I don't know how I'll repay you, Vickie."

"You don't have to. These are gifts of friendship, not a loan." I gathered her up and went to my carved walnut desk, inlayed with leather and tooled with gold. I handed Josie two one-hundred dollar bills. "Go shopping and buy yourself something. I'll join you, if I can."

She departed.

I had to return to Washington, D.C. for the N.W.S.A. meeting starting on Wednesday, January 10, a new moon. I would draw the energies necessary to move the campaign forward during the waxing of the moon. The Senate Judiciary Committee invited Elizabeth Cady Stanton to meet and address the committee on the twelfth.

I planned to travel south on Monday. Instead, I found myself heading north, accompanied by James. We trained to Brattleboro, Vermont, to attend the funeral of Jubilee Jim Fisk, Jr., who died in the early morning after Ned Stokes shot him. Many from the financial world would be in attendance.

We met with J. P. Morgan in the dining car. We talked briefly about Big Jim, Tammany Hall's losing the election, and the markets. J. P. returned to his sounding the alarm over the costs of the transcontinental railroad and especially the primary construction contractor for the Union Pacific, Crédit Moblier of America.

Speaking in whispers, he told us, "If W & C brokerage holds any stocks, sell them now while they are high. Go short on railroads and banks…"

"But, J. P.," I interrupted, "our trading capital is sorely depleted."

"I'm sorry, I did not know." He looked confounded, probably wondering how we could use up or lose all our money so quickly.

The Colonel queried, "How long will we have to support the short positions? If it becomes a prolonged period, say over half a year, we simply cannot." Sadly shaking his head, my husband added, "It has been a long time since we worked with the Commodore." Both men looked at me.

"What?" I asked.

J. P. seemed to be calculating things in his own head. "I'm trying to figure a way to lend you the money and split the profits. The problem being the timing of the markets is tricky and never a sure thing. You would have to pay for the shorts if the shares don't fall."

James questioned, "Will it take more than six months, J. P.?"

"It may take a few months or up to two years. There is no way to know. A crisis is definitely coming."

"Thank you for your ongoing guidance, J. P." I spoke my heart. "W & C simply cannot afford an open-ended liability at this time."

"After all you have done for me, it is but a small expression of the gratitude and debt I feel," the increasingly powerful financier acknowledged.

At the funeral, people quoted the Commodore, who reportedly eulogized Big Jim, saying, "James Fisk, Jr. played big. I admired him for that. I did not always like the way he played. I have lost a powerful adversary, one of the few who kept me sharp and keen. Perhaps now, he'll give me stock tips from beyond."

The Reverend Beecher declared: "The grandiose Big Jim Fisk was a man of giant appetites and absolutely void of any moral sense." The self-righteous Usurper slithered further into his poisonous hypocrisy.

Two days later, I appeared at the opening session of the National Woman Suffrage Association on the platform between Elizabeth and Susan. Lizzybeth wore a heavy black silk toilette; I donned a blue broadcloth suit and double-breasted chinchilla coat; Susan came in a high-neck, silver and black gown with a white collar and blue tie. Joining us were Isabella Beecher Hooker and Lucretia Coffin Mott.

Several days ago, Elizabeth and I had argued with the other leaders to allow men to attend and support our convention. Though some resisted, they acquiesced, perhaps due to the fact I printed the programs for the convention at no cost. James sat in crowded Lincoln Hall with Pearly at his side.

As president of the association, Elizabeth spoke passionately. She implored that unless the current session of Congress passed a declaratory act, women must go to the courts to secure voting rights. Elizabeth also took the time to challenge all who would discard me and declared unequivocal support for me as an N.W.S.A. spokesperson.

Susan spoke next. She reported she had traveled 15,000 miles and pleaded the cause in every state in the Union. Then, she confirmed she knew of no better warrior and leader than Victoria C. Woodhull to push the movement forward. She concluded by criticizing the President. "President Grant, in his message, has remembered all classes and conditions of men to Congress, but never said "woman" once! We have made up our minds, he is not the woman's candidate for the White House." She returned to her seat during a standing ovation.

I began my speech quietly, in the third person, forcing people to listen intently.

> The president of the American Association of Spiritualists stands before you, as the present bearer of the standard of the Equal Rights Party. She has, as gallantly as she knew how, breasted the dark clouds and storms that have risen over her path, but she has done so devoutly and reverentially, always recognizing that she is but a humble instrument…

I reached out to labor constituents, promising I would be their voice in a later speech. I promised to lift their spirits and banners high. They applauded. Then, I spoke to the spiritualists, raising my voice phrase by phrase.

> Let all spiritualists and all reformers and all evangelicals for radical change tear from their political banners the names of Democrat and Republican, which have become a stench in the nostrils of all thoughtful

people, and tie to the breeze that more comprehensive name "Equal Rights"… Let them battle for it stoutly and devotedly, never faltering until it shall be planted in the hearts of the populace, on the dome of the Capitol and in the hands of the goddess of Liberty, in whose keeping it may be entrusted for all future ages.

This is our destiny.

Isabella rose and looked at me in admiration. When she arrived at the podium she opened, "If all of us, reformers and spiritualists alike, have brains enough to comprehend and souls enough to come up to the position to which Victoria Woodhull invites us, then we, together, will rule this world."

After Isabella, the *grande dame* of our movement stood and approached the podium. On her way, Lucretia Mott acknowledged me, taking my head into her hands and kissing my forehead. Then she kissed my hands. I started to cry, and the crowd went crazy.

Everyone who spoke took the time to affirm my importance to the N.W.S.A. This was not entirely altruistic or loving support. I had helped many of them obtain highly paid speaking appearances. After the "Free Love" speech, as requests for speaking engagements deluged our offices, I provided many in the hall endorsements and recommendations.

Nonetheless, I felt humbled and relieved to be back in favor with my sisters.

The following day, I delivered the keynote address as the last speaker of the evening. I returned to the core subject expressed in my "Memorial." I admonished Congress to issue a declaratory act supporting the proper interpretation of the Fourteenth and Fifteenth Amendments. I told the assembly, "American women shall lead the way to forming an international, worldwide Constitution of the United States of the World!"

I was interrupted when the convincing orator for spiritualism and one of its leaders, Laura Cuppy Smith, rose from her seat. She declared to the assembly:

"Mrs. Woodhull told you last night we already are citizens under the provisions of the Fourteenth amendment, and we should no longer petition Congress; but if they failed to pass a declaratory act, we should invoke the Constitution and rally about us the people who elect Congressmen and Presidents. We shall pass our measures over the heads of Congressmen and leave them to be educated by the results. I am not a hero worshiper, but my whole soul does homage to the principles of which I deem this grand woman to be the inspired representative."

Thunderous applause broke out. Anthony tried to call for order, telling Laura she did not have the podium. Laura continued to boom her voice throughout the hall.

"In the few remarks made by Victoria, a sensation was created. The earnestness of her manner, the apparent truth of her convictions, and the real gift of imparting to an audience her own enthusiasm riveted the attention of the audience. She answered the objection that suffrage would result in unsexing woman."

Susan B. Anthony screamed at Laura Cuppy Smith. "You are out of order, madame, and you must be silent." Susan rapped her gavel over and over. The crowd jeered her. Laura went on:

"I am certain neither Victoria Woodhull, myself, nor any other of our sisters on the platform are here for their own sake, but for the sake of all our children and those who should come after them. We stand here, advocating truth as we understand it; realizing we are opening the door for thousands of men and women who shall come after us."

Before Susan could start rapping her gavel again and screeching her objection, Elizabeth Cady Stanton reached over to still her hand.

"Let her speak," the activist Abigail Scott Duniway shouted. She and her husband published a suffrage news weekly, *The New Northwest*, in Portland, Oregon, which commenced its publication a week before *Woodhull & Claflin's Weekly*. Mrs. Duniway turned to the crowd. She raised her hands up to motion all who remained seated to rise. She turned around to look at Susan and then pointed to Laura Cuppy Smith, "Let her speak!" The entire assembly picked up the chant.

Addie Ballou, a powerful delegate from Wisconsin, then called a motion which flamed the already fiery enthusiasm. She stood up and declared, "I nominate Victoria Woodhull as our association's nominee for President of the United States."

Numerous shouts of "Second!" "I second," "I call for a vote," "Victoria for President!" filled the hall as it began a new chant, "Vote! Vote! Vote!"

Susan tried to speak, but the assembly shouted her down. She shot me a deadly look. I put my hands upward to quiet the crowd and impose some semblance of order. I thanked the assembly for its confidence and suggested others on the podium with seniority should be rightfully considered. Eventually everyone calmed down. I continued my planned speech. I presented the full legal arguments and answered anticipated objections. To conclude, I challenged Congress thus:

> Woman, as citizens, have the same rights under the Constitution as all other citizens. We have the power to inaugurate it. I do not propose we shall wait fifty years, nor even five years, for justice. We want it here. We want it now.

I drew a deep breath, raised both my arms, raised my eyes to the heavens and proclaimed, "*Here and now.*"

Lincoln Hall exploded into chants of "*Here and now. Here and now.*"

Almost as one body, the crowd rose and stood up continuing

their chant. They chanted, "*Here and now,*" as they filled the isles and headed for the exits. "*Here and now,*" accompanied the crowd all the way out to the street.

I called after them, "Good night, good ladies. Go forth and bear the message to all."

As James and I entered the dining room of the Willard, after fighting through the smoke-filled, boisterous lobby, Joseph Willard nodded in our direction from his table. His wore his woeful countenance as a sackcloth. My heart went out to him. I stepped away from my husband, and went over to allow Joseph to kiss my hand. He motioned to my table and said, "Please enjoy our hospitality. Perhaps tonight, without my sad tale influencing, you will be able to finish your dinner."

"May James and I join you for dinner tomorrow night?"

"Of course, Victoria. It would be a pleasure and an honor." He smiled at me. "I hear you are conquering our little town, yet again." Before we departed, he offered, "Colonel Blood, perhaps I can save you from the company of so many commanding women. We could enjoy a gentlemen's dinner, followed by a cigar and brandy."

James looked to me, "Perhaps it would be best, my darling." I nodded my consent.

"Well, I will be jealous of you having the pleasure of Joseph's company two evenings in a row." I kissed my husband, nodded to Joseph, and traversed the dining room.

I walked to the table where Elizabeth, Susan, Esther Hobart Morris, Matilda Joslyn Gage, Dr. Mary Edwards Walker, and Belva Ann Lockwood were seated. Esther, from the Wyoming Territory, a contemporary of Stanton, became the first female judge in America. She had introduced an amendment that gave Wyoming women the right to vote in December, 1869.

Matilda, a decade younger than Stanton, grew up in an Underground Railroad safe house. Her parents hid and transited escaped slaves to freedom. Her politics ran as radical as mine, if not more so. We both agreed woman need not argue legalities. Indeed, woman has natural inalienable rights as citizens by birth. Both Mary and Belva were accomplished women in their own right, and six and eight years my senior, respectively.

"Will Tennessee Celeste not be joining us?" Dr. Mary E. Walker asked, clearly disappointed. "I swear, your little sister does more for dress reform in one appearance than all my essays and articles."

It was an impressive statement coming from the Civil War heroine. Dr. Walker served as the first woman surgeon in the United States military. She crossed battle lines to care for the wounded of both armies and civilians. Due to her bravery and constant risk to help the wounded, Mary received the highest military honor, the Congressional Medal of Honor. General William Tecumseh Sherman and General George Henry Thomas had recommended Dr. Walker for the medal, and President Johnson on November 11, 1865, pinned the shining medal displayed on her chest.

"I'm sorry, Dr. Walker, Tennessee will not be able to join us. She has several speaking engagements and is taking care of our brokerage and newspaper businesses."

"Call me Mary, Victoria, unless you intend to salute me." Everyone at the table laughed.

"I know Tennie read your *Hit: Essays on Women's Rights*, published last year. She often quotes your arguments on the medical benefits of loose, non-constraining clothes for women, as justification for her... very liberated manner." Again, some mild laughter circulated the table, with the notable exception of the ever-stern Susan B. Anthony.

Mary replied, "She does take everything a step or two further, but then, you both do. I applaud it!"

I had read her articles and essays on clothing reform. Dr. Mary thought it unhealthy for women to be weighed down by a score of pounds of lacings and petticoats and crinolines. I also knew her citation for the Medal of Honor:

> Whereas it appears from official reports that Dr. Mary E. Walker, a graduate of medicine, has rendered valuable service to the Government, and her efforts have been earnest and untiring in a variety of ways,... and that she was assigned to duty and served as an assistant surgeon in charge of female prisoners at Louisville, Ky., upon the recommendation of Major-Generals Sherman and Thomas, and faithfully served as contract surgeon in the service of the United States, and has devoted herself with much patriotic zeal to the sick and wounded soldiers, both in the field and hospitals, to the detriment of her own health, and has also endured hardships as a prisoner of war four months in a Southern prison while acting as contract surgeon;
>
> Whereas by reason of her not being a commissioned officer in the military service, a brevet or honorary rank cannot, under existing laws, be conferred upon her; Whereas in the opinion of the President an honorable recognition of her services and sufferings should be made. It is ordered, That a testimonial thereof shall be hereby made and given to the said Dr. Mary E. Walker, and that the usual medal of honor for meritorious services be given her.

Dr. Walker wore a simple, rustic, long-sleeved, dark green tunic over a man-styled linen shirt, suspenders, and brown heavy woolen trousers. The medal hung on a short blue ribbon with thirteen stars in white, in rows of two, four, four, and three. A five-pointed star rested on a laurel leaf crown. Each section of the pentagram had a green laurel leaf displayed before it tapered to the star points.

Her shoes could only be described as utilitarian. She wore no makeup at all. She moved haltingly due to a muscle illness acquired as a result of being held in close confinement as a prisoner of war in a Southern military prison.

I asked Dr. Walker, "How does it feel to be the most honored woman in the Civil War?"

"Don't know if I am!" She laughed. "There is Sallie Gordon Law, 'The Mother of the Confederacy.' She had a hospital for all wounded soldiers, gray and blue. Sallie came to my aid when she visited me in prison and demanded better treatment for a fellow officer. My condition changed; I moved to private accommodations with sanitary conditions. She probably saved my life."

We took a minute to order our suppers. Elizabeth and Susan ordered the same dish, the mutton stew. Belva and Matilda ordered the roasted pheasant, and I ordered the pork shank slowly cooked in port wine with roasted potatoes.

Dr. Mary said, "Normally, I do not recommend cuts of pork, no matter how tasty. But I do like the taste, and I trust the Willard kitchen, so I will join Victoria with a shank of a pig."

"May we *please* dispense with all discussion of accouterments and food? With all respects, Mary!" Susan paused and looked at me to emphasize her lack of respect for me. Mary turned to me and shrugged. Most would not dare dismiss so out of hand a recipient of the Medal of Honor.

Susan seized control of the discussion. "We are gathered to help Elizabeth prepare for her comments to the Senate Judiciary Committee tomorrow, are we not?" She gave each of us a chastising glare.

Susan motioned to Belva, "Let me introduce Belva Ann Bennett Lockwood. She is a year and a half away from completing her law degree at the National University of Law in Washington, D.C. next to Georgetown. She…"

"I think I can make my own introduction. Thank you." Belva spoke clearly and formally.

I had reprinted in the *Weekly* a *Chicago Tribune* article about her, reporting that the trustees of the Columbia Law School had rejected her application… "because her feminine form would surely distract the male students."

Belva handed out copies of something she wrote. "I have drafted resolutions for your review, approval, and submission to the committee to confirm and adopt into law the proper interpretation of the Fourteenth and Fifteenth Amendments to the United States Constitution." She paused and formally nodded toward me. "I based the resolution on the arguments in Victoria's "Memorial," delivered to the Congressional Committee last year."

We all perused the resolutions. Belva wrote in the language of legalities and government, very different from my oratory.

"Well done!" The daughter of a judge on the Supreme Court of New York state, Elizabeth Cady Stanton, who studied the books in her father's library, proclaimed for all of us. "I will read these into the record at the Senate tomorrow."

Matilda Gage pitched in, "I agree. This is perfect. Exactly what we need."

"We will all be there to support you, Lizzybeth," I announced. Susan sneered at me. *What has gotten into her?*

After the main course, Susan walked over, took my arm, and guided me away for a talk. A few steps away from the table, she whispered, "You have had your way all convention long." She dug her fingernails into my wrist. "Tomorrow is Elizabeth's day, not yours!" Her mouth got close to my ear. "If you must attend, be mute."

I left her to go to the bathroom. James saw me and started to get up from the table where he was dining with Joseph Willard. I shook my head and raised my right hand, fingers pointing upward with a slight push to tell him to stay in place.

During dessert I asked Belva, "What are your goals, Belva? What do you envision yourself doing with a law degree?"

Before she answered, I had a vision of her future. She would stand before the Justices of the Supreme Court to argue cases. She would write and convince the government to allow all females and people of color who are duly qualified to practice law in all federal courts. I even saw her running for President in some future election. She would become a well-known advocate for suffrage, equal pay, and especially equal legal rights. As I returned my focus to the present, I saw she watched me with fascination.

"Where were you, just now?" Belva asked.

"I had a view of the future… your future." Before she could ask me about it I restated my inquiry. "Your vision, Belva?"

"Equitable legality. In other words, equal rights under the law. Every woman should hold all the legal rights of any man." She paused and thought about her answer. "I want to pave the way for other women, just as Dr. Mary here has done, and as all of you are doing. I want to practice law at the state bar level and argue before the Supreme Court!"

"Most laudable," I commented.

She concluded, "As long as woman is not accorded full legal rights, respect, equal pay for equal work, and suffrage, I shall not rest."

I took both of her hands in mine. "Belva, you will have a long and rewarding life, accomplishing many of the things you desire. Some, like universal suffrage, will not occur in your lifetime." I looked into her eyes. "You will become an instrument for universal equality. This is your destiny."

I let go of her hands, and quietly uttered, "And so it is."

Several women constituents of the senators on the Judiciary Committee met me in the enormous, marble-floored rotunda of the Senate building. Senator Matthew Hale Carpenter from Wisconsin exited the Judiciary Committee chamber and tried to ignore our group. He wore a grey three-piece suit with blue pin stripes. His vest revealed an expensive gold fob. He parted his receding hairline far to the right, allowing a few thin strands of hair to cover his baldness. I noticed his unusually small hands.

"Senator Carpenter," Addie Ballou shouted, "I am a constituent of yours from Wisconsin." She rushed over to him. The pack surrounded him.

"That cannot be, my dear." Senator Carpenter gave a snide, sardonic grin. "To be a constituent you must be able to vote to put me or someone else in office." He flummoxed Addie into silence.

"Do you not know to whom you are speaking, Senator?" I planted myself directly in front of him. "Addie Hart Ballou is a highly honored Civil War veteran; known to troops as 'The Little Mother,' and commissioned by the Surgeon General Erastus B. Wolcott. She is a favorite daughter of your state."

"Nice to greet you, Mrs. Ballou. I am sure we will be friends in the future." He tried to push through our wall of women.

"Senator," we blocked his path. "I am Victoria Woodhull." His eyes widened. "You are an important lawyer and key member on the Senate Judiciary Committee. Do you not intend to hear Elizabeth Cady Stanton address your august committee?"

Exasperated, the Senator said, "I will read the full record later. I assure you a majority of the female gender in Wisconsin are my friends."

"Yes!" I replied. "And according to gossip and rumors, scores of other ladies as well, in several other states." I heard Senator Carpenter rivaled the depths of hypocrisy of the Usurper, Henry Ward.

"Watch your tongue, woman! I have had reporters and other

rabble-rousers placed in federal custody at Fort Stevens for less than your insolence."

I remarked, "This from the same lawyer who secured the release by hung jury of Sherman Booth, the abolitionist charged with raping his fourteen-year-old babysitter, Caroline Cook."

"You are an indecent woman!" the Senator declared.

"If my memory serves, Senator," I continued, "young Caroline claimed that one night while caring for his children overnight, Booth had fondled her and later raped her. I believe you described the young girl to the jury as a "little gypsy" and "strumpet" to exonerate Sherman Booth."

"You have been warned. I will summon the Senate Guard and place you in custody."

"Fine!" I challenged the Senator. I raised my arms to touch my wrists together, "I await the shackles. I have no objections." I shouted. "I do not resist. *Arrest me!*"

People in the large hall turned their heads in our direction. "If every woman who is overpowered by a male and forced into the sexual act is a strumpet, gypsy, or spell-casting witch, then please make me a martyr for woman suffrage. Go ahead!" I shouted.

I calmed myself. I raised my right arm and extended my middle and forefingers to point at him like a curse. "Arrest me today, and tomorrow five hundred women will fan out across this nation to inform the public of the character of the office holders such as you, who *mis*represent them!"

Senator Carpenter forcably moved Addie aside and ran from the lobby.

Out of the corner of my eye, I could see Susan B. Anthony pursing her lips and glaring at me like some angry schoolteacher.

I had no idea what she objected to. More importantly, I didn't care.

Chapter 17

INDOMITABLE

New York City
February–April, 1872

To carry the nomination of a national political party, I would have to incite the working class of men to rebellion. I sought to foment revolution. We started to lay the groundwork for what needed to be formed. We gave it a temporary name, The People's Party.

Saturday, February 17, was an eventful day. First the *Weekly* published an announcement that I would deliver a new speech, "The Impending Revolution," on Tuesday evening, February 20, at the New York Academy of Music. Tickets sold out before the evening, and over the next ten days, the resale price skyrocketed from $0.50 to over $10.00. Everyone wanted to hear what I had to say next, after my "Free Love" speech the previous November.

Second, *The Newark Register* published a review of Tennie's and my new books. The book review complimented and encouraged:

> We have received copies of two books, which just now possess considerable interest for many people. They are entitled respectively, *Constitutional Equality, a Right of Women,* by Tennie C. Claflin, and *The Origin, Functions and Principles of Government,* by Victoria C. Woodhull. We have examined these books carefully, not only for the sake of the subjects treated of, but because of the discussion which has

been called out in the past few weeks about these two remarkable women.

Careful examination of their book fails to show anything so very startling in the doctrines put forth in them, however distasteful they may be to many. They advance many strong arguments for giving the women the right to vote, for a remodeling of the marriage laws, and, in fact, for the general renovating and making over of society. Some of these are new, and some not so new, but they are very well put, and will be found not uninteresting, even to those who are opposed to the doctrines advocated.

Third, *Harper's Weekly* published an egregious cartoon from the satirical pen of Tom Nast, captioned, *Get Thee Behind Me (Mrs.) Satan*!

I appeared with a black cape attached to large bat-like wings with claw points along the fringes, and snake-like horns growing from my forehead over my hair. I held a placard stating: "Be Saved by FREE LOVE." Several steps behind me on a rocky cliff overlooking a deep canyon stood a woman with a cane walking perilously close to the edge, facing the abyss. The woman walked bent over, burdened by one baby in her arms, a second tied to her waist, and bearing the entire weight of a husband holding a liquor bottle high on her back, his feet not even touching the rough stones.

After dismissing the cruel portrayal of me as Mrs. Satan, Tennessee and I had to laugh. Unwittingly the cartoon justified the demand for equality and fanned the flames of curiosity, adding to our popularity.

Tennessee declared, "Nast is despicable, but..." she broke out laughing until she could control herself to continue," what a perfect depiction of our cause! Not only is the woman horribly burdened by prevailing laws and morality, unless she follows you, she will plummet,

along with her two children and drunken husband, to certain death."
She laughed for a long while more.

"It hurts to see myself demonized!"

"Vickie!" She pointed at the cartoon. "You are trying to lead her to safety, across the narrow precipice."

"I do see your point, Sister, but how many readers will see it your way?"

"I believe it was you, older sister, who taught me that a message need not be blatant to be clear, that a coy aversion of the eyes could be more compelling than a declaration."

"Yes. Rosie calls it a "sub rosa" communication, obscure but with a lasting impact."

"Exactly!" Tennessee pronounced, her enthusiasm contagious. "The great Tom Nast, no doubt completely unawares, just showed the world that you are their only salvation!"

"Certainly not his intention!" I started to laugh with Tennie.

The huge red brick building housing the New York Academy of Music stood at East Fourteenth Street and Irvine Place. The four-thousand-seat venue designed by Alexander Saeltzer, who designed the Astor Library at about the same time, had four tiers above the main hall and housed the opera. I loved how sound amplified inside the massive structure.

Just after sunset, small streams of people started forming on the streets around the theater. By 7:00 p.m., a crowd on foot inundated Fourteenth Street past Third Avenue and up to The Union. Irvine Place, Fourth Avenue, and Broadway were all shut down.

Tennie came to me backstage as I prepared for my appearance. She informed me, "When the doors were opened, a mad rush ensued. Speculators on tickets who waited until the last moment to get the highest price lost out, as the ticket takers ran for cover." She continued to distract me. "People were trampled, Vickie. The police could not maintain order. The crowd collapsed an entire wall, which fell out onto the floor of the lobby."

"Is everyone okay?" I asked. "Do I need to go out there and calm things down?"

"*No!*" Tennie said, terrified. "Wait until they all find a seat or place to stand."

She ran out to gather more information and report back to me. I wanted to go out to the lobby, but harkened to Tennie's advice. She came back after a few minutes. I went over my speech, but her excitement broke my concentration.

"Fuller than full, Sister! There is not a single inch of space in the entire theater. Beyond the seats, it is filled half again with people—everywhere!"

Gathering myself to walk out onto the stage, I requested, "Tennie, please make sure all the windows and doors remain wide open. Otherwise I fear I may faint from the heat... too many people..."

"Vickie! What do I always say?"

We answered together. "You'll be fine!"

I gathered myself, fluffed my shoulder-length, loose, curly hair, and straightened my black velvet dress with three flounces. I wore a black satin pannier under a cutaway blue jacket and a large, royal blue necktie. As I walked to the podium and spread my notes, the rambunctious crowd shouted, jeered, and pounded their feet.

I knew my theme. Only a revolution could move us from the authoritative suppression and injustice of the present to equality, freedom, and justice in the future. We simply had to believe all humanity is one, the very same no matter what their gender or station in life.

Despite the cacophony, I began:

> A Vanderbilt may sit in his office and manipulate
> stocks or declare dividends by which in a few years he

amasses fifty million dollars from the industries of the country, and he is one of the remarkable men of the age.

The crowd became silent as I named the richest man in America.

But if a poor, half-starved little girl should take a loaf of bread from his cupboard to appease her hunger, she would be sent to the Tombs.

Several hearty, "Aye's" circled the hall.

An Astor may sit comfortably in his sumptuous apartments and watch the properties earned and bequeathed to him by his father rise from several million of value to fifty million, and everybody bows before his immense power.

But if a tenant of his, who has been discharged by his employer because he did not vote the Republican ticket, fails to pay his month's rent to Mr. Astor, the law places such tenant and his entire family into the freezing street.

Applause broke out as I took small sips of my water.

Mr. Stewart, by cunning practices, succeeds in twenty years to accumulate from customers whom he entraps into dealing with him thirty million dollars. He does some public works and suddenly the world proclaims him a philanthropist.

But, let a wretched immigrant come along with a bolt of cloth from the old country, which he smuggled into the country and thus can sell for a lower price, and then Mr. Stewart, who paid the tariff, is authorized by the law to place the man in prison *and* seize his fabric bolt.

I talked to the guilds, labor reformers, unions, finance reformers, free lovers, spiritualists, and suffragists. Each group's supporters cheered when I finished addressing them. I concluded with a challenge to all these groups.

> Christianity of today is a failure. Jesus himself would decry many who speak in his name. True religion will not shut itself up in any church away from humanity; it will not stand idly by and see the people suffer from any misery whatsoever.
>
> It is naïve, foolish, nay imbecilic for a Christian to say, 'I have nothing to do with politics.' It is the bounden duty of every Christian to support that political party which bases itself upon human rights, and if there is no party existing, then go about to construct one.

The noise multiplied many fold when I finished. Luckily, the police sent for reinforcements and there were enough on hand to manage an orderly disbursement of the crowd.

Reading through the papers the next morning, I sat dumbstruck. I turned to look at my husband.

"Is it really possible only one newspaper covered the speech last night?" I asked. "Only one?"

"Only the *World* ran the entire text of the speech, even though they were all there." The Colonel sighed. "The *Herald* and *The Sun* mentioned the crowds around the Union, but nothing from the speech. The rest were silent."

"How can that be, James?"

"Last night we attacked the one true sanctity in this city. The ruling power—money!"

On March 2, the *Weekly* announced the planning of "a grand consolidating convention" to take place in May, concurrent with the anniversary convention of the N.W.S.A. A less-than-enthusiastic response trickled in. Susan wanted suffrage to be a plank in the platform of one of the major parties. I did not think her attempts pragmatic, and while pursuing them she further factionalized the suffragist cause.

The same issue of the *Weekly* took other newspapers to task for lack of coverage and conducting a campaign of disinformation.

"Woodhull has at last secured an audience," wrote the *Herald*.

I answered in the *Weekly*:

> Has the Herald forgotten her audience at Lincoln Hall, Washington, D.C. of 2,500 persons; at Cooper Institute shortly after, of 3,000 persons; at the Rink, Cleveland, of 4,000 persons; at Steinway Hall, according to its own report, of 3,000 persons; and at Music Hall, Boston, of 3,000 persons? Verily it is convenient for this great paper to be slightly oblivious to facts contained in its own columns....
>
> As we have said, the Academy of Music was crowded... The most radical and revolutionary doctrines were enunciated, the great mass of that great audience accepted them, and the great mass of the people will accept them when permitted to hear dispassionately.
>
> They may not approve of our methods, but our purposes and principles are so in accord with the spirit, necessities, and tendencies of the age that the people can only be made to reject them because they are not allowed to fairly consider them.
>
> If the press do not, the people do, concede that our civilization and our religion are failures. The intelligence

of the age, presented in editors and politicians, is wholly unable to solve the simplest problem in the purposes of government. They do not understand any of the great questions demanding answer, in the hands of a people ready for remedy or revolution.

Scurrility, slander, ridicule are fit weapons in the hands of such men, and for a time conceal their ignorance, incompetency, malevolence, and dishonesty, but the mask must fall, and then the people will lose confidence in editors just as they have in political hucksters and tricksters.

We do not object, we court, fair and honorable criticism. We are ready to publish such criticism; for we have no interest in error. But such the press of New York is incompetent or unwilling to render. So editors are steeped in corruption—the creatures of party and plunder—educated in the school that accepts as axiomatic: "To the victor belong the spoils."

What more can we expect, than dishonorable and dishonest renderings. But the day of retribution is at hand, and not one who has bartered principle for commercial gain, political, or party purposes shall escape.

There was another fact connected with the meeting, which, though of considerable significance, was not noticed by the press. On the stage were two large banners, bearing the following inscriptions:

"What lack I yet?" Jesus said unto him; "Go sell all thou hath and give to the poor."
—St. Matthew XIX. 21, 22.

"Neither said any that what he possessed was his own; but they had all things common."
—The Acts V. 32.

A few days later, after a deafening silence and my emotions spiraling downward, a beacon of hope and providential solidarity arrived in the form of an epistle from my dear friend, the woman I considered to be my true mother, Elizabeth Cady Stanton. Reading the words in her flowing script and seeing the seal with her initials fortified my resolve. I published the entire text in the next *Weekly*.

THOSE WHO KNOW US.
Tenafly, N.J., March 10, 1872
Victoria Woodhull—
Dear Madam:

In answer to an article in your paper of last week, "A word to the wise," let me say, that, as far as I am concerned, I ask no higher praise than to have it said that you—maligned, denounced, cruelly and wickedly persecuted by priests, politicians, press and people— ever find a warm and welcome place in my heart, and by my side.

You are doing a grand work, not only for your sex, but humanity. I have read all your speeches and bound volumes on political and social equality, and I consider your arguments on the many national questions now moving popular thought, able and uncontradictable.

Do not let the coldness and ingratitude of some of your sex wound you, while such noble women as Lucretia Mott, Martha C. Wright, Paulina W. Davis, Matilda Joslyn Gage, Mary J. Davis, Susan B. Anthony, and Isabella Beecher Hooker, are one and all your sincere friends.

The latter spent a few days with me not long since, and one night, as we sat alone hour after hour, by the bright moonlight, talking over the past, the present, and the future, of woman's sad history and happier destiny, and of your sudden and marvelous coming, she abruptly exclaimed, "that little woman has bridged, with her prostrate body an awful gulf over which womanhood will walk to freedom."

Many of us fully appreciate the deep ploughing, sub-soiling, under-draining you have done for public and private morals in the last year, and while the world sneers at your blunders, we shall garner up your noble utterances with grateful hearts. The Weekly is all that the most fastidious could ask this week. I specially liked the editorial, "Positive and Negative Reform." I am amused in reading the Republican and Democratic journals to see how firmly fixed these old parties are to the faith that they are to live on indefinitely, when the democracy per se has been in the grave at least four years, and the Republican party is in its dotage, so weak in the knees it cannot bear its own weight, and so blind it cannot tell its own friends. The Labor party, in refusing to do justice to woman, has sealed its doom also.

Now is the time for the advance guard in all reforms to organize their forces into a "People's Party."

Those who understand the true principles of government, if they would save what we have left of freedom, and secure equal rights for all, must now come to the front and be leaders of numbers, as well as leaders of thought. If we desire a peaceful solution of the many questions now looming on our political horizon, the best men and women of the republic must assemble at an early day, and take counsel together. When we get the united thought of man and woman on national questions we shall have the complete humanitarian idea, that harmony in political action hitherto unknown.

It is strange men do not see this; and yet, not so strange after all; for when we talk to them of the "feminine element" they think of the frail specimens of womanhood who preside in their households, and say what possible benefit could these bring to us? Forgetting that the poor, cribbed slave would be transformed in freedom, and in her native dignity, develop powers that he never dreamt she possess. Today, in a constant state of dependence, she reflects the man by her side, not her own true nature, or her God.

We shall never know what a true grand womanhood is, until woman has the full liberty to bound her own sphere, and you, dear friend, are doing much to usher in that glad day.

ELIZABETH CADY STANTON

We had to move from our gilded home, a reflection of the last two years' blind commitment to avarice, when the landlord informed James and me he could no longer allow us to stay.

"Too many of the neighbors and the vendors in the area have complained about your conduct! Here is your Notice and Termination."

Tennie wanted to challenge him, and James wanted to argue. I told them to let him be.

"Cowardice will always succumb to public opinion." I stated. "Let us focus on a smooth transition."

We moved in with my oldest sister, Margaret Ann Miles. The tiny house forced us to let the children sleep in our room. The sole benefit of such tight quarters: The rest of the Claflin horde could not follow us. I apologized to Maggie, who had to sleep on the couch across from the hearth. She acted glad for the company.

Sadly, on April 6, my first husband, Dr. Canning Woodhull, died. Utica, my sister born between me and Tennie, told the coroner she suspected foul play, an intentional overdose of narcotics. All the papers carried the story, and once again reported the depths of my moral turpitude and depravity. The autopsy showed my first husband had died of pneumonia, his body ravaged by drug and alcohol addiction for over twenty years. Hardship dominated my life with Canning, but he did help me at age fourteen to escape from my pa. I would always remain grateful for that and for the children.

The same day Canning died, *The Weekly,* as planned in advance, issued an invitation to a new national party. This time a group of "The Undersigned Citizens" endorsed a convention of a People's Party for the purpose of nominating presidential and vice presidential candidates to be held at Steinway Hall concurrent with the May 9 and 10 third-anniversary convention of the N.W.S.A. The undersigned included the entire podium and speaker roster of the Washington, D.C., convention and more. I included the name of Susan B. Anthony, although she traveled the Midwest and could not be reached.

Mail from everywhere flooded our offices at *Woodhull & Claflin's Weekly.* Daily, new constituents confirmed their attendance at the formation of the new party. Each week new names were added to the full roster of the previous undersigned. Many of the letters arrived stuffed with cash.

Isabella Beecher Hooker sent me word she wanted to meet at my sister Margaret's home late afternoon on Friday, April 26. I arrived at the house as Maggie served a steaming pot of tea with some toast points slathered with fresh butter.

"Mind if I join you?" I jested as Isabella jumped up and turned to give me kisses on both cheeks. "Dear Bella, you have been crying."

"I fear he is going to kill himself." Bella sniffled and then broke out sobbing. She pulled out a handkerchief and blew her nose. Her nostrils were inflamed from repeated irritation of blowing into the cloth. Clearly, she had been sobbing for quite some time. Her facial resemblance to Henry Ward always amazed me.

"Bella, surely your husband is not that ill."

"What? Who?" Bella questioned me.

"I hope you don't mean John!" I said, exasperated.

As usual I found myself at a quandary, trying to help my troubled friend. She started sobbing anew. She reached into her purse and handed me two letters. At least now, I might be able to find some foothold in her swirling despair.

The top letter showed the flowing script of Isabella. I read it out loud:

> Dear Henry,
>
> Mrs. Stanton told me precisely what Mr. Tilton said to her when in the rage of discovery he fled to the house of Mrs. Bullard and before both narrated the story of his own infidelities as confessed to his wife, and hers as confessed to him.
>
> The only reply I made to Mrs. Stanton was that if true you had a philosophy of the relation of the sexes so far ahead of the times that you dared not announce it, though you consented to live by it.

I read the rest silently. Then I turned to the second page. The scratchy, very slanted scrawl made the note difficult to read.

"Is his writing always this difficult to decipher?"

"Yes. We used to joke about it in the family." Bella smiled wanly.

My Dear Belle,

I do not intend to make any speeches on any topic during the Anniversary Week. Indeed, I shall be out of town. I do not want you to take any ground this year except on suffrage. You know my sympathy with you. Probably you and I are nearer together than any of our family. I cannot give reason now for all my decisions.

Of some things I neither talk nor will I be talked with. For love and sympathy I am deeply thankful. The only help that can be grateful to me or useful is your silence and silencing influence on all others. A day may come for our converse. It is not now. Living or dead, my dear sister Belle, love me for always.

> *Your Loving Brother,*
> *HWB.*

I didn't know whether to applaud, laugh, or vomit. I had heard the variations of this cornered beast before. The manipulation of the sympathetic Bella exhibited masterful artistry. Bella eagerly swallowed the bait full. So transparent in intentions, it approached both satire and hysterics. The letter accurately demonstrated the machinations of the Usurper. I wanted to retch. I had to address Isabella, who was quivering and shaking before me.

"I want you to stay with me a fortnight…"

"But Victoria, I can't." She recommenced bawling.

"Or as long as you want, sweetheart." I reached up and gently guided her head to my chest. "I will send word to Frank and Emma Moulton to assess the situation daily and report the minute they believe there is any sign of danger."

After a few moments, Bella stopped her wailing. She sniffled and blew her nose.

"Thank you, Vickie, I just didn't know whom to turn to."

"I'll put you to work on arranging the N.W.S.A and People's Party convention. Please keep Stanton informed."

"How can I thank you?"

"Your love and support are all I ask. I think I am getting the best of the bargain. I really do need your help setting things to run smoothly."

The sins of Henry Ward Beecher, combined with his uncanny abilities for getting people to do or not do the things he wanted, astounded me.

Chapter 18

I ACCEPT THIS NOMINATION

May, 1872

ay and June were the months national conventions chose their platforms and elected their nominees.

I received reports the first week of May stating two of my errant knights traveled to Cincinnati, Ohio, to attend the Liberal Republican convention from May first to the third. Cincinnati was southwest of Homer, where the townspeople ran my family out and I watched my home burn to the ground. It took a six- to seven-hour train ride to cover the one hundred and fifty miles.

Theodore Tilton and Whitelaw Reed met Susan B. Anthony, who attended in a misguided attempt to force suffrage onto the platform. Whitelaw, seeing an opportunity and probably wanting to restore the dignity of another high-minded newsman, hired Theodore to report on the convention for *The New York Tribune*.

According to my sources, the convention evolved to oppose the corruption and cronyism under President Grant's leadership, or lack thereof. Recently acclaimed for *The New York Tribune's* exposure of Big Boss Tweed's ring suffocating New York and national politics, Horace Greeley seized the position of the popular gentleman among the "liberal and progressive" (for men!) delegates.

On the sixth ballot, Greeley outlasted Charles Francis Adams, Sr., the former United States Minister to the Court of St. James, and former vice-presidential nominee with Martin Van Buren in 1848. To win the nomination, Greeley agreed to select the current governor of

Missouri, Benjamin Gratz Brown, as his running mate. Once word got out Brown supported Greeley, enough delegates followed.

The choice of Horace Greeley ended any possible chance for the party to exercise influence on the current political structure. The suffrage movement did not lose anything, as Susan failed to convince anyone to insert a single word into the platform for suffrage. In fact, Tilton proclaimed, "Woman's rights would not be an issue in this campaign." Scorned and ignored, Susan gave the press a statement. "None but the liberals deride us now, and Theodore Tilton stands at their head in light and scurrilous treatment."

On the days leading up to the combined conventions of both the N.W.S.A. and the People's Party, I spoke every evening to gather support through attendance. Monday, speaking at the American Labor Reform League, I encouraged financial reformers to participate.

"I hope this league will take an active part in both the organization and the campaign."

I spoke at Cooper Union to the American Anti-Usury Society on Tuesday. Wednesday, I addressed a collection of free-love advocates. Thursday, the night before the convention, I took the ferry across the Hudson to address a convention of the Spiritualist Society at Union Hall in Jersey City.

All the travel made me tired, but the opportunity ahead energized me anew. On May 8, upon arriving home late at night, I received a brief note From Lizzybeth:

> Be advised, I support you. If Susan continues and
> tries to block you from unifying the People's Party with
> the NWSA, I will not support her. In fact, I will resign
> and then give the keynote as planned denouncing any

further fractionalization of the woman movement. As you have so boldly proclaimed, UPWARD and ONWARD! You have my vote.

The stage was set. Now it was time to see how the actresses would play things out.

On the propitious Friday morning of May 10, 1872, Steinway Hall filled to capacity with both women and men. Many were my guests, exhorted to attend to lend support to a unification of the N.W.S.A. with the People's Party. The crowd displayed their impatience, shouting demands for the meeting to commence. On the rostrum, Susan B. Anthony, Elizabeth Cady Stanton, the President of the N.W.S.A., and Elizabeth Stuart Phelps sat in three dark green satin and velvet wing chairs, tufted by brass buttons.

Phelps founded the Woman's Bureau. She actively supported Susan and was a prolific writer. I admired Phelps. A profound spiritualist and active political reformer, Phelps worked with Dr. Mary Edwards Walker to reform woman's dress. Phelps and Dr. Walker delighted in Tennessee's widely publicized disregard for the constricting norms of modern fashion.

The press lambasted Phelps for an alleged indiscretion of stealing less than a $1.00 worth of candies from Macy's Department store, and I rallied to support Phelps in the *Weekly*. We accused the rumor mongers of waging a campaign of false facts and distorted proportions, in order to discredit a powerful and openly verbal female critic. She surprised me by still supporting Miss Anthony.

Susan rose to speak.

"We shall maintain a strict order here in this third convening of the National Woman Suffrage Association." Anthony removed her reading glasses and scowled at the crowd. "No person shall approach the lectern unless duly recognized by myself as convention chair."

Thanks to the janitorial staff familiar with me, I emerged from the wings and shouted. "Well then, please recognize me, I am Victoria Woodhull." I waived and blew kisses to the crowd.

The attendees went wild. It took a while, but I calmed them down so I could continue. "The eyes of the world are upon this convention. Its enemies have sneered and laughed at the idea of combining reformers for any organized action. They deem woman knowledge insufficient to organize, and therefore *we* are not to be feared as political opponents. Are they right?"

"*No! No! No!*" The crowd rose to their feet. I had to stop for the unified chant.

"You are out of order!" Susan tried to shout over the reverberating voices.

"*No! No! No!*" The crowd enjoyed overriding the chairman.

"*Order! Order!*" Susan screeched at the top of her voice.

I motioned the crowd to quiet down. It took a few moments, but they settled back into their seats.

"I have even heard some professed reformers say they don't want anything to do with 'Those who do not belong to our clique.'" I lifted both hands and shrugged as if to ask what the crowd thought.

Loud booing interrupted me. When the booing subsided, I went on.

"This elitism will not be tolerated and will not succeed!" Cheering arose.

"I hope that all friends of humanitarian reform will clasp hands with one another and together form a more perfect union, a movement for change!" A long ovation ensued.

Susan yelled. "You are not recognized and have no right to speak!" She pounded the gavel in her hands over and over… to no avail.

The crowd settled down so I could speak. "I move the N.W.S.A. agree to an open dialogue to discuss consolidating with the People's Party."

Boisterous shouting and stentorian applause thundered. Then they chanted, "Victoria! Victoria! Victoria!" My name resounded throughout the hall.

Susan hammered her wooden gavel on the podium. She screamed, "The chair does not recognize any motion and asks the lady to remove herself from the stage."

Shouts of "Second!" resounded in the hall. Then a new chant went up. "Let us vote. Let us vote."

Susan gave me one of her looks that could freeze blood, and screamed again, "There will be no vote." She rapped the gavel so hard it broke in her hand. "The lady is out of order." Seeing no tangible response, she moved up to the edge of the stage, as if blind to the abyss separating her from the people. She vehemently yelled at the crowd. "The Hall is for the *exclusive* use of the N.W.S.A. Anyone who does not like my decision can leave the hall."

Loud booing ridiculed Susan. Elizabeth Cady Stanton rose and walked toward her lover. I overheard Stanton's words to Anthony. "Sit down, Susan. You are making a fool of yourself!" Susan turned to say something. Stanton raised her hand stopping any response. She added, "Your myopic obsession with control has once again divided the movement placing woman against woman." She motioned Susan to return to her seat. "I will not be a part of this." Shocked, Susan stumbled to her seat.

The crowd sat down, waiting to hear what Mrs. Stanton had to say. She walked to where I stood, kissed me on both cheeks, and addressed all the attendees.

"This saddens me, terribly." Silence descended on the hall like a final curtain. "I have served as President of the N.W.S.A. since its formation three years ago." She stiffened her body, I believe, to set her resolve. "If we who claim the right to vote cannot even honor the first amendment and hear all voices, then I shall not serve."

She turned and looked at Susan. "Madame Chairwoman, I accept your directive. I do not abide your decision, and I will leave the Hall. I will return this evening to deliver the keynote address out of respect to *my friends*." The last word smelled like burnt flesh.

Susan stood up, and shaking her head she approached her partner. She wailed, "No. Lizzy, no!"

Lizzybeth reached out her arm with the palm of her hand facing Susan, commanding her to stop and keep her distance.

Elizabeth Cady Stanton turned to the crowd with a trembling lip and announced, "I hereby resign as President of the National Woman Suffrage Association." She quickly walked off the stage.

I moved to the edge of the stage and proclaimed, "Come one, come all. All voices will be honored and heard tomorrow morning at 8:00 a.m. at Apollo Hall."

Cheers broke out as I walked down from the stage by the side steps and walked along the front row to the center aisle. I heard the voice of Elizabeth Stuart Phelps.

"I nominate Susan B. Anthony as the new President of the N.W.S.A."

Many from the audience began to stand to exit Steinway Hall, but they waited for me to pass first. Ada Kepley, the very first woman to graduate from law school in America, and forbidden to practice law in her state of Illinois, yelled out.

"I second the nomination!"

I proceeded to climb the center aisle toward the exit. At least two-thirds of the entire crowd filled the aisles and followed me out. Just as I walked from the theater into the lobby, I heard Susan call for a vote. Many voices said, "Aye." There were no "Nays."

Susan finally got the helm to captain the N.W.S.A. ship. I wondered, *Does she know her command is rapidly sinking?*

We draped the Apollo with long, white banners printed with declarations and trimmed in ribbons of blue and red:

UNIVERSAL SUFFRAGE OR REVOLUTION

THE WORLD IS OUR COUNTRY

TO DO GOOD, OUR RELIGION

GOVERNMENT PROTECTION AND
PROVISION FROM CRADLE TO GRAVE

INTEREST ON MONEY IS A TAX ON LABOR
PAID TO THE WEALTHY

NATIONALIZATION OF LAND, LABOR,
EDUCATION AND INSURANCES

EQUAL RIGHTS, EQUAL PAY FOR EQUAL WORK
PEACE AND CO-OPERATION

THE UNEMPLOYED DEMAND
WORK FROM THE GOVERNMENT

Apollo Hall filled with attendees, about half men and half women. A more disparate group of opinions and passions had likely never assembled. We sought unification under one banner. Each and every faction mattered, but each promoted its own agenda. We needed to bring them together into a single party and movement. I hoped to forge solidarity.

At 8:00 a.m., James DeNoon Reymert, my good friend and lawyer *par excellence*, opened as the convention chairman.

"Come to order. Find a seat. Come to order!" He quickly seized authority, like an experienced cowboy breaking a wild horse. As the crowd quieted down, he laid the foundation for the convention.

"We have a lot of work to conduct." Reymert began to orchestrate. "We must ratify a name for the party, deliberate and ratify a platform, and finally nominate candidates for President and Vice President of these United States."

Yelling and cheering bounced off the walls. Without a gavel in hand, Reymert calmed the crowd down. "We have many diverse groups here." As I looked across the hall, I noticed Lizzybeth and Isabella Beecher Hooker were absent, no doubt sitting in the audience at Steinway Hall out of compassion for Ms. Anthony.

Reymert proceeded to call out each group as if conducting a roll call. "I see Belva Lockwood, Laura Cuppy Smith, and Ada Ballou sitting with suffragists. Hello to the spiritualists gathered around the Horace Dresser lecturer Dr. Caroline Hinckley Spear and her husband John, who founded the utopian community Kiantone in upstate New York." He nodded his head in their direction.

"There you are, the financial reformers sitting with Angela Tilton." Reymert laughed at the juxtaposition of opposing views, "J. S. Sands, I see you lead a group of Christian capitalists, while William West to your right leads the Christian communists." Many in the crowd laughed.

"Ah, there are the free love advocates gathered with the well-known abolitionist, Moses Hull." I knew Mrs. Hull gave her blessing to Moses to tour and practice "divine impulses" with his partner Mattie Sawyer. "Ezra Hervey Heywood is at the same table. The man has a wide reach of beliefs. He is an abolitionist, financial reformer, and anarchist, and he strongly supports woman rights and free love. We may need your help, Mr. Heywood!" Again, the convention laughed cheerfully.

"Here are the Communist International constituents organized by Theodore Banks and Marie Stevens Howland. Looking across the floor, I see labor unions, guilds, and agricultural and political reformers."

Reymert addressed perhaps the best-known delegate. "Dr. Edward Bliss Foote, your book *Medical Common Sense* about sex education, sexual hygiene, and teaching women how to avoid conception, has some sales, I hope." The crowd roared with laughter as Dr. Bliss waived his hand. His book had sold nearly three hundred thousand copies! He presented to the public many of the things I had learned from Rosie.

Reymert declared, "Every one of you will be heard, if you so desire… *And* you will let me move the business of the convention forward." Again, cheering broke out.

"The first order of business will be to formally ratify a name."

So many names were presented that any given a loud approval when announced would be paired with another. Reymert announced the pairs one-by-one and asked which name the assembly preferred. Human Rights Party won over People's Party. National Radical Reformers won over Cosmo-Political Party. Equal Rights Party won over both National Radical and Human Rights Party. Eventually, everyone cheered the new name: The Equal Rights Party. Everyone had a voice, worked together, and made progress. A grand start.

"You see," said J. D. Reymert, "together we can work effectively. The chair recognizes Tennessee Celeste Claflin, who will speak prior to our forming committees to deliberate on the planks of our platform."

The crowd cheered and applauded my sister as she walked to the podium. She wore her provocative blue silk suit, the one she had worn to the Washington, D.C., meeting of the N.W.S.A. some sixteen months ago.

"Thank you, thank you." Tennie gestured to the crowd to settle down. She nodded to the suffragists and the spiritualists, and continued to make eye contact around the hall. "My message today is short and simple—unusual for my sister or me!" Applause filled the hall.

"*Unity!*" She proclaimed. Loud cheering ensued.

"We are gathered here to unite and consolidate! This must be done. Divided, our voices will not be heard... even if some of us are beautiful!" My twenty-six year old sister preened. The crowd went wild. Tennie acknowledged their adoration by blowing kisses in all directions.

Tennie became serious. "Let each of us approach our committees with this thought in mind. Our time is now. We are one." The roar of the crowd almost overpowered Tennie. She waited a few moments and then continued.

"*Unsere Zeit ist jetze, wir sende eins,*" Tennie declared, and the Germans howled. "*Notre temps est maintenant, nous sommes un!*" Tennie spoke, and the French cheered. "*Il nostro tempo e adesso. Noi siamo uno.*" The Italians stomped their feet.

Tennie beamed radiantly. She had united them... by speaking their languages. "*Wǒmen xiànzài shì shíhòu, Wǒmen shì yījiā rén.*" The Chinese heard my sister speak to them, and they stood and yelled at each other, as they did on Mott Street.

Tennie bowed to the crowd, enjoying the moment. Speaking in a heavy brogue, Tennie announced, "I've nay forgottun ya... *Tiocfaidh 'ar la, Taimid ar cheann!*" The Irish rose. The entire assembly clamored, cheered, and went crazy. Our genius languages expert, Pearly, had coached Tennie into a polyglot! Tennie bowed, then curtsied and waved to all. She walked to the wings, blowing kisses everywhere.

It took a while, but the chairman regained control.

"Colonel Blood will moderate the committees. Any disputes you cannot resolve yourselves, bring to either him or me."

The convention divided into twenty committees. Each committee included representatives from each faction. Tennie and I floated from table to table, making suggestions and offering words or concepts designed to appeal to, or at the very least placate, the delegates. On occasion, I promised action on another position if the one at hand got approved.

By 4:00 p.m., after hours of discussions and arguments, one by one, the convention ratified the most progressive reform platform in the history of American politics.

Reymert read the twenty-one planks out loud. They included universal suffrage; equal legal rights; new code of civil law; new code of commercial law; nationalization of monopolies; universal tax; free and open trade with all nations; equal pay for equal work; uniform pay; abolition of the death penalty; government employment of unemployed; government paid vocational training; universal coverage of insurances; work injury compensation; welfare for the needy; equal access to work; child labor laws; freedom of all religions, beliefs, and practices; prohibition of corruption; and sexual freedom.

Reymert proclaimed, "Great work! We did it!" Everyone congratulated themselves and their neighbors. General cheering followed.

"We will break for dinner. Please reconvene here at 7:30, two hours hence."

Cheering filled the air.

Solidarity induced euphoria.

The convention did reconvene at 7:30. At exactly eight o'clock, Tennie and I stood outside the doors of the hall. We choose outfits to prove conformity would never bridle us. In fact, we dressed eager to set new courses in fashion as well as politics.

We wore matching black silk suits with a skirt, polonaise, and long, close-fitting jacket. Our skirts were trimmed on the bottom with deep side-pleated flounce, with wide puffs and narrow side pleating. Our polonaise closed diagonally on the left side and looped at the bottom. Our black jackets were bordered with black velvet faille, as were the cuffs, collar, and pockets. Broad royal blue silk ties adorned our necks. Both of our entire outfits exposed a new departure in woman dress, released of the burden of weight, and slimmed down to the contours of the female form. The only difference between my sister and me was that I wore a white rose in my lapel, and Tennie dressed sans rose, petticoats, or corset. She did enjoy her freedoms… and so did everyone else!

We flung the doors open and marched hand in hand into the assembly. Cheers rose up, and thunderous applause filled the hall. Women and men mobbed us, wanting to hug and kiss. I received this affection, Tennie less so, perhaps because anyone hugging her would intimately feel her body, not layers of unseen clothing.

"Woodhull, Woodhull, Woodhull!" The crowd created pandemonium with the same words repeated over and over.

The chairman asked the tumultuous assembly, "Do you want me to recognize Victoria C. Woodhull?"

Just when I thought it could not get any louder, the sound became waves that could capsize Vanderbilt's ship *The Colossus*, or perhaps a government. They continued their thunder until I reached the podium.

I waved to everyone. Once people finally sat down, I spoke quietly.

> I want to thank all six hundred and sixty-eight delegates from twenty-two states and four territories! And the other thousand plus people gathered here on this momentous day!

After a long pause due to deafening cheering, I resumed.

> Together, we have forged a new political party, smelted from diversity and tempered on the anvil of common purpose.

More cheers.

From this convention will go forth a tide of revolution that shall sweep over the whole world. Go where we may in the land, there we see despotism, inequality and injustice installed where there should be freedom... equality... and justice.

I had to pause for the cheering to calm down.

How can equality rise when one-eighth of our populous is illiterate? How can we plant the seeds of justice when a very few rich hoard all the money produced and own all the land? From what well will freedom spring when the wealthy class poison our waters with corrupt politicians?

I paused to let the crowd scream itself hoarse.

Shall we be slaves to escape revolution? I say *never!* I say, *away* with such stupidity! *We*, together, must *demand* our rights, though the heavens fall. Who will dare to attempt to unlock the luminous portals of the future with the rusty key of the past!

Cacophony interrupted me. I took the moment to gather my thoughts before my conclusion.

Today we have struck the match to ignite the revolution that shall sweep with resistless force, if not fury, over the whole country, to purge it of political chicanery, despotic assumption, and the whole of industrial injustice.

The prolonged chanting of my name seemed a melodious paean of love exalting the namesake of the hall, the Greek god Apollo. I trembled in their adoration. During the ovation, I walked off to the wings of the stage, waving to all.

A booming voice called out. "I place the name of Victoria C. Woodhull for presidential nominee of the Equal Rights Party and future Presidentess of the United States of America!" The voice belonged to the Honorable Judge A. G. Carter from Cincinnati, Ohio, my birth state.

Shouts sounded from everywhere. "Second!"

Chairman Reymert held the nomination in abeyance to pose the motion. "I call for a vote on the seconded motion that Victoria C. Woodhull shall be elected by this convention to become the nominee of the Equal Rights Party for President of these United States of America." He called triumphantly, "All in favor, say aye."

The roar of "ayes" lasted for nearly fifteen minutes. Returning to the podium crying tears of joy, I addressed my people.

"Ladies and gentlemen, I sincerely thank you for the unanimity with which you accord me this great honor." I gulped for air. "For over a year I have worked constantly, heart and hand, in the good cause, sometimes receiving your approval and sometimes receiving your rebuff."

Shouts of "Never," "Not me," "I didn't," and, "Not true," sounded from every direction.

I quieted everyone down. "Now that you thus honor me, my gratitude and humility before you know no bounds." I raised my head and reached my arms wide to embrace the entire convention. I declared, "I shall endeavor to be true to our united principles and the platform of our party." I paused, looked upward through the roof, and then raised my voice to a full forté to be heard in the firmament.

"*Together, we will march into the future.*"

I stood beside Chairman Reymert for close to half an hour before he could address the final decision to be made. He called for nominations for vice president.

I had discussed with several supporters a truly audacious suggestion. I know some of them considered the idea, but I had no idea if they would support it.

Belva Lockwood stood. "I nominate for vice president of the Equal Rights Party, another woman to achieve a full female ticket, Laura Cuppy Smith!"

There were cheers and jeers. From the floor came other suggestions for nominees. Voices nominated General Benjamin Butler, based on his political acumen. A minister nominated Colonel James Harvey Blood, so my husband and I could take Washington, D.C., in the blessed and supportive state of marriage. One Indian tribal leader stood and nominated the Sioux nation chief, Spotted Tail, saying, "Because the Indian had possession of this land long before the colored man and white man arrived." Utopian and heir to his father's industrial fortune, Robert Dale Owen received a nomination, as did the absent, Theodore Tilton and Wendell Phillips. The entire assembly started to factionalize back into its diverse origins.

Finally, Moses Hull, a well-respected advocate for Christian spiritualism, famous for a recent series of debates with ministers and preachers where his clear logic and gifted oratory prevailed, arguing that spirituality is the highest culmination of Christianity while alive on this earth, rose to submit yet another name. I had met with Moses and we talked over my most far-reaching desire for vice president.

He projected his strong voice, knowing how to lead a crowd up to the mountain top.

> I submit a name that will echo throughout history
> as a fitting acknowledgement for a life time of service.
> His nomination alone will create a new level of equality
> for every American.
>
> I nominate the most accomplished and influential
> Negro man of our times, whose career forces America

to think and face complex issues and disturbing history, especially that of slavery. He has spoken, written, published and lectured on a majority of our plank issues, including: Woman suffrage, temperance, peace, land reform, free public education, and the abolition of capital punishment.

I nominate the great and powerful person of color, Mr. Frederick Douglass. The oppressed sex is represented by Mrs. Woodhull, let the oppressed race be represented by Mr. Douglass.

I could not contain myself. I rushed up and joined Moses Hull at the podium. Reymert said, "The chair recognizes our presidential nominee."

"I know Frederick Douglass. I respect Frederick Douglass. There could be no greater imprimatur and sanctification of our ticket than to choose Frederick Douglass." I took a deep breath and proclaimed, "I second the nomination of Frederick Douglas as the vice-presidential candidate of the Equal Rights Party."

The chairman posed the motion, and a healthy if not vast majority voted in favor.

At close to midnight, Reymert told everyone to get a good night's sleep and reconvene on the morrow when the hard work of organizing, fund-raising, and campaigning would begin. He concluded by congratulating the convention.

"You should all be proud of yourselves! We have nominated two representatives, one of woman and the other a Negro man; these are the roots of America. Personally, they are true, honest, and capable. Our country will be happy indeed, when it shall so far triumph in equal rights as to prove its justice to woman and man, without distinction nor prejudice to class, race, or gender."

On Tuesday, the papers ran their coverage of the convention. It ranged from impressed, to neutral (very few), appalled, and outright bigoted. I met for tea with Tennessee, Lizzybeth Stanton, Isabella Hooker, and Laura Cuppy Smith at the Colonial Fraunces Tavern at 54 Pearl Street, where Paul Revere and General George Washington met upstairs in the Long Room.

"Congratulations Vickie, or should I say Madame President?" Isabella asked.

"Oh, stop it!" Everyone but Lizzybeth laughed. Clearly, the split with a twenty-year ally and partner, hurt her deeply.

Tennie joined the banter. "I think 'Your Highness' would be more fitting."

"You might as well take a few days to enjoy it, Vickie," Laura Cuppy suggested. "We are all still giddy with the excitement of the nomination."

I rose and lifted my teacup. "I propose a toast to woman in every country to the far reaches of the globe. United we stand!"

Four woman pioneers repeated, "United we stand."

Elizabeth Stanton sat silent. Then she spoke solemnly. "I am not so sure about united. We have created a powerful precedent and meaningful bridge for others to follow into the future. But," Elizabeth's eyes welled with tears, "we are so divided… three separate divisions!" She wiped the tears from her eyes. "Who will take us seriously?"

"I hope everyone, if we do our jobs right," I said.

Stanton set down a priority. "Raising funds is paramount. We have to assign districts."

I responded, "We sold only $5,400 of the bonds Colonel Blood and I designed and printed. I must say, the tiny amount disappointed. Perhaps we will sell more after the other conventions." I tried to remain positive.

Isabella pitched in. "Really? They were so professional-looking. I thought one of the banks issued them."

"Victoria," Lizzybeth addressed me, "I have read your bonds. The principal is entirely at risk, and no assets are pledged." She hesitated. "I am not sure I can or want to sell them."

Laura spoke up. "I will cover the West Coast. California will provide funds. I will also work the spiritualists.... After all, we can communicate in the ethers!" She paused to smile knowingly. "I am sure Albina L. Washburn will cover the West out of Denver, and Abigail Duniway the Pacific Northwest."

"I'll handle New York, Connecticut, Pennsylvania, and New Jersey," Tennie pledged. "I'll get what we can from the labor unions and a few capitalists." She shrugged her shoulders.

Stanton raised her head. "I will work the suffragist networks, asking for money and encouraging all to get behind the only train willing to take women on as passengers." She paused to look each one of us in the eye.

"Each of you has to take a solemn vow, starting now, to convince five score to become advocates for our cause. Each one of them must convince a score more and then ten for every one of those. Every night until November, twenty thousand women or more should be speaking every night!" Seeing her immersed in her vision warmed my heart. Her fire rekindled. I knew it would help her to deal with her loss of Susan.

"I will work with all of you," I pledged. "Moses Hull will work the Midwest and South from Kentucky." I looked across at our Beecher. "Bella, you can work New England as best you can; I know the other Beechers will try to thwart your every effort. Perhaps Ezra Heywood could be of some assistance."

"I will," said Bella. "But I do not know how successful I will be." She took out a copy of yesterday's *The Boston Advertiser*, which reran a commentary from Isabella's second oldest step-sister, Harriet Beecher Stowe, published after my "First Pronounciamento" sixteen months ago, back in April, 1870. The headline read:

TRUE THEN, TRUER NOW

Whoever sets out to be President of the United States must be ready to have his character torn off from his back in shreds and to be flailed, mauled, pummeled, and covered with dirt by every filthy paper all over the country.

And no woman not willing to be dragged through every kennel, and slopped into every dirty pail of water, like an old mop, would ever consent to run as a candidate.

It's an ordeal that kills a man. It killed General Harrison and it killed old Zach Taylor. And what sort of brazen tramp of a woman would it be who could stand it and come out of it without being killed?

"I am so sorry, Vickie." Bella assumed a burden not hers to bear.

"You never have to apologize to me for anything, Bella." I wanted to break the shackles her family imposed on her. "I am grateful for your loyalty. We can only be responsible for our own words and deeds." She stood and came over to me. I rose to embrace her.

Sitting back down, I wondered, did Harriet Beecher Stowe think so little of woman? Did she believe a woman could not manage the country? Perhaps she just thought I would go away or be killed. Either way, I intended to prove her wrong.

I closed our little session with, "Upward and onward!"

In unison all four repeated, "Upward and onward!"

As everyone said their goodbyes with warm hugs and kisses all around, I tugged on Lizzybeth's arm to stay behind.

"Lizzybeth, have you heard anything from Frederick? South Avenue?"

"No, nothing."

"Do you think he will respond?"

"I know Frederick well enough to say with confidence he would have wanted to be asked in advance of being nominated. Something you might have thought about, my dear."

Tennie spoke to me about an idea.

"Vickie, since Jim Fisk, Jr.'s death, has anyone tried to take the honorary lead of the 9th Regiment of the National Guard?"

"Not that I have heard of. Since it's all colored, it's chronically short on funds. What are you thinking, Sister?"

"I believe the heroic men of the all-Negro unit could use our patronage and publicity."

"I don't think the Colonel wants to return to military uniform, especially after the parade."

"Not him… me!"

It took me a minute, I realized what she proposed would affect another breakthrough for woman. "Is this something you really want to do, Tennie?" I knew the answer from the zeal in her eyes.

"Yes. I think it sends an important statement that we see no difference between man and woman of any religion, origin, or color in the ability to serve our country."

"You won't have to go off to war, Tennie."

Tennie smiled her best combination of a winsome and coquettish grin. "No, but won't I look dashing in the uniform I'll have made up?" Tennie glowed.

"Indeed, you will!" We both laughed. "How are you going to go about it?"

Without hesitation Tennie presented her plan of attack. "We will deploy as practiced." She giggled at her use of military terminology. "We will not approach them directly, we will be indirect from the sides and rear, and we will use the press to create momentum!"

"Do so in English alone, dear sister." We both giggled. "Study the Regiment and its history. Contact the former commanders." Tennie impressed me. I wanted to contribute.

She jumped up and ordered, "Forward, march!"

"Yes, Colonel!" I stood and saluted the honorary colonel to be. Tennie laughed and I smiled at how many times I had said that before—to James.

Cleverly, Tennie delivered a letter to Joseph Tooker, the manager of the Grand Opera House, the former domicile of Jim Fisk, Jr. Tooker did exactly as Tennie assumed he would. Seeking publicity for himself and the Opera House, he delivered a copy of the letter to the *New York Herald*. He also forwarded the original to Captain Griffin of the 9th Regiment, an all-colored unit of the National Guard. The *Herald* printed this copy:

Dear Sir,

I understand that the Colonelcy of the gallant 9th regiment of the National Guard made vacant by the death of James Fisk, Jr., still remains unfilled.

I protest that it would be wrong to the memory of the dead leader to select as his successor anyone who lacks the magnetic influence he possessed over his soldiers.

The brave men of color of the 9th, known as 'Hawkins Nouaves,' fought gloriously under General Benjamin F. Butler to take Forts Hatteras and Clark in North Carolina. They served valiantly in six other battles, including bloody Fredericksburg.

Your connection with the Grand Opera House brings you in social contact with the committee having the selection of colonel in hand. See the gentlemen please, and tell them

I will accept the position and pledge myself, if elected, to give such impetus to recruiting, that in thirty days the 9ᵗʰ Regiment will be foremost in the state.

There can be no objection to me, save that I am a woman. Permit me to remind those who urge such position, that Joan d'Arc was also a woman. While I do not make pretensions to the same military genius she possessed, I may state that it has always been my desire to become actively connected with the service, and I have always gratified a passion for studying its rules and tactics, in which I am well versed.

I have no doubt that this communication will at first sight occasion incredulity as to my intentions, but permit me to assure you I am deeply and forcibly in earnest in the matter.

Yours very sincerely,
Tennessee Celeste Claflin

On June 4, Elizabeth came to see me. She appeared to me as visibly shaken as at the commencement of the N.W.S.A. convention.

"Victoria, Frederick's house in Rochester has been burned to the ground."

"Oh, my God! Please tell me he and Anna survived."

"They both survived. But the fire consumed the entire house. Apparently, he lost precious journals, his personal histories of the last two decades."

I lowered my head. I thought back to our discussion the night we shared the stage for a lecture near the beginning of my lecturing career. I told Lizzybeth.

"He told me once, in that deep, rumbling voice of his, 'There is an unseen danger the more recognized you become. Some will exalt you, but others will swear to destroy you.' I told him, I had received threats." I looked up into Lizzybeth's eyes and cringed at the fear mixed with the anger I saw. "He warned me, 'They're not idle threats, please pay attention.' I remember him pressing my hands and gazing into the distance."

"He gazes into the future, just as you do."

I told him I understood, but for him that did not suffice."

"What else did he say?" Mrs. Stanton spoke, abrupt and demanding.

"He admonished me, 'Be alert and try to envision and foresee the consequences of each of the choices you make.' I tried to convince him I would, but he continued. 'At the risk of belabored redundancy, I reiterate, not doing so can invite catastrophe.' I should have listened and followed his advice."

I hoped Lizzybeth would offer me some compassion, empathy, or forgiveness, but she simply stepped back and away from me.

"Your recklessness has injured two of my best friends, first Susan and now Frederick." She looked up at me with neither mercy nor malice. "Sometimes you make it hard to support you, Victoria, very hard."

The Republican convention took place in Philadelphia at the Academy of Music Hall. I had spoken there on a few occasions. The three tiers of galleries above the mezzanine, a few steps up from a wide orchestra, comprised a grand venue.

The telegraph kept everyone up to the minute with reports going long into the night. This made the event the most talked-about political convention in history. The public got to participate. It was not a normal convention, at least not as to the presidential nominee, although the choice of vice president held some minor intrigue. The entire procession celebrated the past four years with the confidence of another great four years to come.

The wire described the interior as transformed into a Garden of Eden with fragrant floral arrangements, bunting along the face of the galleries, and huge portraits of Washington, Lincoln, and Grant. They draped the entire outside of the building with long flowing flags from every state, as well as the national flag. Delegates worked on the orchestra level, ticket holders filled the mezzanine, the public filled the balconies to overflowing, and listeners populated telegraph offices across the nation.

The public gathered to hear the dots and dashes converted into words, creating three days of total national absorption. Senator Henry Wilson, Chairman of the wartime Committee on Military Affairs and the Militia, won the nomination for Vice President over Schuyler Colfax, the incumbent.

Susan B. Anthony tried to get a plank declaration about universal suffrage. According to reports in the papers, she assailed anyone who would see her, offering support of suffragists—who could not vote. Her efforts resulted in the following language, immediately after the third plank, which prevented discrimination of all rights for any reason, with the singular omission of gender.

The fourth Plank of the Platform read:

> The Republican Party is mindful of its obligations
> to the loyal women of America for their noble devotion
> to the cause of freedom. Their admission to wider fields
> of usefulness is viewed with satisfaction, and the honest
> demands of any class of citizens for additional rights
> should be treated with respectful consideration.

Elizabeth sent me a wire:

THE PHILADELPHIA SPLINTER!

Cowardice caused Mr. Tooker, the manager, to cancel the mass meeting to ratify my nomination scheduled to take place at the Grand Opera House. I went and demanded a full cash return of our fee. He would not return the funds!

From Eighth Avenue and Twenty-Fourth Street I went directly to Cooper Union, between Third and Fourth Avenues below Seventh Street. I knew Steinway Hall and the Apollo were booked. I went to see if I could possibly rent the basement hall two days hence.

The manager of bookings told me both Coopers were on the premises. He went off to ask if they could see me. Peter Cooper, the industrialist and magnanimous benefactor of The Cooper Union, always treated me with generosity and kindness. His son, Edward, the current chairman, respectfully took all the advice and input his father wished to impart.

The manager returned looking disappointed. "Sadly, the Messrs. Cooper are presently involved in a large planning meeting." So many old friends and associates were turning their backs on us.

"Please express my gratitude for all their past support." I turned to leave.

"Mrs. Woodhull, wait." I turned around to face the manager. "I apologize, I should have conveyed the good news first." He smiled. "Mr. Peter and Mr. Edward said to tell you to 'keep up the good fight,' and that they believe in you and what you are trying to do. They have invited you to use the hall on the sixth," he paused and grinned a big smile, "free of any charge."

"Oh, my." I felt embarrassed for leaping to the false conclusion of lumping the generous Coopers with the other naysayers in my life. "This is wonderful news. Thank you!" I pressed the hands of the gentleman before me. I almost cried. "Please, thank the magnanimous Coopers for me."

"I will." His smile broadened. "Something I forgot to communicate," he pressed my hands back, "Mr. Edward said he would attend the meeting. Mr. Peter has to be in Philadelphia for the Republican Convention."

I knew Peter Cooper had worked closely with President Grant on Indian affairs through a privately funded Indian Commission and through the recently established United States Board of Indian Commissioners. I appreciated that he would still host an opposition party, despite his announced support of the President.

Thursday, June 6th, The Equal Rights Party and the public were invited to ratify the nominations. Crowds inundated Cooper Union, and twice as many had to be turned away as the ones lucky enough to get in. The floor could not be seen anywhere, as bodies packed the hall wall-to-wall.

Two companies of Negro soldiers, the Veteran Guard and the Spencer Grays of the 9th Regiment, were seated on the stage. Captain Thomas Griffin of the Grays commanded both units.

Reymert reported on the convention and asked the crowd to ratify the selection of Victoria C. Woodhull as the nominee of the Equal Rights Party for President of the United States. The crowd cheered.

"So ratified." Reymert savored his position. I have the pleasure to introduce your candidate for President, Victoria Woodhull."

I walked to the podium to a standing ovation to recite a small portion of an article written for the next *Weekly*.

> The grand effort which is about to be put forth in the interest of humanity demands the best and most self-sacrificing devotion of every living soul which can feel and appreciate its great need. To promote such a cause I am willing to depart widely, if it need be, from the well-

beaten track of all my predecessors and contemporaries, and stand boldly before you, advocating the cause which is equally dear to all our hearts, and urging upon you all to lose no opportunity to help in the glorious work.

A huge cheer interrupted me.

Look to where we may, to whatever class of people or condition, and in place of equality, we find the greatest, gravest, aye, the most terrible distinctions, existing in everything which law has aught to do. Everything is made to turn on the rights of property, and nothing upon the rights of humanity.

We should remember, that unless we have the courage to endure even to death, we are not worthy to count ourselves the sons and daughters of the men and women, who barefooted trod the wintry roads of Valley Forge, blood marking their way.

In this city there are one hundred and twenty-five thousand workingmen's votes; but is there even one working man sent to Albany? Or to Washington?

The wealthy class knows that the time is near at hand when their accumulations will be taxed out of their hands. If a person who owes on his property ten thousand dollars is taxed up to two and a half percent in the form of interest, then Mr. Stewart who has his fifty million, must be taxed, say, twenty-five percent – under such a system.

For the twenty-five hundred million dollars that *We The People* are said to owe to bondholders full payment of interest and principal will amount to five thousand million dollars.

I know that the true policy of the workingmen has been felt in many of their hearts, and spreading from this, all the noble hearts in the country, which have been borne down by toil, will catch up the glad inspiration. When our course shall have ended, not so much as a single arbitrary inequality, not a single injustice shall be left in power to prey upon the laboring masses.

Thunder filled the hall. Sadly, Frederick Douglass did not attend. He had publicly declared his active support of President Grant.

As planned, I introduced the Civil War hero and captain of the Spencer Grays, Thomas Griffin. The crowd roared its approval as he approached the podium. The captain's deep mellifluous voice addressed the hall.

"Through the efforts of two noble women, Woodhull and Claflin, and in the face of discouraging opposition, the world has been forced to recognize the existence of this party that guarantees equal rights to every intelligent, respectable being in the land, without regard to caste, condition, or sex.

"With the help of these two sisters there is a new unit of four hundred well- equipped men to answer the call to protect the city, state, and country. The leading officers of this unit have resigned paramount positions in the honorary command in favor of Miss Tennessee Celeste Claflin as colonel of the battalion.

"Colonel Claflin, I wish to present the troops. Men, attention!" All the military men on the stage rose. "Present arms!"

Tennie emerged from the wings and walked over to the captain. Along the way, she released her full-length cape and revealed her stunning outfit. She wore a royal blue military coat with embroidered gold piping on the shoulders with rows of tassels. Down the front were two rows, widely apart, of shining gold buttons. Tenny had the circular gold brocaded seal of the State of New York embroidered onto the coat. Flanking the state's motto, "Excelsior" (ever upward), stood two women. Lady Liberty wore a blue Roman gown gathered by a yellow sash, with a plebeian Phrygian hat on top of her walking stick. Lady Justice stood blindfolded in a yellow gown with a blue sash, and she held the scales of justice in her left hand and a sword in her right. Tennie's trousers hugged her body. Gold brocade stripes along the sides narrowed to a tight fit above her ankles encased in riding boots. A Union cap adorned her head with a military crest on the front brow and a large, white feather on top.

Boisterous reactions sounded throughout the hall. Tennie C. looked at the men and commanded, "At ease." They obeyed. "As you were!" They all sat down.

Tennie looked to me in the wings and turned to the crowd. "Our candidate for president, my sister, Victoria C. Woodhull."

I walked over to my sister and we raised each other's hand.

The pandemonium was glorious.

Part IV

Paradise Lost

Chapter 19

DESTITUTE AND ABANDONED

New York City
Summer, 1872

The live telegraphing of the Republican convention reached so many people that the national election in effect ended before the convention closed. Any chance we might have had in raising funds by selling the bonds we printed became more and more remote with every dot and dash from Philadelphia.

On the 15th of June, James sat on the bed. He motioned me to join him, so he could cradle me in his arms. He gave me a hug and turned me around to face him. He held both my hands.

"Vickie, I don't know how to say this. We are simply out of cash. On top of everything else, no one will rent to us."

"I know, James. I have heard it too. It is as if they were all given the same script to read. Surely we still have assets and our trading accounts."

"Sweetheart, you have been so busy you have not kept your promise to the Commodore."

I withdrew my hands. "What does *he* have to do with this?"

"I won't say 'calm down,' because I know the words only infuriate you. He tried to protect you when he admonished you to always know all your positions."

"I do! I…" I stopped. The Colonel spoke the truth. I had no idea what the firm held or how we were doing. I had lost track with the all the politicking. I tried to calculate everything in my head. Could it really be this bad?

"Ever since you named Vanderbilt in your speech, "The Impending Revolution," the brokerage firm lost most of its business. You know as well as I, many depositors and traders used the firm thinking they were following Vanderbilt when taking our advice."

I pushed James for information. "What about the railroad stocks I bought on margin?"

"All of our margin positions have been called." He cringed, telling me the dire straits of our portfolio. "The two railroads you purchased have declared bankruptcy."

"What? We didn't get out in time?"

"Vickie, no one did… other than the manipulators. Most everyone on the street who bought lost their capital. At your insistence we margined, so we lost more."

"So, what is our net cash position?"

"Negative, by a lot. Woodhull & Claflin brokerage is completely bankrupt."

I felt a fear I had not known since we first met Cornelius. I'd sworn I would never be broke again. I knew destitute.

"What about the *Weekly*?"

"We will have to shut it down, or at least suspend publication."

"What? I thought we were making money."

"We were. After you named the industrialists and denounced capitalism, we lost half our subscriptions. Now, after your nomination, the list has been cut in half again. If we print past next week, the twenty-second of June, we will not be able to hold onto the presses."

My mind left my body. I traveled through my past. I relived all the terrible things that happened. I felt the heavy oak rod soaked in water as it thudded against my backside, and the willow switch as it split my skin. I heard Ma screaming and Pa telling me I was worthless and would end up a whore. I felt the pain, hunger, and cold of the births of both my children… my hysteria trying to bite through and tie off Zulu's umbilical cord. I smelled the awful smell of the cancer ward and my return to New York with Tennessee. I had to hold my breath to avoid the terrible offal smell.

I viewed a beautiful young Antonia Ford Willard as she sat in the dark, shivering from the cold in the Capitol Prison. I saw blood spurt from Antonia's mouth when she coughed at the table at the Willard. I watched the blood stain the embroidered napkin, until the mark grew and covered me in a bloody shroud.

I felt the gentle breeze and watched Mary Surratt hanging from the gallows, swinging to and fro... to and fro.

"Victoria!" I heard a hard slap across my face. Somewhere someone shook my body. I heard yelling.

"Respond to me, damn it!" I blinked my eyes and saw James Harvey Blood looking at me.

"Colonel Blood?"

"Tennie, *help me!*" the Colonel shouted.

Tennie rushed in, took one look at me, and interrogated the Colonel. "How long this time?"

He gazed downward, slowly shaking his head, and replied. "Probably ten minutes to a quarter hour."

"James, please fetch me some cold water!" Tennie turned to me. "Victoria, do you know who I am?"

"What's wrong with you?" I asked, before I looked up into her face. I saw the terror in her eyes. "How long?"

"James said ten to fifteen minutes, and you did not know him."

"Sister," I wailed as Tennie held me and rocked me back and forth, "we're penniless!"

All at once, the same persons we believed were friends or supporting the same cause began vomiting forth gall and wormwood against us.

One after another, they used every means to stab us when our backs were turned, and then kick us in the ribs when we were fallen.

Susan B. Anthony, acting like Harriet Beecher Stowe, decried me at every turn. Susan aligned herself with the A.W.S.A. in support of President Grant. She became an aggressive, public, hostile adversary. She even had the temerity to accuse me in print and personal letters of trying to blackmail my friends and associates, many of whom were members of the N.W.S.A., when in fact, I had contacted them to support our campaign and buy the bonds.

Susan now worked with the duplicitous philanderer Henry Blackwell, who helped manage the A.W.S.A. Henry nightly violated his marriage vows with the homely Lucy Stone, while both actively declared, "Free love means nothing more than free lust and leads to the destruction of civilization itself."

The press picked up on all these accusations and defamations. The papers maliciously added to "Mrs. Satan," a new moniker of my character, "Blackmailer."

I remembered what Rosie had told me, "Printed words have a special magic. They create a realness in the reader's mind, whether true or not."

Could it be only three years ago?

Theodore Tilton transformed into a living Janus, with two faces peering in opposite directions, more of a small lap dog than a god. He forsook a full range of his ideologies and sought the approval of his new master, Horace Greeley. Teddy became the campaign manager for Greeley and a contributor to the *Tribune*.

Once an adamant critic of President Grant's Reconstruction as being too slow and too lenient, Teddy now, in an effort to court Southern support for Greeley, promoted abandoning the program entirely. On June 15, Teddy used *The Golden Age* to publish his new position:

We believe the anti-slavery battle has been fought out. Slavery is abolished, and the Thirteenth Amendment makes its re-enactment impossible. The Negro has been invested with the right of suffrage, and the Fourteenth and Fifteenth Amendments make his disenfranchisement impossible. Legally, the Negro stands exactly where the white man does. Socially, whatever stigma rests upon him is far more oppressive in the North than in the South.

When I read these words, I saw clearly a future where a new form of slavery, the institutionalized degradation of the Negro, would rise from the ashes of our brutal war. Confirming this apprehension, I received a letter from "The Beast," my champion, General Butler. It read:

Dear Victoria,

Frederick Douglass visited me yesterday. Sadly, I must inform you, Frederick will be actively campaigning for the re-election of President Grant. I trust this disappointment does not come as a total surprise.

I write to warn you, Mr. Tilton is no longer the man we both thought. Teddy refused to assist Mr. Douglass in bringing national attention to the plight of the young and courageous James W. Smith, the first Negro cadet in the history of U.S. Military Academy. For three years Mr. Smith endured unconscionable, brutal savagery at West Point. Cadet Smith was dismissed for failing a test (so they say at the Academy), one he alone of his class had to take. This took place immediately prior to graduation and Smith becoming a commissioned officer in the Army.

I requested Theodore to assist me to draft language to create a provision to integrate the education of the white

*and the Negro throughout the nation. He flatly refused
my request.*

*Victoria, be very wary of Theodore. North evades his
moral compass. He is very much a changed man. As best
you can, watch your lovely backside.*

Sincerely,
Your dutiful Servant always,
Gen. Beast.

Anna Dickinson, one of my closest friends, started denouncing free love as an immoral doctrine. I wrote to her. "I do not comprehend your switch in advocacy and loyalty. How can you, dear Anna, when you are the exemplary, longest lasting, living proof of the happiness the free love doctrine yields?"

I referred to the identity of her long-time secret lover, three decades older than her, who had been her lover since she reached fifteen years old. While only a handful of people knew this, they had hidden it so well, the man was none other than the great abolitionist and woman rights protagonist, Wendell Phillips.

I received her coded reply.

Dearest Victoria,

*I trust in your discretion. Yes, you are right in asserting
that my position is veering in a new direction. Something, my
dear Vickie, we have in common, the mercurial willingness
to leap into new beliefs.*

*I have been approached by both major campaigns, Grant
and Greeley, to conduct a series of speaking engagements.
They both offer ungodly amounts of money. Though I fear it
may be to no avail, I have chosen to stay loyal to Whitelaw*

Reid and the Tribune. I am confident you can surmise my
reasons all too well.

I remain your friend always and forever.

A.

Her letter hurt, but I could not summon the anger to judge her,
nor waste any more of my effort thinking about her.

New York City itself turned against us. Not one landlord or hotel
would allow us to rent a home or even rooms. We offered the full
sum paid in advance, still no accommodation. The newspapers and
political cartoonists were heartless and relentless. Each day they
had either put me in prison, flogged me, scythed me like wheat,
or burned me at the stake. "Mrs. Satan" and "Witch Woodhull"
appeared repeatedly.

New York had welcomed us to compete with men in commerce
and newsprint. They welcomed the entertaining sideshow of our
posturing and Tennie's ongoing defiance of convention, especially in
clothing. Now, we had profaned the plutocracy and the one and only
true religion of the city—money. We were outcasts.

The entire nation followed in (un)kind. One-by-one, each of
my scheduled speaking engagements cancelled and demanded the
advance fee be returned. I started to keep a list of the places I vowed I
would never again appear. Within days the list became so long I had
to cease my notations, and I burned the list.

With no place to stay, all five of us, the Colonel, Tennie, Byron,
Zulu, and I, slept at the offices of Woodhull & Claflin at 44 Broad
Street. We had to inform Ginny, our receptionist and secretary who
had joined the family, we must let her go.

"Oh, Mrs. Woodhull and Miss Claflin, I am so sorry this is all
happening to you." Her American accent thinly veiled her inherent

Irish brogue. Amazing. This sweet girl worried about us when she had just been fired.

"Thank you, Ginny. I am sorry, too." I replied.

Tennie responded, "Thank you, Ginny, we will miss you. We could try and help you find work, but honestly you might be better applying for work based on your skills and not our references."

"The thing is ma'ams…"

"Please," I interrupted, "call us Vickie and Tennie. We have asked you before. Now it is demanded by circumstance."

"Okay, Mrs…. Victoria." She flustered at the change. "The thing is, I pay my rent by the night. Without pay I will not be able to stay in my present room."

"Ginny, we have to let you go, dear heart; we do not have any monies to pay you," Tennie informed her.

"Oh no!" Ginny seemed unduly stunned. "I did not say it right." She took two deep breaths and counted to six, the way Tennie and I had shown her. "I wanted to offer to keep working and take care of Byron and Zulu or anything else, if you would allow me to sleep here and be near the family."

"But Ginny, I don't know when or how we will be able to pay you," I tried to explain.

"I don't care!" She raised her voice and shocked even herself. "You two and the Colonel are the only family I know."

I caught a glint in Tennie's eyes. She took Ginny's hands. "Ginny, we welcome you to be part of our traveling circus troupe. Thank you for wanting to join us and to help with the children. You are now and forever forward our little sister. Everything will work out just fine."

I shrugged my shoulders in acceptance. Out loud, I blessed the decision: "And so it is."

Last winter had been tame, but the summer of 1872 turned unbearably hot and humid by mid-June. The putrid smells from all the rotting waste made it unbearable.

The toll of the vitriol and constant attacks resulted in the desired effect. Our health, stamina, and purse seemed paralyzed and stagnant. We ceased all business at once. I suffered from deep fatigue and exhaustion. Both Zulu Maud and I became sick, surely due to the barrage of daily attacks and rejections of housing. Every night we had to find somewhere to rest.

I received a telegram the day before the last issue of the *Weekly*—at least until we could resume. The night would be a full moon, summer solstice; June 21 arrived, the longest day of the year and the turning point toward the longest night.

Rosie had lectured me, "The longest day of the year is a turning point and we celebrate the sun and all its glory. Litha, or Midsummer, also shows us the cycle of life as moving forward. After the solstice, days will shorten until the longest night at winter solstice, and we ask for the return of light. One day, Victoria, you and I will watch one of the most enchanting sights you will ever see, the rise of the sun on Litha at Stonehenge in Wiltshire, England."

The telegram read:

> *I told you a long time ago,*
> *You are not alone.*
> *Feel my love.*
> *When the moon is waned, go to Gilsey House to*
> *renew.*
> *Your entire stay is prepaid. Eat freely,*
> *until the moon is full again.*
> *Reservation for three rooms is under...*
>   "BY ANY OTHER NAME..."

I called out and gathered the family around me.

"We've been saved!" The faces before me were downtrodden, confused. "Our Aunt Rosie has been kind enough to provide the family two weeks of luxury at the newest hotel in New York."

"Is this really true?" Tennie asked. She looked off to the east. She viewed what was to come. "Ah, yes, she wants to help and will do even more in the future."

The Colonel spoke, "Thank God for her kindness." He turned to the children, "We will be able to clean ourselves, and eat fresh food." He looked into my eyes. "Perhaps we can cure your and Zulu's nasty coughs."

Tennie announced, "Ginny, you will stay with the children in one room. Sister, you and the good Colonel will have the privacy you much deserve. I will keep my own company," she smiled brightly, "and perhaps entertain a few others."

"Tennie, the kids!" The Colonel exclaimed.

"Yes. This will be such a relief." I motioned for the children to come hug me. Tears flooded my face. "Thank you, dear Rosie, thank you for hearing my prayers." I felt Rosie kiss the top of my head.

In the last issue—I hoped for only a short time—of *Woodhull & Claflin's Weekly*, on June 22, I took up the issues I thought had to be addressed. I worked hard to get everything right and sent out some galley proofs to solicit the reactions of people. In my accompanying letters I prostrated myself, confessed my hubris, and humbly appealed for help with lodging, food, or funds. The number of people whose opinions mattered to me dwindled rapidly.

The first of only four pages carried different stories with a few advertisements in the lower third of each page.

PRESIDENTIAL choice: Corruption or Senility.

ECONOMY at precipice: alarming rate of bankruptcies.

HYPOCRISY: The private lives of public figures.

THE *WEEKLY TAKES A BREAK*:
Woodhull & Claflin's Weekly suspends operations.

We described characters and circumstances, but no names were printed, except for the candidates, President Grant, Horace Greeley and me, Victoria C. Woodhull.

The heat and humidity continued unabated through the summer months of July and August. We did move on the new moon, the day after Independence Day, into the Gilsey House Hotel. The marvel of architecture accentuating ornate wrought iron loomed upward at 1200 Broadway and Twenty-Ninth Street.

The eight-story, three-hundred-room hotel featured brand new, luxurious rosewood and walnut décor, with marble fireplaces, tapestries, and big bronze chandeliers in each room. The Gilsey impressed.

Byron would go around saluting each laborer, as all of them wore military-like livery. He particularly delighted in the dining room, and so did the rest of us. French and German professional chefs delivered the incredible cuisines of their countries. The chefs had arrived from some of the best restaurants in Paris and Berlin. While the Willard served a hearty and savory stew, the *boeuf Borguignon, coq au vin, bratwurst, sauerbraten* and *schnitzel mit kartoffelnudeln* (potato noodles) instilled a new appreciation of food. One novelty became our favorite side dish; we always ordered *pomme frites*, potatoes sliced into long, narrow strips and cooked in hot oil until crisp and then salted. We took leisurely meals and relaxed.

On the sixth day of daily Sabbaths, Tennie and I emerged from lunch at the restaurant. The manager of the hotel rushed up to us. "You must follow me at once!" the man announced rudely and led us out of the lobby to the side area beyond the carriage drop and into the luggage room. As we rounded a corner, four handsome Negro soldiers in new uniforms snapped to attention and saluted Tennessee.

"Colonel Claflin." Captain Thomas Griffin of the Spencer Grays saluted his honorary commander, "The troops await your inspection at the battery."

"At ease," Tennie ordered the men. "I will have to go up and change into my uniform. You gentlemen can have a bite to eat in the restaurant while I am getting dressed."

"No, they will not!" The manager said in a huff. "I know your true identities, Mrs. Victoria Woodhull and Miss Tennessee Celeste Claflin." He said our names as if he had swallowed something terribly distasteful. "These Negroes shall not cross the threshold of the hotel."

Captain Griffin spoke up. "We have no desire to do so, sir." He looked sternly at the manager. "We will wait wherever you wish; in a room, outside, or down the street."

"Nonsense," I blurted. "These men fought valiantly during the war." I turned on the manager. "Where did you serve and what battles did you see?"

The manager ignored me. "Outside and down the street."

"I order you four to sit inside the lobby until I am ready." Tennie glared at the manager.

"I'll have you all arrested!" The manager threatened.

"For what?" I turned on him. "I am a candidate for President of these United States. My running mate is none other than the great Frederick Douglass, a person of color!" I paused. "We survived a great struggle that claimed many lives to treat these men as our equals. Their brothers sacrificed their lives on behalf of the Union on several battlefields."

"I will summon the police." The intractable manager threatened.

"Good," Tennie declared.

"Go ahead!" I agreed.

"*Wait!*" Captain Spencer shouted. "Colonel, I have to respectfully request you release these men and myself from your last order. If not, I will submit my resignation, as I cannot and will not place my men, nor my commander, at risk."

Silence. I watched Tennie struggle with the predicament.

"Captain," Tennie issued a new command while not taking her eyes off the manager, "take your men and wait for me halfway down the block, south on Broadway."

"Yes, ma'am, Colonel." The captain acknowledged his orders. Four soldiers responded with crisp salutes, and Tennie saluted them back with flair. They marched out of the Gilsey baggage area and into the street.

"I hope you are satisfied," I challenged the manager.

"In fact, no, I am not," the manager answered. "The Gilsey has put up with your scandalous behavior long enough. Why, your imbecile son goes around saluting every employee while he drools on our carpets."

"You are an indecent man. I will talk to the owner."

"I already have." The manager answered me with a smirk I wanted to slap off his face. "In fact, I am telling you both now. If Miss Tennessee once more appears in our lobby wearing a uniform, or is seen in the company of Negroes, the Gilsey will gladly turn you out."

When Tennie returned several hours later, she found our family in front of the hotel with our newly acquired luggage and a few new costumes by the door. Luckily, the Colonel and I had acquired some cash by returning merchandise for greenbacks. We could hire two carriages.

"They did not!" Tennie looked at us in horror.

"We must return to the offices." I stated the obvious.

"Mommy, did I do something bad?" Byron cried and tugged on my shirt. I could not lift him, he was a full-grown man at seventeen.

"No sweetheart. None of this is your fault. I love you, By." I trembled.

Rachel tickled him and started singing a soothing song. I sat next to Rachel listening to the song as I held baby Tennie. I smelled smoke and heard the crackling of fire. I looked into the eyes of our Homer, Ohio neighbors, and saw flaming fires or cold black coals. I watched as they torched my childhood home and burned it to the ground.

I shook my head to clear my vision. My childhood friend Rachel died in Homer, Ohio, before we were run out of town. I looked at my son and thanked the Lord. Ginny sang and held him. Her eyes were their normal hazel color.

"*Victoria!*" Tennie must have felt my momentary shift. "Are you okay?" I felt her hand grip my shoulder.

I nodded my head; I didn't trust myself to speak. Byron patted Ginny, trying to imitate the song's rhythm. I wondered about his always tapping on her breasts. She ignored it.

"Sadly, I see no other alternative," my husband surrendered.

"We shall persevere," Tennie encouraged. She looked at me intently. "Sister?"

"Yes." I said softly. "We shall."

I did not share her conviction.

Chapter 20

REVELATIONS:
THE BEECHER-TILTON SCANDAL

Eastern Seaboard
September–November, 1872

Days later, I wrote to Henry Ward Beecher on stationery I
procured while at Gilsey House:

Dear Sir,

*The social fight against me now waged in this city is
becoming rather hotter than I can well endure, standing
unsupported and alone as I do. Within the past two weeks
I have been shut out of hotel after hotel. After five days in
one, I am hunted down by a set of males and females who
are determined I shall not be permitted to live, if they can
prevent it.*

*Now I ask for your assistance. I want to be sustained in
my position in the Gilsey House or another hotel. They all
refuse me because I am Victoria C. Woodhull, the advocate
of social freedom. I have submitted to this persecution as
long as I can endure. It must cease. Will you lend me your
aid in this?*

*Even a docile animal transforms into a ferocious
adversary under the duress of fear and hunger. Please help
me not to be so transformed.*

No reply, not even a courtesy response, nothing at all. Perhaps the Usurper thought himself beyond worldly reproach.

Our lives had been reduced to small fractions of the large numbers we once controlled. It seemed everything we attained fell off a lofty perch and shattered into fragments on the hard earth. One by one, as quietly as possible, we sold all our beautiful belongings at one-eighth, one-twelfth, one-twentieth, even one one-hundredth of their value.

I withdrew into my own personal sphere. Many times, I cried as each piece of the life we had built disappeared like "a clod be washed away by the sea...." I felt the pathos of John Donne's poem, "For Whom the Bell Tolls." I knew it tolled for all humanity. I hurt.

"You must *go!*" Tennie beseeched me.

"Indeed, you must. This will be good for you, my dear." The Colonel entreated.

They wanted me to attend the annual meeting of the American Association of Spiritualists, scheduled for September 10. We talked at our new offices and temporary domicile next door to the old ones. The size, another fraction, totaled about one fifth of our previous offices. I stared at the clean-floor outlines of our bedrolls against the accumulated dust on the rest of the floor. How low could we fall?

"Sister, Husband, we can barely eat and pay rent by liquidating everything we own. None of us can afford to travel to Boston, that hateful city of Beechers and Brahmins, even to see our most ardent supporters."

"Nonsense. You are simply afraid!" Tennie saw my reaction and adjusted her tone. "Vickie, I have already talked with our dressmakers and they are creating stunning new outfits for both of us... on credit."

"Victoria," the Colonel's deep voice rumbled, "you need to speak to a crowd. Why not start with one at least one-half inclined to your perspective?"

"More fractions!" I yelled. They both looked at me with such curiosity and confusion, I started to laugh. The laughter deepened and then became infectious. Even Byron and Zulu, who were playing in the corner with Ginny on top of three stacked-up bedrolls, started laughing.

The Colonel gained control. "What are we laughing about?" He giggled and we all laughed again.

"How in the world are we going to pay for this?" I exclaimed through my laughter and then ceased laughing.

"I'll take care of everything," Tennie announced.

Everyone except Byron stopped laughing. He laughed while crawling all over Ginny, trying to tickle her. When she saw my look, she calmed him down and returned to the game they were playing.

"But how, Sister?"

"The royal chairs." Tennie motioned to the only two remaining pieces of furniture from our magnificent offices next door. The Commodore had commissioned the chairs back in April, 1870, just prior the publication of the "First Pronunciamento," my declaration to the public I intended to run for President.

It felt so long ago, when the chairs were delivered to our offices, everything looked "Upward & Onward." I wondered what fraction of their worth our two royal chairs would fetch.

Are you sure, Tennie? I know how important they are to you." I nodded my head, resigned to our fate. "Perhaps just mine?"

"I'll tend to it. Thank you, Sister, for caring about my feelings."

"Always." I capitulated to my sister's liquidating the gift from her Corney. *At what fraction?* I pushed away the screaming inside my head. "All right, if we can really afford it. I will go to Boston to publicly announce to the A.A.S. convention my resignation as president."

Somehow, Tennie managed to get top dollar for the chairs and also got three first-class passages to Boston for free. She must have seen Cornelius.

General Benjamin Butler, the honorable congressman from Massachusetts, booked us into the Presidential Suite at Young's Hotel in Boston. George Young had built his hotel on the site of the Old Cornhill Coffee House in the middle of the Financial District. The mahogany wainscot rooms were opulent, especially the Presidential Suite. We found a huge floral bouquet, and on a side table an equally large bowl of fresh fruit. A telegram sat tucked into the flowers:

> *Welcome!*
>   *Rooms and dinner are on me, it is my pleasure.*
> *Hope you enjoy the bath.*
> *V be sure to eat something in the morning!*
> *Speak your mind tomorrow. Be intrepid!*
> *I look forward to seeing all of you, soon!*
>   *Yours dutifully,*
>   *General B.*

I smiled at the subtle innuendo and reminder of our encounter at the Hoffman House.

Tennie must have used a lot of credit to get my costume. Bands of black velvet and dark crimson ribbons, cords, and tassels trimmed a fine black faille toilette. The trained skirt fit the body tightly, accented by two rows of velvet trimming and several rows of heavy, crimson cord. The plain waist, laced behind and cut away at the sides, was edged with the velvet trim up to and over the right shoulder to suggest a scarf. The sleeves gathered just below the elbow to fall open in large, flowering points decorated with draping cords and tassels. I looked majestic. A regal Queen Victoria.

Since I had lost so much weight the last couple of months, I wondered how Tennie knew what to tell the dressmakers. Ah, another fraction. I started to weave my hair into a bun, but Tennie undid the pins and released the cropped curls to rest at my neck.

Tennie unpacked her blue pants and the cut waistcoat she had worn to the first N.W.S.A. meeting in Washington, D.C., and several times since. I realized she spent all of the monies on me. She did transform her former outfit. The pants had a new military flare with deep crimson ribbons matching mine, sewn at the outside seam of her pants.

"Tennie, I wish you would have bought yourself a new outfit."

"But I have, Vickie. Wait."

She proceeded to place a sash, consisting of ribbons, over her gauze-like linen shirt. She strapped the ribbons around her waist, the ends reached upward between her bosoms, over her shoulders, and down before being tucked in and tied at the small of her back. She put on her blue jacket, affixed a crimson and gold insignia pin on the right side and… left the jacket open! Her breasts moved freely, their accentuated outline clearly visible. She achieved her desire, an unencumbered outfit both highly memorable and provocative.

"Vickie, I think I will still draw a wee bit of attention in Bean Town." Tennie jested.

"Ha! If they don't arrest you for indecency!"

"Wouldn't that make the policemen happy!"

We both laughed as James came in.

"Tennie, are you going to wear *that* outfit outside this room?" The Colonel asked. His face turned red as he spun toward me.

"Why, do you think it too conservative?" Tennie giggled.

"You look lovely, Vickie." He turned back to Tennie and bowed, "Thank you."

"I simply followed your orders, Colonel," she smiled and curtsied.

"Husband, this is your doing?" I looked at James.

"Ours." They said together.

James spoke next. "We both decided you should look your very best, because we are both confident you will give an incredible speech."

I looked into their eager faces. My stomach started to knot. Thank God, I had eaten something, as General Beast suggested. "I'll do my best."

"Your best is always amazing," Tennie said, hugging me.

"We need to proceed to Andrew Hall." Colonel Blood took command.

I waited backstage, studying my prepared speech. I would resign effective immediately. I would declare that only through the guiding light of spiritualists could social change come to prominence and legislation. The work ahead remained critical.

"Just speak your mind, Vickie." Tennie repeated the Beast's instruction.

"Tennie, I feel queasy. I cannot go on the stage."

My sister pushed my shoulder. "You always do, Sister. You will be just fine."

"I have to tell them I cannot serve. No one wants me to continue as president of the Association."

Now I heard Laura Cuppy Smith building to a crescendo in her introduction. I turned to walk out to the wings.

"We'll see!" My sister shouted.

Laura climaxed, "The incredibly courageous, valorous, and unstoppable Victoria C. Woodhull."

The assault of the ovation startled me. I thought I would cry. I felt disoriented. *Just make it to the podium.* I walked over to Laura. She kissed me on both cheeks and turned me around to the crowd to display my costume. The enthusiastic reaction lifted my spirits. *Breathe! Remember to breathe.*

I shook my head, which jiggled my curls, and the crowd erupted again. I saw some of the same women who had ignored my pleas for help, stand and cheer. *Were my letters as Juliet's to her Romeo, undelivered and foreshadowing death and doom?* I forced myself to focus and started to speak.

"Thank you. Thank you." *Let go of the past. Stay present!*

"I am grateful to be among my own people. You have remained my steadfast, loyal, and supportive fraction."

Realizing my mistake, I stopped. Silence descended onto the crowd.

"*Faction*, not fraction." I hesitated. *Don't you dare leave this room!*

I looked out at so many friends and supporters and felt sad at having to surrender the presidency and leave their company. I saw looks of concern mixed with eager encouragement. *I started to float away.* I opened my speech, but could not read it. The letters danced on the page, unintelligible.

Some woman called out, "We love you, Victoria!"

The crowd began chanting, "We love Vickie! We love Vickie!"

I blinked my eyes and then had to close them to the bright lights from the burning gas lamps. Suddenly, I felt a glowing green and golden presence. *"I am with you, Victoria,"* Demosthenes said. *"Tell them the truth."*

At once, I returned to the hall, and the entire setting became clearer than crystal clear. The spiritualists knew I had just had a vision. A few would know Demosthenes stood by my side, guiding me. An overwhelming gust of inspiration took control. I swiped my prepared speech off the lectern and watched the pages waft to the floor. The crowd roared.

We are burdened as Spiritualists, because we know things most cannot see nor want to know. The knowledge is an affliction for us to bear in silence.

Throughout history those of our ilk, who have

spoken openly and shared their visions, have been
ostracized, hated, and cast out of society.

Some before us were burned at the stake, hanged,
or put to the question in the inquisition. So we learn to
hold our tongues, lest they be cut out.

The crowd sat silent. They waited anxiously for my next words.
Empowered, I poured out onto the ears of the assembly the Beecher
and Tilton scandal in Plymouth Church. I shouted my words like
thunderclaps!

> I can *not*!
> I will *not*!
> I must *not* submit to the lessons history has shown,
> that *retribution* to our kind is harsh, yet a shadow of
> bearing the burden of unspoken *truth*.

I had to pause as the crowd erupted.

> Hypocrisy is well-anchored in the personage of the
> most famous and beloved man in America. While his
> popularity and influence are unmatched, he is a known
> adulterer.
> I speak of Henry Ward Beecher, whom I will not
> call Reverend, for he is a usurper sitting on a throne of
> morality. I congratulate and wish him well on the fact he
> is a prolific adulterer.
> He lives the doctrine of free love. Yet, he actively
> denies the very doctrine he practices. I say to Henry Ward,

I pointed an accusatorial finger at his imagined presence.

> Thou shall not lie!

The words lifted away an enormous burden, and my spirit soared into the firmament. The crowd waited in silence.

> You will ask, "How can I know?" I know because at first I sensed it in the way which all of us here are familiar. Next, I know because I heard it from the cuckold husband whose wife wants only to be with her lover, Mr. Beecher. I know, as I heard it from the woman herself, and several of my friends are fully aware of this pattern of behavior, including the most independent of his sisters. The oldest sisters, who are insufferable elitists, yell "Heresy!" while they hide the truth in a heavy shroud.

I paused, studying their faces.

> I see your shock. "How can this be?" you ask. Our doctrine of free love and radical sex is nothing more than the public statement of doings, common in private. Our subject, the Usurper, I will call him by no other title, is open-handed in his ministrations of free love. On any given Sunday, he preaches to as many as a score of his own bastard children issued from unions with the proper lady members of Plymouth Church. Who are sitting in their pews robed in silks and satins and high respectability.

A few people stood up and walked out.

> Again, I cannot stress enough, I wish all three in Henry's current melodrama happiness and peace. But forsooth, tell the truth to your followers and the public. Stop castigating and defaming advocates for your precise

behaviors. I call on upon you, Henry Ward Beecher—openly express the truth of your way of living.

I am here. I am speaking. I am telling the truth as you yourself confirmed to me pleading I never reveal it. Theodore Tilton and Elizabeth Tilton, come into the light of truth, and be set free. Free to love as you wish, with whom you wish, and when you choose.

Harriet and Catherine Beecher, you have chosen to falsify the facts plainly before you for the past two decades. How long will you promulgate misdirection and dishonesty?

To be clear, I find fault with the Usurper, for the exact opposite from the reasons for which most will condemn him. He holds, on conviction and by behavior, substantially the same views as I entertain on the major social questions. However, incomprehensibly, he upholds the old social slavery, sitting aloof and on high to judge others. He opposes our knowledge of love as true and sacred. He denies us our religious freedom, and he seeks to destroy any one of us who proclaims our beliefs.

If you are sinless, Henry Ward Beecher, I invite *you* to cast upon me the first stone.

I went on as if the lid of a boiling kettle had lifted off and all the pent-up steam released at once.

Henry Ward Beecher is by no means alone. There is a predatory criminal by the name of Luther Challis, who fancies himself a financier. At a public ball, he seduced two girls under the age of fourteen, and enticed them to go elsewhere with him. He urged a few of his fellow *sporting men* to join in.

One of the girls turned up dead the next day, drugged, repeatedly raped, and savagely beaten. Authorities found the second maiden held against her will at one of the lowliest whorehouses on the docks. The girl had been brutalized, ruined and bled from every orifice. That poor girl.

Shouts of "Scoundrels!" "Villains!" and "Curs!" sounded around the hall.

How can it be only the woman, in an act requiring two participants, can be guilty of debauchery? Why is the male participant praised by his fellows, and exempt from the accusation of debauchery? Why is a man who rapes someone's daughter, praised by his associates? This sexual and social double standard is the evil arm of slavery, condemning woman to live in servitude.

Finally, I challenged spiritualists to cease shielding those among us whose personal conduct negated the positions they advocated publicly.

The sinister pen of S. S. Jones, editor of the *Religio-Philosophical Journal*, lives the very life he regularly attacks in his columns. This Bostonian, mad avenger of morality, keeps a mistress and pays for her entire existence to render him satisfaction whenever he so desires.

Do I condemn him for his exploits? No! All lives are private, their conduct private, their values private, until they publicly assert such behavior is evil and seek to destroy the advocates of their exact nature and precise behavior.

I condemn anyone who lacks the integrity to expose the two-faced men and women in our society who argue against free love and live by it. Attack us not, and we shall leave you to your own contradictions.

I took a moment to pause. I knew I had crossed a threshold from which I could not return. I had leaped off the precipice into the chasm. I realized I had to flap my wings and fly!

Some will claim me libelous in my statements. I welcome the lawsuits, for everything I have said here tonight is not only absolutely true, but provable.

And, if you dare attack spiritualism and its practitioners, know you attack not only me, but also a strong-willed group that will not bow to your authority.

So, help me God, we shall speak the truth.

Everyone stood, yelled and shouted. Laura Cuppy Smith came up on the stage and raised my hand. She leaned into to me so I could hear her.

"Brilliant, my dear, simply brilliant. Vickie, no doubt new speaking engagements are already commenced. You will once again be touring widely."

Then a chant started and in unison the crowd shouted, "Tell the truth! Tell the truth!"

In the wings, Tennie and the Colonel were waiting for me.

"Sweetheart, you continue to amaze. I am so proud of you." The Colonel embraced me.

"Nice to have you back, Victoria!" Tennie kissed my cheeks. I pirouetted for my sister and swirled in a circle with my train swishing across the floor.

"Thank you both for staying stalwart." I hugged them both. Tennie stepped back to address me.

"Sister," She placed her right hand over her open mouth in mocked surprise. "You have sworn profanely against those the public consider impeccable."

"I swore not profanely, I swore divinely." We both laughed, and held one another in a long embrace.

Events proved the prognostication of Laura Cuppy Smith. By acclamation the association elected me president for another year. By the time we got home from Boston, over twenty telegrams were stacked on my desk. Those who had cancelled my engagements clamored to reschedule them on the same terms.

Ginny pointed to the telegrams and asked, "Mrs. Wood... Sorry! I mean... What do you want me to do with all the telegrams, Victoria?" Ginny still trembled at having to use my first name.

"Apparently, scandal is more profitable than the politics of reform." I said to Ginny and my sister.

Tennie took charge. "Ginny dear, stack the telegrams by date of appearance. Then we can review them in terms of priority."

"Yes." I had new terms to impose. "For now, answer each telegram with one from me. Let it read:

> *Happy to appear, thank you.*
> *Reschedule / deposit fee set at $300.00.*
> *New Terms: balance 15 days in advance.*
> *Respond in 3 days or we are cancelled.*
> *Graciously,*
> *VCW*

My husband cautioned me, "Vickie, I believe the new fee may be too much. We do need the cash, but..."

"Nonsense!" Tennie interrupted. "They will double their ticket prices or more. They are lucky we are honoring the original price."

Tennie stopped. She looked off into the distance and after a few moments turned to all three of us. "They will all agree."

I placed my right hand in the space between the four of us. Tennie and the Colonel placed their right hands on top of mine.

"You too, Ginny," I instructed.

In unison, we lift our hands upwards and invoked,

"All for one! And, one for all!"

Some bargained, some bickered, and some were outraged at the new fees. Yet they all agreed rapidly. As money came in by wire to our account at The Bank of New York, I left for a speaking tour planned to last three weeks.

While I traveled, I read claims of slander, denials, and artfully worded non-statements. It amazed me the participants thought they could hide the facts by wallpapering the public with false newsprint. For once, the public became aggressive, demanding explanations. They did not relent, not with the scent of carnage in the air.

I had sparked two brushfires, the public's desire for scandal and the newspapers' desire for increased sales. I recognized the familiar formula—scandal sold papers. The heat of one flame attracted and magnified the other. The fires burned hotter and hotter, until they scorched the earth of our nation and leapt overseas.

Demands to appear could have kept Tennie and me appearing every night. Ginny booked only those reservations for speaking engagements that contained a $500 deposit. We started charging double what we had charged in the past. We finally could afford a modest house to rent.

James gathered us in the office of the *Weekly*. Stephen Pearl Andrews, Tennie, and I sat down, as well as Ginny, who helped the typesetters get ready for the print run.

My husband rose from one of the tufted red leather chairs Tennie had re-acquired at multiples of the prices we had received.

"Should I make any attempt to dissuade you two?" My husband asked in a stern voice. "The consequences may be dire."

"Yes," I replied, then jested, "You are welcome to voice any opinion, and it will be weighed with due consideration."

"Wife, Victoria dearest, why, when I offer caution, do you always react by charging forward?"

"Husband, Colonel most dear," I smiled, "am I being compared to a bovine? I believe Whitelaw did so once, but only once." Everyone laughed.

"Well, I seem to wave a red cape I fail to perceive." With a pained expression, James pressed his point. "This summer has shown how precarious our lives are. Can we proceed with more deliberation, a modicum of caution rather than openly declaring war?"

"The die is cast, the course set. Come whatever may, from now on, woman will speak her mind without hesitation." I paused and went over to James. "Yes, beloved, even if it takes being a martyr to create a different future."

"I don't want you as a martyr, Vickie. I want you warm and well and by my side, kissing me." His eyes filled with tears. I had to look away.

Tennie declared, "I do like the sound of the new banners." she read the top one out loud:

PROGRESS! FREE THOUGHT!
UNTRAMMELED LIVES!

Everyone except James applauded.

I held up the printed type. "I am especially proud of the new lower banner declaring:

BREAKING THE WAY
FOR FUTURE GENERATIONS.

I basked in joy. We were solvent. We had our newspaper back, resurrecting our voices. We did have to concede the first page to our advertisers, who were mostly financial. They signed on after the Banking House of Henry Clews & Company bought the top billing, flanked by their current securities offerings. Both Tennie and I wrote editorials on page two.

James's comments addressed two long narratives Tennie and I had prepared. Starting on page nine, I addressed in full detail the Beecher-Tilton scandal:

THE BEECHER-TILTON SCANDAL CASE
A DETAILED STATEMENT OF THE WHOLE MATTER
BY MRS. WOODHULL.

I propose, as the commencement of a series of aggressive moral declarations on the social question, to ventilating one of the most stupendous scandals, which has ever occurred in any community. I refer to that which has been whispered for the last two or three years through the cities of New York and Brooklyn, touching on the character and conduct of the Rev. Henry Ward Beecher in his relations with the family of Theodore Tilton.

I intend that this article shall burst like a bombshell into the ranks of the moralistic social camp.

I am engaged in officering, and in some sense conducting, a social revolution on the marriage question. I have strong convictions to the effect that this institution, as a bond or promise to love another to the end of life, and forego all other loves or passion, all gratifications, has outlived its day of usefulness; that the most intelligent and really virtuous of our citizens, especially in the large cities of Christendom, have outgrown it; are constantly and systematically unfaithful to it; despise and revolt against it, as a slavery, in their hearts; and only submit to the semblance of fidelity to it from the dread of a sham public opinion, based on the ideas of the past, and which no longer really represent the convictions of any body.

The article filled thirteen long columns of print, over five full pages! I went on to present everything I knew, the full cast of characters, all salient details of every discussion or written communication. I exposed the reasons behind Beecher's marrying Abbey Sage McFarland to Albert Richardson on his deathbed. I guarded no person, nor held back any fact in the entire matter. I loved how I concluded:

The whole evil in this matter, then, lies elsewhere. It lies in a false and artificial or manufactured opinion, in respect to this very question of what is good or what is evil in such matters. It lies in the belief that society has the right to prohibit, to prescribe and regulate, or in any manner to interfere with the private love manifestations of its members, any more than it has to prescribe their food and their drink. It lies in the belief consequent upon this, that lovers own their lovers, husbands their wives and wives their husbands, and that they have the right to complain of, to spy over, and to interfere, to the extent of murder with every other or outside manifestation of love. It lies in the compulsory hypocrisy and systematic falsehood which is thus enforced and inwrought into the very structure of society, and in the consequence and widespread injury to the whole community.

In conclusion, let me add, that in my view, and in the view of others, Mr. Beecher is today, and after all that I have felt called upon to reveal of his life, as good, as pure and as noble a man as he ever was in the past, or as the world has held him to be, and that Mrs. Tilton is still the pure, charming, cultured woman. It is, then, the public opinion that is wrong, and not the individuals, who must, nevertheless, for a time suffer its persecution.

Mrs. Isabella Beecher Hooker has, from the time that I met her in Washington, stood my fast friend, and given me manifold proofs of her esteem, knowing, as she did, both my radical opinions and my free life. I have been told, not by her, but upon what I believe to be perfectly good authority, that she has for months, perhaps for years past, known the life of her brother, and urged on him to announce publicly his radical convictions, and assured him that if he would do so she, at least, would stand by him. 1 know, too, by intimate intercourse, the opinions, and, to a great extent, the lives of nearly all the leading reformatory men and women in the land; and I know that Mr. Beecher, passing through this crucial ordeal, retrieving himself and standing upon the most radical platform, need not stand alone for an hour, but that an army of glorious and emancipated spirits will gather spontaneously and instantaneously around him, and that the new social republic will have been forever established.

VICTORIA C. WOODHULL

Tennie commenced on the same page where my article ended. Her article on page fourteen presented an exposé about the treatment of women.

THE PHILOSOPHY OF THE MODERN HYPOCRITE

From the lowest of material forms up to and including lovers of the organization of society there are balances in all departments of nature, which must be maintained to secure the general well-being of all.

If a person finds and exposes a gathering of material filth, insidiously distilling its noxious miasmas into the atmosphere for society to inhale, and thereby contract terrible diseases, he is considered a public benefactor, and the agents of society at once lay hold and remove the poisonous stuff. And the same thing is true when the cause is in the financial or political arena. But when the social arena is involved, when anybody presumes to uncover the stench-generating pools of filth, debauchery and rottenness in which so many of the most respectable male citizens wallow and riot, society stands back horrified, and denounces the presuming individual as the incarnation of diabolism; and as especially damned, if it be a woman.

Nevertheless, put a woman on trial for anything— let her even so much as go before the courts to obtain pecuniary justice—it is considered as a legitimate part of the defense to make the most searching inquiry into her sexual morality, and the decision generally turns upon the proof advanced in this regard.

How is it with regard to men? Who thinks of attacking them in regard to their sexual morality? If a man be arraigned as a thief, forger, traitor or murderer, who thinks of attempting to prejudice his case by proving him lecherous? A man being even the President of the United States, governor of a state, pastor of the most popular church, president of the most reliable bank, or of the grandest railroad corporation, may constantly

practice all the debaucheries known to sensualism—
many of which are so vicious, brutal and degrading as
to be almost beyond belief—and he, by virtue of his
sex, stands protected and respected, so much so that
even the other sex cry shame on the exposer when the
rottenness is laid bare; and the newspapers pretend not
to know that anything detrimental to public morality
has transpired. But let a woman even so much as protect
herself from starvation by her sexuality, lacking the
sanction of the law, and everybody in unison cries out,
"Down with the vile thing;

She went on to the specific conduct of Luther Chaliss, together
with a *bon vivant*, young, and handsome blueblood (Charles Maxwell)
called "Mr. Smith" at the French Ball at The Academy of Music in 1869.
Tennie portrayed the indecent, felonious, and despicable account,
how the two men seduced and drugged two young maidens. Tennie
wrote as if testifying in the court—of public opinion:

MR. L. C. CHALLIS THE ILLUSTRATION

… You, the public can rest assured I followed those
girls up and got the history of their connection with
these men. The maidens of age fourteen were drugged,
seduced and taken to a house of prostitution. Then, they
were robbed of their innocence by these two scoundrels,
Chaliss and "Mr. Smith," who each took one girl and
finished debauching her virginity, then switched to
assault the other girl.

This scoundrel Chaliss, to prove that he had seduced
a maiden, carried for days on his finger, exhibiting in
triumph, the red trophy of her virginity.

After three days of the Lotharios exchanging beds and companions, and when weary of this, they brought their friends, lined up out on the street, to the number of one hundred and over, to repeatedly debauch and destroy these poor young girls—mere children. Within days one girl was found dead, the other at the lowest establishment on the docks, incoherent and terrified.

We have not told the half here that we might; but this is sufficient to show the world that when women are debauched there must be two parties to the debauchery; and we would ask why they should not both be held up equally to the scorn of the world, instead of being called the "worst women and best men."

Mr. Challis made his fortune by proving on the late trial that he was a man of good moral character. The children he has seduced and debauched have now no way open before them than the prostitute's road to hell. Yet, the way is open for him into the very heart of good society; the way for them is the way of the pariah, out into the wilderness of sin and shame. Such is the real character of men high in social and financial life. But what of their victims? We hold that there can be no service of equal magnitude rendered woman beside that of unmaking the sham morality by which men override women.

Scandalous!

TENNESEE C. CLAFLIN

On Saturday, October 26, a full week ahead of the publication date, we sent out issues of the new *Woodhull & Claflin's Weekly*, dated November 2, 1872, to all the newspapers. In the evening, newsies, the hawkers who shouted the headlines to sell papers, lined up in front our printing office door, despite the fact the release date remained a full week away. To liberate them and afford the children to use the interim time to make other money, I addressed the group from the top of the steps with Ginny by my side.

"Ginny will give you each a number according to your place in line and write your name in a ledger next to your number." The crowd of children cheered. "Come back in two days by eight o'clock in the morning on the twenty-eighth."

"Thank you," "God bless you, Mrs. Woodhull." and "You've been the best story we ever had," shouted many.

Seeing some girls in boy's outfits, I turned to the crowd. "You young men are going to be gentlemen tonight!" Confused faces looked up at me, as if I had spoken in Greek. "Girls, you young women in the crowd, *come to the front.*"

Boos accompanied jeers and shouts of "Not fair," "Why them?" "They shouldn't be here at all." Then they started chanting "*Not fair, not fair.*" They jostled and prevented the girls from coming forward.

"Young men!" They would not quiet down. I yelled "*If one girl* receives a higher number than you boys, only the girls will distribute the *Weekly.*"

New shouts of "Get to the front," "Let them through," "Okay," And "All right" replaced the "Not fair" chant.

I spoke to all of them. "I want to thank you young gentlemen for your courtesy to women. In my eyes, you are better than most of the rich, the famous, and the aristocracy of our city."

They all cheered.

On the morning of the twenty-eighth, the few girl newsies lined up at the front. I huddled them together and told them, "When you go out, sell them for no less than one dollar." They looked up eagerly at me. "You girls will get two bits per paper sold. Then get back as soon as you can for a second round. Might even be a third."

We started handing stacks of twenty-five newspapers to the boys; the girls were already returning for their second round.

One of the girls shouted out. "How much should we be sellin' 'em for this time, Mrs. Victoria?"

"Two dollars!" I shouted for all to hear. "You all will keep four bits for each copy you sell."

"Hooray!" The newsies yelled.

"Thanks, Mrs. Woodhull."

"You're the best, ma'am."

"Such a fine lady!"

By nightfall, after running the presses all day—each copy sold for as much as three dollars—we gave all the newsies six bits. Both genders earned the same wage. Hadn't I proclaimed, equal pay for equal work?

Over the next three days we sold an additional one hundred and fifty thousand copies. The newsies made more money on those three days than in several years.

"I'll set up guards around the clock." Police Captain Thomas Byrne declared, walking into the office with two off duty policemen. "Until we can transfer the bags of silver coins and contents of the safe to the bank for you."

"Thank you, Captain Byrne," Tennie replied.

"Ah, think nothing of it," the captain smiled. "I'm sure you'll be making a generous contribution to the Policeman's Retirement Fund."

I accepted his terms. "Indeed, we will, Captain Byrne."

Rumors had the paper selling as high as forty dollars!

New requests for speaking engagements poured in. Ginny's desk filled with letters, many containing cash. We had to decline several after allocating one to me and one to Tennie. We made referrals with personal letters of recommendation to capable women speakers who lived near a requesting venue. We provided income for our fellow women, whether the women had been faithful and supportive or not.

On October 31, under a new moon—propitious for drawing in good fortune—as the festival of Samhain began, we gathered at our new abode. Stephen Pearl Andrews, James, Tennie, Henry Clews, and even Theodore Tilton came to celebrate. I lit candles and drew the circle to close us inside. We took turns and invoked the energies of the four corners of the compass, and then the God and Goddess.

At the end of the rituals, conducted the way Rosie taught me, we thanked and released the four corners and the God and Goddess. We opened our circle and chanted, "The circle is open and mischief is afoot…" over and over. We all danced in a circle, laughing, hugging, and kissing. I believed it would be a great new year. We ate honey cakes and warm savory loaves that filled the house with the aromas of baked bread, melting butter, cinnamon, rosemary, thyme, and garlic. Everything tasted delicious.

Stephen decided he would deliver, in his high, squeaky voice, a dissertation on the history of Samhain, the pagan new year. Henry Clews encouraged him instead to drink the fine single malt Scotch he brought.

The twenty-year-old whisky had the same effect on the gentlemen as Tennie had on all men—intoxicating!

Chapter 21

PERDITION

The Tombs Prison, New York City
November–December, 1872

Tennie and I were en route to deliver five hundred freshly printed copies of the *Weekly* on Sunday, November 3. Suddenly our driver stopped, and three men jumped into our carriage. I saw our driver thrown down into the street.

One man flung himself on Tennie and locked her arms above her head. While two strong men restrained me, the one on top of Tennie groped her bosoms through her clothes. He reached down to the hem of her dress, spread her legs, and forced his hand upward.

With two men holding me down, I could not do anything. "*Stop!* You have no right…"

"Shut up!" The bigger man holding me squeezed my jaw, forcing me to stop talking.

Tennie's body went slack and I saw a faraway look in her eyes. She spoke in an eerie voice, "Go ahead," and continued without stirring, "molest me." She still did not move as she said, "I will learn your name." She turned her head and looked directly at her attacker, "And every night for the rest of your life, I will haunt your dreams."

"*Christ!* Stand down, you *idiot!*" The big man commanded. He released my jaw and pulled the other man off Tennie. "Help hold this one… *gently!* I don't want any bruises."

"I demand to know who you are and where you are taking us!" I asserted. "By what right…"

"I'll give you one more chance, Mrs. Woodhull," the commander interrupted. "You can keep yourself still and silent," he looked at me menacingly, "or I *will!*"

We arrived at Ludlow Street jail. Beside the skeleton Sunday crew of jailors, five men conducted an informal hearing. I recognized four of them as parishioners of Plymouth Church and ardent supporters of Reverend Beecher.

Without asking a single question or allowing us to make a single statement, the committee consigned us to a cell to wait for a proper hearing on a regular business day.

One of the group sneered at us, "You are charged with *obscenity*, for now. Make no mistake, you are here as a result of a gross libel on a reverend gentleman whose character it is well worth the while of the government of the United States to vindicate."

Incarcerating my sister and me on that Sunday appeared to be of higher service to God than attending church. No official arraignment could be conducted until the morning.

On Monday, we had to pay an egregiously high bail of eight thousand dollars to secure our freedom. The legal action stemmed from an obscure, never-enforced statute regulating the distribution of obscenity through the mail. The charge cited Tennessee's use of a biblical phrase. Luther Chaliss had "seduced a maiden, carried for days on his finger, exhibiting in triumph, the red trophy of her virginity."

We published the truth. This was retribution.

The authorities used their statutes to arrest us three more times, on grounds of malicious libel, pornography, and mail fraud.

Incarcerated on the national election day, I could not vote for myself, nor encourage anyone else to do so. I heard that upstate, Susan B. Anthony succeeded getting sixteen women to place their ballots in the polling boxes. Police came to Susan's home and arrested her the next day. After she refused to pay a one-hundred-dollar fine, she sat ten days in prison. Authorities released her because of growing pressure on officials.

Tennie and I were interned and released so frequently at Ludlow Street prison that somebody made sure we had beds, down pillows, linens, carpet, and a dresser with a wash basin, ready at our designated cell to accommodate our comings and goings. Bails increased with each arrest, reaching an impossible amount of *sixty thousand dollars*.

On November 23, after a fourth arrest, the arraignment judge ordered Tennie and me transferred from our comfortable cell at Ludlow Street to await trial in the Tombs, located between Centre, Elm, Franklin, and Leonard Streets—the most feared prison in America.

The broad square granite exterior to the Halls of Justice and Detention sat upon a collecting pond. The architect, John Haviland, meant to mimic an Egyptian castle. The entire area occupied the middle of the Five Points crime nexus, and it stank. The prison was known for executing its occupants with unbreathable vapors and diseases bred in the unsanitary murky waters covering its floors.

Don't dare fall asleep. Darkness—danger everywhere.
I have to survive this night.

Fates worse than death fueled my fears. I tore the thin fabric of reality and created an absurd, macabre focus. The obscene brutality of guards thrusting and grunting transposed into an imagined composition of rhythms in counterpoint to the pianissimo whimpering and stifled, submissive sobbing, a nightly lullaby of beastly sexual domination.

I blanked my memory. I didn't hear the crack of bones or thuds of nightsticks landing on flesh, nor did I feel the inches of frigid water that covered the floor when it rained. I tried to block out the repugnant smell of raw sewage running through the groove in the middle of the stone floor. Whenever the accumulated rain overflowed the drain, human waste floated freely, until the flood receded.

I never left my small cement bed. The darkness was harsh, the relentless cold and dampness worse.

Tonight, like the last sixteen before it, I had to stay alert, awake, on guard, to make it to morning. Whenever I started falling asleep, I forced myself to stand in the inches of shockingly cold water and sewage. I had to stay awake. I napped in the mornings when the matrons returned in their high waterproof boots, bundled in layers of clothing and wearing their gauze facemasks.

Time slowed down at night to an excruciating pace. My pulse and heartbeat became a grandfather clock, tick… tock, tick… tock, inside my head. Each pause became an endless struggle. Thoughts of James, Zulu and Byron, Tennie, and friends were torture. I knew my mind was slipping away.

I have to survive this night.

Obscenity!

This was an ancient and unforgiving society of the disenfranchised, with its own rules, rituals, and menacing etiquette, a perversion of normal, enforced chaos with any transgression brutally punished. Here, one either learned fast or suffered dire consequences. The only answer to any question was a monosyllabic "yes" or "no." Without explanation, no clarification, no "but"; just cruel binary simplicity.

Everything was inverted down here in Hades, in my six-by-eight-foot cell. Right was wrong, friend was danger, guard was perpetrator, safe was precarious, and sleep offered no rest. Nothing was logical, and gravity pulled from the ceiling, causing nausea and dizziness.

Everyone hated me because I dared to succeed, dared to tell the truth, dared to be honest and true. I was shunned, despised, and completely alone.

So far, I'd been in hell one million ticks of despair and a million tocks of deterioration.

The first several days in this dungeon, Demosthenes filled the cell with his shining light. He brought Napoleon Bonaparte and his first wife, Empress Josephine, to talk with me. The Emperor cautioned me against chill in the lungs and something he called the grippe.

After five days in the Tombs, they came to take Tennie away. I could not see her, as the guards placed her in a cell two down from my own. We had held each other with our words throughout the night. We'd sing songs or tell stories.

Now, somehow, someone got Tennie released. When they passed her by my cell, Tennie asked them to stop.

"Vickie, I don't want to leave you, but I have no choice. They have orders to release me." My sister looked horrible. She had lost weight, her pallor was gray, and her eyes had no sparkle in them at all. I recoiled from the sight.

"That bad?" Tennie shook her head.

"Sister, you cannot leave me here alone. You know my fears, please don't abandon me." I pleaded.

"Victoria, I have no choice."

I wondered if one benefactor or another could help me. "Was it Whitelaw, or Henry Clews? Did your Corney arrange your release?" I reached for her between the bars, "Please ask them to get me out of here."

"I will do what I can, Sister. Do not let your mind go too far away. Commune with your spirits, talk with Rosie, but make sure you always come back. Imagine a mooring, see yourself tie a bright ribbon to it before you go, to guide you back when you are far away."

"Tennie, please stay!" I whimpered.

They yanked her down the corridor.

As the guards dragged her away, Tennie shouted, "I will talk to the men at Horace Greeley's funeral tomorrow night, to see if one of them will champion you."

I screamed, "Do not forget me, Tennie. *Please* do not *forget me*." I convulsed sobbing.

The press called the Tombs the worst prison in the North. Only the Old Capitol Prison in Washington, D.C., where Antonia Ford Willard was held and destroyed, earned such a horrific reputation. This dungeon, with its poisonous vapors, smelted humans down to the crudest common denominator, survival.

Antonia coughed and covered her mouth. I watched the crimson stain on her dinner napkin spread over the embroidered "W."

One by one they abandoned me. The jailors imposed limitations on my visitors. James could come only once a week, and I refused to allow the children to see me. Tennie would come with James, but only one could visit me in the cell.

The royal couple, Napoleon and Josephine, stopped visiting me. My dead sisters stopped playing games with me. I could no longer summon Demosthenes. I had not connected to Rosie… since before Tennie had left.

Rosie's parting words to me were, "It will get worse. Know this Victoria, you will survive this long, black night. You have the important half of your life ahead of you."

Four days after Tennie departed, a big brutish policeman with a lame arm brought me a bucket to wash myself. Prisoners were allotted clean water to bathe once a week. He made a point of delivering the water last to me. This meant that all the others had already used this *clean* water. After handing me the bucket, he planted himself outside my cell, staring at me. Then he started to open the buttons on his trousers.

"Not so high and mighty now, are ya, Victoria Woodhull?" He sneered.

I recognized the policeman who assaulted Ginny when she had sneaked under the police line on the day of our grand opening. He punched her in the stomach and then lifted her up from the frozen street to punch her face. Running to protect another woman whom I did not know, I stood in the path of his blow. Luckily, it never landed.

The police captain used a big burl-headed wooden club to smash the attacker's arm.

"I know who you are." I challenged. "Leave me be."

"I am just taking my break. Right here." He snickered. He moved his good fingers into his pants. "You have eight minutes to disrobe and wash yourself… be another week before you get another chance…." He continued to taunt, "Who knows what little beasties are crawling in and out of your holes?" Despite the cold, his face glistened with sweat.

I dumped the wash bucket on my head, then scooped up a bucket full of filth and splashed it on him. I stood on my concrete bed at the end of my short cell and screamed.

"No one will come." He grinned a hideous smile. "One night, I'll come in after everyone else is gone and teach you who's the boss." I heard him slosh away.

I don't dare fall asleep.

I must survive this night.

I developed a hacking cough and had rubbed my nose red from wiping. The mucous made it hard to breathe, but at least it deadened the smell. I started fainting and several times woke up spitting out the putrid water. When the rains stopped, my old friend, a large rat, returned to my cell. I gave her the food I would not eat. She often returned at meal times. Then more rain came and it got colder and darker.

At night, no one. Fear was my only company.

I felt and watched my spirit drift away from my body.

I was completely alone.

James must have made a plea for mercy, because both he and Tennie were in my cell… I think. Was it wistful fantasy, or did I hear him say, "Soon, darling; we will get you out soon." Tennie must have touched my forehead where I got a big bump from falling over. She cried, so I cried too. What were we crying about? I don't know. Then Tennie said something about Yule. I thought Yule was in late December. They brought me some new clothes, but they were several sizes too big on me. Tennie felt my ribs poking at my skin. James felt my shoulders and gently touched my collarbone.

My breasts have shriveled up and fallen off. I cried.

Before my visitors left, the woman tried to get my attention. She said something about focus... soon... hold on. Then they were gone and again, I was completely alone.

One more night. If only I can survive this night.

Stay awake, Victoria!

Was that me?

If I make it to morning, the daily rituals designed to break the will and defeat the soul will be a relief. No matter how dreadful, familiarity bests darkness.

Maybe tomorrow my name will be called to face a judge and I'll find out my fate. Maybe tomorrow I will leave this nightmare.

I see my frail body shattered on the cement bed like a dropped mirror. A jagged piece in my fingers cuts me. My blood flows out of me and stains the putrid waters.

I must try and glue together the sundered pieces of my life. Each shard I pick up to examine cuts me again, and I bleed more. Each new piece I grab cuts me. My hands are so bloodied I won't be able to put the mirror back together.

Slowly, steadily, hope creeps away. Where are you, hope? Have you, too, abandoned me?

I find myself on the bow of small boat in a hurricane, cupping my hands, desperately trying to keep a small candle flickering.

Don't let Pa in. He'll hurt me. He'll hurt me bad.

I feel my innards burning.

There's a fire. Everything is burning!

Help! Women screaming. Animals are braying. Help! The smell of burnt flesh assaults my nostrils. I can't breathe. We will all die. Help me!

No answer. No voice. Alone.

I don't dare fall asleep. Get to another day.

I'm so tired. I want to let go. I'm weary... time to stop... time to let go... go far away... go... time to surrender to sleep eternal... perchance to dream, aye there's the rub.

No! No! No!

Stay alert, Victoria!

Survive this night.

Chapter 22

TRIALS

1873

"**C**ome, my dear," James guided me up the steps to the courthouse. "We will be through this quickly." James treated me with extra kindness. "You promise not to speak?"

"It is important, Vickie." Tennie flanked me on the other side.

"I promise." Didn't they know returning to any prison terrified me, especially the Tombs? My fears doubled when my vision about a fire next door proved true. The thatched roof of Barnum's Circus next to the Tombs caught fire. Seven working girls at a laundry on Fifth Avenue burned to death. All the circus animals died in the flames.

Only a shift in the wind prevented the Tombs from burning. Many of the prisoners died from smoke asphyxiation.

I choked on the suffocating smoke. I would die with the others. I tried to breathe and could not. I gasped.

"Vickie!" James pounded on my back to clear my cough. He lifted both my arms into the air to fill my chest.

"Too bad the conflagration failed to destroy hell itself." I spurted the words between coughs.

"Vickie! Are you all right?" Tennie touched my chin so I would look at her.

"I'm afraid." I wailed and grabbed my sister. I closed my eyes. I tried not to think of my dungeon cell.

I sink into the cold wastewaters. I can't breathe. I feel my own warm blood streaming from cuts on my hands, staining the frigid sewage, like on a linen napkin. I shudder.

"Tennie, she can't appear in court like this! *Victoria!*"

I heard a man shout my name, but I could not see him.

"*Sister!*" Tennie gripped my chin, forcing me to look at her.

"I can't go back." I mewled. I opened my eyes in time to see Tennie shaking her head from side to side, looking desperately at James. I sniveled, "I will do whatever you two tell me."

"Then stay with me, Vickie!" Tennie ordered. "We both need you to stay with us in the here and now."

"Sweetheart," my husband kissed my hand, "you have to stay present in the courtroom."

"Don't speak!" Tennie ordered. Both of them nodded their heads.

Another arraignment, hearing, or trial… there were so many of them. I could not keep them ordered or separate in my mind. Anthony Comstock constantly appeared to swear to my crimes. Somehow this inconsequential commissioner in charge of obscenity and impure literature for the Young Men's Christian Association in Brooklyn Heights had become my Grand Inquisitor. The zealot, an ardent congregant of Plymouth Church, fervently followed his minister, the Reverend Henry Ward Beecher.

The five-foot ten-inch-tall and thick common stock of a man with his devilish fiery-red mutton-chop whiskers and eyes of a flaming torch pursued me from court to court. This self-appointed guardian of Christian souls mounted a national crusade against "undue influences contaminating our society." Comstock vowed to destroy any obscenity or impurity, particularly if it might lead to the forsaken act of masturbation, which destroyed the soul—apparently, with each stroke.

Case by case our herculean lawyers lopped off and seared with fire the heads of this modern-day Hydra, only for it to regenerate with another charge, a new case, another arrest. The original obscenity charge claimed delivery by The U.S. Post Office of the November 2 issue of *The Weekly*, which contained the phrase: "on his fingers the red trophy of her virginity." The Judge dismissed the case for two reasons. First, a technicality: Comstock had filed his affidavit the same day the papers were mailed and thus could not have received them. Second, Comstock asserted, that a specific quote constituted obscenity. When our counsel identified the same words as having been used not only in the plays of William Shakespeare and the poetry of Lord Byron, but also plainly and clearly in the King James Bible, Comstock would not surrender his position.

"Now, Mr. Comstock, I solicit your opinion of the following phrase." He opened the Holy Bible. "I read from the King James Bible, Deuteronomy 22:17. I quote:" Counsel paused to raise the Bible high above his head before bringing to eye level. "the red tokens of the damsel's virginity." My question to you, sir: Is this quote in your knowledgeable opinion an obscenity?"

Comstock placed his hand over his heart and testified, "That is not obscene; it is holy!" Baffled, the judge, who would not dare identify as obscenity the words of the King James Holy Bible, threw both Comstock and the case out of court.

Authorities repeatedly arrested me, each time mortifying me more than the last. Sometimes they arrested Tennie and/or the Colonel as well. One time, the police came to the printing presses and took all the men and also Ginny. I felt bad for them, but they were released the same day.

One thought constantly terrified me. I kept seeing my jailors ripping me from our special cell at Ludlow Street to drag me down, back into the underworld of the Tombs.

I can't go back. Please don't make me. I won't survive. Please!

Bails became an instrument of punishment. They went from unprecedented amounts, to gargantuan, punitive obstacles. Big Boss Tweed, who swindled the citizens of New York for perhaps two hundred million dollars, received a bail of four thousand dollars. As Comstock rose to prominence and power with his boots firmly planted on the necks of two women, Tennie and me, our bails reached *sixty thousand dollars* each. Outrageous!

In February, 1873, Comstock created the New York State Society for the Suppression of Vice, which sought to obliterate "obscenity" in any form, including impure literature, pornography, lewd personal letters, any mention of contraception, any reference to sexual disease—specifically, manuals on prevention, abortatives, and medical study books of anatomy.

With the momentum built by our prosecutions, Comstock appeared before the new Congress. He sought a redefinition of the Civil War era bill authorizing U.S. postal inspectors to inspect all mail and remove any pornography. On March 3, the Senate and the House passed the Comstock Act, criminalizing the use of the United States Postal Service to distribute erotica, contraceptives, abortifacients, sex toys, personal letters alluding to any sexual content or information, newspapers, weeklies, or magazines containing any information regarding the above items. Upon the determination by postal inspectors, any sending party could be imprisoned until a judge determined a fine.

The Congressman from Massachusetts, General Benjamin "The Beast" Butler, sent the following card to every newspaper in country:

> There is a duty incumbent upon me, as sure as my service in the Union army, to warn the republic when threats arise to challenge the basic foundations of our nation. This is a matter of dire importance, an ominous threat to our country, greater than the secession

rebellion over which so many American lives were lost.

The recent passage of The Comstock Act violates one of our most sacred and fundamental rights, vested in the First Constitutional Amendment, which states:

CONGRESS SHALL MAKE NO LAW RESPECTING AN ESTABLISHMENT OF RELIGION, OR PROHIBITING THE FREE EXERCISE THEREOF; OR ABRIDGING THE FREEDOM OF SPEECH, OR OF THE PRESS; OR THE RIGHT OF THE PEOPLE PEACEABLY TO ASSEMBLE, AND TO PETITION THE GOVERNMENT FOR A REDRESS OF GRIEVANCES.

From the earliest cases regarding freedom of the press dating back to 1733 and 1744, when under colonial rule the British governor William Cosby tried to silence *The New York Weekly Journal* for its outspoken criticism of English rule, America has honored and promulgated freedom of the press.

The First Amendment is a simple and elegant departure from egalitarian rule which stifles any dissent. To state the obvious, take as example the American Revolution. Information, ideas and opinions are free to exist without any interference, constraint or prosecution by the rich, the ruling, or those temporarily in charge of government.

The new Comstock Act violates these rights by empowering appointed—neither elected nor approved—officials the right to read my and your private mails, placed into the heretofore safe-keeping of the U.S. Postal Service, to determine what is moral and what is not. The Act further empowers such postal inspectors the unilateral right to place potential violators in jail to be held indefinitely, without bail until a judge can adjudicate the claim, thus violating one of the oldest principals of Medieval English law, HABEAS CORPUS.

The prerogative writ or legal recourse of habeas corpus is known as the great and efficacious writ in all matters to curb illegal confinement, an authorized remedy available to the disenfranchised facing the empowered, the meanest against the mightiest, and carries the force as if ordered by a judge. It is addressed to the custodian, a prison official for example, and demands that a prisoner be taken before the court, and that the detainer present proof of cause for internment and further detention. If the prima facie burden of proof cannot be established, then the prisoner must be released.

The implications of granting anyone the right to read our private mails to unilaterally determine what meets a subjective, temporal, and potentially capricious if not sinister definition of morality, is both abhorrent and perilous. I suggest that such a grant may well be unconstitutional as it violates the First Amendment as presented paramount.

Should any one of us choose to quote a famous poet or nothing less than the Holy Bible, should we be fodder for righteous prosecution at the sole disposition of one person? What if we tenderly and romantically convey the appreciation and memory of a caress or God help us a kiss? Should this communication of private sentiments be subject to anyone's review, interpretation, and judgment?

Sadly, my home state carries upon its soul the inexpungible bloodstains of trials based on the interpretation of words and assumption of thoughts and intentions—the Salem Witch Trials. Are we to return to those unenlightened times?

I say *Nay*!

I have spent my entire career, risked my own life, and ordered far too many young men into harm's way to defend our most basic human rights. Your government has abdicated your rights of privacy and to express your own thoughts, and your ability to privately share your thoughts with another.

Our country was founded on dissent and challenge of the status quo. How dare we, your public representatives and servants, squander your inalienable rights. I implore my fellow citizenry, rise up, dissent, and proclaim your objection.

Shout *Nay*, while you can.

In late spring, 1873, encouraged by Comstock, Luther Chaliss brought charges of libel against me, Tennie, and Colonel Blood—grounds for yet another arrest. This time, Molly de Ford, the famous madam, risked losing her business by coming forward. She testified the facts as reported in *The Weekly* were accurate and true. Once "Mr. Smith" the blue-blood gentleman, Charles Maxwell, entered the courtroom to acknowledge his actions, the case rolled out of court like a decapitated head. I did note that Mr. Chaliss and Mr. Maxwell never faced criminal charges. Obviously, the law and society condoned their behavior, but not ours as servants of the same public for accurately reporting it.

Hydra sprouted a new head when Anthony Comstock filed new charges of malicious slander. This time the Reverend Henry Ward Beecher would publicly accuse me and deny the "untrue stories" under oath. It would not be the first stone, but finally Henry

Ward could smite me down. He only had to swear before God and country and give false testimony. The first time he failed to appear, the court expressed its sympathy upon hearing claims of illness and postponed. The second time, the court indulged the claim the elderly Reverend Beecher could not endure to travel in the inclement weather. The third time, the court refused to listen to any claims and discharged the case. The judge solemnly admonished Reverend Beecher for wasting the court's time and causing undue suffering to the plaintiffs—my family!

In and out… Ludlow Street prison, to and fro… court after court, smells of burning flesh… charge after charge, we were once again impoverished by all the legal costs and the only true obscenity, the punitive levels of bails.

On June 6, 1873, the anniversary day of my ratification as the Presidential nominee of the Equal Rights Party, I felt my health failing. Nonetheless, I went to every editor of a major newspaper in New York City. They each made me wait, but finally allowed me to see them. Time after time, the interview with a few variations followed the same pattern.

"Thank you for taking the time to see me."

"An interview with The Woodhull is always a pleasure, even more so, had Miss Tennessee accompanied you."

"Thank you for your flattery. I will convey your appreciations to my sister."

"Mrs. Woodhull, I must say you look quite haggard and pale. Are you feeling well?"

"No. I am not. I am ridden with anxiety and my health is failing. Tennie and I are working ourselves to the bone to secure enough money to continue to pay our legal fees and post those ludicrous bails."

"I am saddened to hear this. Please take care of yourself."

"Everyone knows the pulpit of Henry Ward Beecher and Plymouth Church direct each and every legal motion."

"Powerful people, Mrs. Woodhull, powerful people! The constant prosecutions must be very difficult."

"Surely, you mean to say *persecutions*."

"Yes, they do seem both malicious and pejorative."

"Then help us!" I would invariably shout. "I come to you, not only on behalf of my family and as a fellow member of the press, but also on behalf of the principle of freedom for all newspapers to accurately report the great, the good, the bad, and the ugly."

"Our newspaper agrees with your legal assertions. We would not have gone about it the way you did. However, we certainly support the premise that the First Amendment as it applies to journalism and an independent press is sacrosanct and an essential pillar of our democracy."

"Then, I beg of you, I plead with you, please report the obvious persecution of your fellow journalists, and implore the public to demand a delay of the federal trial for obscenity on the near horizon."

"As much as we would like to help you, Victoria, you yourself are the best evidence. It is perilous to do so in the present environment. We cannot afford being sued or arrested in multiple cases."

"Tell me you will *not* keep your heads down and your presses still in the face of such coercion."

At the first several encounters I would assail the editor. After the fifth conversation, I simply acquiesced. By the end of a very disappointing day, each apostle of a free press had forsaken us, *The Weekly*, and journalism. I returned to our Broad Street offices. My sister took one look at me and immediately summoned a carriage to take me home.

"You are precariously close to the veil, Vickie. You must rest."

When we arrived at home at 6 East Thirty-Fourth Street, Tennie assisted me up the staircase. My legs felt light and the staircase seemed endless. I faltered and fell, and everything went dark.

Total darkness.

Suddenly a single candle appeared.

The flame fascinated me.

The ocean blue at the base gave way to an arc of soft, melding colors progressing from azure to violet to a shade of silver. The entire outline appeared as the thinnest band of bright yellow that turned into a light gold. The top arc at the tapered tip of the flame embedded a white light in a deep amber chamber.

The colors of light mesmerized me. I felt completely comfortable and at peace, as if I had arrived home in the bosom of a loving family. I joyfully watched the hypnotic flickering motion until I no longer witnessed.

I became the light!

I danced with pulsating energies, bending, lifting, and undulating in flashes of radiance. A wondrous feeling of absolute ecstasy filled my entire being.

Then, somehow, a gust or breath blew me out and I diminished to a dying flicker, my wick quickly turning from blue, to red, to black. I panicked, longing for the glow of the radiant light.

Just as wisps of smoke rose from me, I re-ignited and burned bright, my golden beams illuminating an infinite spectrum surrounding me.

An endless multitude of other resplendent flames engulfed me. In awe, I joined with every other flame, a feeling of complete acceptance and union. I knew a love, constant and pure, that I had never known to exist. My ears filled with alluring, heavenly harmonies.

We all flickered, dancing, swirling to the sounds of an angelic choir. We would all illumine the same or different colors, creating majestic brush strokes. The colors would streak across a vast and endless universe. We shared an infinite unison and communion. I knew I had finally come home to celebrate and enjoy every precious moment as love. Love beyond needing. Pristine, unadulterated, simple Love.

Unending Community... Joy... Love. Infinite love. God-Glorious Love!

It seemed everyone whom I had loved or who had ever loved me, even the energy of endearing moments, places, or objects hovered close, quivering and dancing as one. In utter fulfillment, I surrendered to bliss.

"Isn't it astonishing?" I heard her voice as an ethereal presence. I remained immersed in a celestial symphony of flames, enveloped in an all-embracing love.

"Rosie! Are you here?"

"I told you I would never leave you."

"As did I," the deep male voice of Demosthenes spoke into my ears.

"Can I see you?"

They both laughed a gentle laugh like a cool zephyr on a hot day.

"You are!" Rosie cooed. Suddenly two flames grew in size and power. The corporeal forms of my beloved Rosie and my Majestic Guardian emerged as illuminations. My heart overflowed with joy.

"Who else is here?" I wanted to go touch them, but remained in light form. Then I felt their embrace and my radiance gleamed brighter.

"Everyone." The rich tone of Demosthenes' voice announced.

"And everything," Rosie sang with her laughter like a cascading waterfall.

"It is all so wonderful." I called out, my delight plenary.

"Yes," both responded in heavenly harmony. "And... you have to go back."

"What? Leave here? But why?" I felt the weight of gravity pulling me downward.

"Your work is not done, Victoria." Demosthenes wanted to cast me from paradise?

"Please, no!"

"Yes, Vickie. You have so much more to do." Rosie whispered into my mind. "Have no fear. We will both be with you. Now you know the truth... you were never alone. Everything is the pure energy of Divine Love. We are with you. You are part of everything." Her laughter sounded like sleigh bells, "Always together. Eternally. Forever and a day."

I felt Rosie's smile and laughter enter my body. She guided me into a boisterous splashing of rapids in a river where all the flames disappeared.

"You're back!" My sister, Tennessee shrilled. "We thought we had lost you this time." She turned to the doorway and shouted. "She is awake!" She hugged me. "Colonel Blood, come quickly."

My husband entered and knelt on the floor beside me. He gently caressed my cheek and gave me the most loving kiss on my forehead. "You have been gone for four days, Vickie. Three doctors declared you dead." Tears streamed down his face. "I prayed to God not to lose you." He rested his head on my chest.

I spoke through a veil or haze. "You cannot lose me, my darling." I looked into his eyes. "We are bound forever."

Tennie looked at me intently, then announced, "You have seen beyond."

I grasped my sister's hand.

"Yes, I have seen."

"Victoria Woodhull Dead"

Newspapers across the country reported my death based on reports from the three doctors who came and tried without results to revive me. They administered the traditional tests: feeling for any pulse, a looking glass in front of my mouth, the prick of a pin, and tickling my bare feet with a feather. Each one pronounced me dead.

After my return to the living, many asserted my family conspired to manipulate the press as to win the public favor before my federal case. I did not care anymore. I might feel insulted, but I knew what was true. I experienced a love and connection not of this world waiting for all of us.

I saw the love around me. I knew Laura Cuppy Smith would understand. The one person who had remained unflinchingly loyal. Laura visited me in prison each day, when allowed. She stayed with Zulu Maud and Byron when we could not. When Laura had to leave, she provided for Ginny to take care of Byron. Laura always sat directly behind me in court, holding Zulu on her lap. One could not ask for a more steadfast friend.

One by one, they came back and supported me, some with more vigor, some with less. Elizabeth Cady Stanton sent the newspapers a copy of her letter to Isabella confirming she and Susan had learned the precise facts as the *Weekly* recited from the same named individuals. Miss Anthony told the press she had heard the stories as the *Weekly* had referenced. Even our arch nemesis, Mary Livermore, published in the *Woman's Journal,* a vehement tirade against the persecution of woman, including "The Woodhull and Miss Anthony!" Despite the attestations and recognition, no one invited me to speak at any gatherings for woman rights.

A tide of doubt and wave after wave of contempt crashed upon Plymouth Church and its principals. The public began to realize the vulnerability of each person with the Comstock Act disregarding privacy and unilaterally appointing independent judges of morality.

The evening of June 24, after my federal trial commenced jury selection, I received an unexpected visitor. Henry Bowen, the founder of Plymouth Church, arrived at our domicile at 8:00 p.m. accompanied by four others, two sons, one of the church investors—named Claflin, though no relation—and a stenographer. Bowen wasted no time on civilities.

"Mrs. Woodhull, we have had our differences," he declared.

"I see you are truly gifted in the art of understatement," I retorted.

"Please, allow me to state my purpose, and then I will retire at your request."

I did not feel safe. I clasped the Colonel's hand resting on my shoulder. Tennie came into the room and took a seat.

"Mr. Bowen." She addressed him curtly.

I motioned him to remain seated and continue.

"I have come to your home to make amends. In turn, hopefully, this will encourage you to surrender to my safekeeping letters from certain individuals with whom we are both aggrieved."

"This is an abrupt…" Tennie began.

"Please," Bowen waived his hand interrupting my sister. She scowled, but did not speak. "I solicit your indulgence to let me speak to the end." He nodded his head as a courtesy to my sister. This man never asked permission to direct a conversation. "As a sign of good faith, I will disclose to you certain information you will find useful." He must have seen the look on our faces. "I acknowledge my part in the conspiracy to discredit and if possible, destroy you all by means of continual trials, arrests, and bails."

My husband could not restrain himself. "What kind of man are you, Bowen?" The Colonel rose from his chair to walk away from Bowen, no doubt controlling the urge to strike him, or perhaps retrieve his pistol. "How dare you come into our house, and sit there calmly to inform us you are the progenitor of undue suffering and pain." James stopped. He looked at Bowen as if he were the enemy across the battle line. "For God sakes, man, I nearly lost my wife."

"What kind of man, you ask?" Bowen bowed his head. "An unhappy one, Colonel Blood. I have been blinded by the allure of gold, and betrayed by those I trusted the most."

We were stunned.

Bowen spoke. "I will provide you a copy of a tripartite agreement between the Reverend Beecher, Tilton, and myself. Each of us promises to hold ranks and to disavow any and all wrongdoings against the other. Together, all three of us agreed to cooperate in censuring anyone who dared to expose any facts related to the affairs and the conspiracy to hide Henry Ward's philandering."

Our most heinous antagonist sat before us confirming the grotesque aberration of manipulated persecution over the last eight months. For some reason, the man before us wanted to earn my trust. I shrank further back into my seat, repelled by his composure.

"There are things I believe you do not know." Bowen wanted to say more.

I tried to listen carefully, but the hissing sound at the end of his words distracted me. I tried to stay present.

Bowen proceeded with his confession. "After your exposé in the November 2 *Woodhull & Claflin's Weekly,* your friend and loyal supporter, Isabella Hooker, wrote to her brother, imploring him to admit his folly and ask Plymouth Church, the public, and even you for forgiveness. She even threatened Henry Ward that, if he did not come clean, she would make public disclosures." Bowen paused.

Tennie looked alarmed. So did my husband. I suddenly realized they had kept something from me. No doubt they sought to protect me from further stress, but I felt heat rising up in my body. I clenched my fists.

In the dark, I felt the earth rumble beneath me and shake the house. Who can I trust? Is there anyone to tell me the truth?

I returned to the room. "*Go on!*" I commanded Bowen.

"Yes, ma'am." Surprised by my tone, he flinched. "Henry Ward convinced the ever-pliant Theodore to go to Isabella to disclaim any conversations he had with you, Mrs. Woodhull, regarding his wife or his preacher. Bewildered, Isabella supplicated herself before her older brother, swore loyalty from her knees, and begged forgiveness."

"Oh no!" *I heard my own voice as if it were far away.*

"As reward for her loyalty, knowing the true facts would make her more tempestuous than ever, the good Reverend Beecher consulted with Dr. Harold Butler. He diagnosed 'monomania due to over-excitement from exposure to Mrs. Woodhull.' Henry had her committed to an asylum for the insane out on Long Island."

"Enough!" Tennie yelled.

I looked into the distance.

I felt Isabella being tortured with hot water, cold water, a million pin-pricks, and starvation.

To and fro… Mary Stewart swayed.

Antonia's blood spread on the linen napkin with the embroidered "W."

I choked on the filthy cold waters in the tombs.

Air, I needed air.

… must survive this night.

"Victoria!" I heard my sister's sharp voice. I opened my eyes to see my sister's face. "Remember the candles!"

The flickering candle, surrounded by all the other candles.

I felt warmth and the bliss of being at peace… at home… pure LOVE.

My husband's hand tightened on my right shoulder. I gasped, shook my head, and returned to the room. Bowen watched me intently.

I addressed him. "What is it you want from us, Mr. Bowen?" I asked, stalling for time, seeing fear in Tennie's eyes.

How long was I away?

Bowen spoke as if nothing had happened. "I want the original letters, or in the least, allow the stenographer to make a certified copy of the letters in your presence."

"You wish to destroy your golden goose?" Tennie cut to the chase. "What of the golden eggs you gather daily?"

"If the Reverend were a lad, I would whip him myself. For now, I wish to secure the leverage of proof to direct his future actions. He has caused me egregious and multiple harms, as I believe you know all too well." Bowen stopped himself from saying more.

We all knew he referred to the Reverend's affairs with both his wife and his daughter. His face turned red; admitting to being a cuckold embarrassed the man. Beecher's affair with Bowen's daughter resulted in the enraged, vengeance-seeking man before us.

A moment of silence ensued as I watched through the glass. The kerosene flame flickered, and wisps of frail black smoke wafted into the air. I spoke, looking into the fire.

"The letters I have received are tantamount to confessions of multiple sins." I hesitated, watching the colors dance. "Including the transgressions visited upon your family." I looked at Bowen and made a decision. "If and when you can return Isabella to her home, and demonstrate to me you can terminate the persecutions of myself, my sister, my husband, and his brother George, and of course the *Weekly*, I am predisposed to grant your request."

"I would prefer..." Bowen began.

"Stop!" I stood up and looked Mr. Bowen in the eyes. "Set Bella free and prove your influence on the court. Then, and only then, I will provide you either the originals or a full certified copy of the letters to which you refer."

"Mrs. Woodhull, thank you." The man got up and had the effrontery to smile. "You will see. You shall have your proofs on the morrow."

They left.

"Our worst suspicions are proven true." My husband announced.

"I don't trust the man." Tennie announced.

I looked at both of them and remembered what Bowen had said. "How long have you known my beloved Isabella sits in an asylum on Long Island?"

James approached me, "Please Victoria, we can address that another time." He moved toward me, but I turned away.

"Your husband is right, Sister. You need your rest before court tomorrow."

I slowly climbed the stairs to my bedroom.

Conspiracies everywhere, without, within. Where to turn with no one to trust? Behind each door danger lurks. Rats scurrying across the floor.

At the top of the stairs I spoke without looking back. "Goodnight, then."

Before proceedings began in court the next morning, the presiding judge, who as district attorney had first arrested my family, declared to the jury that due to the fact an 1873 revision of the cited Federal law specifically included the words, "weekly," and "paper," the statute in the 1872 filed case could not apply. The judge dismissed the jury and declared us innocent by operation of law.

Later in the day I learned Isabella had returned to her home, albeit a shattered woman. Not wanting to further traumatize her, I chose to wait to visit her until she reached out to me. I wrote her a brief note:

> *My dearest Bella,*
>
> *I did not know until last night. I am so sorry. Please forgive me.*
>
> *As for you, rest your heart. You have done nothing for me to forgive.*
>
> *I love you eternally,*
>
> *Vickie*

I never had to deliver the letters to Bowen. Henry Ward Beecher tried to preempt any disclosures from either Tilton or Bowen and publicly demanded that anyone with any hard facts come forward. This proved to be disastrous for the ultimate bully. Samuel Wilkerson, the custodian of the original signed copy, released the Tripartite Agreement to the *Tribune* and the *New York Daily Graphic*. Every newspaper in America picked up the story, and the eyes of the nation looked away from us and peered with zealous scrutiny, full of indignation and frenzy, at Plymouth Church and Reverend Henry Ward Beecher.

We were finally free. All the other lawsuits were dropped. Anthony Comstock turned his attentions to others, and many of our friends suffered. No one suffered more persecution than George Francis Train. At the beginning of our travails, Mr. Train had offered to post security for our bails. The *bon vivant* millionaire and co-founder of Crédit Mobilier, purposefully and publicly baited the Protector of Morality by repeatedly publishing suggestive passages from classic literature and the Holy Bible. In response, Comstock had Mr. Train, the original funder and co-founder of *The Revolution* with Stanton and Anthony, imprisoned and held without a hearing or bail in the horrid Tombs.

Our presses destroyed, our financial resources exhausted and with mounting debt, we took to the road. Finally vindicated in the legal matters, we enjoyed a brief period of renewed popularity. By late spring, Tennie and I would deliver speeches wherever and for however much we could get paid—once again, fractions!

On July 9 in the late afternoon, after days of violent rages, my little sister Utica finally succumbed to the poisons, alcohol, and drugs she ravenously consumed. Because malicious rumors spread claiming she died of venereal diseases, I asked the coroner to conduct an autopsy. The coroner certified that Utica died of Bright's disease, which had destroyed her kidneys. I knew she rested in a better place, quietly flickering and feeling loved, among all those other flames.

Chapter 23

COLLAPSE

New York City
Fall, 1873

Early in August, I received two telegrams from J. P. Morgan. The first read:

> *Convert all assets to cash.*
> *Close all bank accounts.*

The second was terser:

> *OUT NOW!*
> *PREPARE FOR STORM.*

I met with J. P. at our home on Saturday evening, September 6. It had been a hot, sunny day, and a bright silver moon illumined the night. As my private banker and financial mentor sat down in our drawing room, I poured Mr. Morgan a tall glass of one of his favorite single-malt whiskies, Oban. Sadly, I could only purchase an eighteen-year-old bottle—we could not afford a prized thirty-two-year-old. He savored the smell and swallowed a goodly amount.

"Have you heeded my warnings?" The now powerful investment banker inquired.

"J. P., we don't have the resources to invest or divest anything."

He looked concerned. "But you are keeping all your cash out of the banks?"

"Indeed." I sighed and sat down next to him, placing the bottle on a circular lamp table. "There is nothing to deposit."

"Then you have no short positions, as I suggested on the way to the burial of Horace Greeley?"

"Mr. Morgan!" I leaned back. "Four governments raced one another to seize or destroy our assets during our many incarcerations. The city government grabbed moveable assets, the county illegally conveyed property titles, the state took as forfeiture funds we held in state banks, and the federal government did the same where we held funds in national banks. Your own firm released funds under our name."

"We tried to delay or stop them, Victoria. Impossible." He lowered his head, clearly distraught.

I laughed. "Save your sorrows, J. P. I have heard the same from John Banker at the Bank of New York and from Henry Clews at Fourth National."

"So, you really have no liquid resources?"

"Absolutely none. Is that more than none?" I jested. "Why are you suddenly so concerned, John?"

"It is all about to collapse. The entire economy!"

"Well, that spoils celebrating our hard-won freedom."

"Yes, congratulations, but be serious, Victoria!" He spoke, annoyed. "Before the month ends, the financial sector will completely collapse. I came to warn you and to help you safeguard any funds you might have."

"Why now?"

"The simple economic answer..."

"Please be brief, J. P." I interrupted his erudite brain, which reminded me of Stephen Pearl Andrews. I had neither the stamina nor patience for an advanced lecture in economics. My once voracious appetite to learn financial matters had long disappeared.

He nodded and continued. "It all comes down to leverage and debt—without risks properly factored in."

"I have often noticed leverage is the narcotic of economics while debt is the alcohol. Both lead intelligent men into folly." I realized I spoke to myself as much as to J. P.

"Brilliantly put, Victoria!" He looked at me admiringly. "You must return to banking and investments quickly." I nodded my head to accept the compliment. "Liquidity, the immediate access to cash will become paramount!" He stopped, and after a moment he chuckled. "I, for one, will maintain intoxication in the liquid form." He motioned for me to refill his empty glass with the remainder of the potent single-malt scotch. I emptied the bottle of Oban 18.

After a long drink, J. P. Morgan stood up, reached for both my hands and bent his knee to allow me to remain seated. "I shall always be indebted to you, Victoria. You have an unusually keen insight into the behavior of people and markets." I waited for the typical addendum, "… for a woman," but none ensued. I smiled.

"Thank you, J. P."

"When you have need of a banker or a friend, please remember to call on me. I will remain always your humble servant."

He stood and made his way to the door. On the round lamp table before the hallway he placed a thick wad of one-hundred-dollar bills and, without looking back or waiting for a thank you, saw himself out.

The Great Depression of 1873 put capitalism itself on trial. The public finally realized the precarious frailty of the U.S. economy. While my family personally benefitted, the Gold Scandal of 1869 identified the inherent risks of *laissez-faire*— manipulation, leverage, and debt. No questions were asked. No commissions formed to investigate. No charges filed. There were no legislative reforms after the brink of disaster, when one more day would have collapsed the entire economy. Of course, the Commodore

Vanderbilt intervened, conveniently buying up most of America for pennies on the dollar.

The diseased system continued to fester, untreated; Daily disclosures of abuses and political corruption of the Crédit Mobilier scandal during the financing of the Transcontinental Railroad obliterated the public's confidence. Congressmen, senators, and even former Vice President Shuyler Colfax all took free stock in exchange for absurd and irresponsible amounts of U.S. government loans, the *entire amounts* of which defaulted.

Jay Cooke, the financier who War Secretary Solomon Chase contracted as the sole agent to sell five-hundred-million dollars' worth of U.S. War Bonds—known as Five-Twenties, callable in five years and maturing in twenty—received a twenty-million-dollar commission on the war bonds. Cooke and Associates invested heavily in railroad stocks. Mr. Cooke planned a second transcontinental route far to the north, from Duluth, Minnesota to the Pacific Northwest. Cooke's newly formed North Pacific Railroad secured new federal government financing and sold bonds to commence operations. The founders structured the entire enterprise without any equity, completely leveraged—all debt. Thus, the owners and operators could not lose any money; they had no skin in the game.

On September 17, the press stated the federal government reneged on a three-hundred-million-dollar loan commitment to N.P.R.R. On September 18, Jay Cooke and Associates' attempt to instill new life by selling new bonds arrived stillborn. The market collapsed like a house of cards. Stocks and bonds plummeted in value. By noon, lines formed in front of Jay Cooke and Associates filling the streets and reaching down two blocks, as account holders demanded their cash balances. Cash ran out within an hour. The next day, thirty financial institutions declared insolvency and shuttered their doors.

Unlike back in 1869, Cornelius Vanderbilt would not ride his stallion onto the trading floor to act as savior! Panic shattered the economy like frigates burst by bombardment barrages from broadside canons. Investors scurried about to liquidate anything they could, like rats abandoning ship.

Dear Henry Clews, who had always helped Tennie and me, had to close the Fourth National Bank before noon on the nineteenth, as more than two thousand people blocked Nassau Street from No. 20 past Wall Street and continuing down Broad Street past our former offices.

The New York Stock Exchange closed indefinitely on Saturday, September 20, 1873, as the moon waned to new. The financial markets could not tell if the moon would wax again, nor if the sun would ever rise.

Freedman's Bank became one of the earliest victims of the collapse. After the war, the bank had built its business on the strength of small deposits by freed slaves. This single institution held the aspirations, hopes, and dreams of all Negroes. Six months earlier, the founding trustees solicited and secured the honorable Frederick Douglass to serve as president of the bank. This boosted confidence, and deposits soared. Within months, Mr. Douglass learned the original founders were Klux Klansmen and had raided the bank from within with false loans to themselves, members of the U.S. Senate Committee on Finance, and Klan programs.

Douglass petitioned President Grant, whom Frederick had supported (while nominated as my running mate) to intervene. Grant would not even meet. Without any outside assistance, the honorable Douglass arranged for depositors of Freedmen's to receive eighteen cents per dollar. This turned out to be the highest payout to depositors of any failed bank.

I sent two letters to Frederick but received no response. He did publish a short statement to explain how he and his race had been bamboozled:

> It is now revealed that The Freedmen's Bank has been the black man's cow, but the white man's milk.
>
> The moral atmosphere is more than tainted, it is rotten. Avarice, duplicity, falsehood, servility, fawning and trickery of all kinds, confront us at every turn.
>
> You claim you have emancipated us. Legally you have, and I thank you for that. But when you turned us loose, you gave us no acres. You turned us loose to the sky, to the storm, to the whirlwind, and worst of all, you turned us loose to the wrath of our infuriated masters.

Shunned and avoided, I received no invitation to attend or speak at the Woman Congress in New York City. Instead, I spoke at Cooper Union the same evening, October 17. I did not feel well and I thought my clothes reflected this fact. I wore a simple pleated black skirt and a black braided jacket gathered at my waist with a starched white shirt underneath. I did adorn myself with my signature ornamentation, a single half-opened white tea rose on my lapel.

I titled my speech "Reformation or Revolution, Which? Or Behind the Political Scenes." The crowd once again exceeded the legal limit as four thousand packed the hall to overflowing. The boisterous assembly shouted off the stage the scheduled preliminary speakers. I realized I no longer felt the dread I used to feel. Instead, confidence buoyed me; even though I suffered a sore throat and a slight fever, I spoke my truth. After introductory remarks, I pressed my purpose:

> The action of about fifty men in destroying a cargo of tea, brought on the revolutionary war. If fifty men,

out of three millions of inhabitants at that time, with the limited dissatisfaction that existed against the crown, could bring about a revolution, how many men and women out of forty millions inhabitants are required, with the widespread dissatisfaction now existing, to bring about revolution?

... Two years ago, when I was importuning Congress to do political justice to women, which was denied, I found the wiser portion of Congressmen feared the country was drifting into revolution. ... Do not deceive yourselves. Negro slavery was not so great a cause of dissatisfaction then, as are the more subtle slaveries of today. Nor were the slave oligarchs any more alarmed about their slaves, then, than are the political, financial and industrial oligarchs for their possessions now.

The bondholders, money-lenders and railroad kings say to the politicians: If you will legislate for our interests, we will retain you in power, and, together (you and the public offices and patronage and we with our immense dependencies and money), we can control the destinies of the country, and change the government to suit ourselves. Now finally, comes in the threatened church power and it says: If you will make your government a Christian government, we will bring all the 'Faithful' to your support. Thus united, let me warn you, they constitute the strongest power in the world. It is the government, all the wealth of the country, backed up by the church against the unorganized groups of reformers, every one of whom is pulling his or her little string in opposing directions.

... The developments over the past two years— the corruptions, frauds and failures—are sweeping condemnation of the system under which they have flourished. From Tammany down to the latest Brooklyn expose, first and last, one and all, they speak unmistakable tones of the approaching culmination of the system. They prove beyond cavil that the government has degenerated into a mere machine, used by the unscrupulous to systematically plunder the people.

... What does the City of New York, this Christian city, with its numerous churches, laden with gold, dedicated to God and Christ, care for the thousands of children who live from its slop barrels, or the thousands more who die from partial starvation and neglect! ... I arraign this thing that goes by the name of Christianity, as a fraud; and its so-called teachers as imposters. They profess to be the followers of Jesus of Nazareth, while they neither teach, preach, nor practice the fundamental principles He taught and practiced.

... Then, when we will have accomplished the good work to the future, will begin the long-time sung and prophesized millennium, in which Love instead of hate, equality in place of aristocracy, and justice where is now cruelty, shall reign with undisturbed and perpetual sway, and peace on earth and good will among us abound.

Because I see this for humanity, in the near future, I have been willing and able to endure what its advocacy has cost me of personal discomfort and of public censure. Finally, in conclusion: May the God, Justice; the Christ, Love and the Holy Ghost, Unity—the Trinity of Humanity—ascend the Universal Throne, while all nations, in acknowledging their supremacy, shall receive their blessings—their benedictions.

The newspapers reported that the applause shook the rafters and floors of Cooper's Union for over a full hour.

By the end of November, fifty-five publicly held companies declared insolvency. Over five thousand other businesses failed. Bands of hungry, homeless, and unemployed men roamed the streets. The island of Manhattan, especially the financial district, became a dangerous place, with roving gangs of starving men willing to risk the nothing they had to attack anyone to get coin for a loaf of bread. If arrested, all the better; at least they would get something to eat.

After a three-year presence in the financial district, Woodhull & Claflin, a registered brokerage, announced in the *Weekly* the Broad Street offices were closed and now housed at our residence on West 23rd Street. No loss, business had entirely died off.

In December, we set out by train to St. Louis. The family of my older sister, Molly, stayed at our home to join Ginny in watching over Byron. Sometimes Ginny would contribute some money. I did not have the heart to ask what work she had found.

As if traveling back in time, we crisscrossed the Midwest by covered wagon. Tennie and I delivered speeches wherever people could pay a dime as an entrance fee. To the bitter consternation of Tennie and James, Roxy and sometimes Buck accompanied us. Roxanne took care of Zulu; Buck, when he joined us, was Buck.

We did not celebrate Yule.

The New Year dawned unhappy and bleak.

Chapter 24

THE STORM

1874–1876

The year 1874 displayed brutality from the start.

Daily, scores of frozen corpses—the death caused from starvation and exposure to the harsh elements—lined the snowdrift-covered streets. Wagons would collect America's newest form of waste, the bodies of young and old alike, the ones the elements and we, the people, had sentenced to death. The Great Depression deepened. It became more and more difficult to separate the financial toll from the human carnage.

Every single market day, more names of once-powerful corporations were erased from the annals of the New York Stock Exchange. Scores of influential men could reconcile neither their books nor their downfall, and suicides became epidemic.

Through the dead of winter, we traveled through the warmer South. It seemed the farther away we traveled from New York, Washington, D.C., Chicago, and other major cities, the local people who lived closer to the land fared better by comparison. Not well, but better. Tennie and I would speak, or conduct spiritual séances for whatever we could get. We asked for voluntary contributions, bartered for lodging, a hot meal for the family, or some mason jars filled with fruits or vegetables. By March we had to make our way back to New York City. We were all sick and exhausted.

The one person I least expected called on me at our home. James and Tennie were off preparing a new edition of the *Weekly*. The range of emotions I experienced surprised me. I had thought I would feel only contempt.

"Theodore!" I remained seated and motioned him to a wing chair across from where I sat on the parlor settee. "I am surprised to see you." I directed him away from his hesitant and awkward attempt to approach me.

I watched as he removed his gloves, revealing the long fingers. I remembered how his hands used to caress my body, and the words of adulation he had scribed in my biography. I did not look up and seek his eyes. His voice punctured the screen I tried so hard to impose.

"Thank you for seeing me, Victoria."

His strong voice transformed into something frail. I looked up and beheld a crumpled man, his eyes downcast. Gone were any vestiges of confidence, elitist *esprit de corps*, and the posture of assuredness. He seemed to have aged fifteen years in as many months.

"I have come to confess and to ask your forgiveness."

I watched him as his myopic vision focused on the floor below him. I felt a rage rise up in my body. "Oh, for God's sake, Theodore, be a man and look at me!" He briefly raised his head, glanced at me, and returned to his intense preoccupation with the floor.

He sat there mute. My scorn grew by the second. I broke the silence. "I am neither confessor nor absolver. You have your reverend for that."

He recoiled from my words. "There are things you do not know, Victoria. I have wronged you and the ones you love—those who trusted me most. Please permit me to recite my egregious behaviors. Things will make more sense once you learn what I have done."

"I will *not* allow it." I yelled. "For the simple reason it may give you some relief. A relief you are not due." The dam inside of me burst, and my vexation gushed forth. "You have *destroyed* innocent Isabella! "I shouted at him. "Why do men commit atrocities against our sex, thinking women will not know of it?" I took a deep breath. "Damn you!"

"I am damned."

"I do not believe you, Mr. Tilton!" He flinched at his proper name. "I perceive no differentiation between Faust pleading for clemency when the pact is already set, nor the serpent offering a taste of knowledge to Eve, and the spineless man groveling before me."

"You are being cruel. You know you cut me deeply. Perhaps I deserve it."

"*Cruel!*" I stood and walked away from him and paced the room. "*Perhaps!*" I wrung my hands. "To think I once held you as my knight, above other men, the most enlightened, upstanding and pure."

"I had no choice. Your silly biography cost me dearly. I was ridiculed and marginalized. I had to abandon you." He looked at me with his big doe-like eyes that used to hold mine for hours.

"That 'silly biography' splayed me wide open in front of the entire world. I call it an endeavor of love."

"Your charms blinded me." He retorted.

I snorted my disgust. "Why not say bewitched? Isn't that what your kind claim to avoid any responsibility for their actions?" I broke into a tattling child voice, "The witch cast a spell over me."

"I said blinded."

"Oh Teddy, you are a wordsmith. You can equivocate all you want. Your lack of faith blinded you... to truth!" I wanted to spit out the bile I tasted. "What you have abandoned is yourself." I looked into the distance. "Reviewing the course of betrayal and misery you have left in your wake, your expedient mercurial turns and capricious comings about of loyalty prove positively you have had no self at all." I looked at the decrepit man. "Do you even have a backbone?"

"What would you have me do?" He rose in anger and towered over me, his right hand forming a fist. He smashed his fist into his hand in front of my face and retreated a few steps.

I stepped back. It took me several moments to calm my breath. "So, passion still abides in thee." I breathed deeply twice more. "Albeit a small fragment of your former glory remains, it is buried deep." I intentionally goaded him, "Behold, you can still hold yourself erect, when properly excited."

"Victoria, your taunts and barbs are trivial against my self-torments. I ask you again. *What would you have me do*?" He bellowed.

I thundered back at him. "Break with the devils and expose them. *Damn you!*" I had to slow down. "Return to serve the public, reclaim the citadel! Be a lighthouse and illumine the darkest corners and hidden secrets you have agreed with Mephistopheles to protect."

"And expose to the world my own cuckold?"

"Ha!" I laughed, before I could hold it back. "Do you really think there is a single soul who does not already know of it?" I looked straight into his eyes. "Seize control, Mr. Tilton." I wanted him to return to a glimmer of his former self. "Stand up tall and strong. Account, expose, and accuse by the most public means available the vile behaviors of your master."

"I am sorry, Victoria." He rose to leave.

I let go the anger and looked upon my former lover with compassion. I stood and offered him my hand to shake. "We will not meet again, Mr. Tilton, except by circumstance in public." I let go of his hand. "Know I wish you well." I hesitated, turmoil swirling inside of me. I decided to give him this hope. "I have seen the other side, Theodore. What you will learn during this life or after is that we are all flickers of the same flame. Universal Love is the one truth, our common life force. Do *not* forsake it."

In June of 1874, Theodore Tilton published the entire truth of the affairs of Henry Ward Beecher. He proceeded to file a lawsuit against his former minister and mentor for alienation of affections of the plaintiff's wife, Elizabeth Tilton.

From January through June, 1875, poverty slit the underbelly of America wide open to spill its guts. The relentless exposures of excesses from the top down deadened the national soul. The citizenry longed for some form of distraction.

The lawsuit against the most famous man in America, Reverend Henry Ward Beecher, finally proceeded to trial. Every newspaper in the nation and most major newspapers abroad offered their readers a daily balm to the Great Depression, the grand entertainment of "The Trial of the Century." This single story kept most publications solvent when all else was falling apart. Even the starving would spare a penny to witness the morally righteous, high and mighty fall.

Due to the public obsession with the ongoing trial, the fees for Tennie or me delivering a speech returned to one hundred dollars an evening. Our remuneration never did return to the one thousand dollars I once commanded, but less money went much farther as precious few had any at all. The family toured months on end without rest.

I delivered one hundred and fifty speeches during half a year, even as far away as San Francisco, full of memories of my youth, acting and loving with Josie and Rosie. Seemed to me another life; hard for me to imagine it happened only a decade and a half ago.

Most talks I quoted the November 2, 1873, exposé in the *Weekly*, and then delivered various renditions of "Reformation or Revolution, Which?" that had been first presented at the Cooper Union back in October, 1874.

As always, coin expanded Pa's love for his family. Buck returned like a vulture to a battlefield. Colonel Blood grew increasingly impatient and hostile to everyone in the family except Tennie, Byron, and Zulu. The constant contact of living in a covered wagon and a cupboard, crammed into a train car, or sharing a couple of hotel rooms fueled hostilities.

My husband would often depart our traveling caravan for months. He would return to New York to work with George on the *Weekly*. Often, Tennie would leave to distance herself from our parents. I finally returned to New York tired, but financially recuperated, with most of our debts negotiated and settled in full.

After six months of daily shenanigans in court, providing pure entertainment for the public, the "Trial of the Century" jury could not reach a verdict, and the judge declared a mistrial. Fabricating their own myth, the congregants of Plymouth Church embraced the *vindicated* Reverend Beecher, as did no doubt many of its women parishioners.

As the trial ceased to be the prevailing scandal, our speaking engagement fees once again plummeted. By the end of 1875, as the national economy approached comatose, we were penniless—again.

For all the hardship and despair, I had a new light burning inside of me, a new message I wanted to deliver. I would heed the advice I had spoken to Teddy.

I would shine a new beacon of truth and hope.

As 1876 arrived, Elizabeth Cady Stanton provided a moment of respite when she granted a New Year's Day interview at her home in Tenafly, New Jersey. The reporter asked her if The Woodhull had destroyed the woman rights movement. Her comments were reported on January 2 in the *Newark Sunday Call*:

> Victoria Woodhull has done a work for woman that
> none of us could have done. She has faced and dared
> men to call her the names that make women shudder,

while she chucked principle, like medicine, down their throats. She has risked and realized the sort of ignominy that would have paralyzed any of us who have longer been called strong-minded.

She has risked leaping into the brambles that were too high for us to see over them, she broke a path into their close and thorny interstices with a steadfast faith that glorious principle would triumph at last over conspicuous ignominy, although her life might be sacrificed. And when, with a meteor's dash she sank into a dismal swamp, we could not lift her out of the mire or buoy her through the deadly waters. She will be as famous as she had been infamous, made so by benighted or cowardly men and women… In the annals of emancipation, the name of Victoria Woodhull will have its own high place as deliverer.

Encouraged by Lizzy Beth's statement I spent a couple of weeks trying to find a way to communicate what I saw and felt when I died for four days back in 1873. Before bed one evening in late January, I handed a new speech, "The Garden of Eden," to James to read and make notes. The speech expressed my new purpose. I recounted the misdirections I had pursued.

When I awoke, James had already descended downstairs. I donned a winter robe and joined him in the parlor. The tone of his voice indicated my husband's fierce mood.

"Victoria, this goes against everything we have stood for, everything we believe in!" He shook the pages.

"Husband, this is what I saw when I died."

"That's not fair, wife. I cannot argue with or apply logic to your visions. What you relayed to me does not mean you have to negate all we have fought for."

"Colonel Blood, I have always spoken my truth."

"Yes, when you spoke the words well-crafted by those loyal few of us constantly in your service."

"Do you think for a moment disparagement will dissuade me?"

"No, Victoria. I would never assume I could ever in any possible way persuade The Woodhull one way or the other on any matter. In fact, you have proven time and again my advice is of little consequence in your determinations."

"I have always sought your counsel and listened to you," I insisted.

He screamed at me. "Do not deny or recreate our history to me!" He rose and started to pace—never a good sign. "You rarely sought and even less often heeded any vantage different from what you had already decided." He cast the pages onto the lamp table. "You are the most obdurate, stubborn, and impenitent person I have ever met!"

"Then why do you stay with me? Why force me to support you?"

"*What?*" He wheeled around to confront me. "I have sacrificed everything to support and defend *you*." He turned from me, "I will not tolerate these ill-conceived refashionings of our lives. Perhaps you have been making up stories and re-inventing yourself for so long, you can no longer tell the difference."

"I remain true to what I believe. I am loyal." I argued back.

"Really?" He sneered. "In this speech, you cast away all that is precious and dear, everything *I* have worked for." You state in this speech that to you *free love* always meant God and Christ would welcome one's love and return it. *You sound like Henry Beecher!* Then what were all those affairs, wife? How were they expressions of your love for God?"

"I believe in every word I have ever spoken. I have faith!"

"Oh yes, completely blind faith." My husband took no measure to protect me from his vehemence. "You are willing to abandon history and truth to some misbegotten fancy."

"I speak what I know to be true and do it for us. *I do everything for us! I sustain us!* And I *always* listened to you." I shouted the words, but felt no strong conviction.

"Of course, you do." He sneered. "The habitation of your parents and family in our home proves it. They steal from us, Victoria, they seek to destroy you, and you don't even see it. They will never love you!" He roared.

"You injure me, husband."

"*No!* It is *you* who injures *us*. You have proven your independent willfulness to the point of our total ruin, time and again."

He paused, no doubt to apologize for his spiteful words. I waited. He grabbed up the pages and continued to admonish. "Why must you repudiate everything we have stood for? How can you disavow free love? Will you now abandon rights for women as well?" He rattled the pages in his hand. "Are you a traitor, Victoria? This is tantamount to *apostasy!*"

I stopped myself from reaching for my temple with my right index and forefinger, the way I used to when I did not know a word. I disengaged and walked away, without asking the meaning of the word.

"This is pointless!" I kept walking.

"Why are you willing to abandon everything we hold sacred?" I heard my husband moan behind me. After a moment he screamed, "Don't you *dare* walk out on me."

I did not turn. I did not stop. I did not look back.

I remembered feeling the first tear in the fabric of our marriage, way back in April of 1870, when James conducted a meeting over the behaviors of Buck—specifically about how he stole Emily Astor's deposit of $3,000.

I suffered a cramp in my stomach. I grabbed the bannister to steady myself. I sank to the steps. I heard the door downstairs slam shut. Sadly, I knew that, before the year would end, the sacred union with the man I had loved for over a decade would be cleaved apart and rendered irreparable.

From April on, I focused on the speech that had so upset my husband. "The Garden of Eden: Paradise Lost and Found" set forth my vision of the proper interpretation of the Garden of Eden as representative of the female body and Tree of Life, specifically, the female reproductive organs. Woman embodied the holiest of holies, and as such must remain true, faithful, and pure.

> The soul of the weary pilgrim when traveling the tangled paths of life's tempestuous journey sometimes sickens and faints by the way. But there is that within the soul that will not repose.
>
> What can be more sublimely beautiful, more entrancingly sublime than the thought that within ourselves—in our bodies—there is the power to create an immortal soul, and an immortal residence for that soul, if we will but learn aright—if we will but learn the truth, which, by being known, shall make us free indeed....
>
> We are now prepared to assert that The Garden of Eden is the human body, that every body is a Garden of Eden, and that the second chapter of Genesis was written by Moses to mean the body; and that it cannot mean anything else... What more complete idea could there be formed of paradise than a perfect human body—such as there must have been before there had been corruption and degradation in the relation of the sexes? The Garden of Eden, in which the Lord God put the man whom he had formed, "to keep it and to dress

it," and in which He created Adam and Eve—universal thinking man—was the human body....

In the Gospels, John saw that these fruits were to be fully realized in the new heaven and the new earth, meaning the new man and the new woman, when told, "to him that overcometh" and is able to pass the cherubims and the flaming swords set at the gates of The Garden of Eden—the sentries guarding the Holy City— shall be given to eat "of the hidden manna".... When this shall come, then "there shall be no more death, neither sorrow nor crying, neither any more pain."

And in the understanding that this perfection is coming to the world, hear the sounding of the seventh angel who comes to herald the doom of death, and realize the prophecy of Paul, who said: "The last enemy that shall be destroyed is death."

Shall we enter through the gates into the holy city, by "The straight and narrow way," and find eternal life in the sunshine of thy everlasting glories, O, enchanting Garden!

... In God's good time, as He shall be able to draw Himself, and enter his children into their rest to know no sorrow more forever; but in glad anthems of never-ending progress, expand their souls, until they shall be one with God, and see Him face to face. That is what it is to enter once more into the Garden of Eden and to live bathed in the glory of its pleasures and delights.

Inevitably, I would be asked if my present view was consistent with my previous advocacy for free love? I would answer, "Yes. God, Himself loves his children freely. And each one of us is free to love Him and be returned to the Garden of Eden."

I removed Stephen Pearl Andrews as editor, and without the active support of Colonel Blood, *Woodhull & Claflin's Weekly* declared on June 10, 1876, after seventy-three months since our premier issue, that the current volume would be the last.

On September 18, I went to the Hall of Justice in Brooklyn to file a petition for dissolution of marriage between Colonel James Harvey Blood and Victoria Claflin Woodhull. To secure the divorce, I had to claim James had committed adultery and specify his accomplice. Knowing the Colonel's code of honor would not allow him to contest, I swore to spurious charges.

On October 9, I received a sealed envelope from Judge J. O. Dykman in Brooklyn. The letter contained an official court decree of dissolution. When hounded by the press for a comment, the gentle and kind man, Colonel Blood, said:

"A magnificent woman has turned her back on me. I will say no more."

In the late stormy afternoon of New Year's Eve, 1876, Tennie returned from seeing her Corney, the Commodore Cornelius Vanderbilt. I knew the Commodore's long-time physician, Dr. Jared Linsley, had arranged for a few meetings between the Commodore and my sister. Each time, it revitalized the frail eighty-two-year-old patriarch. Tennie entered the house and ran up the stairs to her bedroom.

I followed and heard her sobbing. I tested the door and found it unlocked. Without being invited, I entered her room. She crumpled onto the bed.

"He is in such pain. I could only slightly abate his suffering." She cried out. "The only man I will ever love is going to cross over very soon."

"Surely he is rejuvenated and given new vigor seeing you." I tried to encourage her. "Dr. Linsley must believe…"

"Wouldn't that be so very convenient for you, Sister!" Tennie bitterly interrupted me.

Despondent, she wailed.

I could not stop myself. "You know what awaits. You know the glory."

"Stop it!" She curled herself into a fetal position and cried. "He lies dying, and I will never see him alive again."

I dared not speak.

"I want him to live." She gasped. "I want to feel his moist breath on my neck, his rough hands caressing my breasts, his crusted fingers teasing my nipples. I want to hold him so close I infuse life force back into him. He can take all of mine!"

"You two will be…"

"Don't!" She abruptly stood up, pushed me aside, and faltered to a chair. "I know he will let go very soon. I want to be with him to guide him, as I did so many during the War, and with the patients at the cancer clinic."

"Tennie, both you and I…"

"Do you really think you can comfort me, Sister?" Her tone froze me. "Stop! For just once, be *silent!*" She screamed hysterically. She looked up at me accusingly. "I am condemned to a long lifetime void of the love I never knew until he taught me it exists." She staggered back to the bed. "I will suffer a fate worse than Prometheus. All I have to look forward to in the future is a giant eagle tearing through my barren body and plucking at my womb, day after day, after day…" She rocked herself to sleep.

I had to stand off and resist my impulse to hold her.

I watched over my sister as Tennie slept through a fitful night, contorting herself, twisting and kicking, only to fix in a fetal position. She would call out "Wait!" or, "Don't leave me," stretching her limbs and extending her hands to grasp hold of something, someone. When the lightning flashed through the rain-streaked windowpanes, the bed appeared awash in a river of tears drowning my sister.

As I entered twixt sleep and awareness, I heard Rosie's wonderful laughter. Then her voice of dulcimer bells spoke to me.

"Come to me, Vickie. It is time."

THE END

ACKNOWLEDGMENTS

We live in a magic time. Changes that Victoria Woodhull fought for are finding root and changing the landscape. The recent momentum of awareness and discussion, and illuminating deep dark secrets in the light of full disclosure remains a marvelous incentive to continue my work. So, I start by thanking each one of you, dear reader, and all who are willing to take a hard look at ugly things and want and need to change them.

Volume Two of The Victoria Woodhull Saga was tough to write, and for many, certain passages will be tough to read. I promise you it is worth the effort. I self-imposed a standard to achieve and excel the highly acclaimed OUTRAGEOUS—a daunting task. I wanted to get it right. This second volume explores the heart and consciousness of Victoria and Tennessee—the reason I started this whole effort. The way these two fearless women were treated by the society they dared challenge to change, remains SCANDALOUS.

Paramount, I want to thank Teri Rider of Top Reads Publishing, LLC. Without Teri's almost daily support and encouragement this new work would not be published. The appearance and content of the entire work, especially the physical book is all Teri—cover design, back cover design, interior layout, print design; even the stock and covers are alive with the smell of excellence and quality due to Teri's professional dedication. Thank you, dear friend, for making the book the best achievable presentation of my writing. Indeed, you have made me better as well.

I want to thank a couple of my teachers in high school. Robert Karlsrud, Professor of American History Emeritus at Sonoma State University, showed us how much one's belief system influences their recording of history. Mrs. Lillian Young, who in the eleventh grade had us read James Joyce's, A Portrait of the Artist as a Young Man, gave me the gift of loving literature and enjoying the effort it took to fully appreciate it. And then there was the playful Frederick Holtby who put up a huge banner across the entire room that read: ESCHEW OBFUSCATION—and refused to tell us what it meant, so we had to discover it ourselves. We don't praise our teachers nearly enough. I thank all the wonderful teachers who engender in young people a new passion and desire to learn more.

The quality of what you hold in your hands is the direct result of my work with my toughest and most brutal critic, the masterful mentor, Win Blevins, my editor, and his accomplished wife and writing partner, Meredith Blevins. Last year Win received the Owen Wister award from the Western Writers of America for lifetime achievement in writing literature and history of the West, was inducted into Hall of Fame of Western Writers, and displayed in the Buffalo Bill Museum in Cody, Wyoming, and once again achieved being listed on the coveted top 10 New York Times bestseller list. Win has taught writing for over forty years. Maestro, thank you. I am so honored you chose to work with me and challenge me word by word.

Throughout the writing of Volume Two, I imagined Maestro Win yelling. "Shorten it! Too flowery! Get back to the story! I want to feel hungry, not read about it!" I would also sometimes hear the compassionate voice of Meredith gently soothing, "keep working it, Neal, sometimes the right words have to be mined." Win's unfaltering accuracy is the hardest thing to accept; damnably, he is invariably correct. I know, Win, you want me to shorten these two paragraphs into two sentences and lose the exclamation points!!! Rebellion is sweet.

Victor Villaseñor, National best-selling author, three-time Pulitzer Prize nominee, and passionate women's empowerment advocate, provided a Rain of Gold -en comments that enhance the entire tapestry. Victor is uncanny at getting to the pith of things and suggesting a few perfect adjustments. Victor also suggested that I visit Oaxaca, where I now live. Gracias, Amigo. Abrazos grandes.

For this second book, I had a wonderful new source of historic materials, Victoria's own words! Thanks to the New York Public Library,

I read the pages of the first American newspaper owned, edited, and published by women, Woodhull & Claflin's Weekly; I also acquired volumes of Victoria's speeches. The Bibliography identifies several sources and the wonderful history books I used to study Victoria and her times. Without these incredible prior works, I could not have written my books. Special mention to Debby Applegate, who portrayed all the complexities of one Henry Ward Beecher.

If you forego traditional publishing, effectively releasing a novel requires an army of consultants and contractors. Meredith Blevins, your constant humor and support guided me well. Lynette M. Smith, thank you for your meticulous line editing. I apologize for never learning some basic grammar rules.

My network of friends and family are tremendously supportive. Together, we create a healthy community that gives me the strength to stay on task. Arne Liss, Ph.D. and Mojgan Jahan, Ps.D. thank you for your reviews that contributed to an accurate psychological rendering. Thanks to Vera A. Weisz for all your contributions of in depth scrutiny, as if it was one of your major briefs for court. Thank you Patrice Perillie for inspiring my next work.

Alex Katz, Amber Reimers, Leetal Katz, Julie Ann Katz, and Nina Barbara Lott, Ph.D., thanks to each of you, I love you. My Mom was a prolific writer, she passed over leaving many unfinished manuscripts. Dad took me along to business meetings as if I were his apprentice, so I learned entrepreneurism and finance at an early age. Clearly, this book combines some of the best of both my parents, I am sure they are smiling.

I wish you well.
Neal Katz
San Andres Huayapam, Oaxaca, Mexico
2018

BIBLIOGRAPHY

The following books helped me tremendously. Like Victoria and Tennessee I like defying convention, so the books are listed in order of significance of contribution to Volume Two.

SOURCE MATERIAL:

The Woodhull & Claflin's Weekly: 1870 – 1876 Archives: The New York Public Library

Woodhull, Victoria C. (Author), Michael W. Perry (Introduction), *Lady Eugenist Femisint Eugenics in the Speeches and Writings of Victoria Woodhjull, Seattle, WA, Inkling Books, 2005*

Woodhull, Victoria C. author; Carpenter, Cari M., editor *Selected Writings of Victoria Woodhull: Suffrage, Free Love, and Eugenics (Legacies of Nineteenth-Century American Women Writers)*, University of Nebraska Press, 2010

Woodhull, Victoria C. (Author), Michael W. Perry (Introduction), *Free Lover: Sex, Marriage and Eugenics in the Early Speeches of Victoria Woodhull* Seattle, WA Inkling Books, Reprint December 2, 2005

Woodhull, Victoria, *The Garden of Eden: Or the Paradise Lost and Found, 1875, DoDo Press, 2005*

HISTORY BOOKS:

Applegate, Debby, *The Most Famous Man in America: The Biography of Henry Ward Beecher*, New York, Three Leaves Press, Random House, 2006

Sachs, Emanie, *The Terrible Siren, Victoria Woodhull 1835 – 1927,* New York, Harper and Brothers Publishing, 1928

Goldsmith, Barbara, *Other Powers: The Age of Suffrage, Spiritualism, and the Scandalous Victoria Woodhull*, New York, Adolph A. Knopf, Random House, 1998

Fox, Richard Wightman, *Trials of Intimacy Love and Loss in the Beecher – Tilton Scandal,* Chicago, The Univeristy of Chicago Press, 1999

Frisken, Amanda, *Victoria Woodhull's Sexual Revolution, Political Theater and the Popular Press on Nineteenth-Century America, Philadelphia, PN, University of Pennsylvania Press, 2004*

Stella Blum (Editor), *Victorian Fashions and Costumes from Harper's Bazar, 1867-1898 (Dover Fashion and Costumes)*, New York, Dover Publications, Inc. 1974

Macpherson, Myra, *The Scarlet Sisters, Sex, Suffrage and Scandal in the Gilded Age,* New York, Hachette Press, 2014

Gernsheim, Alison, *Victorian and Edwardian Fashion A Photographic Survey,* New York, Dover Publications, Inc. 1963

Stiles, T. J., *The First Tycoon: The Epic Life of Cornelius Vanderbilt,* New York, Alfred A. Knopf, Random House, 2009

Gabriel, Mary, *Notorious Victoria,* Chapel Hill, North Carolina, Algonquin Books of Chapel Hill, Workman Publishing, 1998

Underhill, Lois Beachy, *The Woman Who Ran For President: The Many Lives of Victoria Woodhull,* Bridgehampton, New York, Bridge Works Publishing Company, 1995

Renehan, Jr., Edward J., Commodore, *The Life of Cornelius Vanderbilt,* New York, Basic Books, Perseus Books Group, 2007

Preview

AUDACIOUS

THE VICTORIA WOODHULL SAGA
VOLUME III
PARADISE REGAINED

Excerpt from Audacious
PROLOGUE

10 Washington Place
New York City
Late Afternoon, June 4, 1877

"That's obscene, Victoria!" Declared William, the son of the Commodore Cornelius Vanderbilt, a truly great man. He sat behind his father's desk in his father's chair, both too big for him.

"I have become quite the expert on what does and what does not constitute obscenity, William Henry. There is nothing obscene here except for your complete lack of mourning your father's death over the last six months."

"I don't give a damn what you or anyone else thinks!" He put his clenched fists on the table and raised himself up.

I shook my head and looked away from him. "Your father would not hesitate to pay ten percent, as was his practice."

Turning red in the face, William squealed, "Ten percent would be ten million dollars." He started to sit back down and bounced back up. He screeched, "*Preposterous!*"

"William, you have neither his foresight, his fortitude, nor his grace. All you care about is being accepted by High Society. In case you are not informed, they like your money, William, only your money. They don't accept you—not in the least."

"I told you, I don't care what you think, Victoria Woodhull."

"The courts and your relatives do. My sister and I have been subpoenaed to produce all written correspondence and to testify at the estate trial."

"Nothing you or your harlot sister could say will damage me."

"Watch your mouth! Be very wary of what you pronounce, William Henry Vanderbilt." I stared at him and could see no humanness. "I surmise with you about to inherit one hundred and five million dollars, your already untethered arrogance is beyond restraint."

"I won't react to your insults. You are an unseemly woman."

"Good, then. You always were an elitist little prick!" I intentionally goaded him. "I don't expect you to be generous like Corney would have been." He blenched at my use of my sister's nickname for her lover. "Still, netting ninety-five million dollars might be better than you will fare in the courts, when Tennie and I reveal what we know and *what is written.*"

"I do not respond to idle threats," he declared smugly.

I took my time to let my words penetrate the imbecile before me. "I am sure the love letters from your father to Tennessee in your father's hand will be fascinating to everyone. He despised your threats and Machiavellian manipulations. Oh, yes, it is all written down."

"I'll pay you for the letters, but not anywhere near your wild fantasy price!" He tried to shame me. "Ten million dollars—outrageous!"

"Ah," I smiled. "So now we are negotiating." I raised my hand and counted one finger for each point as I proceeded. I raised one finger. "Your betrayal of your mother to Dr. McDonald's asylum would come out." I raised a second finger. "You locked your own mother away so you could maneuver whom your father married." I raised my third finger. "Then there is the glowing praise of your father's virility and his own pride at such when he and the woman you call a harlot were intimate." I continued to bore into his eyes. "And of course," I raised a fourth finger, "your denial to him of not only effective but proven medical treatment, according to Dr. Linsley and written complaints in your father's own hand."

I knew William had swallowed the hook.

"Stop. Just stop it." He spoke clearly defeated.

"Of course, you will still get... what do you think? Half the money? Perhaps a little more? Perhaps a lot less!"

The son of a great American seemed to turn green.

to be continued...

Thank you for reading!

Dear Reader,

I hope you enjoyed *Scandalous: Fame, Infamy, & Paradise Lost*. My desire is for Victoria Woodhull and Tennessee Celeste Claflin, women who overcame so much to become intrepid, empowered women, will become iconic models for young women everywhere. Speak out, work for and live the change you want to see, and beware of divisiveness—it held women suffrage back for five decades.

Fear not! While tempered on the anvil of scandalous mistreatment, Victoria and Tennessee go ever *Upward & Onward* to live lives of luxury and accomplishments in Europe, always forwarding their progressive beliefs. The third volume of the series, *Audacious: Paradise Regained* will cover the balance of their amazing lives.

As an author, I love getting feedback. I would love to hear what your favorite part of the story was, and what you liked or disliked, please share your thoughts with me. You can write me at neal@ thevictoriawoodhullsaga.com and visit me on the web at www. thevictoriawoodhullsaga.com.

Also, I'd like to ask a favor. If you are so inclined, I'd love a review of *Scandalous* on Amazon (http://amzn.to/2FJlGgM) and Goodreads (http://bit.ly/SCANgoodreads). You, the reader, have the power to influence other readers to share your journey with a book you've read. In fact, most readers pick their next book because of a review or on the advice of a friend. So, please share! You can find all of my books on my author page here: http://amzn.to/2zMOuSL

If you have not read *Volume I, Outrageous: Rise to Riches*, I highly encourage you to do so! *Outrageous* tells Victoria's and Tennie's story from the very beginning, and won ten literary awards.

Thank you so much for reading *Scandalous: Fame, Infamy, & Paradise Lost* and thanks for spending time with me, Victoria C. Woodhull, and Tennessee Celeste Claflin.

Upward & Onward,
Neal Katz
Oaxaca, Mexico

neal@thevictoriawoodhullsaga.com
thevictoriawoodhullsaga.com